THE LEGEND OF THE BLOODSTONE

The Legend of the Bloodstone

TIME WALKERS BOOK 1

E.B. Brown

KIRKBRIDE

Contents

ALSO BY E.B. BROWN

The Legend of the Bloodstone
Return of the Pale Feather
Of Vice and Virtue
A Tale of Oak and Mistletoe
Time Walkers The Complete Collection
Ghost Dance
Season of Exile
Through the Valley
Song of Sunrise
The Pretenders
Time Song

PART ONE

1

James County, Virginia
October 2012

"STUPID FREAKIN' BARN," she muttered. There really was no good reason for her to be out in the old barn this late, but she would lose what was left of her composure if she sat in the empty house any longer. She could hear grandpa as if he stood there beside her, his accent slurring his words together as it did when he was angry.

"Maggie-mae, yer head is full of bricks, I swear it, girl!"

Although she wanted to smile at the thought, she could not. It was still too fresh, too raw. Her lips twisted downward, and she shook off the flash of anger that surged as she thrust her fists into her front jean pockets and took a swipe at a tuft of loose straw with her boot.

Death sucked; there was nothing much more to say about it. No one to blame, no way for her to fight the advance of time. The Reaper claimed him, and there was not a blessed thing she could do about it.

Making things right around the farm? Well, there was a problem she could manage, and she had two good hands and two strong legs to work with. At least it was something.

Sunset dipped away beyond the horizon and the crimson orange sky streaked with that glowing time of peace before nightfall, her anger seeming like an intrusion into the cycle of nature. The wind kicked up, fluttering the edges of her red parka so she zipped it fully closed, putting off the luxury of mourning when there was so much work to do. She heard the roar of the waterfall beyond the meadow, the riverbanks swollen to overflowing from the recent storm. It left the ground saturated, like an overused sponge.

Her hood fell back off of her head with the next gust of wind and the rain soaked her long hair as she walked through the courtyard back to the barn, the damp earth squishing beneath her boots.

The old dairy barn loomed first on her to-do list. Over one hundred years old, the field stone foundation stood crumbling in some spots, in dire need of reinforcement. Maggie was determined to ready it for the upcoming construction work by doing some of the labor herself, so she worked to clear the debris most of the afternoon. It was a solitary task, one that kept her occupied until early evening, but she was pleased with her efforts and glad for the distraction. It would be quite useful as a private foaling box when it was finally finished, far enough from the main horse barn to provide a birthing sanctuary for the broodmares.

She shook the stiff work gloves off of her soiled hands and threw them onto the bale of musty straw at her feet. The muscles in her shoulders ached and her legs cramped at the effort, yet she bent to tighten the laces on her sodden work boots anyway. She rested one hand against the cold stone wall to balance herself, but as she straightened up she noticed a handful of loose rocks cluttering the ground. She considered ignoring the debris, then felt foolish after she worked so hard all day. What difference would it make if she spent a few more minutes picking up rocks? She had nothing else to do anyway.

"Move yer lazy ass!" she berated herself. A laugh escaped her lips at the thought of how silly it was to be talking to no one in an empty barn, and she promptly bent to the task. She grasped the hem of her parka upward until it pouched, then tossed a few of the smaller stones into her makeshift bucket. As she reached out closer to the wall to chase a stone poking out beneath the scattered straw, something sharp jabbed her fingers and she drew back at the flash of pain.

"Damn it!" she muttered. She jerked her arm away and sat back on her heels, grasping her throbbing fingers with her other hand and trying to contain the rocks in her parka with her elbow. A trickle of bright red blood dripped from two torn digits, both sliced clean across the fin-

2

Something tasted gritty and damp when she tried to moisten her cracked lips. She figured she must have slept like a rock if she was waking up with a cottonmouth, but when she tried to swallow all she could taste was dirt. Maggie sighed and rolled over, and when she opened her eyes, nothing made sense at all.

The palms of her hands were caked with wet earth when she pushed herself into a sitting position.

"What the hell?" she groaned. She blinked a few times in an effort to clear the sleep from her eyes, and when her gaze finally sharpened, she was dismayed to find she truly was sitting on the ground. It also appeared she had rolled around in the dirt, because as she extended her arms away from her body she could see the mud slathered on her skin.

A crescent moon was shining overhead illuminating the evergreens in a silver glimmer, the sounds of a busy forest smothering her senses. She was sitting in a patch of damp earth in the middle of the woods. Her fingers dug into the ground as the heady scent of evergreen needles fell upon her, and she could still taste the bitter blood residue in her mouth from her wound.

Ok, she knew what was going on. She must be dreaming. It was the only explanation. *Time to wake up!* She closed her eyes again, knowing when she opened them she would be safe in her own bed, snug and cozy like she was supposed to be. Not sitting on her ass in the middle of the night in a forest.

She gave it a go. Eyes closed, she counted backward in a methodical manner from ten to one. Yup, that should do the trick!

Oh, goo• Lor• Jesus!

It did not do the trick. She remained there on her wet backside, just as before. Unease nagged her consciousness, turning into a rising howl as she glanced down at her hand covered with dirt and her own dried blood. Before she could make another attempt to wake from her curious dream, she heard the snapping of branches and could see the brush ahead separating. Something was making its way through the undergrowth, pointed in her direction.

Maggie had never seen a bear so close before in real life, so it was a bit of a shock to see how immense the creature looked in her dream. Ah, okay! If she was trapped like a dirty little pig in an insufferable dream, she might as well get to a look at it up close! She smiled at her predicament and hoped she would remember it when she woke up.

Walking on all fours, the massive bear was a solid chunk of dense brown fur. He lumbered toward her in a lazy swagger, his enormous head swinging back and forth. The creature's head stopped abruptly when his deep brown eyes swung her way and his weight shifted somewhat backward on his haunches, although he did not actually sit down.

Maggie stuck her dirty palm up and waved, as if the bear was sitting behind a fence at the zoo.

"Hey bear," she whispered. It seemed odd that she could feel the dampness through her denim jeans as she rolled forward onto her knees. She was fine with ignoring that bit of information, much more focused on getting close to the animal in her dream. As she reached for him, the beast opened its mouth and uttered a snarl, and she scrunched her nose. Rancid breath, indeed!

The beast rose upward on his hind legs, still roaring his displeasure, his front limbs extended outward so close to her head she could see the round pink pads on the underside of his paws. She pushed off with her feet and scrambled backward on her bottom, then turned over to crawl away faster. Dream or no dream, she did not want to be eaten by a wild animal.

Di•n't someone once say if you •ie• in a •ream, you •ie• in real life?

She was not willing to test the theory. She was still considering that idea when she felt the blow to her right shoulder followed by a searing pain as she was slammed flat to the ground, evacuating the air from her lungs in one painful rush. Her mouth again tasted like dirt as she struggled to gasp for air.

"Tkali-a!" A shrill voice whooped from very near her face. She could not see with her cheek pressed down into the ground, but she felt the air above her swoosh and the weight of the massive paw was suddenly gone from her back. The bear sounded angrier at the intrusion, his roaring mingled with the sharp rapid cries coming from what sounded like a man. Maggie pulled at the ground with her broken fingernails and struggled to breathe but her crushed ribs refused to expand. She managed to curl into a half sitting position and backed away from the melee at her feet. Her shoulder screamed in protest with every move and a steady trickle of blood trickled down the front of her parka.

The scene in front of her was very much like a movie. The brown bear stood on his hind legs, his front paws extended outward, looking as if he was about to give the man standing in front of him a hug. Except that the bear was truly, really, there in front of her. Moreover, crouched between her and the bear was a dark-haired man, lithe and quick on his toes, wielding what looked like a rather small knife in consideration of the size of his opponent.

"Tkali-a nusheaxkw!" the man roared, as if in challenge to the beast.

The stranger danced away from a swipe by the bear, eliciting another frustrated bellow from the beast. Maggie could see the muscles of his legs flex through the leather leggings he wore, and there were colored beads attached to a belt at his waist that bounced when he jumped. She had not gained enough breath back in her lungs yet to scream, but if she had, she would have been screaming by now from the sheer absurdity of it all.

The bear aimed another seeming half-hearted swipe at the man, and then gave his massive head a shake as he dropped back down on all fours. The man remained crouched between her and the beast, his fist extended with the knife pointing at it, the veins on his muscled arms standing out like cords against his skin. With one last series of groans and roars, the animal tossed his head and then abruptly swung his shoulder around. The beast lumbered back the way it came through the underbrush. It appeared to have lost interest in the fight.

The man watched the bear retreat. When he was satisfied the animal was gone, the stranger turned to Maggie. She could see beads of sweat sliding down off his brow along his black hair. There was a thin braid down the left side of his face where his hair laid flat just past his bare brown shoulders, but she was perplexed to notice the right side of his head was shaved clean in a crescent shape from temple to nape. She could see the bone-handled knife he still clutched in his hand as he glared at her. His hands were fisted at his sides and his chest heaved with the effort of slowing down his breathing. Maggie was too stunned to speak, but even just staring at him in return of his sharpened gaze was too much. She felt her head spinning as if she would vomit, but the last thing she wanted to do was throw up in front of the stranger, so she leaned forward and put her head in her hands.

"Keptchat!"

She heard the utterance that sounded like a curse, and felt his presence when he kneeled down beside her. Her limbs felt like rubber and she felt she was going to lose her head to a moment of panic. None of it made any sense. The warm hands that settled on her upper arms sent a shock through her bones, and the man holding her was most certainly not a dream.

Everything that had just happened was real.

The man muttered words she did not understand, as if talking to himself in another language. Maggie felt fingers grasp her chin and then the wet rim of some sort of container of water as he pressed it to her lips. She took a few sips and then shook her head to show him she had enough.

"Aptamehele," he muttered.

He sat back on his haunches in front of her, now an unmoving statue as he surveyed her. Maggie returned his bold gaze this time. She imagined she should feel uncomfortable with the way his eyes raked over her, but she did the same to him so she figured they were on equal footing. Other than his brown leggings and knotted rawhide beaded belt, he was adorned with leather ties above each bicep and a pendant necklace decorated with beads and two black feathers. The necklace hung in the center of his broad chest, banging against his skin when he moved. Some sort of hanging flap was secured around his hips by a narrow cord; was it a *breechcloth?*

His features could not be called handsome by the standards she was accustomed, but there was a fierce strength in the sharp lines of his face that paralyzed her. When she slowly returned her gaze back to his eyes, she was startled to find they were a luminous deep blue. A corner of his mouth slanted downward as he met her appraisal with his own.

"Why are you here, stupid woman?" he asked in clear, but hesitant English. She did not care for the mocking tone of his voice nor the way he raised his eyebrows to wait for her answer, as if he held some authority over her.

"I—I don't know," she managed to stammer. "Why are you here?" she countered. Her response was clearly humorous to him, as it caused him to laugh aloud and smile.

"Maybe you should be glad I am here. Lucky for you that bear was not too hungry."

Maggie closed her eyes and shook her head. Yup. Still there when she opened her eyes and looked again. The blasted man was grinning as though she had provided him endless entertainment. *How on Earth was she sitting in the mi••le of the woo•s after being attacke• by a bear, with a man •resse• in an In•ian costume laughing at her?* Maybe she had been sleepwalking and stumbled onto...onto what? Wait, Halloween was next month! Yes, that had to be it! An early Halloween party and some adults running around in the woods in costumes, perhaps taking things a little too seriously. Hell, the guy was probably drunk, especially considering the way he shaved the side of his head for one silly costume event!

She could think of no other explanation that made sense. She knew she was missing something important, but her brain seemed to be in a fog and the self-preservation of denial was controlling her senses.

"I really don't know how I got here, mister, but—"

Maggie snapped her mouth closed when remnants of memory began to rush back. She could recall picking up stones in the barn, and then cutting her hand.

The air surged like an electric charge as she looked down at the ground and the fine hair on her arms pricked up when she focused on the object. Lying on pine needles beside her was the dark green stone.

She slowly reached out and picked it up, its weight not too heavy but definitely substantial as she raised it in front of her face. It was still stained with her blood.

The man dropped to his knees beside her and snatched her wrist in his own large hand. His blue eyes widened and he drew back somewhat as he slowly raised his gaze to meet her own. She tried half-heartedly to pull her hand away, but he held it firm as his eyes remained locked with hers, a flutter settling down deep in her belly at the connection. She could see him swallow hard and his lips closed together in a tight line. Finally he spoke in a low, even tone, but his eyes remained fixed on her.

"Sawwehone Shacquohocan," he said. "This is a Bloodstone. How did you come by it?"

"I found it in my barn. I was cleaning up. I dropped it, I guess," she stammered. Her answer was an honest one, but it seemed to incite his agitation.

"You say you found it? Or stole it?" he asked.

"No! I didn't *steal* it! I just found it," she tried to explain. "But I didn't steal it. It's just a rock, for Christ's sake!" she insisted. She had no idea why she was trying to justify herself to him. Despite the fact that she still felt disoriented and had been nearly mauled to death by a wild animal, she felt like she had to make him understand.

He plucked the stone from her hand and a hiss escaped from between his clenched teeth when they both saw the burn on her palm. A twist of lines scarred her skin where she held the stone, tender to touch and disturbingly...organized. As if a strange knot shape had been branded to her skin.

There was no more time to ponder her predicament because the man swiftly scooped her up and stood to his feet, holding her in his bare arms as if she weighed nothing at all. One hand rested gingerly around her shoulder where the bear had scratched her, and it was only then that she began to feel the sharp burning ache the claws had left in her skin.

"I can walk just fine, thank you," she protested. He glanced down at her.

"Your wound needs to be bound. You have lost much blood."

His purposeful gait cut a path through the underbrush, the tall growth brushing against his leggings as he navigated to a nearby clearing. When they entered the spot where a sorrel horse stood patiently ground tied, he let Maggie's legs drop down but still he held his arms around her waist and kept her close. Her chin was even with his collarbone, and her cheek brushed against his chest. The scent of sweat mixed with evergreen and smoke bonded to him, overwhelming her senses. With a sickly feeling in her bones, Maggie glanced around the clearing. A panic began to rise as she looked at her surroundings and realized they were familiar.

They were standing at the entrance to her barn. Only it was not there.

She was aware it was damn impossible, but she knew the farm better than anyone did. They were standing on it—on her property. Two tall ancient Cyprus trees marked the spot behind the barn, overlooking a steep drop off that tumbled down to the river below. The view was unmistakable. There was a winding gravel trail to navigate the slope, which still appeared to be there. She could hear the roar of the waterfall beyond the clearing.

The trees were shorter than they had been earlier in the day, the trunks a smaller diameter and their branches not yet as full. An old split rail fence had guarded the drop off to the river below for as long as she could remember, but it was not anywhere to be seen now. Her fingers curled into fists and she barely felt it when her nails dug crescent-shaped daggers into her palms.

"You said you found the Bloodstone. When did you find it?"

She knew it made no sense, but the truth was the only thing she could cling to with any certainty in the midst of rising panic.

"I found it today. This morning, the fifth of October."

At this confession, he placed his fingers on her chin and twisted her head gently upwards to meet his stare, his head cocked to the side. His brows furrowed and his eyes searched her own in a question he could not seem to put to words. She did not understand what she was doing there, or who the man was. She was willing to wager he was just as confused as she was.

"It is now the month your people call September," he replied.

"But it can't be September," she insisted. "That doesn't make any sense! I was just here today, and I cut my hand— I think I passed out."

He shook his head.

"This is the place I buried the Bloodstones one year ago. The ground is not disturbed. No one knows this place but me."

"What...what year did you bury them?" she whispered, the words rushing out before she could stop the ridiculous question.

"The year your people call 1621."

She felt relieved that his arms still held her as her knees buckled and the blessed darkness swallowed her one more time.

"I know not what hos-tel is, but you will stop your fight!" he growled.

He uttered something harshly under his breath and sat abruptly back, causing the horse to drop its haunches and slide to a stop. Maggie twisted around and tried to pry his arm away from her waist, but the bastard was too strong and determined. How dare he refuse to release her! She wanted to wipe the grin off his smug face. She made another attempt to jump off his lap but he anticipated the motion, defeating her attempts to flee. Who the hell did he think he was? She'd damn well get down if she wanted to!

Frustration washed through her, surging over her body like a rapid. She wanted to argue, to make him let her go, and then – then she would just go home. It sounded like a simple plan, but stark reality confirmed she was terribly lost. She panicked with the knowledge that her current predicament was not a dream, and that the raven-haired man who held her was very, very real.

"Stop fighting, woman," he said, the words even but ground out in a hoarse whisper. "There is nowhere for you to go."

"Stop calling me *woman*, my name is Maggie," she stammered, her eyes imprisoned by his softened gaze. Frustration remained in the pit of her stomach, tinged with fear of her impossible situation. The impatient glare on Winn's face faded and he cocked his head slightly to the side as he studied her. His eyes darted a glance at her flushed cheeks, then traveled downward to her lips. She knew her cheek was chafed and smeared with dirt-laced tears, and she suddenly wished he were not so damn close.

His hand slipped upward and his fingers pressed against the back of her neck, his grasp large enough to cup her face and tilt it toward him so that their eyes met. She had an abrupt awareness of his closeness and tasted the salt of her own tears on her lips. His blue eyes captured her gaze, holding her prisoner more securely than his arms ever could.

"Stop it then, *Maggie*," he whispered, enunciating her name in his peculiar accent. "There is nowhere for you to go."

"I want to go home. Just let me down."

His eyes softened as he shook his head. "You cannot return to your place. You must understand. I am...sorry."

The smothering panic that gripped her eased, his touch like embers against her skin despite the chill of the evening breeze. His fingers moved in her hair, as if he meant to comfort her, the gentle soothing motion an anchor which helped her slow down her hammering heart and get some sort of handle on the panic.

Flung through time by someone unknown force, saved from imminent death by a fearless stranger—none of it could be rational, and submitting to such an implausible scenario caused her to question her own sanity. How could she possibly accept it? Could he be real—could it all possibly be real?

They both heard the steps of horses coming their way. His face remained close to hers and she could see him become tense. She chastised herself for clinging to the man, but she let him hold her all the same.

"What meaning is Maggie? A strange name," he asked, her name drawn out as he tested it on his tongue.

"Maggie? It doesn't mean anything, I think."

"You belong here now," he said. His hands left her face and he let out a sigh. "My brothers are near. They will ride with us back to the village." He gathered the reins together and the horse snorted, hooves stomping in response.

"*Ntënuyëm!*"

Winn uttered the greeting as a shriek and the two newcomers answered immediately in kind. His horse began to prance, lifting its hooves in place in anticipation as the two riders approached.

They dressed similar to him, in leather leggings and beaded adornments, bare-chested as well. If he had not told her they were his kin, she would not have guessed as much. One man, shorter than Winn but with slightly more breadth to his shoulders and waist, stood silent behind a round creased face. His brown eyes held a careful tolerance as he deferred to his companion. The second man compared to Winn in stature, but when his hostile black eyes fell sharp on Maggie, the fear that Winn had chased away returned. His dark copper skin gleamed with sweat, its shade quite different from Winn's lighter brown. The two men wasted little time in survey of her before they spoke to Winn.

They spoke in short, tight responses, the cadence of their exchange abrupt. She had no idea what they were saying or what language they spoke, but she was pretty sure the two newcomers were angry. The shorter man said little since the other seemed to dominate the conversation. The black-eyed man shot a glare at Maggie, then at Winn, and erupted into a furious stream of shouting. Winn listened without interruption, but then something the other man uttered caused him to snatch Maggie's bloody hand and hold it up for them to see.

"Sawwehone Shacquohocan!"

Although his body was tense behind her, the words he spoke were calm. Not knowing what they were saying infuriated her, especially since she seemed to be the target of the other man's anger. At the sight of her hand, the two men fell silent. The silence stretched as they stared.

"What is going on?" she asked, half turned around in Winn's lap. She snatched her wrist away, a motion that brought laughter from the shorter man. The other remained silent, his lips pursed in a tight line.

"Your woman has a loud mouth, *nimahtes*. Maybe you should tame her first, then come back home," the short man laughed. His eyes brightened and he crossed his arms over his chest as he chuckled. The second brother did not smile.

Winn's horse stomped the ground and tossed his head.

"She has a wound that must be tended. I will tame her after it is healed."

They spoke in English this time, but Maggie did not like the conversation any better in her own language. What happened to the man who comforted her so sweetly, as if he wanted to chase her fear away? Why was he laughing with his brothers about *taming* her? Scarlet warmth rose from her neck to her cheeks at the implication. She was raised by the men in her life as an equal voice in matters, and even if she was trapped in some never ending fantasy nightmare, it simply was not in her nature to be dismissed as if she was simply a piece of property to be managed.

She decided enough was enough. Winn's hold lessened a fraction as he spoke with the men. Maggie took advantage of the distraction and jumped down off the horse, taking off in a sprint out of the clearing back into the woods. The wound on her shoulder screamed in protest at the effort, and a fresh surge of blood saturated her torn parka. How could she be so stupid, trusting a stranger? Maybe she was trapped in another time, but she did not have to act like an imbecile, and she was certainly not going to be *tame* by any man!

It took him mere seconds to catch her.

His fist caught her around the waist, knocking her off balance and sending them both sprawling into a heap on the forest floor. Maggie kicked and tried to scratch him, but his hands were quick and he proceeded to shove her fists above her head into the dirt. She cried out at the searing pain in her shoulder and tried to catch a breath through aching ribs. His strapping legs entrapped her kicking limbs, and his hips pinned her to the ground. He panted shallow with the effort of containing her struggle, and seeing his frustration felt like a measure of triumph. He glared at her, wordless, as she tried to scramble away, and she felt the cold earth against her bare back. Her torn shirt exposed the strap of her pink lace bra at one shoulder and his gaze flickered as he glanced downward and his eyes fixated on the bright color. The hand holding her hip traveled slowly upward and his fingers brushed the edge of her lacy undergarment.

"Oh, no you don't!" she exploded. She slammed her head up against his, and his blue eyes flared as a scowl creased his face with a low uttered curse.

"Enough!" he shouted.

Blood dripped from his mouth as he thrust his hand into her hair and slammed her head back to the ground. She cried out in pain and surprise at the reaction and frustrated tears formed across her lashes. She understood immediately that her plan to get away was a foolish one. The man who chased her tears away was gone, replaced by a furious warrior bent on submission.

"Do not run from me again!" he said.

"I won't stay here! I don't belong here!"

"You *o* belong here." His cold glare betrayed no emotion other than anger and she knew she tread a dangerous path with her resistance. She expected some sort of retribution but was shocked when he produced a long cord of rawhide and began to wrap it snug around her wrists.

"No! Damn it, let me go!" she screamed. He ducked to evade her head butt and continued to tie her hands, otherwise ignoring her outburst as blood from his split lower lip dripped down his set jaw. She cursed through gritted teeth. "You bastard! No! Let me go!"

He dragged her to her feet, and when she kicked out at him he snatched her chin painfully in his fingers. He spoke the warning low, a hiss that only the two of them could hear.

"I will bind your legs if you kick me. I will bind your foul mouth if you speak. Do you understand?"

She glared at the face now shrouded in an unreadable mask. Her wrists ached against the binding, and her shoulder throbbed where the bear claw marked her. There were few options available to her. She closed her eyes and nodded one time in reluctant submission.

He grunted a word she did not understand and then hoisted her into his arms with disturbing ease. The obedient horse waited a few paces away. He placed her back on the beast and swung up behind her before the other two men joined them.

There was no more talking.

4

Winn did not look at his two brothers as he rode with the woman. She remained silent now, her fire subdued for the moment. He regretted the need to threaten her, but he was stunned by the way she fought him. Memory of the manner in which she defied him in front of his brothers caused a scowl to darken his face again. He knew she was from another time by her odd clothes and strange way of speaking, but even so, he could not fathom why she dared challenge him. Did women in her time disobey their men and just do as they pleased? He could not let her defiance go without reprimand, especially when his brothers stood by as witnesses.

He gripped the reins tighter and sighed. Maybe the Great Creator made a mistake. The irrational desire he felt to keep her close was surely just a product of his anger. He looked down at her head lying against his chest, her amber locks sprawled across his skin. By the Gods, she was beautiful, but so willful! He remembered the way it felt when she fought beneath him, the way she held nothing back. Even then, with anger clouding his thoughts, he wanted to possess her. When she made him bleed, it took every measure of strength he had not to tear her strange clothes from her body and ravage her in the dirt. Only the knowledge that his brothers were nearby dampened his lust.

The Great Creator must have made a mistake. *She coul• not be the one he was meant to kill.*

His brother Chetan laughed no longer, although he seemed to enjoy questioning Winn's manhood when the woman first tried to get away.

Makedewa, however, kept a tense silence. Other than his original out-burst of disbelief that Winn did not slaughter the woman on sight, Makedewa kept his thoughts to himself and rode ahead alone. Winn suspected it was not the last he would hear from his temperamental younger brother on the matter, but at least he had sense enough to let it be until they returned to the village.

It was good that the men remained silent since he was in no mood to respond to any more of their jibes. With her sleeping in his arms he could barely concentrate on guiding the horse, let alone argue with his brothers. Closing his eyes gave no relief, damn her. Even her scent maddened him, a sweet honeysuckle aroma that drifted to his senses with each pace of the horse.

Winn shook his head, confused at the pull this woman held over him. He grew up listening to tales about the Time Walkers, how some-day one would arrive who would end the life of the Great Weroance. All young braves longed for the chance to kill a Time Walker and bring honor on the tribe for the sacrifice. After all, Time Walkers were the most powerful of the Blooded Ones who once lived among them. Everyone knew the prophecy, his brothers included, and they all had reasons to anticipate the coming of the next Time Walker. Many wished for another sacrifice to gain favor with the Weroance, with the belief it would bring prosperity to their decimated Paspahegh tribe. Long ago, Opechancanough bestowed the greatest rewards on those warriors who served him the head of a Time Walker. Yet those gifts had been the heads of men, never a woman.

Winn let his chin rest against her for the briefest of moments. He did not want to wake her, giving her less opportunity to cause trouble in front of his brothers. As much as her presence was a shock to him, it was even more so to his brothers.

Winn knew not why he failed to kill her on sight. Perhaps because she was a woman. Or was it because she brought out something raw in him, something primal, driving him senseless just as it made him afraid? Once his uncle learned of her arrival he would be bound to act, her gender of no consequence.

The bundle of sleeping fire in his arms stirred, her rose-stained lips falling open as she sighed. He needed badly to shift his weight, but he did not want to wake her. Her battered body needed rest, and he needed to regain some semblance of control.

Her hand slipped down across his waist as they rode. She was a curious thing. She was not tall, about the same height as the women of his village, perhaps shorter. Her skin was creamy ivory like the bone-handled knife in his belt, her hair scented with meadow flowers. Dirt smudged her face and neck and leaves tangled in the bright auburn hair that flowed nearly to her waist. He wished to take her to the river and bathe her himself, but he knew his sister and mother would not allow that once they laid eyes on her.

Despite the surge of possession that railed through his bones when he looked at her, a current of anger remained. How could this slip of a woman defy and belittle him in front of his brothers? If he had any sense he would end her life now and leave her body to the wolves.

How coul he follow through with what he was boun* by honor to *o?*

He uttered a half-snort, half-growl at his own thoughts, eliciting a curious glance from Chetan. Winn ignored the wordless inquiry from his brother and continued the ride in silence. If the woman was powerful enough to cause him both barely constrained anger and uncontrolled lust in the span of one evening, he feared what any more time in her presence would wreak on his self-control.

He wondered again if the petulant gods made a terrible mistake as he glanced down at her. He could see the curve of her body pressed against his chest, covered by the remains of her torn clothes. Winn grinned as he recalled how she exploded when he examined the strange pink fabric covering her shoulder, her eyes alight with fury as she fought him like an animal. Of course, she must have feared the worst by his actions, and for that he was sorry, since he meant no harm. *Ah, she probably thought he was a *og, pawing at her like that!*

He let out a groan as he adjusted her sleeping body in his lap.

Perhaps the Great Creator enjoyed watching him suffer.

5

"Shh, shh, Maggie, it's only a dream." Marcus wrapped her in his burly arms, smoothing the hair back off her tear-stained face as she cried. She shook with the force of the nightmare. Although she knew Marcus would never let anyone hurt her, she still feared the darkness. Once the lights dimmed again and he left her alone, the shadows would dance across the walls and her toys would begin to talk. The mischievous teddy bear on her dresser would grin, and the string puppet hanging from a hook would taunt her until she was again screaming.

"Please don't go! They'll come back!" she sobbed.

"Aww, lamb, it's all right now," he soothed her, his deep voice humming through his chest. He took something from his pocket and placed it in her hand. "Here, you hold onto this. It keeps the nightmares away."

She looked down at the gray stone figure. Heavy in her hand, it was the size of her palm, the edges pitted and scarred. It was a bird, its wings just beginning to lift in flight, with a slightly open beak that seemed to cry out some unspoken promise.

"It will keep them away?" she asked. He nodded.

"Of course. It's a raven, a great brave bird. The raven keeps safe those he loves."

"Well," she sniffed, "how do I know he loves me? He just met me!"

Marcus chuckled.

"He's always known ye, lamb. He's loved ye forever."

It was the second time Maggie woke in a strange place, but this time the disjointed feeling lasted for only seconds as the echo of her dream dissipated. She could not explain how or why she was in another time, however she was painfully aware of the reality of her predicament as her hands twisted against the rawhide ties. Her damaged shoulder throbbed in time with her rapid heartbeat as she glanced furtively around the unfamiliar place.

Above her a rounded roof over a circular walled structure protected her slumber, and Maggie vaguely recalled something about Indians who lived in wigwams. Lined with thatch and shingles of rough-hewn tree bark over a bent sapling frame, it confined the warmth from the fire into the space, giving it a cozy ambience. A soft pile of fur cushioned her spot on the ground, and she could feel the lick of the flames warm her skin as it funneled upward in a wisp to escape through a soot-stained smoke hole. Across the fire, she could see a girl in a rawhide dress bent over a large basket, rummaging through the contents.

When Maggie tried to push herself up and failed, the girl noticed. She left the basket, shaking her head at Maggie as she muttered to herself in that other language. The agitated gesture tossed her two dark braids around her head as she kneeled, and Maggie bit back a scream when the girl produced a knife from her waistband. Was the girl going to stab her? She had done nothing wrong!

Maggie scrambled backward as the woman crawled toward her.

"No! Please, I didn't do anything!"

The girl paused and tilted her head, then her lips widened in a smile.

"Shhhh! Be still!" the woman laughed, her English stilted but easily understood. Maggie thought it was decidedly not funny, but she did as the woman demanded and prayed it was the right thing to do.

With a quick practiced flick of the knife, the woman sliced the rawhide binding around Maggie's wrist. She then sat back on her heels and chuckled, continuing to shake her head in amusement.

"I'm glad you think that's funny," Maggie replied. She rubbed her sore wrists, happy to see the skin was not broken, just a bit raw. Her wristwatch remained intact, shimmering in the firelight. The woman reached for her hand and Maggie let her examine it, figuring she would be dead already if the girl wanted to kill her.

"You wear a strange bracelet," the girl said softly. "And you carry the Bloodstone." Maggie nodded.

"I—I didn't steal it. I already told him that."

"I know. It marked you. It belongs to you now," the girl agreed. She smiled again and closed her small brown hands around Maggie's fist. "I am Teyas, sister to *Winkeohkwet*. I cleaned your wound. The bear marked you, make a deep cut. You understand?"

The girl spoke slow and careful, her English edged with uncertainty but still understandable enough. Grateful to her for her kindness, Maggie smiled back.

"Yes, I understand. Thank you, my shoulder does feel better."

Both women relaxed in a mutual appreciation and curiosity. Maggie allowed the girl to remove what was left of her parka, and watched as Teyas examined it in fascination. The girl rubbed the fabric between her fingers and squealed when it made a scratching sound, then she held it to her nose to catch a scent. Seeming satisfied, she placed it aside and reached for the basket. Made from woven reed, the large flat basket held an assortment of garments similar to the ones Teyas wore. Maggie did not want to undress in front of the girl, but she was fearful of damaging the tenuous bond between them so she did what the girl asked. Her cheeks flushed as her exposed skin remained bared longer than necessary, since Teyas insisted on careful inspection of each item of clothing removed. Maggie eventually ended up in a plain tan dress with bits of rabbit fur on the edges, her legs wrapped in fur-lined leggings and soft flat moccasins decorated with colorful beads.

Teyas picked up an object that tumbled from the heap of clothes. It was the heavy raven figurine. Maggie held out her hand for it, hoping the Indian girl would return it. After turning it over in her fingers a few times, Teyas placed it in her palm with a smile.

"My friend gave it to me, it's just a toy," Maggie explained. "A raven to keep bad dreams away."

"Raven? Ha!" Teyas snorted with a giggle. "They bring trouble. Just ask my brother."

Maggie shook her head. She tucked the raven into a fold of her soft new dress.

"Uhm, that's okay, I'd rather not."

Her shoulder ached, but the bleeding was finished and the bandage wrapped snugly around her gave it support. She gladly took the cup Teyas offered, not knowing what it was, but too thirsty to care. It was a sweet, thick fruit nectar that did little to quench the dryness, but felt warm as it settled in her belly.

"Thank you," she said after finishing the entire cup. Since Teyas said she was Winn's sister, she wondered if the man was still nearby, and if so, what were her chances of leaving? He made it abundantly clear she was here to stay, whether she objected or not. She wondered why the man seemed at ease with the notion that she was from another time. Maggie was in tentative acceptance of the idea, but still had hope of waking up in her own bed at some point. Winn, however, almost behaved as if he expected her to drop into his lap. *Did he know something about how she arrived? And if he did, could he send her back?*

The bearskin door flap being pushed aside interrupted her musing. An older woman with one long grey streaked braid entered the enclosure, followed by Winn. She was dressed in a simple doeskin skirt, with a loose fur shawl covering her shoulders. Winn had discarded his leggings and stood glaring at her behind the woman, his jaw rigid and any emotion he might have had well hidden. Anger welled inside her as she recalled what he had done to her and she boldly glared at him in return. His eyes widened for a moment and his lips parted as if to speak, but he quickly clamped his mouth shut and his face returned to a blank slate.

Teyas tugged at her hand. The older woman spoke, and both Teyas and Winn deferred to her with the respect of their attention. Teyas smiled and nodded, but Winn remained silent. He said nothing until the woman folded her arms across her chest and gave an emphatic nod. At that point, Winn said something abrupt and tense. It was frustrating to have no idea what was being said, especially when she could plainly see they were discussing her. After a terse exchange, they turned to her.

"Maggie, my mother, *Chulensak Asuwak*, gives you welcome. She is happy to meet you." Teyas drew her name out into one long breath as Winn had done earlier, but it was close enough so Maggie did not attempt to correct her.

Teyas served as translator, listening to her mother and then relaying the message with careful enunciation. Winn observed, but remained so tense she could see the outline of each muscle across his folded arms.

"I, uh, please tell her I said thank you. And for the clothes, and for taking care of me, as well," Maggie stammered. At least they were including her in the conversation, but it would take some time to get used to speaking through translation.

Teyas nodded and smiled, and relayed the message. Her mother nodded as well, but there was more she wanted to say.

"Mother asks from what time you traveled, and she says she wishes you had a good journey."

"What time? You mean...what year?"

Teyas nodded. "We do not keep time like the English, but we understand it. Yes, what year?"

The words felt alien on her tongue, but akin to a confirmation of reality. It took her a few moments to compose herself before she could reply.

"Two thousand twelve. The year 2012. That's what it was when I left," she answered. Winn muttered a sharp retort in response but otherwise kept silent. The older woman kneeled down beside Maggie and patted her hand. Maggie could not help but smile at the comforting gesture.

"It must be very different, the time you come from," Teyas said, her eyes wide.

"Yes, I guess it is," Maggie agreed. She looked up at Winn. Although the two women settled down beside her on the furs, he kept his distance, arms crossed and legs planted in a rigid stance. "Where am I? I mean, what is this place called? None of this makes sense to me."

"We are the last of the Paspahegh people, of the Powhatan tribe. This land is called *Tsenacommacah*, where all Powhatans live. Does that have meaning to you?"

Maggie swallowed back the lump in her throat as she nodded. Yes, it did have meaning, but it still seemed ridiculous.

"Teyas, I don't understand how this happened, how I got here. I just really want to go home."

She noticed Winn stiffen when she made the confession. Why did it matter to him if she left? The man bordered on infuriating. The span of emotions he incited in her within one day was enough to make her head spin. First, he saved her from certain death, and then he tenderly comforted her through her fear. Then he turned into an angry, stubborn ass that tackled her like a linebacker and proceeded to fondle her bra. Yet he stood there glaring as she spoke, obviously bristling at the notion she wanted to go home.

Well, he could take a flying leap. If he refused to help her, she would find someone who would.

"Maggie, we cannot send you home. The Bloodstone magic is very powerful, but we do not control it. You are here for a reason," Teyas tried to explain. Chulensak Asuwak spoke rapidly and Teyas struggled to translate her message. "Mother says she gives you her protection. She remembers the summer when the Blooded Ones lived among us. Many of them were Time Walkers. We have never met another woman Time Walker since then, and she tells you she will not let harm come to you."

"That is very kind, but I don't understand—what reason do you think I'm here for? Why would anyone want to hurt me?"

"You have traveled here with the Bloodstone. Our Weroance seeks death of all Time Walkers."

Maggie did not protest when Teyas took her hand, squeezing it in her own, but she swallowed back the stiff lump in her throat at the implied threat.

"Death?" she whispered. She knew she was not ready to hear any more, nor would she ever be, and when she saw the puzzled look Teyas sent to Winn, her worst suspicion was confirmed.

"We will keep you safe, Red Woman. Winn did not kill you, he brought you here to us. There has been no other woman Time Walker since the Pale Witch. The Great Creator must have sent you to us for a reason."

So they would not kill her – for now. Maggie reached up and twisted a strand of her own hair between her fingers. It gleamed against the shimmer of the firelight. *Re‹ Woman, in‹ee‹.*

Teyas and Chulensak Asuwak left the house after showering her with embraces and welcomes. Numbness seeped through her skin, and although she appreciated their heartfelt acceptance, she could not yet process what had happened or what she should do about it. The absence of the two women was purposeful and it left her alone with Winn. The blasted man still stood there, silent and brooding. She must have misunderstood what the girl meant. It had to be some mistake; she was part of no prophecy, especially one that meant to see her dead. She was just Maggie McMillan, a terribly lost twenty-one-year-old woman in a strange place.

The silence between them stretched as tense as the muscles in his crossed arms. Maggie remained seated on the furs at his feet, and the irony of the position suddenly occurred to her. Is this what Winn expected of a woman? Submission and silence? Of all the places time travel might have deposited her, the irony of being a twenty-first century woman stranded in the seventeenth century did not escape her. She tried to stifle the insane reflexive laughter bubbling up in her throat.

"What is funny?" he demanded.

"Everything," she laughed, letting it out in a glorious release. "Me? I must look like a filthy mess. And you? You look like you'd rather be anywhere but here!" Frustration waned for the instant as she rocked back and laughed so hard tears squeezed from her eyes. His eyebrows rose and his eyes gleamed cobalt in the light as he watched her laugh.

For a moment she feared he would be angry, but she was relieved to see his shoulders relax and his arms slowly fall to his sides. The corner of his lip twitched and eventually turned upward in a lopsided grin.

"You may be right. You do need a bath," he agreed as he laughed with her. Her laughter slowed when he held a hand out to her. His grin remained but tightened somewhat as he waited for her to respond.

She knew it was an offering of peace and she would be foolish to refuse him. Maggie placed her palm in his and he clasped his larger one around it. He pulled her gently to her feet, the skin of his fingers calloused but warm against her own hand. She tried not to grimace at the burning pain the movement elicited in her shoulder, but the limb was stiff and Winn was not a man easily fooled.

"I would show you my village, but perhaps you need rest."

The trauma of the last few hours had wreaked a fatigue on her body she had never experienced, as she certainly was unaccustomed to blunt force blows wielded by a bear. The truth of his observation gave her weary body permission to accept it for now. Maggie felt her shoulders sag and her back relax as she nodded in agreement.

Winn led her toward the back of the yehakin, where a thick pile of furs lay over a mat woven from coffee colored reeds. His intent was clear so she started to sit, surprised to feel his hands at her waist to assist her to the ground. She murmured a word of thanks which he did not acknowledge, but instead he turned away to rummage through a covered basket along the wall.

Maggie watched him, mystified by his presence yet still fighting twinges of irritation. She knew she was too tired to argue anymore, she would have to regroup and save it for another time. Besides, the way her shoulder burned, she feared more damage than could be treated without modern medicine, and with one less functional shoulder, she was as good as useless.

Winn found what he was looking for and returned to kneel at her side. He held out a smooth wooden bowl to her, which he placed in her hands. Her stomach rumbled at the sight of the ripe red berries and strips of dried meat that looked like jerky. There was something soft and brown and shaped in a ball that seemed the consistency of corn-meal, and he broke it apart and handed her a piece. Past caring what the food was, she was grateful for anything and quickly dug in. Winn sat down facing her with his legs crossed, watching her devour the meal. He smiled as she shoved berries into her mouth, and when she realized he was laughing at her she stopped eating, mortified.

"I'm sorry. Here, have some, you must be hungry, too," she said as her cheeks filled with crimson. He waved her off.

"No, little one," he laughed. "You eat. I am a good hunter. I will need to hunt every day to feed you."

For a moment she considered dumping the bowl in his lap, but she was too hungry to waste any food so she tried to take his teasing grace-fully. She went back to eating with a scowl, shaking her head and biting back a smile. He reached over and plucked a few berries from the bowl then tossed them in his mouth as he continued to watch her. When the bowl was empty, he passed a cup brimming with sweet apple juice to her, which she found delightful as it ran down her throat thick and warm. She finished in one long swallow, then quickly wiped the back of her hand across her dripping mouth and handed the cup back to him. Winn refilled it and took his own taste, downing the entire cup as she had, but with much more control and finesse.

"Thank you...Winn," she said when he put the cup down. He said nothing for a moment, but then nodded.

"You should sleep. You will be safe here in my *yehakin*."

He pulled a loose fur from the pile and reached forward. Maggie held her breath as he entered her space, his arms closing around her as he placed the fur on her shoulders.

"This...house...*yehakin*...it belongs to you?" she asked.

"Yes. I will send Teyas to stay with you. She will be good company."

Maggie wondered where he would sleep and nearly asked him to stay, more for want of someone to remind her she was not dreaming than for actual companionship, but ended up flushing pink again as she reconsidered. He raised an eyebrow in response and Maggie dropped her chin to avoid his stare.

"Okay. Thank you, Winn," she murmured.

He made a low grunting noise in reply and stood up.

"Good dreams, Maggie."

When she looked up, the bear hide hanging over the doorway flapped closed. He was already gone.

6

Maggie walked beside Teyas through the center of the village, glad the younger girl's arm was laced securely through hers. The packed clay beneath her feet lined a wide lane throughout the heart of the town, smooth under her moccasin-clad toes. The girl chatted gaily, pointing out the Great Long House that formed the hub of the community, taking care to explain how important it was to her people. It stunned Maggie to see how comfortable Teyas seemed with the idea of her time travel. The girl was patient and thorough as she gave Maggie lessons on their ways, focusing frequently on the role of women and how they were expected to behave.

Although Maggie listened, her scattered memories of history lessons competed with what Teyas said and it was difficult to resolve it all. Teyas said the small village was Paspahegh; from what Maggie recalled, the Paspahegh people were the first Native American tribe that English settlers to Jamestown encountered after their arrival, but the Paspahegh disappeared from the written historical record shortly thereafter.

The numerous horses were another peculiar matter. Teyas explained that many years before, her people had helped Spanish survivors of a shipwreck. Most of the crew were lost, along with all their supplies and cargo, but many of the ponies swam to shore. The handful of Spaniards that survived gifted the Paspahegh with a half dozen ponies, and eventually the foreigners left to search for their own people they believed were settled somewhere in the south.

Listening as best she could while taking in the busy village, her attention peaked when Teyas spoke of her family. She explained how the lineage of the Chief, or *Weroance*, came from the maternal line, and how their Great Weroance Opechancanough was brother to Chulensak Asuwak. She was not surprised by the role women played, since she knew a bit about the early settlement of Virginia and had once found stories about the First People quite fascinating. However, the reality of living it was a different matter entirely.

Maggie dared a question at that point, hoping she would not offend Teyas or cause a stir.

"So where is your father, Teyas? Does he have light eyes, like Winn?"

Teyas shook her head. "No, Winn and I do not share fathers. Chulensak Asuwak is second wife to my father, Pepamhu. He lives with his people, the Nansemond, and sometimes he visits. Pale Feather is the father of Winkeohkwet."

"Sounds complicated," Maggie said. Teyas smiled and nodded to a group of women seated in a circle working hides. Maggie followed suit and smiled, not too surprised to see a few glares returned among scattered shy smiles. Teyas noticed the somewhat unfriendly greeting and pulled Maggie to a stop in front of the women.

"Chitkwesikw! Eholekw toholao!" the younger girl hissed. Several pairs of eyes widened at her words and a few heads ducked to the ground in shame. Teyas hooked her arm back through hers and continued walking.

"What did you say to them?"

"They are jealous women. I told them to be quiet." Teyas squeezed her arm as she smiled.

Maggie swallowed hard and did not reply, but squeezed back. She was at loss over how to get out of the situation, knowing she had no weapons in her arsenal to combat the predictions of an Indian prophecy. She changed the subject back to where they left off.

"So Pale Feather has light eyes then?"

"Oh, yes. He is like you. A *weopsit.*"

She gasped and swallowed so fast that she choked, ending up in a coughing fit. Teyas patted her back, eyeing her strangely.

"Does Pale Feather know how to use the Bloodstone?" she sputtered, trying to catch her breath and get more information before Teyas clammed up again.

"Of course. He used one to leave many summers ago, before Winkeohkwet was born."

The sliver of hope she allowed to surface found a quick death. The only person she knew so far who could help her besides Winn was gone. Could it be any more unfair?

"Oh. That's too bad," Maggie said, more to herself than to Teyas.

Two familiar warriors approached, just as Maggie gritted her teeth against the pain of a sharp rock stabbing through her moccasin. She was fairly certain she would never get used to the clothes or shoes, and failed to accept why she couldn't just wear her own boots. After all, it was not like it was some big secret that she came from a different time; everyone she met so far acted as if it was a perfectly normal occurrence.

"You look much better today, Red Woman," Chetan said with a shy grin.

"Thanks," she replied. Teyas seemed welcoming to the men, and Maggie wondered how they were all related after the mini-genealogy lesson she received. Makedewa flanked Chetan, his demeanor much less flattering, and Maggie again felt a twinge of unease in his presence.

"Did the mare drop her foal yet, Chetan?" Teyas asked, pointing toward a lean-to and corral where several horses stood eating.

"Yes, but neither will live. The mare bleeds, and the foal will not stand. They will die soon."

"What mare?" Maggie interrupted. Chetan waved his hand toward the corral.

"She lies there. The colt is too big and his legs too weak. Go see," he offered, moving aside to let them pass. Maggie pushed in front to see what they spoke of, and was sad to see a large sorrel mare lying motionless inside the lean-to. Her barrel heaved with each breath, her silken nostrils flaring with the effort to push the air through her lungs. Her belly was slathered in sweat, and her eyes sallow.

Maggie did not think to ask permission. She lifted her leg and ducked under the wooden rail, sinking to her knees in the straw beside the mare. The sorrel twitched her ear forward and made no other movement, except to shift her eye back to the male foal at her side. Lying in a heap, gangly legs curled under his body, the nose of her colt lay buried against her lathered flank. He could not reach her teat to nurse, nor could she move to help him.

"He can't reach her—he needs her milk," she said when the man reached her side. Chetan squatted down beside her, but Teyas and Makedewa hung back, silent.

"Yes, he will die without her. He is not even strong enough to stand. I know little about this mare, she came as a gift from the English. She is much different than our Spanish ponies," he answered. He ran his hand down the neck of the mare and patted her softly. "Go in peace, *nehenaonkes.*"

Maggie already knew the mare was past hope from the pale color of her gums and the way her skin hung limply from her muscles. She had lost too much blood in the birth, but the colt might still be saved. If she could get him to nurse, perhaps he would stand, and then he would have a chance. Her eyes darted around the corral, and when could find nothing of help she turned to Chetan.

"Do you have a sack? Like you can carry water in?" she asked.

"Sack?" he frowned. *"Mpiakhakw?"* He held out a soft skin that Maggie thought might be the bladder of some animal, but it was perfect and her face broke into a wide smile.

"Yes, that's perfect! Mpiakh-akw!"

"Do you know horses, Red Woman?"

"I raise horses back where I come from. I think I can help this one, if you help me," she replied. She saw the hesitancy when he glanced back at his brother, but was relieved when he quickly returned to her for instructions.

"Help the new one. What do you need?"

"We need to milk the mare, the colt needs the colostrum."

"The first milk?"

"Yes, we need to milk it from her." Maggie crawled closer to the mare, fairly certain there would be no resistance, but she watched for a swinging hoof in case the dying mother objected to her teat being milked. Maggie never had a mare die at birth, but she had helped milk a sick mare once, and knew she could extract something to help the colt. The mare let out a sigh when Maggie grasped the base of the swollen teat and massaged it downward, but other than that, the horse did not stir.

Chetan bent over her shoulder, nodding encouragement at her work. The milk was slow to start, but then it suddenly began to rush in a steady flow into the bladder skin, filling it quicker than she anticipated.

"We need another, Chetan, hurry!" she called out, unwilling to risk losing even a few drops of the precious liquid. Chetan shouted to Makedewa, who snapped a curt reply, causing Chetan to groan in frustration. Teyas stepped forward, snatched the water bladder from Makedewa's belt, and thrust it through the fence rail at Chetan. Teyas stood on the low rail and leaned over to watch, and Makedewa stalked off amid a growl of what she could only imagine was cursing.

Chetan held the second bladder until it filled, and Maggie stopped milking.

"I need a knife to cut a hole," she said. He did not hesitate. He unsheathed a small dagger from the edge of his legging and handed it to her. Their eyes met for a moment, and Maggie was pleased at the trust in his gaze. They both grinned when she plucked a hole in the bottom of the first full bladder and watched the milk shoot out in a steady stream into her hand. She quickly pinched the hole closed and sat down beside the listless colt, which nickered softly at the scent of milk on her hands. He did not struggle when she placed his over-large head in her lap, but seemed not to know what to do when she placed the makeshift nipple in his mouth. The colt wrinkled his nose and sneezed.

Teyas and Chetan exchanged and anxious glance. Maggie refused to let the colt ignore the life-saving nourishment, and squirted some of the warm fluid into her hand. She cupped her palm to the colt's nose and fought as he tried to weakly pull away, and then suddenly either from exhaustion or her persistence, he stopped.

The colt stuck out his tongue and licked her hand.

She quickly filled her palm again, and the colt licked it dry. She heard a weak nicker from the mare and smiled.

"We'll save your baby, momma," she whispered to the dying mother. She knew it was her last breath. Maggie offered the bladder again to the colt, and he eagerly latched onto it and began to suck. She held the bladder against her breast and cradled the colt's head in her lap, reaching out to scratch him gently along his mane.

"The mother is gone," another voice said. Winn kneeled down beside her.

"I know," she said softly. She slowly raised her eyes to meet Winn's gaze, relieved to see his face soft and his blue eyes shining. *He looke◦ quite han◦some when he was happy*, she thought.

"You have soft hands. My young horse is lucky you care for him. I have no warriors to spare for one sick colt."

"Your horse?"

"A gift from the English. The mare was mine. Thank you for helping this one."

His quiet stare held hers for a timeless moment, his brows shading the slits of his deep blue eyes as the corners of his mouth turned slightly up. She could tell neither if he was amused or just grateful, but the intensity caused her belly to do that strange aching thing and she ducked her eyes downward in response.

"I'll stay and feed him. He'll need to eat several times tonight. And then we need a goat, or a cow, for more milk," she stammered. The colt began to slow his feeding, and she wiped a froth of milk from his whiskers with the edge of her dress. His lips dropped away, and his head felt heavy again in her lap as he lay satiated and began to snore. A sleepy musical whinny filled the silence.

Winn glanced down and noticed the knife, which he plucked from the dirt and held out to his brother. "Chetan, your knife."

Maggie nearly forgot his brother stood beside them. Chetan took the knife, but his eyes met those of his brother and they exchanged a stare she did not understand. Chetan lifted his chin and held the knife out to Maggie.

"You saved a life with this weapon. It is my gift to you, Maggie," he said. Stunned, she was slow to accept the gift, but he reached gently for her hand and placed the knife in her palm. He closed her fingers around it and glared at Winn. He then turned quickly and left the lean-to. Maggie noticed Teyas shoot them a wide-eyed look, and then jump off the fence to follow him.

"You cannot stay here all night, little one," Winn said softly, breaking the silence. She chose not to question the knife exchange for fear of changing his grateful demeanor, especially when she meant to challenge him for the right to stay with the colt. Caring for the animal was something solid she could focus on, a way to find some foothold in the insanity of her predicament.

"I will stay, I can take care of him."

Her breath ceased when he moved behind her in the loose grass, sitting close and leaning his back against the base of a tree. He then reached out and pulled her slowly to his chest, pulling the colt with her to remain snuggled on her lap. The colt continued to snore. Winn tightened his arms around her waist, and she felt his chin rest on her shoulder.

"You argue too much. Sleep. I will watch over you," he grumbled. Maggie smiled at the twinge of amusement in his rankled tone. She settled back against him and let out a sigh. A truce then, and a welcome one.

A series of muffled giggles roused her from her sleep. Her cheek lay flat against Winn's chest, her hand tucked in a fist beneath her chin, and she lifted a hand to swat at him when he plucked at her hair. It tickled, and she was not ready to wake yet. He persisted despite her attempt to smack him, and she opened her eyes to confront his intrusion of her sleep.

"Stop it!" she hissed. A pair of soft brown eyes stared back, attached to the biggest head she had ever seen on a newborn colt. He stood over her on long, but steady legs, chewing a piece of her auburn hair between his gums. A smile washed over her face as she stared at the colt in amazement. He was tall, with strong straight legs and a huge, mischievous face. She felt Winn sit up behind her with his arms loosely looped around her waist.

"Bad horse!" she laughed. "I think I'll call you Blaze." It seemed appropriate, considering the swash of white streaking his face from ears to nose. She could not tell what color his coat would be for sure, but she suspected it would be chestnut considering the shade of downy fur he was born with. She scratched him under his chin and he nickered softly. More giggles erupted, and Maggie glanced up at the commotion. Standing on the middle rail in a row were three children, two girls and a boy, watching them sleep in the horse pen. She moved to get up, but Winn held her in place.

"Stay," he grinned. "Feed Blaze. I will return and feed you."

Her eyes followed him. He made a harsh barking noise at the children, who merely laughed louder, and then he chased them away from the lean-to. He snatched a retreating boy by his breechcloth and knelt beside him, pointing to Maggie and the colt.

"Go fetch her some water, little warrior. You will make my *Tentay teh* happy." The boy grinned, and Winn patted his shoulder, speaking into his ear. "A wise warrior makes a woman smile."

7

Winn wished to ignore Makedewa as he made his way back to Maggie, but his brother was in a temper and refused to be put off. He paused when the warrior uttered a respectful, but curt, greeting, knowing it would be rude to ignore his brother in front of the other men. Winn shifted his sack of food to his shoulder and spread his legs slightly apart, crossing his arms as he waited to hear what Makedewa needed to say.

"What say you, brother?"

"Brother?" Makedewa sneered. He lifted his chin in the direction of the lean-to and flung out a hand to point toward Maggie and the colt. "You fail to kill the Red Woman, then you keep her! You give her your yehakin and sleep alone in the Great Long House? What is this?"

"I found her. She is mine for what I please. It is no matter to you, I have told you this!" Winn straightened up to his full height and his eyes narrowed as his brother continued to rant.

"True, you found the Red Woman. So she is your prisoner. Why does she walk free in our village? You let Chetan give her a knife!"

Chetan moved to stand between the two warriors.

"I gave her the knife for her kindness. And for her protection," Chetan growled. "If you try to kill her, I hope she stabs your black heart!" he snapped at Winn, then turned to Makedewa. "And yours, too!"

"You both have no voice in this. I captured her. She is nothing more than a slave. I will speak on it no more," Winn snapped. He could not believe his brothers. He expected as much from Makedewa, and knew the hot-tempered warrior was angered the woman still lived. But Chetan? Giving the woman a knife as a weapon, a knife to stab him with? He suspected as much when his brother presented the gift, but he had been too pleased with the way Maggie smiled at him to question it further. Curse them, and curse the Great Creator, the woman had him scraping for her affections like a wounded puppy!

Maybe there was some truth to Makedewa's words.

"We leave to hunt. Get your ponies, and tell your women," Winn ordered, his voice calming to a lower octave. He put his hand on Chetan's shoulder before his brother could follow Makedewa. "Tell Teyas to tend to…my captive. I will not see her again before we leave."

Chetan shrugged off his hand and stalked away. As Winn heard the muttered curse his brother uttered he closed his fingers into a fist. He deserved Chetan's curses, and they both knew it.

The hunt was a successful one, and Winn was glad to be headed back to the village after two grueling days of chasing game. What once might have been a half day hunt, or at most, a full day, had become much longer, and it took many more men now to take down enough game to feed their families.

He wondered if it was time to scout for a new spring settlement, a place where they could find more plentiful game and spend more time on their other duties, but they had used their current land since Winn was a boy of ten summers and he was reluctant to make such a change. Furthermore, Winn was only War Chief to his tribe, nothing more, so any such move would need permission of the Council and his uncle, the Weroance Opechancanough. He had led the remnants of the Paspahegh tribe since his uncle appointed him War Chief, but he knew Opechancanough would not approve any change until his plan to drive the whites from their land was fulfilled. Until then, the few Paspahegh people left were trapped living on land that was nearly depleted of resources. All were bound by the Weroance to remain friendly and accommodating to the whites to gain their trust.

He gave a curt nod to Chetan as his brother rode up beside him. The man was shorter in stature, but still not a warrior to have as an enemy, and Winn was glad to have loyalty from such a man. Wide and muscular, he was a fierce fighter who showed no fear of any threat. Since his wife had died last summer, Chetan spoke less and smiled even rarer, so Winn was surprised to see his brother with a secret grin as they approached the village.

"What is so amusing, brother?" Winn finally asked as the other man continued to smirk.

"Well, I look forward to our return home. The men speak of what women to take to furs."

"So what?" Winn snapped, not intending to sound so irritated.

"If you do not take your slave to furs, I will take her. I like her red hair and pretty pale skin."

Winn felt his teeth snap together so forcefully he feared he cracked his jaw.

"I am not ready to share my slave," he growled, incensed at the rage building in his blood. How dare his favorite brother presume to share his captive?

Chetan lifted one corner of his mouth in a wry smile.

"Then claim her yourself."

"Why do you test me, Chetan?"

Winn gripped his reins tighter and felt his fingers dig into his palms, trying to contain the urge to reach over and grab his brother by the throat as the man continued to grin and shake his head.

"If you do not claim her, another man will challenge you. Then I must challenge him, and I do not wish to fight. But if I must save my stupid brother from himself, I will."

Chetan smacked Winn's thigh with the long end of his reins, leaving a welt across his skin and a scowl on his lips. Winn looked straight ahead, refusing to acknowledge the taunt.

"Any man who tries to take what is mine will die a quick death."

"Then stop being a fool. Or I will take her from you and die smiling for it."

Chetan smirked, smacked Winn again with the rawhide rein, and took off in a gallop. The village was ahead up in sight, and the warriors began to whoop and holler in greeting. His blood began to simmer at the thought of their usual return from the hunt. It was common for the men to seek comfort after the task, and there were plenty of widows and wives who welcomed the attention. Winn found there was always a woman eager to warm him and he usually joined in the celebration. But now, as they approached the village and the warriors screamed their success, he felt a fire smoldering in his chest as he thought of the woman who waited in his yehakin.

She belonged to him by right, if not by prophecy, and he would be damned to let another challenge him.

8

Teyas bent over a large iron cauldron, nodding in approval at Chulensak Asuwak as she inhaled the steam from the stew. Thick with venison, it was a special mixture prepared with more meat than usual to celebrate the return of the hunting party. Maggie felt her stomach rumble in response when the heady scent drifted to her nostrils. Although they tended to her needs and appeared quite considerate, Maggie felt hungry often as she was not accustomed to the portions or food the Indians ate. She tried everything they offered, afraid to offend, but she still could not stomach some of the fare and had trouble eating enough to ease her hunger pangs.

Ahi Kekeleksu snuck up and snatched a piece of bread from the rations the women divided, and giggled when Maggie caught him by his elbow. She squeezed the child as he howled in mock disgust at her attention, then whispered a warning in his attentive ear.

"Don't tell anyone I let you have that, you menace," she laughed.

"No, *Tentay teh*, I will not!" he promised in his most fierce warrior pledge voice. She released him, and he sprinted back toward the corral. He was one of the children who watched the first feeding of the orphan colt, and in the days since the warriors had been away hunting, he became a shadow to Maggie. Teyas explained he was Chetan's young son, and had lost his mother only the summer prior. Maggie took an immediate liking to the child, and was pleased to cultivate his interest in the colt by showing him how to feed and care for the orphan.

Maggie watched from afar as the child leaned over the fence with the offering. The colt trotted over, taking the bread from his flattened palm with gentle bites.

"The food will cook longer. We can change your bandage now, sister." Teyas handed Maggie a bundle of rolled cloths they would use to dress her wound. The scratches were healing and the site remained sore, but so far free from signs of infection. Skilled at healing, Teyas tended the villagers with remedies made from herbs and roots, a craft she explained was handed down from elder women of the tribe. Maggie did not know what Teyas applied to her wound, but she was grateful for her care since she knew the alternative was likely death from infection.

Teyas served as her constant companion while the men hunted, leaving her no opportunity to escape the confines of the village. Maggie searched the yehakin thoroughly without success the first night Winn was gone, and with no idea where else he may have hidden her Bloodstone, she felt even more hopeless as the days wore on.

Maggie glanced up at Teyas and smiled. She took the proffered bundle and tucked it under her good arm. As Teyas bent to throw more wood on the fire for the stew, a group of riders entered the village.

Greased with paint but otherwise undecorated, the warriors looked surprisingly fresh after their two day hunt, especially considering the large amount of game they dragged on a sled behind one of the horses. Amid the impatient snorting and stomping, the warriors handed the animals off to younger boys to be tended while they allowed the women to fuss over them. Maggie watched the scene from across the village yard as women flocked to the warriors in welcome. She spotted Winn among them, aware that the breath left her body in a relieved sigh with the knowledge he returned safe. His eyes met hers through the crowd and she saw his lips curl up as he nodded to her in acknowledgement.

"Good, the men have returned," Teyas said. Maggie nodded absently, and Teyas prodded her with a wooden spoon. "He will come for you, just wait," she teased.

Maggie frowned and shook her head. "I don't care what he does. I'm just glad he's not dead, that's all." She felt hurt by the way he left so abruptly, not even wishing her goodbye, but she would not show the arrogant man how he wounded her.

Teyas giggled. Maggie kept her head down to shield her flushed cheeks, but she could still see the group of warriors surrounded by the women. One young beauty threw her arms around Winn and proceeded to kiss him, and Maggie watched as he turned his head from the kiss but picked up the woman and swung her around, laughing at her squeal. Another warrior plucked her from Winn's arms, but two more women blocked his exit with eager embraces. He wore a frustrated smile as he met her eyes again, but this time Maggie looked away. He could have his half-naked women, it was no matter to her. She only needed Winn to return to her own time, nothing more.

"Such a stupid man," she mumbled, much to the amusement of Teyas.

"You should tell him that, Maggie," she laughed.

Maggie sent a scathing glare in her direction just in time to see the glistening warrior swoop in and yank her off her feet. His skin was slick and hot as she squirmed against him, letting out a shriek of surprise at his ardent enthusiasm. Cradled in his arms like a child, her chest heaved with uneven breaths to match his own. His eyes squinted against the sun and a boyish grin graced his face.

"Tell me what, *Tentay teh?*" he demanded as he swung her in a circle. She could not help but laugh as he twirled, then pretended to drop her only to catch her before she hit the ground, causing her stomach to do back flips as she giggled along with him.

"She says you are a stupid man, Winkeohkwet," Teyas offered. Maggie stiffened, afraid Winn would be angry. His laughter slowed and he gripped Maggie tighter in his arms. She felt his muscles tense as she placed her palm to his chest in attempt to steady her breathing.

"Ah, well, we will see," he replied. He raised one eyebrow at Teyas, and then turned abruptly to stalk away with Maggie still in his arms.

"Winn, that's enough, put me down!" she said, eliciting only a chuckle from him.

"Only I give orders in this village, woman."

"Stop calling me that! And put me down!" she shot back. His grin remained.

"You want me to put you down?"

"Yes!"

He smirked and released his hold, and she closed her eyes to prepare for hitting hard ground. Instead she splashed into the shallow creek bed, going under and immediately surging to the surface, spitting up water. He stood waist deep beside her, roaring with laughter as she sputtered.

Maggie regained her footing, and as he continued to laugh, she launched herself at him, tackling him into the water. She was glad the attack caught him by surprise, giving her the upper hand for a split second before he grabbed her in a bear hug and drew them both beneath the water again, bringing them to the surface when she thought her lungs might explode.

He easily deflected her blows as he laughed, finally stopping her onslaught by wrapping her in his arms. Soaked through and shaking, uncertain if anger or amusement drove her, she relaxed her fists. She uttered a half-laugh, half-choke and clutched his shoulders to keep her footing. The creek bed sand shifted easily beneath their feet, and he repositioned to a wider stance yet continued to hold her. His laughter eased when their eyes met. His clear, sparkling blue eyes reflected humor, which she could see rapidly changing into something more. She swallowed back her own unwelcome response, confused by the way his gaze sent a tingling down her spine.

"Have I silenced you yet, *Tentay teh*?" he asked, his voice low and throaty. She meant to look away and laugh, but she only managed to shake her head. He called her *Tentay the* often, and although she did not know the meaning, it sounded nice enough, so she did not mind.

"No. You can't make me stop talking," she whispered.

She regretted the words immediately, for she saw his eyes widen in surprise and a wicked grin creased his face.

"I must try harder, then," he answered. Before she could object, his mouth closed gently over hers and then curled into a smile.

"See? I can make you stop talking," he breathed against her mouth.

Still shaking, her eyes flew open and she yanked away, her cheeks burning. She tried to turn away to escape to the bank, but he held her tight, shaking his head. He glanced briefly over her shoulder, and then his eyes returned to capture hers.

"You're a pig!" she whispered.

"Perhaps. But my men watch, and I would not have them question what is mine." She shivered when she looked toward the bank and saw he told the truth. Several of the warriors stood nearby with the women, talking and laughing as they watched the spectacle in the creek.

"I don't belong to you," she said, trying to keep her voice even.

He paused before he answered, his eyes glancing at the warriors and then back to her. She tensed when his palm tightened on her waist and he pulled her closer as if to solidify his message.

"Stop that!" she hissed.

He spoke again, low and firm, his lips so close to her own shaking ones.

"Why do you defy me? Do women in your world speak to men this way, or is it just you?"

The sincere question caused a surge of despair to swell, which overflowed to darken her gaze before she could stem it. The utter reality of her situation had been easy to put off for the last few days as she spent time with Teyas, but now that Winn stood in front of her making demands, it all rushed back. She was far from home and had no idea how to return – or if return was even possible.

"Women of my time take care of themselves. We don't have men telling us what to do all the time. We call men like you chauvinist pigs," she whispered. His eyes narrowed into slits.

"My men watch, *Tentay teh*. When they watch, you must...obey."

She scowled and opened her mouth to protest, but this time he covered it with his hand.

"When they watch, you obey," he repeated, slower this time. When she finally gave in and nodded, he let his hand drop from her mouth. "It is the way of this time, and my right as your captor."

"Am I a prisoner?" she whispered.

"I found you. It is my right to keep you as a slave if I choose. Or I may give you away to one of my men, if you do not please me." He held her face with his hands so she could not look away. "Do you understand?"

She did not answer, but held his gaze.

"The men choose women to share their furs after the hunt. It is what we do when we return. I would keep you with me now."

"And if I run?"

"Do not run."

She followed his logic and could make no response. She thought her silence would pacify him, but it only seemed to agitate him further. He carried her from the creek then, passing the group of warriors with a nod and making his way back to his yehakin.

A fire in the hearth greeted them, and Maggie's bundle of bandages lay next to the fur-sleeping mat. She reached for the bundle, knowing her dressing needed to be changed and the wound cleaned, but afraid to make her request known to Winn. The man was frustrating beyond measure, and she had no idea why he fascinated her so much. Why on Earth had she let him kiss her? Had time travel warped her brain?

She peered at him from the corner of her eye as she pretended to study the bandages. His confidence alone was enough to send even a modern woman into a swoon. Tight sinews flexed in his limbs as he bent to remove his leggings, then stood and dropped his wet breechcloth to the floor. She glimpsed a dark winding tattoo from one hip to his tapered navel, and gritted her teeth as she quickly turned her back, noting that his flaming eyes met her own before she cowered.

Damn him, she seethed.

She sat down with her back to him and began to unroll the bandages, the motion echoing the unraveling of her senses. What did he plan to do with her?

She stiffened and closed her eyes when he placed a hand on her shoulder from behind, the scent of evergreen and sweat that was distinctly him invading her senses. The truth of her situation hit her like a bolt through the gut. She was trapped in the past and her very survival depended on his mercy.

His fingers kneaded her shoulders, and she bit back a harsh retort as his fingertips brushed over her skin. When he untied the laces of her dress from her nape, she stubbornly held the dress up with her fists pressed into her chest to keep it from falling away. She would not let him continue without a fight.

"I will fight you," she whispered. His fingers paused the gentle massage for a moment at her words, then resumed a lazy rhythm. She remained there unmoving, knowing she could not outrun him, but sure that she could at least hurt him in some way.

"Be still. That is an order." She felt his breath hot against her neck and the command chilled her, but she obeyed it as she awaited his next move. He tugged at the binding of her wound dressing and she felt it unravel.

"I can't," she replied as tremors shook her body.

He removed the remnants of the dressing and a moment later a warm gush of water flowed over her wound. Winn repeated the process several more times before he was satisfied, and then gently patted the wound with a clean cloth. Maggie held her breath as he reached around her for the bowl of healing salve and then smeared it over the wound. What game was he playing? She felt like a toy, twirling aimlessly at his mercy. Motionless and silent, she waited as he replaced the bandage with a fresh one and secured it around the sensitive skin of her shoulder.

Maggie did not expect the pile of clothes that landed in her lap, and she startled at the quick motion. A soft, dry white doeskin dress lay across her legs, along with a pair of small white moccasins, decorated with a delicate pattern of red and black beads. She slowly turned to look at him and was surprised to find him standing near the fire, a frown on his lips and his blazing blue eyes fastened on her.

"Change your wet clothes. Then we will eat."

She held her wet dress up with one hand and clutched the new one with the other.

"I – I'll change when you leave."

He closed the distance between them in three strides, snatching a fur from the bed and wrapping it around her shoulders like a cloak. He grabbed the white dress from her. She noticed his hands were clenched, and she could see he struggled to contain his ire.

"Change now, woman," he growled. "Or I will do it for you."

She returned his challenge by glaring back into his seething blue eyes, then snatched the dress from his hand and turned her back to him. She heard him stalk away, but even knowing he was across the room still sent shivers down her spine as she let her wet dress fall to the floor. She managed to keep the fur wrapped around her as she stepped into the dry dress, but waited to face him again.

She felt the flush of her skin and hated herself for her weakness. Naked skin was nothing special to the Indians, she knew from her observations over the last few days. Women went topless more often than not, or had a flimsy fur shawl wrapped around their shoulders to cover bare breasts. Maggie was grateful for the modest dresses Teyas gave her, but she was aware that she was much more covered than any of the other young women. She struggled to be so confident, as Winn obviously expected, but she failed miserably.

Maggie sat down across from Winn at the fire, keeping the thick fur around her shoulders as they ate. He took a few bits of food from each bowl and passed it to her, keeping his eyes on hers as he slowly chewed.

"Your wound looks like it heals. You are lucky."

She refused to meet his eyes as she ate and nodded in response.

"Thank you...for helping me. I can't reach it very well on my own," she murmured.

He rested one hand on a bent knee and lay back onto an elbow, studying her as she finished her meal. She stole a glance at him over the rim of her cup as she drank, seeing a bemused tilt of his head and a furrowed brow which seemed distinctly non-threatening.

"Women of your time, they have no need of men?" he asked. He twirled a piece of straw in his fingers as he waited for her response.

"Women take care of themselves is all I meant. They don't need a man to tell them what to do, or to look after them." She took another sip from the cup and watched as he struggled to find his words.

"No husbands? The men must be weak to let women behave that way," he declared, tossing the straw into the fire. She smiled despite herself.

"We still *like* men, and women do marry. But it's not necessary to have a husband, it's just... nice."

"And you? Did you leave a man in your time?"

"Yes," she said, although she believed she would regret baiting him in such a way when she saw his jaw clench. "My grandfather. I feel like I left him. He died last month, and I'm not there now to put flowers on his grave...or to take care of the farm. But a husband? No, there is no one."

His tense demeanor relaxed at her explanation, and he met her tentative smile with a wry smile of his own across the blazing fire. Good thing she had not mentioned Marcus. Although the thought made her smile, the ache of missing her home felt heavy in her chest. The orange flames cracked and spit when he tossed in a loose stick, and she wrapped her arms around her knees and rocked back. She rested her chin on her locked hands and stared into the fire, remembering the way it felt when she grabbed the Bloodstone and the sun engulfed her being. She wanted to ask him where the stone was, but feared to damage the uneasy peace between them.

"It is strange for me to talk so much to a woman," he admitted. Now it was her turn to laugh, and she scoffed at his admission.

"Oh, is that so? If you were in my time, I would never give you the time of day with that attitude," she retorted. Her confidence grew as their exchange remained playful, but she knew she tread a thin line with his ancient ego.

"Humph," he snorted. "Maybe so, *Tentay teh*. But here," he said, pointing to the ground he sat on, "here women obey their men, and wait to be spoken to. My men see you defy my words, and they ask why I did not punish you," he said quietly. Maggie stopped rocking, aware the conversation had taken a turn. She pushed a loose strand of hair back behind her ear and noticed her hand trembled. Damn the man and his veiled threats!

"I thought I *was* being punished. You keep me here like a prisoner," she whispered.

"Pishi, I do keep you, it is my right. Not as a prisoner. If that was so, I would have cut out your tongue days ago."

She said nothing as he sat up, his face shrouded now in an unreadable mask as he stared at her across the fire. A not-so-veiled threat? She liked it even less.

"In this time my warriors follow me without question. They wait even now for my command. If I ask them to leave their women, they do so. And their women honor them as they go." His voice dipped as he stared into the heart of the fire. "Warriors do not answer to women. I will not answer to you out there," he pointed toward the door where they could see members of the village taking a meal by a large central fire. "Here, in my *yehakin*, I will hear you. You can call me... *show-vist pig*...and I will hear you."

Maggie stifled a hysterical laugh at his attempt to placate her as she bit back her despair. Winn was clearly throwing down the gauntlet, and her life was held in the balance. She would obey him without question, or she would be punished as women of this time were punished. He understood her own time was very different, so he was giving her a way to talk to him without damaging his authority with the tribe. She wished she could feel more grateful, but the only emotion she could summon was frustrating defeat. She was trapped, not only in his time, but also in his *yehakin*, to be punished at his discretion for any perceived slight.

She would play by his rules, but only until she discovered a way back home. She refused to admit she had little choice, deciding instead to fool him into trusting her. It was the only way to get what she wanted.

"Chauvinist. You're a chauvinist pig," she said softly, enunciating the syllables.

"Pishi," he nodded. "And you may keep your tongue."

He rose from his spot and approached. Her eyes never wavered from his, glaring in muted defiance when he gently pulled her to her feet. He led her to the sleeping mat, and with a few careful tucks, he nested the furs around her, and she closed her eyes.

When she dared to open them again, she saw him across the fire. He lay on his side, head on his forearm, his eyes closed in sleep.

9

A stream of morning sunlight warmed her face when she woke to find the yehakin empty. She should be glad the heathen left her alone, but a nagging voice in her ear wondered when she would see him again, or if he would return soon to continue ordering her about like she was his personal property. Well, he could stay away all day for all she cared. She was not thrilled with the prospect of deceiving him to get the Bloodstone back, but it was the only chance she had.

Her bladder felt near bursting, so she stopped off in the bushes to relieve herself before she made her way to the lean-to. She could take care of Blaze, and maybe come up with a few ideas of where Winn hid the Bloodstone. He had few personal belongings, and she had already searched them thoroughly, so she was certain the stone was not in his yehakin.

She grimaced at her toileting options, leaves or more leaves, and hurriedly completed the task before anyone noticed she was gone. It was bad enough walking around with no undergarments, but to have been observed during such a personal act would be humiliating. She never thought herself a shrew in her own time, yet among the women of the village, she was most assuredly the strange one. Maggie insisted on covering herself, unwilling to wear the skirts the others wore with only a mantle loosely covering their upper bodies, her modesty a well-ingrained trait she was unable to change even if it meant fitting in. Teyas understood, and Maggie felt lucky to have her as a tentative ally. The younger woman took to wearing a full dress very similar to the ones she gave Maggie, as if she gave her silent support by emulation. Maggie was glad for any camaraderie she could get.

Chetan was preparing to mount his Spanish pony when Maggie arrived. Makedewa was already astride, his horse pawing impatiently at the dirt as they waited for the other warrior. She was unsure if she should approach Chetan, but when a warm smile creased his face, she decided it was safe enough and continued.

"Red Woman," he nodded. "Your Blaze grows well, I think he will be a great stallion someday."

They turned to watch the colt, who perked up his ears and issued a shrill whinny at the sight of her. Chetan chuckled and Maggie reached in the fold of her waistband to find a sliver of apple she brought for him, reaching over the rail with the flat of her palm in offering. The colt quickly slurped up the fruit, leaving a slimy mess on her palm, which she rubbed off on the edge of her dress. Chetan watched the exchange, but his smile faded as he took her hand in his own.

Startled by the contact, but unafraid, she watched as he slowly turned her hand over to stare at her scarred palm. It was the hand that she held the Bloodstone in, and it was creased with a healing silver scar, a knot that looked strangely organized as if it was a brand.

"Ah, you have been marked. I see now," he said softly, as if to himself.

"What do you mean, marked?"

"The Bloodstone. It marked you, so you must truly be from another time. A woman Time Walker," he muttered as he shook his head, his round cheeks now more serene than smiling. "Is it a peaceful place, this time you come from?"

"It is very different," she offered. "Peaceful enough." Thoughts of the life she was torn away from were like lead in her throat, and she shook her head against the tears that threatened. "I miss it very much," she admitted. He ducked his head, squinted his eyes, and uttered a nervous cough to clear his throat.

"Maybe you are here because you should be. I think if you open your eyes, you will find happiness here with our people."

She did not answer him, unwilling to argue when he was trying to be kind, so she shrugged her shoulders in response as she remained silent.

"Winn buried the Bloodstones to keep you away, but still you are here. He thought never to disobey our uncle. He was sure he would kill the Time Walker if one ever arrived."

"Everyone would be happier if he just let me go home."

Chetan smiled, shaking his bowed head.

"No, I think not. Not my brother, and not you. I hear your words, but I see your heart. You were meant for this place."

A protest formed on her lips, but she did not voice it. There was no argument she could make against such magical things.

"Do you ride horses as well as you care for them?" he asked. She raised her eyebrows at his words.

"Well, yes, yes I do. I'm a good rider."

"Then come with me. I go to scout our border."

She glanced around him at Makedewa, who she could tell was listening but held his tongue. What harm would it do to take a ride? She was tired of being treated like a prisoner, as if she had no more value than an ear of corn, so perhaps a ride would ease her anxiety for a few hours.

"All right, I would like that. But will Winn be upset if I leave?"

Chetan made a deep snorting sound. "Upset? Yes, he will be. My brother is War Chief, but I am still a man. If you want to ride, you can come with me."

She grinned like a schoolgirl playing hooky when he slung a hackamore style bridle on a spotted pony and gave her a leg up. She was unaccustomed to riding bareback, a pursuit she left behind in adolescence, but she was eager to leave the village for a while and would have submitted to anything to do so. The animal was plump with a thick stout neck, making for a more comfortable ride than a lean horse, and she settled quickly into the motion of keeping her seat with her thigh muscles as they left the village.

They passed by the Great Long House and entered the woods, keeping to a narrow dirt trail winding through the evergreens. There was a gentle cool breeze in the shelter of the trees, and as it lifted her hair from the nape of her neck, she raised her hands high and stretched. Although her healing shoulder ached, it still felt wonderful, and as her chest expanded, the heady scent of the forest filled her lungs. Rocking with the motion of the horse, she let out a deep sigh and replaced her hands back down to rest on her bared thighs. She had never ridden bareback dressed so scantily, but the exhilaration of freedom squashed any doubts she might have had.

Chetan watched her and smiled as she stretched, and she heard an annoyed grunt from Makedewa, which she ignored. They clicked their tongues and urged their mounts into a faster pace, and she squeezed her knees to press her fat pony into an easy lope to keep up. She wondered why they suddenly changed speed, and was dismayed to hear another rider approaching. The men seemed unconcerned so she knew they were safe, but she hoped it was not someone who would object to her presence.

"Did you hear me shout, Chetan?" Winn growled as his pony caught up to them. The horses all slowed to a brisk walk, and Winn continued to rail at Chetan, who slowed his horse as he shrugged his shoulders in amused indifference.

"No, brother, I heard you not. I was too busy enjoying the view."

Maggie turned backward on her pony to look at the two men. Although Makedewa rode off ahead, she was clear on what Chetan implied and she twisted back around before she was tempted to chastise him.

She ignored the brothers as they argued in their own language, and continued on to follow Makedewa, who had pulled ahead quite a bit. Her pony navigated a narrow sandy trail that opened up from the woods onto a wide beach, stretching as far as she could see in both directions. When Makedewa took off, she felt a surge of excitement seeing him gallop away, and before she could contain the urge she tapped her heels against her pony and took off after him. She wound her fingers through her pony's mane and ducked her head against his neck, feeling sand spike up to dart her face like tiny needles as the sound of the surf muffled her peals of laughter. Saltwater splashed out like a wake around them, and seagulls screamed their displeasure at the intrusion as they conquered the beach. Her pony was not as fast, but he had plenty of heart, and it was not long before he was beside Makedewa's mount, their hooves pounding in near sync across the sand. Makedewa's eyes opened wide when he saw her, and although he did not smile, he did not scowl either, so she figured he was not too annoyed that she had followed him.

His pony slid to a stop, and hers responded the same, circling Makedewa a few times before the little beast was ready to cease pursuit. Nostrils flaring, his lips lathered, the pony snorted and stomped, and she patted him firmly on the neck to calm him. She could see Chetan and Winn riding toward them, and when she glanced back at Makedewa, she thought she glimpsed a smidgeon of a grin.

"You ride well, woman," he said gruffly without making eye contact.

"You ride okay yourself," she replied. His jaw was tight as he shook his head, turning his horse in a circle around her.

"I think you are much trouble for my brother."

"I don't want to be trouble for anyone. I just want to go home."

He made one of those half-laugh, half-snort sounds the Indian men were known to utter when they had nothing nice to say, then reached out and slapped her pony on the rump. The horse jumped but did not take off, instead succumbing to being rounded up and sent back in the direction of Chetan and Winn. Makedewa dismounted. He pulled a spear off his back as the other men caught up with them.

"Good ride, Maggie," Chetan grinned. She smiled back, despite the look of irritation on Winn's face.

"Thanks. It's beautiful here," she breathed, looking out toward the ocean. Low waves rolled in, crashing against the reefs to break their splendor before they rushed back toward the shore, creating a haphazard foam barrier along the sand. The water was a deep blue, brighter and clearer than any shore she had ever seen, and she recalled with sadness how sickly beaches of the future looked in comparison.

"Yes...beautiful," Chetan laughed. Maggie saw him shoot Winn a sly look, and then Chetan dismounted to follow Makedewa. She watched them stalk a shallow tide pool, thrusting their spears in to snare the fish trapped in the barrier. Winn's pony bumped into her own.

"Come on. We will ride some more," he offered, his voice controlled with the invitation. His blue eyes seemed cautious, betraying a glimpse of uncertainty, or perhaps bashfulness, both of which perplexed her when she was accustomed to a much different temperament.

"All right," she agreed. Their ponies walked off together so closely that her bare knee bumped against his with each stride, a constant tap to remind her he was still there. Although his shoulders pointed straight ahead, his dark head tilted toward her a bit and his braid fell across his arm, as if his words were meant to be some sort of secret between them.

"Chetan takes notice of you."

"Oh?"

"As do many of my people. Teyas sees you as a sister." His startling blue eyes met hers and held, and she could feel a stirring in her belly as he kept her gaze. He turned away abruptly and looked down at his hands for a moment before he adjusted his rein, then turned his head forward. "You look happy here today. Is your world so different than mine, *Tentay teh?*"

Maggie considered the question for a moment before she responded. Yes, her world was much different in many ways, but how could she make him understand? Loyalty, dedication, a home – they were all things that drove her to find a way back, yet with each passing day in the past, another sliver of her resolve flaked off and dissolved. Looking at his profile, seeing his jaw set against his teeth and his almond shaped blue eyes squinting against the sun, she wished they could just keep riding and somehow their peace could continue.

"Some things are very different. We don't ride horses anymore, that is, most people don't."

"So they travel by water instead? As we do with our *quintans?*"

"Well, no," she explained, assuming he was describing the dugout canoes the Paspahegh used for common travel. "We have these...wagons. Wagons that drive without a horse. There's an engine to make it move."

She could see his face relax and his smile turned genuine as she described cars to him. He snorted when she told him they ran on gasoline, a fossil fuel, and he laughed when she explained how people bought expensive cars to impress each other. Her tales of the future clearly intrigued him, however, and she prattled on with descriptions of indoor plumbing and spring-coiled mattresses.

"Is it from the English that all these things come?" he asked.

"Uhm, I guess. Mostly. But there will be many different kinds of people to come live here in the future, not just the English."

She saw how his smile faded and his eyes dimmed as he considered her response, and she suddenly had a feeling her words meant more to him. He reached out with a fist and grabbed her rein, stopping her mount beside his.

"So where will my people go, when so many whites come? Already our lands are used up, and many of our people forced to move. Even now the Paspahegh are few. What will happen to the Powhatan? When does it happen?"

Her teeth closed over her lower lip, and she pushed a strand of wayward hair back behind one ear. Should she tell him the truth of what was bound to happen, or was this knowledge of the future too much for him to handle? She still was not sure of her role in this time travel business, but with the turn their conversation took she suddenly feared what impact her actions could have. Would changing the past in turn change the future? And was it up to her to do so?

"Winn, I don't think –"

"Tell me," he insisted, his voice betraying that he expected the worst. She sighed with the knowledge that he would not relent without the truth, and tried to find the words to describe the end of the life he knew.

"I'm sorry..." she began. He listened without interruption, and when she finished the tale he remained wordless. His clear blue eyes exposed his despair, the azure depths reduced to empty hollows as the impact hit him. He appeared to pale beneath his dark skin, even the tips of his ears and his soft full lips drained of color. They rode in silence together, her heel tapping gently against his foot with each stride of her pony, until they joined his brothers again.

Makedewa kneeled over a small fire in a shallow pit in the sand, laying several fish pierced on stakes across the piles of rocks he lined the fire with. The fish hung suspended above the licking flames, the searing scent of their flesh cooking rising from the smoke. Chetan walked back from the surf, a wide grin across his round face as he held a snapping crab in his upraised hand. He took a proffered stick from Makedewa and speared it through, then tossed it on the fire with the fish, and her belly made a growling sound at the scent of fresh charred seafood as the food began to roast.

"Uhm, I'll be right back," she said. Winn raised an eyebrow as she dismounted. "I just need a minute to myself," she stammered. She had no idea what words to use to explain that she needed to void, so she was relieved when Winn seemed to understand and made no protest. He pointed over to the trees where they had entered the beach, and she gladly took his direction.

She wished she had even a smidgeon of the confidence the Indian women had, and she was deftly reminded of her failings every time she needed to relieve herself. She walked further back in the woods than was truly necessary for privacy, and when she was content she was adequately hidden, she squatted down and raised her dress.

"Akekweh!"

Maggie shot to her feet at the angry utterance and swung around to holler at whichever man had followed her, her face streaked with crimson at being interrupted. When she did not recognize the intruder, she let the leaves she had gathered fall from her hand and stepped back a pace.

Not just one, but two natives approached. The nearest one spoke to her again, his words a slower but much different cadence of the Paspahegh speech she had grown accustomed to, and he stepped boldly toward her when she did not answer.

"I don't understand," she said, feeling her heart start to pound in her ears. Already backed up to a thick grove of narrow young saplings, she had chosen the place for its natural screen, unaware it would become a prison in a few short moments.

The man continued his approach. Tall and lean, his chest heavily scarred and his eyes hollow beneath hooded brows, his black hair was shaved completely except for a section of long braid trailing from the top of his head down his back. Both men wore only breechcloths, and their skin was stained with black slashes of paint and an array of intricate tattoos. She held her breath as the first man reached out to her, taking a strand of her red hair in his hand. He peered at it for a moment, and then a grin spread slowly over his face when he looked up at her.

"What?" she croaked. His smile was not comforting, only serving to show her the gap where his lower tooth should be, and with his close proximity, the stale stench of his breath. He ran one finger across the black grease pattern on his chest, then reached out and rubbed the fingertip across her forehead, leaving a dark smudge on her pale skin. Stunned, she let out her breath. Perhaps it was a friendly gesture, and he would be on his way.

The men spoke amongst themselves, and then the first one turned swiftly back to her and grabbed her wrist, towing her with him as they went back the way they had arrived. She let out a screech and tried to pull away from him to no avail, and he grunted but otherwise ignored her as he dragged her along.

"No! Let me go!" she screamed. She dug her heels into the ground until he was forced to stop, at which point he turned back to her with a knife brandished. She froze when he held the blade under her chin and grunted something she did not understand, then proceeded to continue dragging her away.

"*Nahkihela!*"

The native stopped so fast that she stumbled into his backside, and relief washed through her when she realized the new voice belonged to Winn.

Great, she thought. Winn would clear up the little misunderstanding and they could go back to the beach peacefully to eat their fish.

She tried to shake off the hand that held her, but it remained locked like binding around her wrist.

Winn made no eye contact with her as he confronted the man, but the muscles in his neck were taut like bowstrings as he approached. The second man swung around to flank him, leaving Winn surrounded as he spoke in rapid Paspahegh to the intruders.

Something Winn said suddenly angered the man, and he snatched her forward and thrust the knife beneath her chin as Winn stepped toward him. At the sight of the knife and her gasp of surprise Winn immediately stopped, his feet planted shoulder stance apart, crouched slightly, his breathing slow and cautious.

"Winn?" she whispered. His eyes met hers, and she shuddered to see the flare of anger held back within as he remained poised to strike. She made her decision, and after taking a deep breath in preparation, she raised her leg up and struck backward with all her might. Her heel made contact with one knee in a sickening snap, and in a blur of copper skin and limbs she was shoved away to fall on the sandy soil at their feet as the warriors crashed together.

She saw the second man move to enter the fray, and since she had nothing with which to fight, she grabbed a handful of sand and threw it at him. He blocked her attempt but it slowed him down enough for her to find a nearby rock, which she also threw at him to little effect. When he unsheathed his knife and approached the two men who fought, she let out a piercing scream. Winn had the other man beneath him on the ground, fully exposed to an assault from the second man.

"No!" she yelled. There was a sickening thump and suddenly the man slumped to the ground, an arrow protruding from his temple and his eyes staring blindly at the sky. Makedewa stepped through the bushes, his bow poised ready for a second shot, Chetan flanking his side.

She scrambled backward on her bottom away from the dead man and watched as the brothers simply surveyed Winn as he fought. It made no sense to her why they did not jump in to help him. Winn rolled the man onto his back, hitting the man with his bloodied closed fist, bone connecting bone with a sickening crunch. Winn shouted at the man, and the intruder seemed to smile through his missing teeth, and when Winn shook him he spit a mass of blood out that splattered Winn's face and chest.

Winn raised his knife and thrust it deep into the side of the man's neck. The intruder went limp, and Winn slowly stepped off the man. His chest heaved then as if he released his anger in one final breath, and when she met his eyes she saw the rabid fierceness slowly fade. He swiped the back of his arm across his face, then sheathed his knife before he approached where she still sat on the ground.

"Winn?"

He kneeled in front of her.

"Are you hurt?" he asked softly. She shook her head. She stayed motionless when he reached out for her forehead and his fingers rubbed the oily black smudge from her skin. His blue eyes burned like two slanted embers when he looked down at her, her heart beating like a jackrabbit trapped in a snare.

"You will never wear the mark of another warrior."

The words were coarse and low from his lips, and in one motion he swept her up into his arms. She rode in his lap back to the village, her riderless pony trailing behind.

10

"Patawomecks. They were scouts," Makedewa said. He inhaled smoke from the long bone pipe, passing it to Winn as he exhaled. They sat with the other men in the Long House, cross-legged on furs in a circle. There were few Paspahegh men left in the village, many eradicated by English raids or white man's diseases, and of the forty odd men, only half were able-bodied enough to be considered warriors. Though only twenty strong, they were still fierce fighters and Winn was confident they could handle the threat from a few rogue Patawomecks.

"What reason do they have to spy on us? We leave their lands to them. We let them trade with the English as they please," another warrior spoke. Pimtune, an older man, sat up and addressed the others. Born with a twisted upper lip, he looked as if he always smiled, even when he was clearly agitated.

"They do not join with Opechancanough. I hear they want no more war with the English. The man I killed said nothing before his death," Winn said. His feet and hands felt heavy as he inhaled the sweet pipe smoke, the slow rush spreading a warmth through his essence as it cleared his troubled mind. He knew the Patawomeck opposed the upcoming attack on the English that his uncle had been planning for years. The Patawomeck had already refused to join the Powhatan and pledged they would remain neutral. Opechancanough had given up trying to ally with them as the time drew near, so this breach of territory worried Winn. There was no good reason for the Patawomeck to be in Powhatan territory, especially in the small Paspahegh lands.

"It is not usual for them to take English slaves, yet they tried to take the Red Woman," Makedewa said. The other warriors looked up at the revelation. Pimtune creased his brows yet remained respectful as he glanced toward Winn. Winn passed the pipe to him, and did not look at Makedewa, unwilling to show his brother how much the statement bothered him.

"What say you, Winkeohkwet?" Pimtune asked.

Winn nodded. "Yes, the dog marked her. It was clear he meant to take her."

Murmurs erupted among the men. A canopy of smoke hung over them, a wisp funneling up through the fire hole at the top of the Long House where the wind whipped above. Rumbles of an autumn storm shook the walls and the wind wailed outside. Winn wondered if Maggie was warm by the fire in his yehakin.

"We will send word to Opechancanough. He will want to hear of this."

The men grunted in agreement with Winn and resumed passing the pipe amongst them.

11

She lay curled under several furs, chilled by the unseasonably cold winds and eager to warm her frozen fingers and toes. Darkness had fallen hours before, yet Winn had still not returned. She waited up as long as she could, trying to keep the fire burning and failing miserably, until finally she gave up and retired to her sleeping space. Her mind would not rest, however, even though the remainder of her body begged to succumb, fatigue not enough of a distraction to keep away visions of the dead warriors.

An arrow to the temple, quick and effective.

A blade jammed into the neck? Equally as efficient, yet somehow seeming much more brutal. She recalled his eyes when he did it, the frigid, focused stare, flaming with violence, intent on bloodshed. Yet Winn came to her afterward, the fire dimmed, his gaze anxious, his touch gentle and calming.

He had killed a man to protect her, taken a life as if it meant nothing. She could not grasp how such violence could be turned on, and then off, like a simple switch to be flipped at a whim. He could turn that on her at any moment, yet some tiny voice inside whispered he would never direct that hatred on her.

She heard the flap of the door covering and knew he returned. With her scattered thoughts still fresh, she did not immediately rise, instead keeping her eyes closed to mimic sleep. She was afraid to face him, wanting to thank him, but unsure if thanking him for killing a man was something appropriate to do.

"*Tentay teh,*" he said softly. Warmth rushed through her when she felt him sit down beside her. Although the furs separated them, she still felt his heat, and his closeness caused her throat to tighten and her palms to moisten as they lay curled under her chin. He ran his hand over her hair, drifting down her chin, then to her shoulder.

She swallowed back against her closed throat and opened her eyes. He seemed unsurprised she was awake. His nearness was disarming, so much so she sat up and put a bit of distance between them. She crossed her arms over her chest.

"I did not mean to wake you," he said.

"It's okay. I wanted to see you." She bit her lower lip, the words seeming to come out in a disjointed mess instead of how she wanted them to. She held her breath as he reached over. He pulled a fur up over her shoulders and enclosed her in it, his fingers brushing her bared arms but nothing more.

"Oh? Why?" He sat back away from her, staring at her with his wide full mouth slightly parted, his blue eyes soft and serene.

"To thank you. For what you did," she replied. He frowned and ducked his head a bit, then met her stare again. She hesitated to explain further, but made the attempt anyway. "Men don't do things like that where I come from. Kill people, I mean. Not over a woman. Certainly not over me," she stammered.

His gaze hardened, and she saw the skin across his abdomen crease as he held his breath. She was confused when he left her side and began adding kindling to the fire.

"Did I say something wrong?"

"Men of your time," he snapped. "Are they all such weaklings? Are there no warriors? I protect what is mine, *Tentay teh.* Until breath leaves my body, I will do so."

Maggie sat back, stunned at his confession, unwilling to move a muscle before she could gather her senses to respond. He continued to toss wood to the flames.

"You think me savage, because men of your time spill no blood? I say your men know nothing of honor. Why do you want to return to such a time?"

"It's where I belong, Winn," she said softly.

"Je fais partie ou la lumiere me prenφ," he murmured.

"Is that Paspahegh?"

"No. French words, from a book. It means 'I belong where the light takes me'. Just as you do."

"Who are you?" she asked, filled with wonder at each snippet of soul he revealed to her. She rose from the furs and approached him. "Where did you learn that? You speak so beautifully."

His shoulders tensed, and she felt him stiffen when she slipped her hand into his.

"You think this savage knows nothing? I know many languages. I can read from your books. I am quite valuable to my Weroance."

She placed her other hand softly on his chest and moved closer to him so he could not avoid her gaze. He looked angry, yet controlled, but she needed to ease the fire and staunch the distance between them.

"I meant no insult," she said, trying to lighten his mood. "I was being nice." He frowned.

"Nice? Humph," he grunted.

"Here, sit. I have a gift for you," she said softly. He let her pull him down next to the fire, where Teyas had left a few supplies for her. A clamshell that fit snug in her hand, a bowl of thick bear fat, and a soft deerskin to use as a towel. When Maggie asked her how to properly thank Winn for what he had done, Teyas assured her that shaving his scalp would show him just how grateful she was. She only hoped she could do it without hurting him.

"Maggie—"

"Please. Let me do this for you."

When he watched her dip her hand in the grease, she saw his throat tighten. She knelt in front of him, and while placing one hand on his shoulder to steady herself, she carefully smeared the grease on the crescent of short hairs over his right ear. His eyes followed her every move-ment.

"Be still," she said. She took the sharp shell in the palm of her hand as Teyas instructed her, and slowly scraped it along his skin. She was pleased when the hair came cleanly away, leaving his bared scalp slick from the grease. His breath felt warm on her neck as she worked with her face close to his, going over the moon shaped patch to ensure it was smooth. As she leaned in to pat his skin dry, he turned his chin, a slight movement, yet enough for his lips to brush the side of her neck.

"Thank you for what you did today," she said.

She touched his cheek softly with her closed lips, meaning to give him something to show her sincerity, but at the contact, he caught her face in his hands, moving his mouth to gently cover her lips. Sweet with brandy wine he kissed her, his palms cupped around her cheeks.

She felt him shudder, and her own hands shook as she placed them flat upon his chest. She meant to move closer, every ounce of her being drawn to him, but suddenly he broke the kiss, breathing heavily as he looked down at her. His gaze flickered down, as if it pained him to face her.

"Go," he said, his voice hoarse, "take your rest. I will see you when the sun rises."

She thought he would kiss her again, yet he did not. He left her there alone by the fire, wondering what exactly had just happened between them.

* * *

"Did you cut him?" Teyas asked.

Maggie shook her head.

"I did a pretty good job, if I may say so myself," she replied. They worked together with the other village women, grounding Tuckahoe root into flour. Maggie would have liked to go out on the boats to re-trieve it, but she was reluctant to make any suggestions since most of the women viewed her with suspicion. She imagined they wondered if she was a slave or a guest, and since she was hardly sure herself, she could see why they might be leery of her.

"Oh, good! He liked it, then?"

"Seemed so," Maggie admitted. The memory of his kiss distracted her, and blood rushed to her cheeks as she dropped her wooden mortar. Teyas giggled.

"Is that so? My brother makes you clumsy. Maybe you should do more wife duties!" the girl laughed. Maggie stiffened and turned on her.

"What are you talking about? Wife duties?" she asked. No, surely Teyas would not be so sneaky! Maggie was fully aware it would take years for her to grasp the extent of the Paspahegh customs. Simple things she saw no meaning in were chock-full of implication in their world, so much so that she was afraid to make any move without prior instruction. When Teyas suggested she shave his scalp as a show of thanks, Maggie suspected nothing of it.

"When a woman shaves a man, she tells him she accepts his court-ing. Do not worry, Maggie, it is the proper way to show love."

"Wait a second!" Maggie sputtered. "I only wanted to thank him! I don't *love* him!" she hissed. Teyas grinned.

"Ah, thanks...love? The same," she laughed. Teyas continued with her grinding, and the women around them broke out in song, perhaps as a way to muffle the strange strangled sounds Maggie was making. Teyas nudged her with her foot, flashing a faux chagrined smile.

"Not funny, Teyas," she seethed. "Not funny at all."

Some of the other women chuckled, and Maggie clamped her mouth shut.

12

The celebration feast lasted three days. Maggie felt her body ache as she helped Teyas raise the large chunks of venison onto stakes for preparation. It surprised her to feel so fatigued from the daily chores the rest of the women churned through so easily, but she imagined her fitness level would catch up soon. Determined to perform her share, she trudged on, but she still looked forward to dusk when everyone slowed down. Then she could spend some time with Blaze. Although she instructed the children how to care for the growing colt, she enjoyed working with the animal and found it a distraction from reality. The best part of the day was also unfortunately the most uncomfortable, since it involved spending time alone with Winn in his yehakin.

Maggie met little progress trying to figure him out, and she was even more confused since he kissed her. Teyas explained he was War Chief of the tribe, a title of great honor to their people. She could see how the tribe respected him, how they deferred to his orders without question. She noticed how the women flocked to him and how Winn rarely stood in a crowd without one of them hanging on him. He acted kindly and near affectionate with many of them, although she noticed he never disappeared with the woman as the other warriors did. Teyas shared bits of information with her in their conversations as they worked, and she giggled about how Winn was blinded to any other women since Maggie arrived. It was meant as a compliment, but it gave Maggie pause. She was more afraid of her own growing feelings than she would care to admit.

Winn spent the mornings with the other warriors and attending to his duties, which was fine with her, especially since he had become much more thoughtful after their conversation of the future. She hardly knew what to say, and the urge to comfort him in some way squeezed her chest so much she could barely speak to him without longing to ease his distress.

Maggie worked to learn some of the language and relieve her frustration, intrigued by the smooth cadence of their speech and eager to communicate. Perhaps if she learned more and behaved as if she was trying to fit in, she could find others who might help her with the Bloodstone. She suspected Winn had something to do with the way Teyas clammed up anytime Maggie asked about the Bloodstone, and she was sure Winn hid the stone from her. Maggie spent many mornings searching the yehakin for it without success.

Maggie sliced her knife through the venison top to bottom, and as she watched the meat yield, a hand fell on her shoulder. She swung swiftly around, the blade clutched in her fist, thinking about how Winn had ended the life of a man with such a weapon.

Winn plucked the knife from her hand, his brows arched in challenge. She bit back a harsh retort and took a breath before responding. She crossed her arms and held her hand out to him, palm up.

"I can't finish without the knife," she said evenly. He nodded.

"Teyas can finish. I would walk with you."

"Are you asking me?"

He sighed, then nodded.

"Yes. Would you walk?"

Teyas smiled as if the exchange was normal courtship, and resumed her chores without complaint. To her surprise, Winn returned the knife to her hand and watched as she tucked it into the cord tied around her waist. She followed when he walked away, wondering where he would take her. He spoke little in the last two days other than to ask random questions about her time, which she tried to answer even though it made her more homesick, so this change in his behavior intrigued her.

She noticed eyes of the women follow them as they walked through the village toward the corral. Other than Teyas, Maggie was not allowed to spend much time talking to the others. She knew she had to earn Winn's trust if she was ever going to make any progress with her plan to leave.

His sorrel horse stood waiting. Winn helped her up and then mounted behind her in one lithe leap. He had not allowed her to ride alone since the attack in the woods. She twisted her hands in the coarse mane and tried to touch him as little as possible, but her attempts were useless when riding bareback with the man. They balanced much easier when she relaxed and leaned back, and she felt his thighs fit behind hers with less effort. He rode with one hand looped around her waist, the other guiding the horse with a single hackamore rein around its nose.

"Where are we going?" she asked.

"A surprise," he replied simply.

The horse trudged up a loose gravel path which became too steep to climb safely, so they dismounted and walked the rest of the way while Winn led the animal. The air felt crisp, cool against her skin as a light breeze lifted her winding auburn hair from her shoulders. She realized they stood on a peak overlooking the village valley. She stood closer to the edge of the slope, amazed at the miles of evergreens covering the valley, scattered by clumps of peaked hilltops entwined along the winding river. Maggie twisted her hair into a knot with one hand and closed her eyes as the breeze flowed over her again. She took a deep breath and let it out slow. How strange she never noticed before how beautiful this place was!

"You can see all of Tsenacommacah lands from here," Winn said. She heard his footsteps and felt his presence behind her when the tiny hairs on her neck stood at attention, but he did not move to touch her. The scent of leather and faint evergreen followed him, a scent she recognized now as belonging uniquely to him.

"It's beautiful," she replied.

"It is yours now as well. This land is part of you."

She bit her lip and tried to soften the blow of her answer.

"I—I can't stay here. I need to go back to my own time, Winn," she said softly.

She felt his chest brush against her back as he let his breath out in a sigh.

"You have no choice. You are here, and it is done." The quiet urgency in his voice left little room for compromise. "I give you this. I give you time to forget your sadness. There is no more time."

"I don't understand."

"Many summers ago a Pale Witch arrived by magic and became one with our people. She had knowledge of the future, and guided our tribe. On the moon of my birth, she saw a Red Woman arrive with a Bloodstone. She foretold that I would fight the bear to save you, a maiden Time Walker." His voice lowered, and she felt his head rest against her hair for a moment. "She said the Red Woman was no sacrifice, and she was banished for her disloyalty to the Weroance. When time came near for the prophecy to fulfill, I took all the Bloodstones of my tribe and buried them. I thought the legend could be broken."

His hands slid down on her arms as his lips pressed close to her flushed cheek over her shoulder.

"My uncle is Opechancanough, Great Leader of our tribes, our Weroance. Long ago my uncle ordered the death of all Time Walkers. It is a great honor for a warrior to bring our Weroance the head of a Time Walker."

She shook her head at the truth, the meaning of his words sinking in. A sacrifice? Bound by a legend, forced to obey by his tribe and his honor, would he follow through by ending her life? For all she knew of him, she believed he felt some care for her, but was it enough to risk the wrath of his uncle? Even if he knew how to return her to her time, she was certain he would never agree to do so now.

"Did you bring me here to – to kill me?" she whispered.

"No. Only to make you see. There is only one way I know to keep you safe, and that is to keep you with me. I will not let you go."

Maggie closed her eyes, relief washing through her at the revelation he did not drag her up the mountain as a sacrifice.

"Winn," she said softly.

"Can you learn to love this land, *Tentay teh?*" he asked. His warm breath caressed her ear as he spoke, sending a shiver down her spine. "I feel sorrow for your pain. I wish you to love my time like your own. Is there nothing here you could stay for?"

She did not expect the surge of confusion his words brought forth.

"There are things I love about…your time," she admitted. "Your uncle wants me dead… is that the only reason you're doing this?"

He gently tilted her head to the side and closed his warm mouth over hers. Her hands found his neck, and his fingers twisted in her loose hair.

"No. I would keep you even so."

She told herself it was only an act, a way to gain his trust. A means to an end. Yet in that moment, her traitorous heart wanted more of him.

She glanced over his shoulder and her eyes fluttered open, her body suddenly frozen as she uttered a scream.

Standing behind them was another Indian male, his body littered with scars, one hand perched on his hip and the other clutching a feather-tipped spear as he watched them. Tall and lean, with a long narrow face and a sneer across his lips, his dark eyes met hers, betraying no hint of embarrassment but rather disappointment the show had ended.

At the sound of her scream, Winn pivoted fast and grabbed his knife, shoving her backward. She could only see his back as he stood between her and the stranger, but she saw the way he straightened as he spoke to the man.

The way the stranger continued to stare at her as he spoke to Winn made her blood run cold. She recognized little of the exchange as they spoke in their native language, but she heard the restrained anger in the words Winn spoke. Her breath caught in her throat as Winn suddenly breached the space between himself and the intruder, his knife gripped in his white-knuckled fist, and the other man raised his spear away from his hip in reply.

Winn spoke to the man, his voice low, yet even she could hear the threat. Silent for a moment in consideration, the intruder glared at Winn. The man then slowly lowered the spear.

"Shewanakuxkwe!" Winn snapped, turning slightly to glance at her. She did not recognize the word, so she simply ignored it. She backed away a few paces, waiting until she was sure Winn spoke to her. When she did not answer, he swung around in a fury and snatched her wrist, his handsome face contorted in a scowl. *"Keptchat!* Come here, now!"

Maggie recognized the word *Keptchat* immediately. Foolish woman, huh? How could he speak to her like that after what they had shared moments before? The memory of the first insults between them sharpened her anger, and before she could stem her temper, she turned on her heel and stalked away from him. She wasn't going to stick around while he insulted her in front of another man.

The next thing she knew, she was yanked roughly into his arms, his fingers gripping the base of her neck in warning. More from anger than from pain, she cried out and fought his hold.

"Let go of me!" she shouted, swinging around. When her open palm connected with his cheek, an accident rather than an assault, she heard the other Indian gasp. Winn's fist tightened on her shoulder when she tried to pull away and she gritted her teeth, vowing she would not let him see how much he hurt her pride. His eyes flashed like glowing coals when she met his stare, and she thought she could feel his body quiver against hers as he spoke.

"Silence your foul tongue," he warned, his words spoke low as she remained captured by his gaze. She started to open her mouth, but the scowl clouded his face and he shook her hard, as if to retain her attention. "Get on the horse," he growled, and then added as an afterthought, "or I will drag you back to the village."

With his last word he released her toward the horse, loosening his hold with more sharp uttered words she did not understand. She stumbled and nearly fell to her knees, but the stubborn resolve to defy him gave strength to her shaking legs and she managed to get back to the horse. Thoughts of escaping him with his own mount were not realized quickly enough, and before she could gather her wits, he leapt behind her on the beast and urged it back toward the village.

13

Nemattanew kept silent as they returned to the village, and Winn was glad. The woman stiffened and squirmed in his lap, causing him to groan and clasp her to his chest. He made little effort to curb the anger that seared his veins, for he knew if he did then fear would take over, and he was no man to lose himself in such a lowly emotion. If the other man saw weakness in him, Winn knew it would be reported to his uncle. Nemattanew was his uncle's most trusted advisor, and if he exposed Winn's weakness, the decision of Maggie's punishment could be turned over to the Council.

Nemattanew would never let Maggie get away with her attack on the favorite nephew of the Weroance. It was bad enough that she tried to walk away from him when he gave her a direct command, but the blasted woman sealed her fate when she raised a hand to him. Yet she still sat in his lap, shaking in rage, and he knew she would attack him again should she have the chance. He regretted the harsh words he spoke to her, but he knew no other way to subdue her when the other warrior challenged him, for as much good it had done. Nemattanew chided him, declaring Winn was no master to the woman, rather he was a slave to her whims. He challenged how a warrior such as Winn could lead their people, if a lowly white woman held so much power over him.

Winn clenched his fists and thighs, and the horse took it as a signal to move faster, jerking Maggie back against him once again. He had no choice but to prove Nemattanew wrong. He swore as his lips buried in her soft red hair and she stiffened, but he was glad she chose to cease her struggles. He had no idea how to make her understand how tenuous a situation her actions sparked. By the way she described a woman's place in her time, he knew there was little chance she could see how her actions put her life in danger. What had men become in the future that they let women act so brazen? They must all be weak fools, he sighed.

When they arrived in the village, he ignored the cries of welcome and rode directly to his yehakin. He leapt deftly off the horse and jerked Maggie down as well, thrusting her into the house before she could add any more credence to the charges against her. Once inside, he let her go, unwilling to let her be the one to shove him away. Her quick-tempered refusal of his attention bothered him more than he cared to dwell on.

"Leave me alone!" she snapped.

"You give no orders here!" he sniped back.

She retreated to the furs, where she stood with fists clutched to her sides, her chest heaving in her rage. He tried to ignore the surge of arousal she ignited as she stood glaring at him like a flaming goddess of fury, his body nearly consumed by the need to finish what they started. By all that was sacred, she was a beauty! Even with her eyes glazed in anger, he still desired her.

He shook his head against the urges. He needed to break the hold the woman held him trapped in, by bedding her or killing her. Perhaps then the wicked spell would collapse, along with the confusing need to protect her from the ways of his world. He moved to step toward her, but balked when she stepped back. His insides clenched at her response, and he could find no words to explain the foreign feeling. He did not care for her outspoken defiance, but he liked even less the way she cringed away from him with fear in her eyes.

Winn scowled. She *shoul* be afraid. He was the War Chief, and he cowered before no woman. He would not—could not— continue to let her defy him at every turn.

"Take your rest now, woman. I will think on your punishment."

Her face twisted with a retort, but she wrapped her arms around herself instead before she whispered her defiant answer.

"You treat me like dirt in front of that – that *pervert*, but I get punished? You'll drag me back to the village, will you? Drag yourself back to the village!"

He covered the distance between them as the black haze of rage clouded his vision. He understood few of her words, but her intent was clear and he would stand no more defiance from her. Still driven mad with wanting her, his skin on fire where it touched his own, he grabbed her by her upper arms and lifted her off the ground.

"I will! I must!" he shouted, shaking her as if the action could force her to understand. "I am nephew to the Weroance, War Chief to my people! You, woman, cannot strike me!"

He groaned a curse when she did just that, hitting him repeatedly with closed fists as she channeled her anger on him. He did nothing to deflect her blows, letting them fall upon his chest until she tired of her assault and let him hold her in his embrace. He once promised her she could rage as she liked in his house, and he would keep that promise. His first thought was to soothe her with an age-old method, his blood screaming to ravish her until she fought no more. But he realized immediately he knew nothing of how to calm this frustrating woman, the product of some bizarre future time.

"You cannot – you cannot raise your hand to me. Nemattanew will not let this go," he said, his voice strained hoarse, her body like a hummingbird in his arms as he struggled to keep her in his embrace.

"Let me go. Just let me go home. Give me the stone, I will leave," she whispered, her damp face pressed against his chest. His hand slid up behind her head, holding her close to prevent her from stealing his resolve with her glimmering jade eyes.

"I cannot let you leave." *I will never let you go. Anything but that.*

"You can let me get away – you can pretend I escaped!"

"It would not be believed, *Tentay teh.*" He inhaled the sweetness of meadow flowers as he stroked her neck, keeping his lips pressed into her hair. He sighed when her body relaxed and she leaned into him.

"What is *Tentay teh?*" she asked.

He grimaced at her question, not certain if his name for her would break their fragile truce. "I call you my Fire Heart," he murmured.

"Oh." She fell silent.

"*Ktaholich kweti kishku, Tentay teh.*" He whispered against her hair, holding her gently as he pledged a promise in words she could not understand. *You will love me one ,ay, Fire Heart.*

She did not ask the meaning and he was glad. He could only whisper such promises in his own tongue, leaving it lashed to his pounding heart where it belonged. Her silence bought them a measure of peace, and when he lowered her to the sleeping pallet she did not protest his motives. With the woman curled in his embrace and her back nestled against him, she finally submitted to sleep.

Winn lay awake as he enjoyed the thud of her heartbeat against his arm and the warmth of her shallow breathing on his skin. He knew he would face questions in the morning and be forced to act on her crime, and he wondered if he was a fool to keep her, but the alternative of letting her go caused his pulse to quicken and a piercing pain in his chest. He should take her life and be glad for it, but he knew from the moment he first laid eyes to her that the path was set. There would be no Red Woman sacrifice to please his uncle.

No, he would not let her go.

* * *

He woke later when his arms felt empty and he heard the shuffle of her feet across the room. Without shifting position, his eyes opened in narrow slits to see what the woman was up to. He suppressed a laugh when he spotted her rifling through one of the baskets where he kept his garments. She must still be searching for the Bloodstone, not knowing he hid it far away from her devious prying little fingers. Did she think he would not hear her leave his furs in the darkness? He hid a grin when she turned back toward him, and quickly closed his eyes.

She was a small thing, but not very lithe on her feet, and her feet scraped with each step she took closer to his furs. Her breath came in warm, shallow spurts and it singed his skin when she leaned closer, placing a hand in the furs on each side of his head. He longed to reach up and touch her, but the urge lay stifled as his curiosity burned stronger. What was she doing?

"Open your eyes!" she hissed. He felt the prick of a cold blade against his neck and readily obeyed.

The crazed woman held her knife to his throat.

By the Gods, the woman surely had no sense! First she dared strike him in front of another warrior, now she threatened him with a weapon? Torn between amusement and anger, his face remained impassive as he raised one eyebrow and glanced down at the blade. His eyes quickly dipped to her breasts, nearly tumbling over the gap in the shift she insisted on wearing to sleep, plump and daring, tempting him to madness. He swallowed hard when she swung one leg across his belly and straddled him, then pressed the knife harder to his throat.

Was she trying to kill him, or tease him to death?

"Looking for something, Maggie?" he asked softly.

"Yes!" she hissed. "You know what I want! Give me that Bloodstone now, and I won't kill you!"

He felt a pinch and a trickle of blood when she moved, her hand unsteady and shaking although fury twisted her face and her eyes stayed firmly latched on his. He raised his brows and slowly placed his hands on her knees. Tracing lightly with his palms as she trembled harder, his fingers came to rest on her hips.

"Stop that! I will stab you, Winn! I just want the stone!"

She dug the blade in and he flinched, but it was only a scratch and worth the risk. He grasped her hips and lowered them firmly against his own, smirking when she let out a gasp. She tried to pull back, but could not keep the knife in an effective position while she squirmed, and he took advantage of her imbalance by pushing her dress slowly up her thighs so she sat naked against him.

"Cut me now, woman, and I die a happy man," he grinned.

She let out a furious screech, and he decided he had been tortured enough. He made no move to take her weapon, but swiftly lifted her and rolled until she lay beneath him. She grabbed the hair at his nape with one shaking fist and kept the knife firmly planted on his neck with the other.

"I have a knife, you idiot!" she shrieked.

"So you do. I don't have the stone, nor will I give it to you."

He settled his hips deeply against her, one hand sliding down, his fingers slipping beneath her buttocks. Sweat glistened on her skin in the glimmer of moonlight through the smoke hole, the salty slickness making a low sucking sound as their skin collided in her struggle. He groaned when she bucked against him and cursed.

"Let go of me!"

"You have the knife. Let *me* go," he countered.

"No. You – you'll punish me," she whispered.

"That is the last thing I will do to you right now."

"You're lying!"

"No, I do not lie!" he growled, his patience wearing at her game and tired of fighting the urge to ravish her into silence. No other woman could have driven him so senseless, nor escaped death after holding a knife to his throat. But for some reason he felt his power drain with her, as if it mattered not that he was the Great War Chief of his people, nor even a man larger and stronger than she was. She battered him to the ground with her stubborn fire, and he could not lift a finger to punish her for it.

The fingers she clenched in his hair loosened. Her gaze did not waver from his. He dipped his head slowly, aware of the knife between them, and gauged her reaction when he ran his fingertips down along her side. She shuddered and closed her eyes, and he saw her throat contract as she swallowed and the knife wavered. He planted a soft kiss against her neck, not sure if she trembled in fear or lust, and suddenly the thought of her panic stopped him.

For all of her threats and demands, she was no more than terrified. He knew he deserved her fear, in fact he made great effort to show her he would be obeyed. Her behavior put her in grave danger from his warriors. She had no understanding of his time, or the ways of his people. He had none of hers, but he could see it was clearly quite different. He wanted nothing better than to keep her, but she believed the worst of him. She had no idea he would never throw question to his honor by taking a woman who did not want him. As much as he wished he were a lesser man in that moment, he drew back from her.

He shifted his body to lie beside her, and pulled her against his chest before she could protest, allowing her to keep the knife if she chose. She was a stake in his arms, her back rigid against his skin, her body shrinking away from his. Let her keep her blade, if it eased her mind. He would show her that hurting her was nothing near to what he truly desired.

"Stop fighting." The hoarse command strained from his lips as he pressed them into her soft hair. He pulled a fur over them and tucked her trembling body closer, noticing her knuckles were white and still clutched around the knife handle. He closed his hand over her fist and let it rest over her shaking one.

"When you must kill a man who means you harm, strike swiftly," he whispered against her ear. "But I am not that man. It is only me, *eholkon*. Sleep now and be safe, *ntehem*."

It is only me – he who loves you. Sleep now and be safe, my heart.

It was a long time before her furious shaking finally slowed and her fight diminished enough to surrender, but eventually her breath eased into a shallow sleeping rhythm. Sleep did not claim him, and he rose at dawn to find the knife still clenched in her hand.

He kissed her softly before he left.

14

He sat cross-legged next to Chetan while Makedewa paced near the entrance of the Long House. His brothers stood by his side against the Council, neither in defense of Maggie or against her, merely showing their support for him by their presence. Winn hoped it would be enough to spare her against the accusations Nemattanew made.

Technically, Maggie was a prisoner, his slave to be precise, since Winn was the one that found her and brought her to the village. Tradition called for the owner to discipline the slave, but if others thought he did not punish her crimes in an appropriate manner, he could be challenged.

On return to the village, Nemattanew demanded immediate audience with the council. Before Winn could speak, the other warrior described how Maggie slapped his face and ignored his commands. Even worse, he told the Council that Winn did not raise a hand to her in return. Thankfully, Nemattanew had no idea Maggie had attacked him with a knife during the night, and for that he was grateful, since that offense would have him kneeling in the dirt before the Council, begging for her life.

As he sat beside Chetan that morning, waiting for word of the decision, he hoped his impromptu lie had been enough to sway the Council.

"Did you truly beat her, as you said?" Chetan asked quietly. Winn avoided his gaze, his throat tight with the lie he would tell his brother.

"Yes. She has been punished."

Chetan snorted in response.

"I hope she stabs you in your sleep. How do you expect her to act? She knows nothing of our time! You must teach her our ways if you plan to keep her. She is in danger by knowing nothing of our people."

Winn sighed, his brother's words hitting closer to the truth than he realized.

"She knows much of our people. She chooses to attack me! I know not how to make her listen," he growled. Chetan glanced over at him, one brow raised, his mouth parted in surprise.

"What do you do that angers her?" Chetan asked.

"Nothing! I do nothing," he snapped. His brother chuckled.

"Do less nothing, and more something, or they will break her," Chetan said, eyeing the Council as they returned in single file to their spots inside the Long House. Makedewa joined them, the strength of his brothers flanking his sides.

The speaker of the Council remained standing as the others sat, his long bear mantle dragging the floor behind him as his horned stag helmet graced his proud head. Diminutive under the trappings of his station, the man had served since the time before the English arrived, maintaining his position through many wars and deaths. Winn looked up at the wrinkled man now, hoping the decision was a fair one.

"Winkeohkwet, we have talked on the matter of your slave."

"Yes, Council?" he said. His back was straight as a pike, his lungs barely moving as he held them without air, his mouth parched with thirst.

"We will leave the punishment of your slave to you. For now. Teach her well of what her defiance will cost in the future."

He wanted to close his eyes and shout his joy, but instead he lowered his head and humbly bowed to the Council.

15

Damn that man to hell. Her waking thoughts brought the events of the previous day back in rapid succession.

She groaned at the flush of warmth in her belly at the memory of their encounters, not sure what enraged her more – his treatment of her in front of Nemattanew, or the fact that he withheld the stone from her. Her fingers clenched down on the bedding and she ground her frustration into the furs, feeling abandoned by her own good sense. *Damn him.* She hated her weakness, despised the way she forgot everything whenever his crystal blue eyes met hers.

The room appeared empty when she risked peeking out from the furs, and she was relieved. She did not want to face him, unwilling to let him tear down her defenses. If he were in her time, he would be a goner after the way he treated her, dismissing her in front of his friend. She was not raised to tolerate that sort of behavior from a man, in his time or any other. A bitter frown formed as she recalled her last real date, disastrous, as it had been.

His name was Josh, a fellow student in her college Biology class, and he had asked her out several times before she said yes. Grampa had been sick for weeks and she was reluctant to leave him, but the old man knew she needed to get out of the house and he insisted she go. It wasn't that she disliked Josh, in fact he was a handsome athletic man and he certainly turned her head when he walked in the room, but she felt little interest in cultivating a relationship. Although she had been attending college for a year, there had been little time to even think about dating.

Between running the farm and worrying over Grampa, her plate was full.

After a pleasant but uneventful dinner, Josh took her to a movie. She recalled putting popcorn between them at one point, but he was persistent in his advances, and managed a few kisses and poorly aimed gropes anyway. Nothing earth shattering, and certainly nothing to cause her blood to simmer.

The night ended with Josh parking his car in the driveway of the farm, a single gravel lane that the main farmhouse shared with the cottage. Maggie didn't mind when he kissed her goodnight, expecting it would be the quickest way to end their evening before she jumped out of the car, but she was stunned when he continued to slather her mouth with his as she reached for the door handle. She was not interested in a petting fest in the driveway. She shoved him off and he came back for more.

"Goodnight Josh!" she snapped when she was able to come up for air.

"Not yet, babe," he insisted. She screeched when one of his hands slipped inside the top of her blouse. Her desperate hand found the door latch, and she fell out of the car onto the gravel. Sprawled on her backside as she righted her blouse, she was speechless when her amorous date was yanked out of the car by a pair of very muscled arms.

Next thing she knew, a hulking mad giant stood spread legged beside the car with her date held by his collar. The veins stood out on his neck in thick cords and his usually gentle face was paved with a scarlet mask and no sign of remorse.

"Agh! Oof! I'm sorry, I'm sorry!" her date gurgled as his face turned purple.

Josh choked out a stuttered apology, and Marcus slowly let the younger man down from where he held him several feet off the ground. Maggie watched as Josh scrambled into his car. He gunned it down the driveway, spewing a cloud of gravel smoke as he retreated.

Maggie burst into laughter at the sight of her date fleeing. She knew it would be a long time before any of her classmates asked her out again, but the notion did not bother her so much. Marcus raised one thick black eyebrow at her and shook his head in disgust.

"Ye think that's funny, Maggie?" he asked.

"Oh, yes, I do!" she laughed.

"Are you all right?" the older man asked finally as her amusement faded. He looked out of character at that moment, still the enormous beast of a man who had been her protector since childhood, but when his shoulders slumped in relief and he reached for her hand, she knew something was more amiss than just her disastrous date.

"What is it, Marcus?"

His lips thinned and his normally twinkling blue eyes clouded over. His brogue sounded thick and hesitant when he answered.

"It's yer grandpa. You better come inside."

Grandpa never did wake up after that night.

Maggie sat up in the furs and brushed back her tears, stowing the bitter memory away. Marcus must be worried sick about her disappearance. But it was no use thinking of the past. Or her future past. Or whatever it was properly considered now. She needed to get it together and figure out a way out of her current mess, regardless of what year it was. The knife lay discarded on the furs. She crawled over to the bowl of water and used it to rinse her mouth, then tied the wayward fastening of her doeskin dress to some semblance of decency before Teyas burst into the yehakin.

Teyas collapsed onto her knees in front of Maggie and took her hands in her own. The girl spread them wide, raking her over with a practiced eye, then broke into a wide smile of relief. Maggie squinted at her, wondering what on Earth the girl was up to.

"I knew my brother told lies!" she exclaimed.

"What are you talking about, Teyas?"

"He told the Council he punished you for your crime. He said he beat you, but I knew he told false," she answered smugly in her glee. Maggie pulled her hands away and sat back on her heels. So that was his game, huh? Tell the other men he beat her into submission? Well, Winn had another thing coming!

"That arrogant—"

"No! Do not be angry, sister!"

"And why not?" Maggie seethed. "He's a liar!"

"Maggie," Teyas smiled, taking her hands back and placing them in her lap between them. "Your ways are so strange. I do not understand your anger. My brother shows great love for you in this way. He risks much by telling a half truth."

"He can shove it. And if he ever touches me again, I will—"

"You will what? Stab me with your knife?"

Both women went silent when Winn passed through the door. With one glance at his agitated stare, Maggie averted her eyes and refused to acknowledge him. She held her breath to keep from returning his taunt with one of her own, aware that she was on precarious ground after attacking him with her blade. She rose from the furs and motioned to Teyas to follow.

"We have chores to do, right Teyas?"

"Ah, well –" the girl stammered.

"I need to see to Blaze, and I am taking my clothes to the river to be washed. My dress is ruined, and my only spare is covered in mud, thanks to that moody bastard brother of yours. Stay if you want, but I'm getting to work," Maggie said. She frowned at the way Teyas glanced at Winn for approval, her mouth hanging open in disbelief. With a shrug, Maggie grabbed her basket of clothes and moved to pass Winn, tucking her knife in the thong at her waist and hoping he did not notice. She should have known it would not have been so easy.

He stopped her with one hand closed around her upper arm, not painful, but still firm. She refused to look at him, but she felt his breath close on the skin of her neck as he bent his mouth to her ear.

"You may go," he said simply. She bit back a harsh retort and jerked her arm from his grasp, annoyed that he felt the need to give her permission to leave and frustrated that she was incapable of submitting to him. With each passing day she felt she was slipping away from the independent modern woman she once was, instead becoming like all the other women around her.

Stepping out into the daylight, she stalked away from the house with a purposeful stride toward the river. She still had her knife, and she would stab him with it if he dared make any more advances on her. He would not find her hesitant again.

She vowed not to cry as she navigated the path to the river. *Damn his blaste, heathen heart.* Perhaps she would jump in the river and drift downstream, surely someone would help her. As attractive as the notion was, she knew it would be foolish. She knew little of this time, nor how to live alone in the wilderness and survive. She was trapped here just as surely as if he tied her to a post. She bowed her head in frustration and kicked at the dirt in her path. When she heard the racket of none too careful footsteps behind her, she swung around in a fury to confront her stalker.

"Leave me alone. I have work to do," she muttered.

Winn grinned when she turned and spoke. She had no idea what he found so humorous, and his chuckle enraged her to the point of violence. She gripped the basket until her fingers throbbed with the effort.

"What is so goddamn funny, Winn?" she asked.

"I should pretend to beat you every day, if that is what it takes to make you work," he laughed. She snorted a low curse in reply and turned on her heel, continuing down the path to the river. She would not let him bait her into attacking him, although every sliver of her being wanted to scratch the smile from his handsome face.

"Nothing to say, *Tentay teh?*"

"Go away."

"I would have words with you. Stop walking."

She stopped on his command, but kept her back to him as she stepped off the path. She felt him beside her, felt his stare sear her skin. His words dripped of heat as they rolled smoothly off his tongue. She refused to look at him, afraid one glimpse of his smoldering eyes would render her senseless.

"Yes?"

"You call me a bastard? The English use that word as well."

"Well, you act like it," she said.

"Why do you have anger at me?"

"You treated me like a whore."

"Whore?"

A deep sigh escaped her as a huff, and she kneeled down to the river-bank where she could wash her clothes. She hoped he would tire of talking and just leave her alone.

"It means – it means a loose woman. A woman who does bad things. One who sleeps with any man," she said, at loss to define it for him and blushing as she tried. He frowned as he considered her explanation, and then grinned sheepishly when he realized her meaning. But Maggie was surprised to see his eyes darken again after his initial display of amusement.

"Is that what you think?"

"Yes, Winn. If we were in my time, and did—we did those things," she stammered, "and then you treated me so badly in front of your friends, I would never speak to you again. You don't just kiss a woman, then toss her around and holler at her. How can you expect me to be okay with that?"

"This is not your time, it is mine," he answered, with no trace of harsh intent. "Women do not challenge their men. I would kill a man for less than what you have done to shame me."

"I'm not your woman."

"I found you. You belong to me."

"This is useless! I just want to go home. Why is that so hard for you to get through your thick head?"

He tilted his head a bit and grinned when he realized the meaning of her insult.

"Why do you not understand I cannot let you leave?"

"Because I can't just give up. If you were me, wouldn't you do the same?"

Neither offered an answer. She filled the silence by slapping her wet dress against a rock to rub it clean. He sat down a few feet away on the riverbank and watched her.

"Yes," he said softly. "I would do the same."

She looked up at him. His eyes were soft blue orbs as he watched her, briefly lingering before he lowered his head, his braid falling over one brown shoulder.

"What fills your day, in your time?"

She startled at the earnest question, and dared a glance his way. He sat cross-legged in the grass, leaning forward on his knees. His eyes followed her movements without a semblance of threat. She felt her skin prickle in a warm rush and quickly turned back to her work.

"It doesn't matter."

"I would hear it."

"If I tell you, will you stop pestering me?"

He considered her offer, and agreed with a curt nod.

"I will go back to the village," he promised.

"Fine! I went to college during the day, and then I came home. I took care of my grandfather. I looked after the farm. I kept it running pretty well."

"You lived with only your grandfather?"

"Yes. Well, no. Marcus lived with us. He was like family."

"Like a husband?"

"No, like family. He looked out for me. He was like—like an older brother. Or an uncle. I never had a father."

He scowled and changed his tactics. Maggie was stunned when he tossed a pebble at her, hitting her backside. The gesture seemed playful, and completely out of line.

"What is college?" he asked. She picked up a sizeable stone and considered launching it at him, but let it drop, annoyed as two more pebbles struck her thigh in quick succession.

"A place people go to learn. We sit in rooms and listen to other people who teach," she answered.

He joined her at the creek and took one of her garments from the basket, which he began scrubbing against the stones next to her. She scowled but said nothing.

"What you told me of your time... my people. Is nothing left of us, nothing at all?"

She stopped squeezing water from her dress, and glanced sideways at him. His furrowed brow sheltered his eyes as he continued to work on the garment in his hand.

"Winn ... I shouldn't have told you."

"I asked you. I wanted to know."

She slipped her fingers over his hand, her anger slipping away and the urge to comfort him as strong as the reflex of taking another breath. She wished she could take away the anguish shadowed in his eyes. How could she comfort such a man? A man she watched rise to her defense against a bear, not knowing who she was, only that she needed saving. A man who acted in the moment, who took the life of another warrior that threatened her, without hesitation or question.

How could she console him, when it was her own words that caused him such misery? The guilt hit her hard. What right did she have to tell him what the future would bring? As for specific dates and years that events would happen, she was useless. She knew the basics, but she had never been an ardent student of history.

"I'm so sorry," she whispered. His calloused thumb moved against her hand, then squeezed it, only a gentle motion, but enough for her to hear the words he left unspoken. She did not want to move, afraid to shatter the tenuous strings binding them in the moment, unwilling to lose any ground when they worked so hard for every inch of the fragile peace between them.

She saw him swallow as he abruptly pulled his hand away and stood up.

Chetan walked toward them on the path, chuckling at the sight of them washing clothes together. His son followed behind, also bearing a curious grin, but too respectful to laugh at Winn as his father did. Chetan obviously had no such compulsion, holding a fist against his lower belly as he goaded Winn.

"Will you wash my clothes as well, brother?"

Winn pursed his lips for a moment, then one corner of his mouth crested into a grin.

"No, you are not quite as pretty, you can wash your own clothes," Winn shot back. He tossed the dress he had wrung out into the basket, and playfully snatched the basket from her hands.

"I'm not done with that!" she said, trying to take the basket back. Much to her annoyance, he dodged her hands, dropping her basket to impishly deflect her attempt to recover it. If she did not clean what few clothes she had, she would have nothing presentable to wear to the feast, and she was bone tired of feeling like the beggar visitor.

"Yes, we are done here," he argued, laughing.

Frustrated beyond measure, she swung around back to the creek bed.

"I answered your questions, now you can leave," she said.

"As you wish!" he grinned. She had no sooner bent back to her task when he swept her up over his shoulder like a sack of potatoes, slapping his palm against her buttocks when she kicked out.

"You liar!" she screeched, furious at being treated yet again like a piece of property.

"I said I would go back to the village. I did not say you could stay here."

She reached out to strike him, but when her fist hit his back he slapped her bottom again, this time with more authority. She realized they had reached the village, and that people stared open mouthed at the warrior carrying the crazed flame-haired woman. She remembered his warning about defiance in front of the villagers and clamped her mouth shut. When he finally entered the yehakin and dropped her to her feet, she stalked off to the corner and sat with her back to him.

"I won't stay here! I have things to do! You left my clothes at the river, now I have nothing to wear!"

"You will stay here until I say you may leave. If you leave again I will tie you. Do you understand?"

"Don't threaten me."

"Then behave!" he bellowed. He kicked a fur closer to the fire and thrust out his hand toward it. "Sit," he demanded. She hesitated long enough to see the spike of rage cross his face, then decided it would be wise to heed his request. Slowly lowering herself down to sit on the fur, she met his furious gaze without yield.

"Opechancanough sends his advisor to see how our people fare," he began. Maggie let him speak without interruption, her curiosity sparked when he spoke of his family. She knew little about him other than what she gleaned from his sister and mother, which was next to nothing. They would not hear of her desire to leave, and placated her with assurances that Winn would keep her safe – as if that was a consolation.

"My uncle has much hate for the white settlers, and he wishes to make them go back across the great sea to their own land. He grows tired of their demands and would see every white man dead." His throat tightened as he continued, and a shadow of disgust fell over his face. "I serve him as council to the whites. I speak their English, and I eat at their tables. I learn their ways, so I can see their lies to my people."

"So that's why you speak English so well," she murmured. He nodded.

"My uncle sent word of his plans to rid us of the English. It will happen soon. He wants my help, as I have always given him." He paused and looked away for a moment, then shifted his eyes back to her. "Nemattanew has heard whispers of a Time Walker in the village...I think he knows you are a Blooded One."

"Nemattanew?" she stammered. "I don't understand."

"Listen, woman! Nemattanew will tell my uncle a Blooded One is here. Opechancanough will demand your death...and it must be done."

Her teeth slid over her bottom lip and squeezed as she felt a wave of nausea surge up her throat. She leaned forward to fight the urge and slowly felt it wane.

"You can just let me go."

"He will hunt you." She grimaced at the words unsaid. If Winn did not kill her, his uncle would.

"You won't kill me," she whispered.

He stared at her across the flames of the fire. "I should end your life. I should kill you and feel no regret," he said softly in return. Her spine stiffened at his quiet admission.

"Then do it," she taunted, regretting the foolish words the moment they left her lips.

"Perhaps I will. If I smother your breath while you sleep, will I still see you in my dreams?" He rose from his spot and bent down in a crouch in front of her. She trembled at the luminous darkness in his eyes, his body tensed and ready to strike. "Perhaps I will cut your throat as you tried to cut mine. Will I still want to touch you when your blood is on my hands? Or will it chase your ghost from my thoughts?"

He held his palms out and considered them for a moment, shaking his head.

"I think not. I think still you would haunt me." She closed her eyes as he reached for her and felt his fingers take a strand of her hair. She felt his breath close and dared not open her eyes for fear of losing the last shreds of willpower she had left. Her heart hammered so loud she was sure he could hear it thump in her chest.

He slowly rose to his feet and put distance between them. He parted the hide covering the doorway and paused, his back turned and his face shrouded from her questioning gaze.

"You will join the women for the feast tonight. You worked hard to prepare it."

She found no power to answer him before he left.

PART TWO

16

Although the remnants of their conversation left her reeling, Maggie went along with Teyas to take the evening meal. Teyas graciously provided another garment for Maggie to wear, since all that she had was still wet from washing. The women sat apart from the men, seated in a group by the large fire burning in the village center outside the Long House, the steady hollow beat of drums echoing through the air and the smoke of their pipes wafting into swirls above their heads. She was glad to be among them, but still frustrated by her slow grasp of their language. Teyas did not seem to notice, giving her a smile now and then as she chatted with the other women.

Dusk settled over the treetops, casting a magical hue on the festivities as near naked children raced through the crowd, shrieking and laughing in their games. Their antics shadowed the behavior of youngsters in a schoolyard, and the bitter reminder of her home brought on the sting of sadness. She would not break down in front of the women. Most of them viewed her with suspicion, and she would not have them see her as a weak simpering fool.

She wished they would hurry on with the meal so she could escape to the yehakin and get some kind of handle on the situation. If she could only find out where Winn hid the Bloodstone, she knew she would be one step closer to going home. Of course, she had no idea how to make the time travel magic work, and then there was the added complication of the feelings for Winn that she tried desperately to ignore.

Winn was seated across the fire with the other warriors, looking more relaxed than he had earlier. She watched as he took a puff from a long handled pipe and then passed it to the man beside him who did the same. He looked sleepy as he laughed, with pink tinges of bloodshot around the edges of his eyes, and Maggie wondered just what exactly was in the wild tobacco blend they smoked. Apparently, it was a luxury only the men enjoyed, not that she wished to partake, but it still intrigued her that women were not allowed the same pleasures.

As she watched the men enjoy the smoke, Winn lifted his head and their eyes met across the fire. Her stomach lurched and somersaulted when he smiled despite the way they left things, and it was all she could do to look away when a crimson blush crept across her cheeks.

Nemattanew did not share the smoke with the others. He wore a multitude of feathers, his back decorated with the full wings from an unlucky swan. He looked like a treacherous angel, the wings spread from his shoulders, fluttering in the brisk night breeze. She quickly averted her eyes when he noticed her gaze. His eyes held nothing but bleak hatred, dark brown orbs full of restrained malice as he stared back at her across the fire.

She needed to get away from them all, even for a few moments.

Maggie made an excuse to check on Blaze, escaping from the happy gathering if only for a short time. If she continued to enjoy their company and take part in their lives, it would only be that much harder when she left. She had doubts about saving her own heart from breaking, but she pushed that indecision aside and concentrated on the colt instead.

She expected to be joined by the children as she tended to Blaze, but she was surprised to see they did not follow her as she made her way to the lean-to. Horses stomped and their hooves made impatient thuds in the straw at the sight of her, and she imagined they thought it was feeding time by her presence. Blaze usually ran to her on sight, and she was puzzled to find him missing.

She twirled around to make her way back to the feast, intent on finding Winn to see what had happened to the colt. Suddenly a hand closed over her mouth and she was jerked into the shadows. She let out a muffled screech against the hand and stomped on his moccasin-clad foot, eliciting a deep chuckle from her captor.

"You fight like a wildcat," he laughed. "Do not fear, it is only me."

"You scared me! You—"

"You left the meal," he murmured as his mouth came down softly on hers. She could not recall what curses she meant to call him, her senses scattered by his touch. The tangy scent of the smoke clung to him, sending a tingle through her lips that slowly changed to a pleasant numb twinge.

"I didn't think anyone would notice," she answered.

"I noticed." His lips caressed her shoulder and she could feel the warmth of his shallow breaths upon her skin. "I missed you," he said softly, his face still hidden against her. They stayed like that for along moment, clutching each other.

She closed her eyes at his admission, for once in her life at loss for words.

"What magic is this that I cannot leave you? Why do I stay here with you, when I should go join my men? Do you cast a spell, *Tentay teh?*"

Maggie shook her head without a response, afraid to interrupt the flow of his words as the dam of his emotions began to crumble. Even if the smoke had clouded his judgment and loosened his tongue, she still longed to hear the words from his heart. Surely, the thing between them meant something to him.

"My uncle calls for your death. If I make you my wife in truth, I know not what he will do. Even he cannot make a man kill his wife. Should I just take you and be damned?"

"You think I would agree to be your wife?" she asked, breathless as his lips traced a path of delicious torture across her cheek.

"You would agree," he murmured, intent on his work as he continued to nuzzle her.

"No I would not," she insisted.

"What if I take you to my yehakin now, would you still argue?"

"Wait a second," she said, tearing away from his seeking lips. "I don't have to marry you if we- if we just *sleep* together."

"This is my time. I can see your fire for me, I feel it in here," he insisted, brushing his fingertips lightly over her heart. "And I promise you, when I take you as mine, it is forever. That is my way." His hand fell to her waist and he pulled her tight against his chest, his face hardening. "Have you given your heart to another before me?"

"I haven't given you anything. You never ask, you just give orders," she stammered.

"Answer me," he groaned, his hand sliding beneath her dress to cup her buttocks. She writhed at the contact and felt him shudder in response.

"No. Never. I have never loved a man enough...to do that," she admitted.

A flush crept over her neck and cheeks when she saw him smile, the sudden understanding of her words apparent in his face.

"Then you admit I have your love?" His mouth closed over hers.

She threaded her fingers in his hair and clutched him against her, and she knew no other answer to give him. For once, she felt no urge to deny him. The words slipped from her lips.

"You do," she whispered, meeting his soft blue eyes with her own.

His mouth covered hers, eager and intense. The possession in his kiss left no question, the words once spoken, never to be rescinded. The shadow of consequence fell away, smothered beneath the urgent need to be a part of him, with him, swallowed whole by the unknown, tempered by his strength.

With one swift movement, he lifted her into his arms. He carried her across the clay packed path to his yehakin, where he dropped the bearskin hide across the door to shield them inside. He let her legs fall so that the tips of her toes brushed the ground, holding her so tightly she could not attempt to flee if she had wanted to.

His fingers tugged at the rawhide tie that bound her dress down the middle, unraveling it slowly as his lips probed lower. She needed his heat, the contact of his skin like a ripple of electric through her body. The only motion she could command was that which brought him closer. One round breast fell free, aching for his touch, and he complied by covering it with his wet mouth. His hands tugged off her dress and he clutched her bare bottom, refusing to release when she strained against him with a cry of pleasure. He kneeled down in the soft furs, his lips tasting her navel, gently biting and licking a torturous path. Right and wrong held no meaning, nothing left inside except an empty ache that longed to be sated. He was a storm, and she was fire, and each touch of his hand inflamed her soul with frantic need. She shuddered with pleasure, the thrill of his caresses chasing away the fear of her nakedness and what would come next.

When he pulled her gently down beside him it was none too soon, for her legs lost purchase and she gladly let him guide her. His breath whispered shivers across her bared skin and the pounding of the drums outside echoed between them, but the sounds were muted to her ears from the roaring of her heart. She wanted to take all of him, to hold his gentleness inside her secret place yet harness the smoldering violence that clouded his soul. There was a surge of panic down in the base of her belly when he parted her thighs with his knee, but she embraced the beast of her fear and meant to meld it to her own doing.

"*Ntehem.* Let me love you," he murmured.

She felt him shudder when she wrapped her hands around his neck to draw him down, the muscles of his abdomen taut at her touch, his head dipping to her shoulder as he moved to join their bodies.

* * *

Maggie felt the warmth of golden sunshine across her face from the smoke hole as the sun rose overhead, gently dousing their skin as they lay together on the furs. Limbs entwined with his, her head resting against his chest, she could hear the thud of his heart beneath her ear. It was slow and steady, humming a peaceful rhythm that soothed her senses back into memory of the night they shared. Her lips curled into a smile, and he must have felt the motion, for he sat up a bit and arched one brow at her, his thick dark lashes opened slightly over sleepy eyes.

"What are you thinking?" he asked.

Although fresh off the intimacy between them, shyness overtook her at the thought of discussing the act.

"Nothing," she lied. It was his turn to smile. He pulled her upward against his chest so that she had to look at him.

"If you want me again, you only need ask, my wanton woman," he grinned. She blushed harder at his taunt and giggled, and he covered her lips with his own. Teasing at first, he nipped at her lip, but his kiss became more wanting when she lowered her head for more. He held her head with both hands and tilted her face, the taste of sweet tangy smoke clinging to his lips. His eyes twinkled with mischief, soft and wide as he gazed at her with a boyish grin.

"No – I mean, yes, but that's not it."

"No or yes?" he smirked.

She buried her face into his chest, feeling the blood rise to her cheeks at the turn of the conversation, at utter loss to explain the questions she wanted to ask.

"Where is Blaze?"

"You think of a horse now? Perhaps I should distract you better," he murmured, tugging playfully on her ear with his teeth. "He's in the meadow with the other young horses, if you must know."

"Okay. What does *ntehem* mean?" she asked. He smiled.

"My heart," he said softly. "More questions, *ntehem?*"

"You've done this before," she blurted out, her cheek still lying hidden against him. "I, well, I haven't. I was just wondering what … wondering if … oh, Christ! I want to know if this was good for you. I mean, if I was good," she stammered, the last of her words trailing off as a mumble. She regretted the question immediately, sure she would be unable to answer him coherently if he chose to entertain her ridiculous conversation.

She squeezed her eyes shut when he slipped his fingers under her chin and raised it up.

"Look at me," he demanded, his tone teasing yet insistent. She complied, grudgingly, and met his steady gaze with her own.

"I just...I just want to know. Was this...special to you?" she said softly.

He opened his mouth as if to speak, but nothing came out, then he clamped it shut. She saw him swallow and he shook his head a bit as if clearing it from a fog, then pushed himself up to sit. She moved with him and settled in his lap, her belly flipping in cartwheels when he settled his arms around her waist.

"Look up, *ntehem*," he said finally, glancing upward with her at the rising sun through the smoke hole, its shimmer too powerful on their eyes to view for more than a moment.

They bowed their heads together and he paused, taking her hand in his and turning it gently over. He considered the scar in her palm, gently tracing his thumb over the silver knot that seared her skin like a brand. He brought it to his lips and kissed it, then laid it against his chest over the steady beat of his heart. She felt the heat, the pounding, the joining of the connection as warmth spread through her body to the deepest recess of her soul.

"A man is only a mountain in the darkness, waiting for the day when the sun will smile on him," he whispered. "But no man can look on the sun without burning. You burn me, but I will not let you go. I have waited too long to feel you smile on me."

He kissed her tears gently away as they slid down her cheeks, kissing her mouth with the tangy taste of salt between them.

"Special? If you need a word, then take this," he whispered. "You are mine, and I am yours. I know no other word for that."

She settled back down deep into his embrace, her questions answered.

17

Maggie and Teyas rode alongside each other as the men rode ahead. When the women were invited to travel to Martin's Hundred for supplies, they both gladly accepted. Maggie was anxious to see the English town, curious to connect it to the little she knew about the history of the settlement. Over the last few weeks as they explored their new-found intimacy, she noticed Winn seemed reluctant to take her to town, so it was a surprise when he made the offer. She had many questions about the English, and she hoped her curiosity would be satiated by the visit.

Her fat pony plodded along, swinging her back and forth in a lazy rhythm. The glutton resorted to grabbing at every piece of tall grass they passed, so Maggie was forced to tap him frequently with her heels to remind him his job was to walk, not eat. Teyas had no such problem with her mount, but she was kind enough to lag behind with Maggie anyway.

"C'mon, you lazy hog!" Maggie groaned, kicking her pony for what seemed the hundredth time. Teyas giggled and helped her along by swatting Maggie's horse with her rein, which did absolutely nothing.

"He only does that with you," Teyas smirked.

"Well, maybe I need an upgraded model," Maggie huffed.

"Upgrade?" Teyas asked, raising her eyebrows.

"A better horse. A faster one," she explained. Teyas shrugged and tossed a round orange fruit at Maggie, which she caught in her lap. It was a maypop, and it seemed ages since she'd tasted anything she recognized.

"Try it. The elders say this fruit holds magic."

Maggie raised an eyebrow but took a bite of the overripe fruit anyway, laughing when a bit of the sweet juice dribbled down her chin.

"Thanks. It's good," she agreed. "A little soft, but good."

They followed the men along the coastline for what Maggie estimated was several miles. Once the beach began to narrow they came to an inlet, suddenly in sight was the outline of some sort of civilization shimmering as a mirage against the sand. Maggie pushed herself up as high as she could manage on the short pony and craned her neck to see.

"There it is!" she said. "Is that Martin's Hundred?"

Winn must have heard her exclamation. He circled his horse around and rode back, trotting up to ride beside her. Sandwiched between Winn and Teyas, Maggie let out a frustrated groan. She wanted to gallop in for a closer look.

"It is part of Martin's Hundred they call Wolstenholme Town. We will get there soon enough, no need to hurry," Winn teased her.

"Are you sure they're friendly? It doesn't seem safe to me," she asked. He made a half grunt, half snort sound and frowned, shaking his head.

"As safe as it always is. I've had no trouble, but I will have you stay with me. No wandering off. Hear me, Teyas?" Winn called over his shoulder. Teyas tossed her long braid over her shoulder with a shrug and retorted with the same grunted admonishment the men frequently used, and Maggie giggled at their exchange.

A shrill whinny pierced the air. Chetan's stallion reared and began to prance as the palisade gates opened, and Winn rode ahead to help steady Chetan's wayward animal. Their party entered amidst shouted greetings and waves of welcome, and as she looked around at the bevy of faces in the crowd, Maggie suddenly felt her body sway as if she were on a boat.

Blurred faces swirled around her, cleared, and then clouded. The strange sensation hit again, and with the threat of losing her breakfast, she leaned forward against the coarse mane of her pony and promptly evacuated the contents of her stomach down the side of the horse. When she let out a groan, Teyas swung back around, and she reached over and grabbed Maggie's reins.

"What ails you, Maggie?" Teyas asked. Maggie shook her head as another wave of nausea came, milder than the last. She was able to straighten up somewhat by the time Winn reached them.

"It must have been the maypop, I thought it tasted off. I'm fine now," she muttered. Whatever it was seemed to be passing, for which she was grateful. She wished she had passed on eating the fruit, since it seemed too soft to her, but the deed was done and now she could only face the consequence.

"You look like an eel, all green and wet," Winn laughed. He held out his arm, and she gladly slid over onto his lap, rather than risk falling off her own mount. She supposed it was all right to behave like a damsel in distress once in a while.

* * *

A damp cloth covered her eyes as she rested. She suspected it was meant to lie on her forehead, but as such things happen, it drifted downward like a mask, and when she pulled it off her face and looked around, she figured she was lucky it had not fallen over her mouth and stopped her breathing since no one would have noticed.

She sat up on a padded bench. She had not noticed much when Winn carried her inside, but now that she had recovered from her bout of sickness, she was eager to look about. Gathered around a long wood slat table were the Indians she had arrived with and several strangers. She seemed to be in the parlor of some sort of store, a saltbox style building as far as she could tell, with whitewashed walls and glass windows. Outside the large picture window toward the open door sun streamed into the room, and she could see what looked like a packed clay road, with the semblance of further similar buildings across the way.

Other less interested people filled the space, some looking at shelves lining one wall. An assortment of glass jars littered the shelves, filled with varying colors of remedies. A second shelf housed multiple sizes of blown glass bowls. A large round basket filled with squares of clean linen sat pushed against the wall beneath the shelves, and several fine trunks were stacked nearby.

In the middle of the room a table was currently occupied by a boy of about five-years-old lying flat on his back, flailing his legs as a curly haired teenage girl held his shoulders in place. The boy knocked her white cap off her head in the struggle, and when she reached to grab it, he jumped off the table and ran for the door. An older woman stood behind the table, a rustic set of hot pliers waving in her hand as she laughed.

"I think the mite wants to keep that rotten tooth, Miss Ellen," the healer laughed. The sprite made it through the door before anyone could snag him, and the younger girl shook her head with a groan.

"Did someone lose this?"

Maggie looked up at Winn's voice. Winn came through the door, the boy hoisted over his shoulder like a sack of grain, kicking and squealing at his captor.

"Winkeohkwet, bring the lad here!" the older woman called. He crossed the room and deposited the child back on the table, then held the child while the woman quickly plucked the tooth from his gaping mouth. The child howled and burst into tears.

"There, there, hush, child! 'Tis the indignity of it all that pains him, not the tooth," she assured to the curly-haired girl who soothed the child. "That tooth was plenty numb from the spirits I gave 'em."

"Feel better, *ntehem?*" Winn asked, kneeling down at her side. He placed his hand over hers and gave it a gentle squeeze.

"Yes. Did I make a mess?" she asked, her pride more damaged than anything.

He chuckled. "You did it quite properly, your horse did not mind. Did you eat enough today?"

"I think so. I'm fine now, really. Just a little dizzy."

One eyebrow dipped down and he made a dismissive hissing noise through his teeth.

"Right, then. Fine? I think not. Stay here, I will be back," he replied. He took Teyas by the elbow and spoke quietly to her. She produced a pouch of dried meat from the satchel tied to her waist, which she proceeded to give to Maggie.

"I'm not really hungry," she said, scrunching her nose at the strong smoked smell of the meat and waving her hand at them to fend off the do-gooders.

"Eat," Winn demanded.

"Can you ever just ask me to do something, instead of ordering me around?" she asked.

He frowned. "Eat...please."

"No. I'm not hungry." She tossed her braid back and turned her shoulder to him, hiding the smile on her lips. He put the meat to her mouth and reached for her head with his other hand as if he meant to shove it down her throat, and she smacked him playfully away. "Ok, ok! I'll eat, give it to me!" she giggled.

"*Keptchat!*" he hissed. He grunted, but she saw him hide his smile as he gave her the dried meat. He watched her chew for a moment and then reached into the small pouch he carried. He fished out her raven and handed it to her.

"My raven! Where did you get it?"

"You dropped it when you were sick, Makedewa found it. Did it come with you when you traveled?"

She darted a glance around to see if anyone listened to their conversation, then ducked her head close to his when she spoke.

"Yes, Marcus gave it to me when I was a little girl. It scares away the bad dreams," she whispered. A secret smile formed on his lips, and she narrowed her brows, wondering what he was up to.

"Do you know what meaning my name has, in your English words?" he asked, his eyes alight, teasing as he gazed down at her.

She shook her head.

"No, why?"

"When I was a young boy, I had dreams that caused me to scream in my sleep. One night my mother took me outside, and she pointed to a great black bird that sat in a tree next to our yehakin. She said the bird would cure my madness and protect me from evil. Since that day, I have been known as Winkeohkwet, The Raven."

Her mouth dropped open at his story as he smiled.

"Fear not, little one. This Raven will always protect you. He has loved you forever."

Her heart pounded wildly as he stood up, the voice of Marcus filling her ears.

"It's a raven, a great brave bird. The raven keeps safe those he loves."

"Well," she sniffed, *"how do I know he loves me? He just met me!"*

Marcus chuckled.

"He's always known ye, lamb. He's loved ye forever."

She shuddered despite the warmth but managed to smile weakly back at him all the same as he dared a quick kiss to the tip of her nose.

Winn left her side to clasp arms with a man near the doorway as a melee ensued, with the two men standing nearly head to head amidst the crowded room. Winn wore a brown tunic over leggings, with tall moccasin boots covering his limbs up to the knees, a living enticement to illicit thoughts as he stood there oblivious of his charm. His hair flowed loose down his back, unencumbered by the usual braid, and she could see the side of his head above his ear was still shaved close. Maggie smiled thinking of how she had helped him with it.

The stranger grinned broadly in greeting, and Maggie could see the gray woolen breeches he wore against a royal blue waistcoat when she caught a glimpse through the crowd. Tall knee-high boots covered his feet, different from the other men who wore flat shoes with square metal buckles. His thick curling dark hair was pulled back with a blue ribbon at his nape. Taller than the others, but standing straight and proud, he was thick through his shoulders and unintentionally demanded a presence from those around him.

The men were too far away for her to hear any of their words, embroiled in such a conversation that Winn took to using his hands to illustrate his speech, and the stranger responded with his own gestures. Hands planted on hips, body arched, the stranger threw his head back and laughed, then thumped Winn boldly over his shoulders while Winn held a boyish grin on his own face.

Maggie rose up off the bench, pleased to find her legs were steady again and her vision seemed clear instead of like a swirling typhoon. Winn met her gaze from where he stood talking to the stranger, cocking his head inquisitively at her, then smiling back when she nodded reassurance to him.

The healer motioned Maggie closer with a tilt of her head and a smile, and Maggie tore her gaze away from Winn and approached her rather than interrupt the men. The curly-haired girl brushed by Maggie on her way out, the child sobbing with his little legs wrapped around her middle and his pudgy hands twisted in the girl's apron.

"Hello," Maggie smiled. The healer nodded. She clenched the front of her white apron and wiped her hands clean, her linen stained with the bloody remnants of previous tasks from the day. Her hair was a bright shade of gold that laid in a thick braid down her back, a few loose strands of gray at her temples the only testament to her age.

"You must be this Fire Heart I hear of. Welcome, dear. I am pleased to finally meet you. You've caused quite a stir in the village, yes?"

The woman held a twinkle in her eye as she gazed at Maggie, the corners of her thin lips turned up in a smile. She had an odd lilt to her voice, not quite the same formal English accent as Maggie had heard the other townsfolk speak with, but something different altogether. Her words, although innocent in appearance, sounded laced with knowing, as if she held some secret knowledge she wished to share.

"Why, yes, I guess I have," Maggie replied evenly. Finola winked and tittered with laughter as she turned and dumped the tongs into a copper pot beneath the table.

"Does my grandson treat you well?"

"Your grandson? I don't know what you mean."

"Oh? Winkeohkwet is so full of himself now, he does not speak of his grandmother? They call me the Pale Witch in his village. Here, I am Mistress Finola, a healer," she said, casting a wink at Maggie. "Witch is a word we do not speak loudly in this time, dearest." Finola turned away to tend to a potential customer and smiled an apology to Maggie.

Maggie felt the color drain from her face at her words. *Finola was the Pale Witch?* Finola knew about the Bloodstones! She wished she could speak privately with her, if only for a few minutes, but she knew the conversation would be too risky around the English ears.

She felt the gentle pressure of a hand on the small of her back. Winn returned to her side before she made a fool of herself by getting sick again, and she gave him a terse smile. The man he had spoken to earlier accompanied him. The stranger extended his gloved hand to her with a genuine broad grin streaking across his face. She placed her fingertips in his hand, and when she looked up at him to smile in greeting, she noticed his kind blue eyes darted downward and a flush crept up his neck.

"Benjamin, this is Maggie," Winn said.

"A pleasure to meet you, Miss," he murmured. "Benjamin Dixon, your servant." He bent at the waist, a considerable task for the tall man, and pressed her fingers quickly to his lips before he released them. She saw his throat tighten and he swallowed before he raised his head with a stunning grin.

"How long have you lived with the Paspahegh, miss? I cannot recall seeing ye on my last visit to the village," Benjamin commented.

Her tongue stuck to the dry lining of her mouth, and her back stiffened at the thought of disclosing anything to him. No matter how friendly he seemed to be with Winn, she was fully aware of the history of violence between the English and Indians, and she was still perplexed trying to make sense of their relationship. She suspected time traveling and Bloodstones would stick her right into the category of witch, so she clamped her mouth shut and shrugged demurely in return.

"She is under my protection," Winn said. He still smiled, but Maggie could see his eyes flicker with caution.

"Ye haven't been raiding, have you?" Benjamin asked. He tilted his head toward Winn and lowered his voice an octave. "You know the folk here willna abide you having a white slave! I beg yer pardon, miss," he stammered, darting a quick look at Maggie. "Tempers are high to-day, man! I heard an Indian left with the Elder Morgan two days ago on a trade run and he hasna been seen since. Do ye know any 'bout that?"

"I know nothing of it, but I will see to it. I'm sure it is just idle talk," Winn replied.

"Then take yer rest at my yard tonight, and I shall speak to ye later on it. I think it best for ye to lay low," Benjamin said, nodding curtly at Maggie. "Especially seeing the womenfolk with ye."

Winn and Benjamin clasped arms in farewell. Benjamin tipped his head to her and made a quick exit.

"What was that all about?" she asked as soon as he was gone. "And your grandmother? The Pale Witch? That information would have been helpful before we arrived, don't you think?" Maggie hissed. Winn moved a bit closer, his breath warming her ear when he spoke.

"So there is something you don't know from your school? I thought you learned all about my people?" he teased. She nudged him with her shoulder in his chest, a little more forcefully than she intended, but she smiled nevertheless when he let out a grunt.

"I don't know enough, Winn. Not nearly enough," she sighed.

18

THEY SETTLED DOWN for the night on Benjamin Dixon's property, which Winn knew was the safest place to rest. Winn watched Maggie from where he sat across the fire, her smile lighting up the night as much as the flickering flames between them. It was a cool night, one of those unsettled days between fall and winter before the cold overtook the warmth entirely, and Maggie sat huddled next to Teyas with a fur draped over her shoulders. He could tell she was chilled by the way she bit her lower lip, her small white teeth closing down as if to ward off trembling. At some time since they arrived, she had loosened her hair, and now her hand darted up several times to push the wayward waves behind her ears. Her red hair shimmered in the flicker of the fire, amber gold against the curve of her jaw, and he had to adjust his seat to a tolerable position as depraved thoughts of her escalated in his mind. As soon as Benjamin left and there were no eyes upon them, he would warm her well.

He glanced over at Benjamin, who sat next to Chetan, the two men sharing sips of rum from a shiny metal flask. Winn noticed Benjamin watching Maggie as if he had never seen a white woman captive before. It was not common for the Paspahegh to have slaves, but it was not unheard of either, so Winn was unsure of why Benjamin was so curious about it. It was quite usual for other Powhatan tribes to have white slaves, however, so it should truly be of no consequence.

Benjamin had always been the voice of conscience, the one to point out the good in every situation, even when the outlook was bleak.

Winn spent two summers in the care of the Dixon family as a youth, and he and Benjamin became fast friends, despite their obvious differences.

Benjamin continued to watch Maggie across the fire.

"Benjamin," Winn called. Benjamin broke the stare and looked over at Winn, one eyebrow raised in question. "Sit with me, brother."

"Ye mean to share my rum, more likely," Benjamin grinned as he sat down beside Winn. Winn took a swig from the proffered flask, smiling as the burning warmth heated his belly and traveled down to his toes.

"Good drink."

"Came in on the last ship from England."

"Ah, well, English are good for something, then."

"Come now, we're not all such rakes," Benjamin grinned, taking a sip. "Speaking of...tell me of the woman. Where did ye steal her from? I cannot help ye if I know nothing of it, and ye know they will want her returned, whoever her kin are."

"No kin will look for her, I promise you that," Winn answered truthfully. "She is mine, that is all you must know."

Benjamin looked back in Maggie's direction where she sat laughing with Teyas. Winn felt a twinge of unease at the way his friend stared at her. Was it curiosity, or something more in his eyes?

"You've never kept a slave woman before, brother."

They watched her stand, make a shrugging gesture at Teyas, and then rub her belly before she set off toward the woods. Winn stood up.

"I must make sure she's safe," Winn muttered, leaving Benjamin with the others. He followed her into the trees, reluctant to let her out of his sight although it was obvious she needed a moment alone.

She had learned to be fast with such things, and Winn caught her as she was righting her dress. She let out a squeak when he snuck up behind her and grabbed her around the waist, but her alarm dissipated as soon as she realized it was him. How he loved to hear her laugh!

"Winn!" she laughed. He kissed the back of her neck, pulling her hips firmly into his, feeling the surge of arousal at the touch of her soft welcoming backside nestled against him. She leaned into him in a teasing manner and giggled, and it was all the permission he needed.

"I cannot wait any longer," he murmured against her ear.

He felt her shiver as he ran one hand up her thigh, bringing her dress up around her hips. She squirmed and tried to turn around, but he held her tight.

"Not here, Winn! They might hear us!"

"Yes, here. Be silent," he soothed her. He pulled her down onto the soft moss, at loss to find a better method among the scattered brush of the forest, knowing only he needed to possess her and that he would wait no longer. He pushed her hands down to the ground and took hold of her hips as she tried to scramble away.

"Winn!"

"Quiet!"

"Oh!"

Her words turned to moans and he thought his heart would pound out of his chest with the force of their joining. Frantic and needful, he buried his fear and longing within her, a lustful sinner comforted by the warmth of salvation as she cried out beneath him, begging him not to stop. She reared back against him as she reached her peak, and he sunk his fingers into her soft white hips at his own release. He smiled at the soft cry she made as he pulled her up into his arms, and they sat there on their knees, clutched together as they tried to steady their breathing.

As she pressed her face to his chest, he kissed her hair, loving the way she fit curled up in his arms. He heard the snap of a branch, and then another, and was stunned when he found the source of the noise as he looked over her shoulder.

Winn saw Benjamin's face as a pale outline against the evergreens, his mouth parted open, his eyes wide. Winn felt his throat tighten as he met the Englishman's gaze. Benjamin quickly turned and left.

19

Maggie was glad Benjamin left before they returned to camp, certain their stolen moment in the forest would be evident on their faces when they returned. Winn showed little surprise his friend retired without seeing them settled, so Maggie brushed off her insecurity and felt no qualm over lying down beside him to sleep. She was restless, however, and thought Winn was in a pleasant enough mood to field her questions, so she turned her curiosity onto him.

"How do you know Benjamin?" she asked. He let out a long sigh and pulled her closer before he answered.

"My uncle sent me to live with the English for a time. I spent two summers with the Dixon family, and Benjamin became my friend."

"Do you trust him?"

"Benjamin? More than I trust any white man," he said. "My uncle wanted me to learn the English ways, so I could help in his plan to drive them away. He was not pleased we became friends." Winn nuzzled her neck and nipped her with his teeth. "Just as he will not be pleased to know I keep a Blooded One here, safe in my arms."

He looked a little sad at this confession, his eyes darkening, and his hands tightening around her.

"Why does your uncle hate the Blooded Ones so much?" she whispered as they snuggled beneath the furs.

"Why do you ask?"

"Just curious, that's all."

"It is a story much older than my years. Blooded Ones lived peacefully among the Paspahegh until Opechancanough had his vision. He saw one of them, a Time Walker, end his life, and after that, they were all in danger. My grandmother was spared death and instead banished by my uncle, but this happened before I was born. I have only known her as the Pale Witch, living here with the English, and I visit her as much as I can."

"So it is true, then, that your father was English?"

Winn shook his head. "My father was white, but not English. He traveled here with Bloodstone magic when he was a boy. Finola told me the tale. They came from a place where they had great long boats to travel far, and his people read from books and wrote in them. Grandmother speaks little of him; I think it pains her to know he is gone."

"Why did he leave without his wife?"

"I know not, and mother does not speak of it. He used his Bloodstone soon after he wed my mother. After he left, she became second wife to Pepamhu of the Nansemond, and bore my brothers and sister."

He lifted the necklace from his neck and separated the black feathers that shielded the pendant. In his palm, enclosed in tarnished melted copper, was a tiny Bloodstone charm. She felt his eyes upon her as she slowly reached out to touch it and then jerked back away before she could make contact. She had no idea how it worked and was not willing to test it any further.

"When a raw Bloodstone is used to travel, it binds to the bearer. You can use no other stone to travel," he said softly. He took her branded hand and turned it over to reveal the healed scar, tracing the delicate knot in an unending twist upon her palm. "I keep this Bloodstone to remind me."

"To remind you of what, Winn?"

"That my blood is not true Paspahegh. My father was a Norse-Man, and he chose to leave with his Bloodstone before my birth. I need reminder of how worthless all whites are, so I will never waver when it comes time to end them," he said carefully. "He knows not what he left behind, and I hate him for that. As a boy, I felt anger for the difference in my skin and that of my brothers, and some English called me Half-Man. Children are most cruel to those who are different."

"A Norseman? You mean a Viking?" she interrupted.

He rubbed her lower back with one warm hand and nodded.

"Some called them Vikings. They were said to control powerful magic."

"I'd say. Those Bloodstones pack some punch," she snorted. She chose to avoid the subject of his father, even as her curiosity rose, knowing Winn had conflicted feelings about the man. "So you went to live with your uncle?"

"I was sent to live with Opechancanough and spent many years there as his favorite nephew. It gave me great status, and when I returned to the Paspahegh, I was welcomed. My return to my own people was to serve as War Chief and lead the few left, serving Opechancanough in his plans. I have watched over them, and always have given my loyalty to my Mamanatowick."

"I thought he was *Weroance?*" she asked.

"*Mamanatowick* means Great Weroance, Great Chief of all Powhatan, of all Tsenacommacah lands. He has many names, and that is one."

"Oh. Sounds like a busy man."

She ran her finger lightly over the winding tattoo on his torso, an intricate swirl across his ribs that ended below his navel. Although they shared a growing intimacy, she remained in awe of his powerful body, each muscle and sinew honed by hunting and fighting, strong yet yielding beneath her touch.

"Does this have meaning?" she asked, placing her palm flat against his navel.

"Some objected to my presence when I went to live with Opechancanough, since I was son of a Time Walker. He marked me to silence them."

"I don't understand."

He sighed.

"Those born to the Weroance bloodlines, like Opechancanough and my mother, may never have such a mark placed on their bodies. Only common men decorate their bodies. I could never be Weroance because of the Time Walker's blood in my veins. He marked me to show the people I am one of them. War Chief is the most honor a common man could hope for in his life."

He placed his hand over hers, and traced over a part of the tattoo near his hip.

"This one, here," he said, "Is for the first man I killed. This part, here, is for the day I became a man. And this, this one shows I am different, that I am not true Paspahegh, that I carry the blood of the whites."

"Does it bother you? Being marked that way, I mean?"

She felt his shoulders shrug, and he made a dismissive sound.

"Once it did, but no longer. It is part of me now."

He grinned, and pulled her snugly against him. She buried her clenched hands next to his skin, giggling when he jumped at her cold touch.

"Here, let me warm you," he murmured. He clasped his larger hands over hers, and gently blew into them to drench her chilled fingers. Dipping his head down, he kissed her knuckles with a smile.

"What does your history say of the Norse-men?" he asked, very softly. She saw his throat tighten and his eyes widen a bit, his brows raised. Her heart lurched at his change, the way his face filled like an expectant boy, almost childish as he asked an innocent question. She paused before she spoke, hoping to say the right words to ease his mind and help heal his ache.

"They were fierce warriors. Stories were written about their journeys— legends, really— that children still read in my time, about all their brave adventures." She pressed her lips to his skin and threaded a lock of his dark hair in her fingers. "Tall, strong, like you. You must get your blue eyes from your father."

She felt his hands tighten around her, only for a moment, a gentle reminder that his feelings for his father were much more complicated than a tale could absolve.

"So the dog gave me eyes like the sky, and then ran away as a coward. Brave? Humph."

Maggie wondered if he could ever let go of the ache, the depth of his feelings apparent as they ran so close below the surface, the hurt little boy buried so far he was nearly forgotten. She said nothing, giving him the choice to continue, barely surprised when he nestled his head to her shoulder and remained silent.

She stroked his hair as his breathing finally slowed into sleep, comforting him in the only way she knew how.

* * *

Ghosts of the future haunted her that night, begging acknowledgement, refusing to be put to sleep.

She placed her raven on the ground as she played on the floor of the old barn. No one would bother her there. Grandpa had no use for the space, but she liked it. It was a secret place, her hiding spot, a place to call her own among the world of adults.

Hinges creaked, and she saw the wood plank door open. A pair of round blue eyes peered at her between the slats.

"Can I come in, Maggie?" he asked. She rolled her eyes. It was the boy, Marcus's son. He wasn't so bad.

"Oh, I guess. Hurry up and close the door."

He slithered in and plopped down beside her.

"Ach, crap, I cut my finger on the stupid door. Gimme your sock, will ya?"

"No, I'm not giving you anything! Go get a Band-Aid, or keep bleeding, I don't care!" she sniped. He shrugged.

When he saw her raven sitting solitary in the dirt, he fished in his pocket for a moment until he produced his own treasure.

The boy held it up, a wide toothless grin stretching across his face.

"See? Da gave you the raven, but I have the eagle. It's better than the raven," he bragged.

"No it's not!" she hissed.

"Aye, it is! My Da said so!"

"You're a liar, and I'm telling!" she shrieked. She jumped up and left him in the dirt.

It was the last time she saw him. Grandpa said not to speak of it, poor Marcus could not bear it. His little son, disappeared without a trace. The police said the mother must have taken him.

Divorced spouses kidnap their kids all the time. It was just one of those sad things that happen sometimes.

She wiped the tears from her eyes and burrowed in closer to Winn. Memories like that, well, they were best forgotten. There was surely enough trouble in this time to keep her occupied.

Poor Marcus. They never found his son, and Marcus carried on somehow. She hoped he did not suffer now in the same manner. If only she could find a way to tell him she was alive, that she missed him. Then perhaps the leaving of him would not ache so much.

20

Winn placed A pile of kindling onto the fire, stirring it with a long stick. Embers of the morning sun darted over the horizon, yet the moon still shone above. Although the men had been awake for some time, they let the women sleep longer, knowing they would need rest to travel on as the day grew warmer.

Makedewa sat on a log near the fire, tossing in bits of a branch he picked apart in his hands. His demeanor was unchanged from his usual angry mask, the same scowl he wore upon waking and the one he walked with each day.

Winn wondered if his younger brother would ever find happiness, or at least something to occupy his anger other than planning the next raid on the English. Oftentimes rash, known among the villagers as a hothead, Winn knew the warrior was a much deeper man than his disguise portrayed. Unlike Chetan, who laughed and loved with no care what others thought, Makedewa lacked such confidence. Winn wished he would not suffer so much for his own pride.

"Nemattanew killed Morgan White. I know not why, but I am sure of it." Makedewa continued to stare into the fire as he spoke, his gaze unwavering.

"Did he admit as much to you?" Winn asked. Makedewa nodded.

"He said the English will never find the body."

Winn let out his breath in a sigh as he shook his head. It served no purpose to agitate the English at this time, and Nemattanew was aware of that fact more so than any Powhatan brave. With one rash act, the foolish warrior had given the English cause to mistrust them all, making it even more dangerous for the Paspahegh to remain cordial with the settlers.

"We should return to the village today. Ready the horses and pack our supplies." Winn stared hard at Makedewa. "My uncle will hear of this, and he will not be pleased. I hope Nemattanew has not brought his wrath upon us."

Makedewa grunted, and set off to dismantle the campsite. Winn looked toward the cabin where Benjamin lived. He wondered if he should wake the man to bid him goodbye. Glancing down at Maggie, sleeping peacefully beneath his furs, he decided against it. The image of the Englishman spying on them in the woods made his chest tighten, sparking his ire.

No, it was better this way. Let things cool between them before they met again. There had never been anything they could not find agreement on, and although Benjamin mediated between the English and Paspahegh, he was still a loyal friend. Winn wondered if things now had changed. He was willing to wager they did, after seeing how Benjamin stared at his woman.

His woman.

Winn tickled her neck until her sleepy jade eyes opened and she smiled up at him, despite him rousing her from her dreams. He kissed her gently along her ear and buried his face in the sweet meadow scent of her hair for a moment.

"Time to wake, *ntehem*. We leave soon."

He resisted the urge to melt back down into the furs with her, instead taking her hand to help her to her feet.

21

She was happy to be back in the village. It was almost funny that she now viewed it as the height of civilization, especially since she never thought she would survive a week within the culture. Yet after she had been exposed to the way the English lived, she was quite content to remain among the Paspahegh. In fact, she would be happy to stay anywhere, as long as Winn were there.

As she sat with Teyas near the Great Fire awaiting the start of the evening feast, Maggie noticed the sounds of whispered uproar throughout the village. She looked up to see what they were fussing about. Across the thruway near the horse corral, a group of men entered the clearing.

White men.

She sat up straighter and stuck her fisted hands in her lap, her eyes searching the warriors who gathered for any sign of hostility. Were the men friends, or enemies?

Their group consisted of a half-dozen Englishmen, all dressed in similar knee-high breeches and linen shirts, wielding rifles which they kept slung over their backs in what Maggie perceived must be a less threatening gesture than if they carried them outright. On entering the village, one bold man led the others, flanked by the reluctant entourage who followed with caution. It was Benjamin Dixon.

Shouts rose from the men, and for a moment Maggie was terrified there would be a violent response. Her fear dissipated quickly when she saw a warrior break from the crowd of men to approach the visitors.

Benjamin clasped arms with the warrior and Maggie saw a broad smile crease his face.

The warrior who welcomed him was none other than Winn.

"Who are those men?" Maggie nudged Teyas, who was watching the exchange as well.

"You know Benjamin Dixon. He is a friend to us. He brings many of the English with him today," Teyas answered with a frown. "Thomas Martin is with him as well, he is the fat one next to Benjamin. I hope they do not need more corn, we have little to share," she sighed.

"Do they always need supplies?"

"Most times. They are lazy people, they grow little food on their own."

"They look like trouble," Maggie said, her voice escalating a pitch. It made her nervous to see the English visit the village, no matter what pretense they offered, since she knew full well how they abused the kindness of the Indians.

Teyas shrugged and shushed her. Winn approached, Benjamin walking in stride beside him. Winn led the white men by the fire next to where the warriors gathered, escorting them to a place of honor apart from the others. Not quite as welcoming as Winn but not hostile, either, the warriors made space for the guests and settled back into the spirit of the feast. The hollow thud of a drum resounded, and the interruption seemed forgotten.

Winn looked in her direction from across the fire where he stood with Benjamin. Their eyes met for a moment, and Maggie glimpsed an edge of something unsettling in his gaze. There was no acknowledgement in his wooden stare, but she could see the muscles in his crossed arms tighten and the way his back stiffened at her inquisitive perusal of the strangers. He quickly broke contact and turned back to the visitor.

"Will Winn eat with us?" Maggie asked. Teyas shook her head.

"No, he will eat with the men."

"Is there some rule that says I can't talk to him now?"

"Shush, Maggie! No, no rule. But we wait to be spoken to at this feast," the girl hissed back, jabbing her in the rib with her elbow. "He will take you to his *yehakin* soon, be patient!"

Maggie scowled as her cheeks flushed at the implication. She ignored the jibe and continued questioning the girl, curious to glean information about the visitors.

"I just want to talk to him," she said.

"You must wait to be spoken to! He will be angry if you go to him now!"

"Well, he can be angry at me later. I just want a second to talk to him."

Maggie stood up, but Teyas was fast on her heels and grabbed her by the back of her dress before she could go very far.

"Teyas, let go!" she hissed as she tried to shake the other woman off.

"Sit down!" Teyas pleaded. Panic laced her words. Maggie suddenly felt bad for causing a scene, and let Teyas pull her back down to sit on the grass. A few of the other woman shot them hard looks and shook their heads.

"Ah, *kemata tepahta*! Now Winn sees us!" Teyas groaned.

Winn was staring at them from across the fire, as was the visitor at his side. Benjamin tapped Winn's arm and pointed at the quarreling women in question. Maggie watched as Winn said something tense to the man and waved his question off, shaking his head, while pushing a bowl of food into the man's hands as if to distract him. Winn clapped Benjamin on the back in a friendly manner and then spoke again. Maggie wished she could hear what they were saying, but the distance was too great and it was enough just to decipher the expressions on their faces. Winn left the visitor and turned to one of the warriors that flanked his sides, his attention shifting for the moment. He uttered some direction to the warrior before he left his position, his destination clear to both Maggie and Teyas.

Maggie prepared to face his onslaught, unaware of what to expect since she knew little of what stoked the obvious temper he was in. She glanced back across the fire and noticed Benjamin was staring straight at her, confusion etched on his face as he squinted to see her in the glare of the setting sun. When their eyes met his mouth fell open, and she quickly ducked her head. No good could come of making contact with the visitors in front of the villagers.

Maggie felt Teyas nudge her in warning before Winn grabbed her arm and yanked her to her feet.

"Ouch! What the hell-"

"Be silent. You will go back to my *yehakin*. Now!" he demanded, his words uttered hoarse and low next to her ear. She allowed him to hold her upper arm, but turned to meet his steel gaze.

"Why? What is going on?"

"Go, *ntehem*. I will meet you soon."

An unsettling surge of fear at the look in his eyes challenged her resolve, as she could see Winn was worried about something. It was not like him to show such emotion in front of others, and with a deepening sense of unease Maggie realized he was afraid. Of what, she had no notion.

"Teyas, come! You will eat with Maggie and tend her wound," he growled. His sister immediately obeyed, taking Maggie's hand and urging her back toward the yehakin. Maggie let out a sigh and succumbed to being led away. Winn stood rooted in place, watching them go. Maggie saw Nemattanew approach and was glad to leave.

"Wait!"

Maggie swung around at the clear English plea. Her eyes shifted to Benjamin, who was standing next to Winn and looking at the women expectantly.

"Please, Miss, if I could have a word with you? Surely you do not mind, Winn?" Benjamin asked. Behind the Englishman stood two other older men, dressed in similar attire but both equally as interested by the astonished looks on their faces.

"The woman was wounded by a bear. She needs her wound tended," Winn replied tersely. The wound was long since healed, but Maggie played along.

"Well, yes, of course! But it will only take a moment, my friend," Benjamin insisted. "Can ye tell me how ye came to be in these parts, Miss?"

Maggie thought a simple white lie was enough to quell Benjamin's curiosity and show the man he need not worry that she was being kept against her will, so she eagerly responded.

"I don't remember. I must have hit my head. The last thing I remember was Winn saving me from a bear attack."

Winn froze at her words and Benjamin's mouth fell open.

"'Tis as I said, Dixon, she is my niece," another man announced.

The man Teyas had called Thomas Martin stepped forward toward Maggie. Towheaded and stocky, but not in a pleasing manner, the gentleman pushed past his companions to approach her. Maggie held her ground as he scrutinized her with tiny piercing black eyes, making her feel like a piece of prime meat on display. The urge to inform him he was sadly mistaken crossed her mind, but she opted to keep her mouth shut for the moment. She looked helplessly to Winn, fully aware she could not tell the Englishman where she truly came from. In light of the manner which Winn barely contained his anger, she stepped a pace away from the man instead.

"She is not your niece," Winn said.

Thomas cocked his hands on his hips and spit on the ground at her feet with a nod. Maggie noticed his gun shift slightly forward on his shoulder in a way it would be easier to grasp.

"Of course she is. This girl is my kin, I think I would know my own dead brother's sweet child! I heard word she was lost in the river on the way to Jamestown. She clearly wandered into the wood where ye found her. My thanks for returning her to me safely," the man said, pausing before he added, with a side glance at Benjamin, "my friend."

"No, I'm not your niece," Maggie stammered, completely confused as to what was going on. Nemattanew stepped forward and placed a hand on the Englishman's shoulder.

"You will take the woman away?" Nemattanew interrupted, suddenly interested in the discussion.

"Well, yes, I paid a great deal of money to bring her here, and I can't rightly leave her with you sav—with your people. You don't expect me to buy her back, do you?" Thomas snorted, the thought evidently causing him much distress.

"Then take her." Nemattanew made the offering, his eyes fixed on Winn.

Her breath caught in her throat as she waited for Winn's response.

"You forget she is not yours to give, Nemattanew," Winn said.

"Then I will ride to speak with Opechancanough, I am sure he will wish to return the woman to her kin," Nemattanew replied. "Our Weroance wishes nothing but peace between our people, Thomas Martin."

Veins stood out like cords on Winn's arms, and Maggie saw the way his eyes narrowed as he stared at Nemattanew. His hand flexed open then closed into a fist at his side.

"Then ride, Nemattanew," Winn answered. "But until then, she stays here."

She felt Teyas squeeze her hand, and saw the look she exchanged with Winn. She did not protest when Teyas nodded to the men and then proceeded to drag her back to the yehakin.

Once they were safely inside, Teyas began to pace back and forth, stopping every so often to peer out through the hide-covered doorway. When Maggie tried to ask a question, Teyas raised a hand in dismissal and urged her silence. Suddenly, Teyas stopped pacing and joined Maggie where she stood at the back of the room.

Winn parted the bear hide and ducked into the room. He gave Teyas a short command in his own language and his sister quickly left the yehakin. Alone with Winn and his flaring temper, Maggie braced herself and let him approach.

"That man is Thomas Martin. He claims you as his kin. He wants you returned to him."

She felt faint as his words struck her.

"But you know I'm not his niece."

"I know."

"But Winn—"

"Listen!" he hissed, "There is no time to argue! Nemattanew has left the village to seek permission from my uncle to give you to the English. If he returns with orders from the Weroance, the Council will support him, and they will release you from me."

"Release me?"

"You became my prisoner when I found you," he said quietly, his eyes dipping down away from her stare. "It is my right to keep you or cast you off. Only the Great Weroance can compel me to release you."

"Your prisoner?" Her back stiffened. "Is that what I am to you?" she replied, the words slipping from her tongue laced with fear and betrayal. It shattered her to know he could rid himself so easily of her after what they had shared.

"You know you are more to me than that," he growled.

"Am I?" she whispered, afraid to hear his answer even as she demanded it. She saw his fists clench at his sides.

"You are. Have I not showed you what you are to me?"

She remained silent. *What could she say to him?* As much as she wanted to hear him declare his love for her, there were much more pressing matters to deal with.

"Would your uncle send me away, against your wishes?" she asked, dipping her head down to avoid his stare.

"When Nemattanew tells him the English claim you, he will order me to give you to them. My uncle seeks to keep friendship with the English above all else, he will not risk angering them. If the English wanted Teyas, or Chetan, or even Ahi Kekeleksu, he would give them away. It only matters to him to keep peace right now."

She glanced up at him, seeing his skin flushed red from his neck to his ears, his jaw clamped and his veins standing out like bowstrings.

"I thought your uncle hated them."

"He does. I do. But for now we give them friendship. It is part of his plan. I cannot tell you more than that." He shook as he glared at her, every muscle across his chest rigid as his hands tightened, his knuckles white from the pressure. He raised his arms as if to draw her close, then thought better of it and thrust them back to his sides, turning his back to her. "I have no choice but to obey my uncle, or bring his anger on my village."

She made the rash decision and crossed the space between them, desperate to draw something other than anger from him. Placing her hands against his back, she slowly slipped them around his waist and rested her cheek against his shoulder. His taut muscles relaxed at her touch, and she felt him take her fist and hold it tight to his chest.

"I know what happens to the English, Winn," she whispered. "I know he plans to attack them, and that he will succeed. Will you be a part of that? Will you just send me to them, and slaughter me with the rest of the English when the time comes?"

He turned rapidly around at her words, his hands closing around her face to capture her gaze. Blazing blue eyes narrowed and brows squared as she met his stare.

"How do you know this?" he asked, his voice strained and hushed, as if he were afraid of ears that listened.

"In my time children learn history. I was taught about the Indian Massacre in school, Winn."

"Indian Massacre? Is that what your people call it?" he hissed.

"It was – it will be a massacre!" she shot back, unafraid of his rising fury. "You're going to kill hundreds of people, women and children! God, how can I love you when you would do such a thing?"

"Love? You would not love a man who protects his people? You would not love a warrior who protects you?" he shouted. She tried to move away, but his hands kept firm around her face as his slanted blue eyes bore into hers, his features clenched and his veins standing out like rawhide against his arms. She choked back tears, unsure of why such words spilled from her mouth but unable to stop them.

"If your idea of loving me is sending me to the English, then no. At least give me the Bloodstone and send me home before you kill them all!"

"No!" he roared. His lips silenced her next protest. It was no seductive kiss like his prior attentions, nor a gentle invitation. It closed her down, consumed her denial, and then he broke the kiss and pressed his forehead to hers, the sound of their shallow panting filling the void their passion had left. She lifted her lips to him again, but after dropping a series of kisses along her eyes and cheeks and chin, he grasped her face once more and forced her to listen.

"You belong to me. I will not let you go," he whispered. "You will stay here while I go to speak to my uncle. I will not let Nemattanew be the only voice my uncle hears."

"Don't leave."

"Stay here until I return." His tone was hoarse but firm, issuing yet another demand. She shook her head furiously at his words, refusing to submit. He pressed his lips to her hair, murmuring words that danced to her ears like the melody of a song.

"I will always come for you, *ntehem*. Do you not know that by now?" His voice thick, he drew her close, pressing his face to her neck. She felt the smoldering anger flicker out as he held her in his arms. "As long as I breathe, I will hold you here," he said, taking her hand to press it against his heart. "I lie to my men, I disobey my Weroance, and curse you, woman, I will do it again!"

She buried her head against his chest in that shallow valley beneath his throat, where his bronzed skin felt softer than the lines of his muscled chest. He murmured words of love in soft Paspahegh, and although she did not know the meaning of them she loved the intent, and she nestled tighter against him.

"I don't want to lose you," she said softly, fearing his answer but driven to say it nonetheless. He cupped her face in his hand and ran his thumb over her pink bottom lip, parted it with the pressure, and then gently kissed it.

"You are worth everything to me," he murmured. "I have nothing to give you, no fine clothes such as you once wore, no land to call my own but where we might rest our heads at night. Can you love a man such as this?"

She placed her hand over his heart, and he covered it with his own.

"I love this man beside me, and that is all that matters," she whispered.

He turned his head to her palm and kissed her cupped hand, pulling her close to fit against his broad chest. There would be no other for her, she realized. The warmth coursing through her body from his embrace chased away even her deepest fears, smothering any lingering doubt between them.

"For my people, when words of love are spoken between a man and woman, they are married in the eyes of the village," he said softly. "You are my wife, in here, in my heart...if you will have me."

She nodded, choking back a sob as her tears flowed.

"Say the words to me, and I will have you."

He brought her hands to his lips and gently kissed them, his eyes never wavering from hers.

"Now you will feel no rain, for I will shelter you.

Now you will feel no cold, for I will warm you.

Now you will never be lonely, for we will be together.

There is only one life before us.

Now we walk as one."

His lips tasted of sweet brandy when he kissed her, the kiss of a man she now called husband.

They both heard Makedewa call for Winn at the same time and saw his shadow across the doorway.

"*Nexasi, ntehem. Lapich knewel,*" he said softly.

"Tell me what that means," she whispered. His lips formed a smile that failed to reach his eyes as he answered her request.

"Be safe, my heart. I will see you again."

22

Winn sat perched on his pony, ready to follow the English back to their town. He glared at the man who claimed to be her uncle, and wondered what game he played as he snapped the reins and sent the horse forward. Winn knew little of the man called Thomas Martin, and he was certain Benjamin had no idea the man was lying about Maggie being his niece. Perhaps the man truly believed Maggie was his lost niece, but Winn suspected there was something afoul in the Englishman's claim and Benjamin was caught in the middle of it. Benjamin had proven his friendship to the Paspahegh and visited Winn often, so he felt some trust for him, but he had none of that confidence for the rest of the English.

Damn that interfering Nemattanew, that sneaky spy his uncle truste↑ so much. Forced to make a decision in front of his people and the English, none of the choices were acceptable to him. Give her to the English who claim her as kin, or refuse to relinquish his right to her as his captive. Either choice would lead to a similar outcome: Nemattanew would inform Opechancanough of the Time Walker in their midst, and his uncle would send her away or demand her blood.

Honor his uncle, and slay the Red Woman. Use the Bloodstone to return her to her own time. Release her to the English. *He woul↑ choose none of those options.*

Finally, when his head cleared, he made his decision. It was a decision that would gain him no support from the English or his kin, but the only one he could bear to live with, the one that kept her safe in his arms and protected from the rising storm he knew would come.

He would see the English safely back to town and then ride to speak to his uncle. If his uncle refused his request to keep her, he would return to the village and take Maggie far away. He had no plan beyond that, not yet willing to face the consequence of betraying his Weroance, but knowing his path was set nonetheless. It was the only way. Winn hoped his uncle would forget about the woman, and leave off with the notion she needed to die like the rest of the Time Walkers. Surely it was not a woman Time Walker that would someday take his life. The prophecy could be wrong. After all, his uncle had once spared the Pale Witch.

"My thanks to you for your escort, Winn," Benjamin offered as he rode up beside him. His larger, leaner mount fell in step with the sturdy war pony Winn rode. Winn nodded in response without turning his head to the other man, his gaze still focused on Thomas Martin's straight back.

"She is not the niece of Thomas Martin, my friend."

Benjamin frowned.

"Of course she is. Who else would she be? Surely Martin knows his own kin."

"I know not his purpose, but I know the truth. You have my word on this," Winn replied, trying to use an assurance that Benjamin would identify with.

"You know I trust ye above all others, Winn, but on this I think ye are mistaken. The man recognized his niece, and it all makes sense. Who else would she be? It is not as if she dropped from the sky!"

Winn snorted. "No. Of course not," he grumbled. *Not the sky, but that assertion was not too far off.*

"Surely ye do not object to returning her to us? You know what that would mean."

He ground his teeth in the back of his jaw at the implied consequence and nodded to the man. He could not antagonize the English at this point or risk his uncle's wrath, and until Maggie was safely hidden away, he was bound to pacify them. Of all the whites to challenge him, how could his friend Benjamin be the one? They had played together as children and he hoped to save him somehow from what was to come, but if his friend posed an obstacle to Maggie, he would kill him without hesitation.

"I wish no war with your people, friend. But I will not release her," he said, the words tasting bitter on his tongue. "She must stay until Opechancanough gives his decision." He omitted the fact that no matter what decision his uncle rendered, he planned to take Maggie far away. Even if by some miracle the Weroance refused to return her to the English, Winn knew it was impossible his uncle would not demand her sacrifice. The old man believed too strongly in his visions to consider any alternative when it came to a Time Walker.

"Well then," Benjamin said quickly. "Jack-of-a-Feather is a swift rider, I'm sure he will return soon with permission to return her to us. Will ye give her up then?"

"No."

"You're acting a fool. Ye cannot keep a good Englishwoman as a slave! I thought ye were better than that!" Benjamin snapped. "She will be returned to us, now or on order of your uncle."

"She is no slave," Winn growled, his ire beginning to rise. Benjamin pushed him too far. "I found her, it is my right to keep her."

"If you found her as ye say, then why are ye so sure she is not Martin's niece? The woman fell overboard during a storm on the way to Jamestown, who can say for sure who she is? She must have lost her wits when she fell from the ship, and she admits she cannot recall anything before ye saved her." Benjamin cast him a pained glare. "I feel that there is more to this than ye have revealed to me. If ye went raiding and stole the girl, I will not judge ye. I just did not think ye did such things. Tell me the truth, and I can assure Martin she is not his niece."

"I did not steal her."

"So she must be the woman from the ship. The Virginia Company sent them here to find husbands among our men."

"A stupid English plan," Winn muttered, ignored by Benjamin as he rattled on.

"Why will ye not tell me the truth? I thought more of our friendship than that."

Winn noticed the way Benjamin squinted as he waited for the answer, and his hands clenched at the implication of his words. He could say he was angry Benjamin questioned his honor, but he knew the English thought his people little more than animals.

"She is here under my protection."

Benjamin let out a sigh.

"I have no doubt ye protected her," Benjamin muttered. "I've never seen ye so taken by a woman."

Winn quickly turned his head to the other man.

"Yes. I know what you see. Is that what English men do, spy on each other like snakes?" he asked, his words slow to form as he suppressed the sickness rising in his gut.

"I am sorry. I should not have followed ye. But I thought I knew ye better than that. Better than a lout who would take advantage of a helpless woman! What were ye thinking? Ye know ye've ruined her, no decent Englishman will take her to wife after ye tire of her." Benjamin said.

Winn ducked his head and his lips formed a scowl in response as he glared at the Englishman. Unwilling to pacify Benjamin any further, he decided his journey with his old friend was over.

"You know nothing of me, Englishman," he growled. "We gave you food and supplies. Take your beggars and go back to your village. Think what you will. As for the woman, I keep her. Try to take her, and I will kill you the same as any other." Winn swung his horse around in a circle, and let out a fierce howl that pierced the silent night sky. He glared at the man he once called brother.

No Englishman will ever take her from me, he vowed, and with that thought, he knew he would risk everything to keep her. He pictured his knife slicing through the belly of his friend Benjamin and then the acrid stench of his innards as they slid through his hands. A painful wave of anger surged through his chest and squeezed the air from his lungs.

Benjamin had been his friend since they were too young to notice the difference in their skins, loyal and true in brotherhood nearly as much as his own blood brothers. Of all men to stand between him and Maggie, would it be Benjamin? He was the only white man he wished to save from what was to come. Until now.

He was glad Maggie was safe back in the village, away from the English, waiting for him to return to her.

His heart thudded a steady beat, and he could feel the sweat break across his skin and moisten his clenched palms against the leather reins. Numbness settled through him like the unwavering truth, a truth that would change his life forever, and that of all those that loved him. He would bide his time and steal his woman away. The course he chose would settle his own fate and he would not be able to turn back, but he realized his path had been sealed the moment he looked into her shining jade eyes and fought the brown bear.

He galloped away from the English and turned his horse toward the river. He would take the fastest route, and get to his uncle before Nemattanew could poison his mind further.

His woman. Maggie was his wife. And he would keep her.

23

She sank back and pulled a thick fur around her shoulders as she sat listening to the beat of drums in the village. The rhythmic thud kept time with the chants of the warriors, their cries of thanks echoing through the bright autumn night and leaving a hollow emptiness within her. She thought of the tender words he murmured against her hair when they slept, and the way his breath felt against her skin. The memory only served to deepen her longing for him and brought the sting of tears to her eyes.

She thought she might suffer remorse for abandoning her own time, and although there was a hint of sadness at never returning, the notion of living her life with Winn ran sweeter through her soul. Relief washed over her like a waterfall, the decision made, carrying her doubts and fears away as she looked forward to their future. Perhaps in some cosmic plane there was a reason for her journey to the past, one they would never discover, and if it was nothing more than the purpose of bringing two hearts together, she could live with that.

She swiped the back of her hand over her eyes. Winn would return for her, she was certain. Hell, she made her own rules and ran her own life in her time, and as such, she should be well equipped to survive on her own in the past for a few days without him. She needed to learn the Paspahegh ways, and learn to be strong when he was away.

Cold, hungry, and more than the least bit agitated by Winn leaving, she decided to solve all the problems that she could and worry over the things she could not change later. She could fix cold and hungry, but there was little else for her to do but keep occupied until her husband returned.

Her husband, she thought, and smiled.

She crawled over to her basket of clothes and pulled out her soft faded blue jeans. Torn at the knee, but still serviceable, she pulled them on beneath her doeskin dress. Next were her suede work boots, which she covered with her fur leggings and tied tight with rawhide cords. Satisfied with her work thus far, she examined her parka. Streaked with blood and slashed from shoulder to waist, it would offer little protection so she left it beside the fire. She could not fathom any useful task for her wristwatch, but she slid it over her wrist anyway.

The night the Bloodstone took her she had been unusually bereft of any technology in her pockets such as a cell phone, not that it would have done her much good in her current predicament. She tightened the laces of her boots and double knotted them, then grabbed a traveling satchel made of beaver bladder with a long strap. She crossed the strap over her shoulder and settled the bag at her waist, then scourged for the few remaining bits of food left in the yehakin. There was not much to choose from since they expected to eat at the feast, but Winn usually kept at least some dried meat and corn cakes to munch on and she added what she found to her sack.

She peeked out the yehakin and saw the villagers engrossed in the dance, and the sounds of the beating drums muffled her footsteps as she left. She crossed behind the yehakin without looking back, thrusting a fist across her cheek when a tear spilled as she made her way toward the corral. Spending time with the horses would soothe her, as it always did, and bundled up snugly as she was she could spend the night with them instead of alone in the yehakin.

"Damn it," she muttered. She shook her head when tender thoughts collided, ones of a soft gentle mouth caressing her skin, a firm hand that held her against his heart, the way he whispered endearments against her ear and sent shivers down deep in her belly.

She cursed as she tripped over a fallen branch, and stopped to regain her sense of direction. She could still hear the hollow thud of the drums and the cries of songs from the village, and she could see the glimmer of the bonfire across the way when she looked back. Had she been so distracted by daydreams that she passed by the lean-to?

With her ears filled by the fading pounding of the drums, she did not notice a snapping of forest debris on the path behind her until the footsteps were upon her. The hair pricked up on the back of her neck and she smelled his dank scent before she swung around to confront her stalker.

Nemattanew stood crouched behind her, slowly rising to his full height as she glared at him. He was planted between her and the village, her only escape being the woods. She moved her hand to the knife at her waist for reassurance and glared at the man as she waited for his next move. Obviously, he had lied about his intent to leave the village.

He took a step toward her, and she backed away an equal amount of paces.

"So the Red Woman stays here."

"Just go away, leave me alone," she said, her voice tapering off as it wavered. "Winn will be back soon," she lied. She darted a glance to her rear to see where to escape, dismayed to see only dense brush and no discernible trail.

They both knew it to be a lie, and a grin stretched over his lips.

"I saw him leave the village. He goes to ask for your life, but we both know he will not get it. What then, Red Woman?"

"You should worry what he will do when he finds you bothering me!"

"No," he growled. "You should worry if I will kill you now, or let you suffer. Perhaps I will keep you until he returns, and let him watch you bleed from my knife." He reached out and snatched her wrist painfully, turning it over. He made a deep growling sound as he glared at the scar on her palm

"Stay away from me!" she shouted, wrenching away from him.

"Winn truly hides a Time Walker?" He raised his head to the stars and let out a chilling howl of laughter. "He thinks to keep you? What a fool he is!"

She fumbled backward and felt the stab of a branch in her ribs and leaves brush her neck.

"Run," he grinned, his words dripping with excitement and malice. "Run as fast as you can. I give you five paces before I gut you." He traced a path on his own chest with one finger from the base of his throat down to his navel. "I will see great honor when I bring your head to my Weroance."

She believed every ounce of his threat and took off in a sprint. The satchel bounced against her kidney as she darted through the trees, wincing at the sting of branches tearing at her face and neck. She jumped over a rotted fallen tree and lost her balance, falling to her knees on the pine-needle-strewn ground. Looking around, she tried to catch a breath, her chest heaving with the effort, and she sighed when she realized he was not pursuing her. When she struggled to her feet, her head still spinning, she was immediately knocked back to the ground by a blow from behind.

She felt his face against the back of her neck as he leaned in close to her ear, with the stink of his rancid breath causing her nose to wrinkle in disgust.

"Where is your warrior now, Red Woman? I see no man here, except me."

He bound her wrists behind her back with a thick rope and hauled her to her feet.

* * *

She sat on her knees in the dirt, a pair of viselike hands gripping her shoulders to keep her as much upright as was possible with her head hanging limp. The return to awareness was abrupt, as if a light switch had been flicked on and suddenly she could see again, but a thick sour smoke filled her lungs and she twisted her head away from the scent. The hands held her tighter, and then she spotted a burning ember smoldering in the hand of another held directly under her nose. She scrunched her nose and sneezed, and struggled to sit back away from the ember and smoke.

"Enough! Stop it!" she snapped. At the sound of her voice, the brown hand with the burning bundle of twigs pulled back away from her face and she coughed out the last remnants of smoke from her lungs.

"Welcome, Blooded One."

Maggie looked up. The voice was stilted but clear, authority ringing through his words as sure as the smoke smothering her breath. It was Nemattanew who stood at her side keeping her upright, but the man who spoke sat on a high dais in front of her. He wore a decorated breechcloth riddled with brilliant colored beads, his arms littered with thick copper bracelets and smeared with bright red paint. His face was creased with age, tanned to a dark hue, a stark pallet of amused disgust gracing his expression as he considered the white woman kneeling in a disoriented heap before him.

"Welcome? This is hardly a welcome!" she replied, prompting a wave of gasps from onlookers. She suspected she was in a long house and with the cluster of people gathered, she could see this was some sort of ceremonial assembly. She desperately hoped that not all the pomp and circumstance was in honor of her appearance.

The man considered her words, his black eyes narrowing into slits. The two beautiful women at his side moved closer to him when she spoke as if to shield him from the advance of the evil Blooded One. Maggie could not help a stifled laugh that emerged as the gloriously half-naked woman clung to the man, equally decorated in finery.

"I am Weroance Opechancanough," he said. His voice betrayed no anger at her words, only a curious tolerance, but his face still was hardened in a formidable mask. The strength of her resolve began to crumble as a sick feeling permeated the pit of her stomach and she realized exactly who the man was and how tenuous her situation had become.

"I'm Maggie," she answered, her voice wavering only slightly.

"Tell me, Maggie," he said. "Do you put a spell upon my nephew, as the Pale Witch put a spell on me?"

"I don't know any spells," she replied evenly, figuring the stronger she sounded, the better. To sit like a quivering idiot and plead for her life would be useless, so if she were going to burn she would do it with a fight. "But I do know what happens to you and your people. Is that why you want me dead?"

His lips pursed tightly and he patted the shoulders of each woman beside him, and then gave a curt nod to the other spectators in the Long House.

"Leave us."

Nemattanew continued to keep a grip on her shoulder, and he made one attempt to argue in his own language before the Weroance issued a final order to dismiss him. The Long House emptied completely in less than a minute, leaving her on her knees at the feet of the leader.

"I wonder why you still have a tongue, with the way you speak. Have you turned my nephew into a fool? Is sharing your furs such pleasure he would forget he is a man?"

"Winn is no fool."

He slid off the platform, with much more finesse and grace than Maggie expected from an older warrior, then squatted down in front of her to eye level. When he reached out to touch one of her thick red braids, she swatted at his hand with her bound fists, which only caused him to smile. It was not a pleasant smile by any means, more forced and maligned, but it kept his hand away and for that, she was grateful.

"Don't touch me," she hissed. She overplayed her hand against his composure and lost, a startled yelp escaping her lips when he snatched her chin in his fingers, his ebony eyes flaring.

"I will touch what I please," he snarled. "You only breathe right now because of my command. Perhaps you should consider that before you speak." He released her chin and she sat back on the ground, her eyes still set warily on him as she fought to control her rapid breathing.

"What do you plan to do with me?" she asked.

"What my nephew failed to do."

"Your nephew is a...a decent man."

One eyebrow rose slightly. "Decent? What meaning is that?"

"It means good. Kind."

His black eyes narrowed into slits and his weathered face hardened.

"Winkeohkwet will not disobey me. No warrior of mine makes such a mistake. You think you are so important to my nephew, you think he would not crush your skull at my command?"

She was sure he meant every syllable, from his declaration of wonder at her protest to his pledge to murder her himself. She swallowed back the bile rising in her throat and closed her eyes.

"I know he would not hurt me," she whispered.

He darted forward and grabbed her neck with one large and surprisingly vise-like hand, the other latched to her shoulder to make it easier to drag her close to his pedestal. There he slammed her head down onto a flat, round stump protruding from the ground, the skin of her neck and shoulders scraping against the roots that anchored the stump to the ground. Her vision split into blackness with shredded stars whirling above, but before she could succumb to losing consciousness, his hand loosened on her throat enough for her to gasp air back into her lungs.

"I have killed many Time Walkers. You are one of many, Blooded One, and you will not be the last."

She saw dark dried blood on the stump, her cheek pressed into the slimy wood that she realized was slick with gore from another recent sacrifice. She gasped another breath of air through her narrowed windpipe, unable to move since his fingers still held her down by the neck. What could she say to save herself? She was no Pale Witch, nor a witch of any kind, and her magic came from her knowledge of her own time, not some spell. Her stomach whirled and dropped when she saw him raise a mallet in his other hand.

"I know when you will die," she croaked. The effect was not instantaneous, but it worked. He slowly lowered the weapon and removed his hand from her neck, and she gauged her actions against his by very carefully raising her head. She kneeled in front of him, hoping her attempt at mimicking other Indian women would show him her deference. Trying to control her rapid breathing as her lungs screamed for more air, she remained hunched over at his command, her cheek caked with wet gore from a previous sacrifice on the stump.

"Then your magic is more powerful than even the Pale Witch," he said, careful and controlled in his response, spoken more to himself than to her. "Tell me, Blooded One, when will I die?"

She made the decision, not certain if it would keep her alive, but afraid it was her only hope.

"I see you trick the English by sharing their food. I see your warriors take many lives in one bloody day, in all the English villages. It will be called the Massacre of 1622. You think it will drive them back across the ocean, but it will not," she said. Her voice gained conviction as she thought up more nonsense to cast doubt in his mind. "A Weroance who knows when his time ends cannot lead his people," she said. "And the man who kills the Blooded One will curse his people for eternity." She dared to look up and saw his eyes opened wide and his mouth slightly agape. "I have seen it...and it will be!"

She clenched her hands tightly but could not feel the pain as her nails dug into her palms, too focused on the way the deep bronze of his skin faded to a gray tinged pallor on his face. The hand holding the mallet twitched and rose slightly, indecisive, before it dropped back down at his side.

"Nemattanew!"

The warrior responded to the Weroance's command with only a few seconds delay, and Maggie realized he had been standing nearby the entire time.

"Take her to the English, since they claim her as kin. She will share their fate."

Opechancanough lowered his head close to her crusted cheek, and though her heart pounded loudly in her ears, his words were clear.

"You may keep your life today, as I spared the Pale Witch once before. When you see her, tell her what was done here today," he whispered. "You will die, but not by my hand. I will not let you curse my people."

He straightened up and nodded. Nemattanew grabbed her by her bound wrists and dragged her out of the Long House.

PART THREE

24

She sat numb on the wagon bench, her head feeling as if an axe had split it, although it remained intact and throbbing. Nemattanew rode silently beside the wagon. The man called Thomas Martin who claimed to be her uncle drove from a bench in front of her, ambling along as if they found a stray Englishwoman every day. She closed her eyes for a moment with a semblance of relief. She was still alive, and that was enough of a victory for the moment.

Whether Thomas had truly mistaken her for his kin or had some other devious plan in mind, she did not know, but she was certain she wanted no part in it either way. She subdued the urge to tell him exactly why she was not his niece, but the warnings from Winn still resonated through her. *No one could know where she came from.* No one would believe her, and the truth would likely get her strung up for witchery. Her only option was to play along with the English until she had an opportunity to escape.

Thomas Martin finally breached the silence by clearing his throat with a cough.

"I am glad to see ye hale my niece. It seems the savages treated ye with kindness. I am saddened to hear of yer ordeal since the accident and wish ye a speedy return to good health."

"W-what accident?" was the only sensible thing she could muster.

"Why, yer fall from the ship. Ye were thought dead in the river. Ye know not what I speak of?"

"Uhm, no. No, I don't remember falling off a boat," she murmured. He cracked the reins against the hide of the horse to urge it faster through the dense wooded trail.

"No memory? Have ye lost yer sense, girl?" he asked.

"No! I just don't know what you're talking about," she lied.

"So there it is. The escorts from the Company said ye took a fall no man could survive. Perhaps it jumbled yer memory a bit," he shook his head in disgust. "I hope ye recover yer wits soon, or I will lose the price I paid for ye passage," he grumbled.

"What are you talking about?"

"Yer speech is queer, niece, did my brother speak so? Mayhap he spoke that blasted Scots like his wife and twisted yer English tongue for it." He shook his head at her expectant appraisal. "No matter. I think young Benjamin has already taken a fancy to ye, so do not worry. He is a good man. Perhaps he will contract for you."

"Contract me?" she choked. One of his eyebrows rose up and he peered back at her.

"Ye signed the contract before you left England, girl. You will wed one of the men in the colony, which is why I paid yer passage. Jack-of-a-Feather is a good friend to us, be glad he returned ye. Your rescue came at a good time, lest I would be lost of my money with no bride to barter with."

"There has been some mistake, I am not your niece!"

He looked sideways at her. "Yes. *Yes ye are.* Hold yer tongue, girl, if ye know what is good for ye." He spit out a dark wad of tobacco and clucked to the horses. "Ye have the look of yer mother, ye know, blasted bloody wench she was."

Maggie had learned something of the time she was stuck in and knew when it was prudent to keep silent. As much as she wanted to jump from the wagon and start running, she had seen enough of the untamed wilderness and knew better than to risk her neck in it with little more than the doeskin on her back. As if he read her thoughts, Thomas looked down at her, a frown on his lips and his heavy brows slanted.

"We will get ye into suitable clothes as soon as we return. Yer heathen dress will surely give yer aunt a fright, but she will make do."

Maggie agreed. She would give anyone a fright with little trouble.

* * *

Nighttime had fallen by the time they reached the town. The wagon came to a stop and Thomas jumped quickly down, but Maggie remained frozen, unable to remove her fingers from where they were clenched around the plank supports.

"Miss?"

Benjamin stood beside the wagon, holding his hand out to her expectantly. She turned slowly and looked down into his clear blue eyes, noting with a flush that the shade reminded her of Winn's odd blue eyes. The man smiled at the color rising in her cheeks, and she imagined he assumed it meant something else. She swallowed back the lump in her throat and took his offered hand, and as she stepped down, she glanced past him.

Still seated on his pony, Nemattanew watched them. His face was a flat mask that betrayed no indication of unease, but Maggie thought she spotted a flicker in his gaze when their eyes met.

She choked back a sob. She had thrived on the strength of her anger, and it fed her resolve to carry on like a dysfunctional crutch. Now, separated from Winn, she felt that urge drain away like a wound gone bloodless, and the sickly taste of fear pricked her soul as she wondered if he would ever find her. She knew her American history, and she knew Jamestown was not a safe haven. Nemattanew was leaving her there to rot with the other whites, getting rid of the Blooded One one way or another.

"Thank you," she mumbled. She turned her attention to Benjamin. Taller than the others, with thick wavy dark hair curling around his collar, he took her dusty hand and tucked it in the crook of his elbow. A stray curl fell over his brow as he dipped his head to speak. She stared hard at him for a long moment in the moonlight, his image reminding her of the hulking protector she left behind in the future. Similar in stature to Marcus, there was something about Benjamin that radiated protection and strength. She wondered if she could trust that instinct in regards to Benjamin, or if her desperate imagination was only reaching for the safe haven she once knew back home.

"Are you steady, Miss? I will carry ye should ye have need. 'Tis understandable if you are weary," he said quietly, heard only to her ears. She shook her head and let him lead her to the house.

Larger than she expected and constructed of stone and wood, she followed Benjamin through the plank doorway inside the house. Thomas Martin had already roused a woman she imagined was his wife, and she was comforted by the kindness in her eyes. Short and pleasingly round with a swath of ebony hair twisted at her nape, she listened to a whispered explanation from Thomas and placed both hands to her lips as her eyes widened. The woman then nodded vigorously and pressed her hands against her heart as she turned to Maggie.

"Welcome home, dear. How do ye fair, yer uncle said ye took a blow to the head? We haven't seen ye since ye were a child, but I am yer Aunt Alice. What a blessing to see ye live and well," she said. She motioned with a hand for Maggie to follow. "Come with me, we shall leave the men to their business."

Benjamin nodded at her as if in blessing, and Maggie let her hand slip from his arm to follow Alice into another room off the main area.

"I fear my dress may be a bit short for you, dear, but it will do until we can fit ye for another. Anything will serve better than that which ye wear—thank our Lord no other women were about to see ye arrive. 'Tis good they know nothing of where ye have been," Alice muttered, pulling a white cotton shift from a wooden chest next to the lone window in the room. Two functional shutters stood open to admit the brisk night breeze through the small high window, the opening naked and free of glass. Alice noticed her staring at the space.

"My husband says he will have glass windows for us before the winter falls. He is so busy now with managing those who work the tobacco fields, he canna tend to it yet. But soon he will remedy that," she assured Maggie. Maggie said nothing as the woman thrust the shift and a wool dress at her, as if Maggie knew what to do with it. "I will tend to the men and return for ye, dear."

Maggie stared blankly at her back as she left the room, pulling the door closed firmly behind her. She sat down on the edge of a narrow cot, one of the few furnishings in the room. Dropping the clothes in a heap on the floor, she put her head in her hands. The tears came fast, staining her dusty cheeks with hot denial. She had no idea how to get herself out of the unbelievable mess she was in. Maggie lay down on the stiff cot and curled her knees to her chest, hugging herself as she cried. She startled at the hand on her hair, relieved to see it was only Alice patting her head when she opened her tear-swollen eyes.

"There, there, dearest. Ye just sleep now. I told yer Uncle ye need sleep before he speaks with ye. The rest will wait for morning."

The older woman pulled a soft woolen blanket over her shoulders and tucked it under her chin, patting her back softly in comfort. Maggie closed her eyes to the gesture and let the exhaustion of sleep carry off her weary mind.

She heard the lock click securely into place when the woman left.

25

Winn ignored the stares and whispers as he rode into the Powhatan village. On his last visit, he was received as the favorite nephew of the Weroance. As War Chief of the small Paspahegh tribe he was given some respect, but many remembered that half his blood ran white and treated him accordingly. For some, it would never be enough that his mother was sister to Opechancanough, or even that Winn had proved himself as a warrior among his people. Within any community there were those with long memories tainted by fear, and the Powhatan people were no exception. To many, he would never be anything more than the son of a white man.

He stopped directly outside the Great Yehakin and dismounted, thanking the wiry boy who ran up to take his tired pony. Winn had ridden hard and the beast panted with the need for water. Although his own throat was stretched dry, he would not see to his own needs until his journey's purpose was fulfilled. It was the only thing within his power to do at a time when he felt control of his life slipping away.

He knew the warriors guarding the Great Yehakin. The older of the two, a man called Assapanick, was one of the most decorated warriors in the village. Winn dipped his head in respect to the man, earning a tap on his shoulder in return. As one of the few who were permitted to enter the Great Yehakin unannounced, Winn was allowed passage.

Once Winn lived among them as an unsure youth, and he recalled the kindness Assapanick had always bestowed upon him. Like Winn, Assapanick had white blood in his veins. It was Assapanick's father that was half-Spaniard and his mother a Pamukey, but others still remembered. There was a time that it garnered him some sort of kinship with Assapanick, yet Winn was acutely aware that his role as one of the Powhatan was coming to an end.

If Opechancanough called for Maggie's death, there was only one choice Winn could make. The acknowledgment of his decision felt like a stake driven through his belly, hard and unyielding as it tore his flesh. The pain of leaving everything he had ever known was harsh, but it was nothing compared to the thought of losing Maggie. He recalled the words spoken the first time they shared furs. In her shyness at their intimacy she had blushed asking him questions, but he quickly deduced the reason for her distress. When she asked if she was special to him, his heart clenched into a fist. He needed to make her truly understand what she meant to him.

"Special? If you need a word, then take this," he whispered. "You are mine, and I am yours. I know no other word for that."

He meant every word he spoke, as he meant it when he kneeled before his uncle. The Great Yehakin was filled with people, including several of the Weroance's wives. It was all he could do to hold onto his temper when Opechancanough tapped his mallet on a stump and bid him to rise.

"I see you kneel before me, nephew, but I wonder what path you will choose," Opechancanough announced as Winn stood up. Winn straightened his back and faced his uncle.

"So Nemattanew had your ear before I arrived. Then you know what I ask of you," Winn replied.

The Weroance grunted with a tight grin stretched across his weathered face. Winn noted that his uncle seemed more tired than usual, his eyelids heavy among his creased skin.

"Eat first, and then we will speak on your matter. It has been a long time since you sat beside me, nephew."

Opechancanough waved his hand and three women immediately responded. They presented him with a bountiful supply of food, placing the best of the nightly meal before him. Winn joined in despite his frustration, knowing he could not refuse his uncle without insulting him. For some reason his uncle was delaying their conversation, and there was little for Winn to do but play along.

The Weroance was in no hurry to finish his meal. Winn refused the offer of English rum, which earned a raised eyebrow from his uncle but no other comment. As the night wore on, Winn felt his ire rise. Opechancanough seemed in no hurry to speak with Winn, despite the fact he had long since finished his meal and he was completely enamored by one of his wives who sat in his lap.

Just as Winn decided to pursue his request, the Weroance turned his attention to him.

"I think you should rest, nephew. We can speak on your matter in the morning, so I have time to think on it," Opechancanough called out. He clapped his hands together, bringing forward several women who were eager to please. Before Winn could object they led him from the Great Yehakin and escorted him to a smaller yehakin nearby. It was a place he knew was reserved for guests of the Weroance, and with a twinge of unease he let them lead him inside. Was he only a guest to his uncle now? On other visits Winn had slept in the company of the Weroance's family members—sisters, wives, or children. To be relegated to the position of guest unsettled him.

He faced the empty yehakin, noting a fire burned brightly and warmed the space well. As he absently shed his tunic, two small hands embraced him and slithered up his chest from behind. He closed his eyes tightly and tried to keep his voice calm. It would do him no good to insult the woman, as insulting his uncle's "gift" would be the same as a challenge.

"Thank you," he said quietly, swinging around to face her. He peeled her hands away. "But I am tired now, and I must rest alone."

She had the look of youth about her, but her eyes spoke of experience when she laughed and continued to pursue him.

"Surely you are not so tired for me?" she asked, placing her hands on his shoulders. He backed away, stumbled over the bedding, and was incensed when she wrapped her arms around his waist.

She laughed as he gritted his teeth and pushed away her groping hands.

"Enough!" he growled. When she tried to kiss him he let out a growl and shoved her – hard.

The motion sent her sprawling onto her backside, and suddenly the woman was speaking rapidly and crying. With the sounds of her crying and the roar of his pulse throbbing in his ears, he did not understand much of what she said.

"Get out," he said hoarsely. "I have no need for you."

His breathing was shallow as he watched her gather her belongings, which she had left conveniently beside the sleeping furs. She paused at the door.

"If you tell him I did not please you, I will be shamed," she said. He closed his eyes for a moment, running his hands over his head. He suspected the woman was a gift from his uncle, and her words were only confirmation of the Weroance's game.

"What did he ask of you?" Winn asked.

Her eyes dipped down and she hesitated to answer. Winn was surprised to see her skin flush, as if speaking to him was much more difficult than bedding him.

"He said I must make you forget the Blooded One. If I fail..." her words trailed off, the unspoken threat left hanging.

It was bad enough his uncle sent a half-naked women to his bed. Worse than that, her fate was now on his shoulders. He knew he could not send her away. He sighed.

"Sleep here tonight on my furs. I will tell him you pleased me well," he muttered.

Her eyes widened in surprise.

"Thank you," she whispered.

Winn watched her place her bundle on the floor near his furs, and then he left the yehakin on his own mission. He was through with the games his uncle played, and after the scene with the woman, he was exceedingly ready to return to his wife. *Damn the tribal rules and damn his uncle, he would wait no longer.*

He pushed past the warrior guards at the door, knowing that by his actions his time as Opechancanough's favorite was at an end.

"So this is the path you choose, nephew?" Opechancanough asked, gently disentangling himself from his wife as Winn stalked toward him.

"I have no time to wait, uncle. I must return to my woman. I only ask that you grant her your protection," Winn said, dropping down on one knee in deference.

"It is said she is a Blooded One—a *Time Walker*. Is it not a Time Walker that will end my life? Did I not see it in a vision with my own eyes? Why, then, nephew, would I give her my protection?" Opechancanough asked. He rose from the furs and picked up his ceremonial mallet, which he held as he made way to a bloodied stump centered in front of his royal platform. Once there, he tapped the mallet on the stump, his eyes fixed on Winn.

"Because I have asked nothing of you, in all the years I have served you," Winn said quietly. "I know that you are a great leader, uncle, and my request is easy for you to give."

"I once decreed I will have the head of all Time Walkers."

"Yet the Pale Witch lives," Winn shot back, eliciting an annoyed grunt from the Weroance.

"She is not the one who brings me to death."

"Nor is my wife."

Opechancanough's eyes widened and after a pause, his lips curled downward in a scowl.

"Your wife?" he asked.

"Yes. My wife," Winn replied evenly.

Opechancanough shifted his gaze, his attention turned to the stump once more. Suddenly he raised the mallet, sending it down to smash upon the bloody wood.

"It was here that I placed her head, and with this hand I moved to end her life," The Weroance said softly. His voice was whimsical, as if he meant to tell a story. The darkness reached for Winn, grasping his gut, twisting it so that he could not ignore the rising terror.

He was speaking of Maggie. His uncle had placed her head on that bloodied stump. He would not—could not—believe that the gore on the stump belonged to his wife.

"Where is she?" he demanded. *Ha# he not left her safe in his yehakin? He nee#e# answers.*

The guards moved inside the Great Yehakin at the sound of Winn's raised voice, taking position on each side of the leader. His uncle smiled. His mouth had very few teeth, his grin appearing more menacing than well humored.

"So you have made your choice," the Weroance said quietly, nodding his head. "I sent her to the Englishman who claims her. She rides there with Nemattanew. Go to her, if you must."

Winn swallowed hard. He tilted his head in acknowledgement and left without further words spoken. The warriors who guarded his uncle shook their heads sadly at him as he left.

Winn knew there was no return from the journey he embarked on. His future was unwritten, tangled within the destiny of one red-haired woman.

26

Maggie kicked at the ankle length skirt restricting her pace as she tried to keep in step with Alice, but her gait was clumsy enough to cause the other woman to pause in wait. Alice pursed her lips but said nothing while she waited for Maggie to regain her bearings.

"I hate this dress!" Maggie muttered. If she had even a notion of where she was at in relation to the Paspahegh village, she would have made a run for it as soon as they stepped out of the house, but being that Thomas already had an idea she might be a flight risk her opportunities to flee were kept to a minimum. Not that she would have made it very far. She suspected that in the clothes she currently wore, she was more likely to fall on her face than escape.

She could feel the sweat dripping down her back and her scent was no better, reminding her of the way sweatpants smelled after a good workout. The stench did not seem to bother Alice as much, and she knew the other woman thought her daft for insisting on a bath that morning. Maggie had a two-fold reason for her cleanly ways, the most of which was the desire to keep her freshly healed shoulder wound from festering in the moist warmth. The other was her fear of becoming too much like the women around her.

"Hush, girl! What else would ye wear?" Alice chastised her.

"I have a few ideas," Maggie mumbled. They resumed walking toward the church. Nervous about her ability to sit through a long Christian church service, Maggie was eager to have it over with. She tried to plead sickness, but Alice would not be swayed, insistent she must do her duty and attend her first church service at Martin's Hundred after her "terrible ordeal with the savages." The constant proximity of either Alice or Thomas kept her imprisoned, and she was acutely aware she had not any private moments other than using a chamber pot. They used an outside closet, but they insisted she not "tax" herself. Maggie was convinced it was just another method to keep her from fleeing.

"Young Benjamin is coming toward us, Margaret. Be kind!" Alice warned.

Maggie had also noticed the tall man striding toward them through the crowd. Instead of going toward the church as the groups dispersed through the town center were, he cut through others with a well-placed smile and nod of apology as he made way to them. His earnest grin was too infectious to miss, and she found she could not be too unkind to him. After all, he was Winn's friend. Perhaps he would help her.

"Good morning ladies! I pray ye will allow me to escort ye to church?"

Maggie was not too affected by him to decline, but Alice squashed her refusal before it left her lips.

"Why, of course, dear Benjamin! My niece takes kindly on your offer, but I will walk with my husband. I see he joins us," Alice answered. Thomas Martin approached as well, and although the crowd parted for him, he did not garner the same glance of appreciation that Benjamin did.

"Thank you, Mistress . I will take good care of Miss Margaret at your leave," Benjamin promised. He waited a long moment with his elbow outstretched before Maggie would take it, and she was certain he would give up if she simply ignored him, but she was surprised to see he continued waiting through the awkward moment until she finally slipped her hand onto his arm. Her brows creased at the warmth of his grin and the way he placed his other hand over her fingers, as if to keep them from slipping away.

"So, how do ye fare since yer return?" he asked when Alice and Thomas were out of earshot.

"I'm fine. Why wouldn't I be?" She bristled at his words, certain it was another display of distaste for her spending time with the Indians. She had heard enough of it from the whispers between Thomas and Alice.

His skin flushed at her words, and his half-smile seemed strained at her response.

"I just thought yer ordeal may have been quite distressing, with the accident. That is all I meant."

"I was not on that boat, and I'm not his niece," she hissed. "You need to help me get away from these idiots!"

"Ah, uh … quiet down," he whispered, his eyes briefly darting around at passersby. "It's not so simple! Thomas Martin swears you are his niece!"

"I'm not!"

"Then who exactly are ye?" he asked. His fingers tightened over hers as she moved to pull away, so she could not disengage herself without making a considerable scene.

"I'm just – I'm just not his niece, that's all," she mumbled. There was nothing she could say to prove her identity. No driver's license, no credit card, nothing of value to illustrate exactly whom she belonged to. As far the colonists were concerned, the word of a man was law, and she was most painfully aware that her word held as little meaning as that of the Indians.

"Ye needn't be afraid of Winn anymore, miss. Ye can tell me the truth of where ye come from. Ye need not return to the Indians."

She squinted up at him. She heard a tremor in his voice, only slight, but enough to cause an undercurrent of unease to wash over her, pinpricks of goose bumps rising up on her arms in response.

"I thought you were his friend," she said softly. His head dipped down toward her ear, and he slowed their pace by pulling back on her arm.

"He *is* my friend! 'Tis the only reason I did not put a bullet through his foolish whoreson head for this!" He raked a hand through his tousled hair, disrupting the binding enough so that scattered curls sprung free. She moved to step back, but he held her arm firm. "I thought more of him than this – that he would steal a good English woman and – and act on his base instincts! He asks too much for me to stand by with no action!"

"He has done nothing wrong!"

"Nothing wrong? Has he blinded yer eyes so much, then?"

"No. It is nothing like that!" she snapped. "And if you are truly his friend, then you will help me go back to him."

"If you want my help, ye will tell me the truth of it. Tell me who are yer kin, and I will return you to them!"

She snatched her arm away with a seething grunt.

"I have no kin."

"Then ye'll have to bear my questions until you recall them."

Alice and Thomas approached. Thomas cocked his head and his brows narrowed as he neared, his cheeks squashed like two purple plums over a pointed scowl. Benjamin notably changed his demeanor, switching gears seamlessly to more gentle conversation. Although his skin remained flushed from ears to throat, his voice was tempered with calmness when he spoke again.

"Winn spoke of a wound ye suffered. I trust it heals well?"

"Yes, it's fine," she sniped.

He squinted a bit at her retort and resumed a pleasant smile. "Yer manner of speech is…different. I admit it intrigues me."

"I'm sure you've never heard my accent before," she shot back.

His skin flushed a bit more and his head ducked down as he smiled. He cleared his throat and patted her hand as if in distraction.

"Ah, yes, then. I would like to ask ye a favor, Miss."

"Maggie. I think you know my name by now."

"Maggie, then. Would you like to ride with me after the service? I would take ye to visit some friends, I'm sure yer uncle would approve."

"That is a fine idea, Benjamin. She will join ye," Thomas interrupted as he joined them. The older man smirked, nodding eagerly at them. "Ye plan to see Morgan White, I suppose?"

Benjamin tilted his head in agreement.

"I hope he has returned. His young son has been worried after him."

"Do ye know which savage he was consorting with? I can't say I trust them as much as ye do," Thomas said.

"Pray he's returned and we need not worry over it," Benjamin replied. Her lips pursed shut when he pressed his hand over hers. She did not care for the way he continued to hold her as she attempted to pry her hand free, but decided her best bet was to play along. She let out a sigh and stopped her struggle and his mouth curled up into a grin.

"It will be a short ride, my dear. Unless ye prefer to return home with yer aunt—"

"No!" she said quickly, causing him to grin mischievously. He knew damn well she didn't want to go back to the Martin house and she did not appreciate the manipulation.

"Well, it's settled then," he murmured. She nodded.

"I will meet ye there," Thomas said. "I've business of my own with Morgan White. No better time to settle it."

"Does that please ye, Maggie?" Benjamin asked.

She considered denying his request, but when she saw the hope in his eyes and the way he feared her rejection, she nodded in agreement. She would take him up on the offer, play on his lapse of judgment, and find a way back to Winn. It would be an easy way to get away from her fake family, and might provide her opportunity to make her escape.

"Good! We will leave right away, as soon as the minister releases us."

The service was blissfully short, in part because the regular minister was absent and the job was taken on by volunteers. Maggie sat daydreaming beside Benjamin, relieved when the final hymn ended and they were able to leave the stuffy stone church. Alice and Thomas seemed content to leave her in Benjamin's care, which she suspected was just another part of her captivity. She imagined they viewed him as a helpful accomplice to keep her in line, and although she still tried to decipher their rules of right and wrong, she failed miserably.

It was no matter. She would ride out with Benjamin and make her escape, and the nightmare of being detained by the English would soon be nothing more than an unpleasant memory.

27

Maggie sat stiffly beside Benjamin, who had been courteous but quiet the entire way as they rode in the wagon. He took her as scheduled to a neighboring plantation to meet his friend, Morgan White, trying to introduce her to other members of the community. Apparently, the widower White had contracted for a wife from England and they would marry later in the week. It would be one of many weddings in Martin's Hundred, thanks to the influx of eligible women sent over by the Virginia Company. Benjamin mentioned that many women had arrived on the same ship Maggie had supposedly traveled on.

Mr. White, however, had been gone for longer than expected on a trading run with an Indian companion, so Benjamin was eager to see if the man had returned safely home in time for his wedding.

He tilted his head and cracked the reins again to speed the horses, and pointed ahead to show her the plantation they approached.

"Your uncle is here," he commented. She expected as much from the earlier conversation, but Maggie was surprised to see the elder Martin had arrived before them. The yard was empty except for a lone horse tied to split rail fence, which looked to be the black mare Thomas rode that morning. Maggie wondered if she could get her hands on the horse.

There was a pleasant small cabin at the heart of the settlement, and it seemed peculiar that there was no smoke coming from the chimney, especially considering the breeze in the air. A shiver of unease stole over her when she saw the empty barn door snapping back and forth in the wind, making a hollow thud each time it hit the barn wall. As they pulled up in the wagon, Uncle Thomas stalked out of the house, followed by a young boy of about four holding a round black felt hat and two young men, dressed in the gray homespun that most servants wore in the colony.

"What happened here?" Benjamin asked, climbing down from the wagon. He offered his hand, and she gladly took it, curious to get a look around. The place looked near abandoned.

"Young Morgan says his father left days ago with that savage Jack-of-a-Feather, and he has yet to return. Then this morning the Indian comes here wearing his pa's hat," Thomas said, clearly riled up.

"He never returned?" Benjamin asked.

"No," Thomas answered, spitting out a slick of tobacco onto the ground. "Jack says he didna kill him, says he had an accident, but the evidence is damning. He's wearing Old Morgan's hat!"

Maggie looked toward the barn and decided to take a better look while they talked. Young Morgan watched her walk toward the barn but he hung back with the men, clutching the hat in his tiny white fingers. His dusty face was littered with pale streaks where tears had washed off the grime. The tow-headed child was dry eyed now and silent in the presence of the adults.

As she made her way closer across the packed clay, she could see two ponies tied to a post in the far side corral, one of which she immediately recognized. "Benjamin?" she called. "Who else is here?"

"Maggie, stay with me!" Benjamin reached her side and grabbed her upper arm to stop her from the path. It was unlike him to snatch her so, but she took his advice and remained next to him as they stood outside the barn since the hair on the back of her neck was standing at attention.

"The boys have the savages tied up in the barn. They said Jack-of-a-Feather rode in alone, and then the other one showed up," Thomas said. He hoisted his rifle up to his shoulder and pointed it toward the barn in practice, then lowered it back to his side. "He must have killed Old Morgan. Jack won't go willingly to the magistrate in Jamestown, and I do not know what to do with the other. Maybe ye can decide, Benjamin, since ye know the savage well. He's from the village."

Maggie saw Thomas shoot her a glare, his lips twitching nervously as he looked toward the barn. She cared very little if they planned to execute Nemattanew after what he had done, but she wondered who the second brave that accompanied him on his misdeeds was. Bile burned hot in the back of her throat. She recognized the horse tied up, and she knew very well it was one from the Paspahegh village.

"If Jack said it was an accident, we must treat him fairly, Thomas. We canna tie them up like animals," Benjamin snapped, taking off for the barn. Thomas uttered a protest but followed him, and Maggie trailed behind.

Benjamin was on his knee, untying the captive's ankles when she made it to the door. Winn sat cross-legged on the ground, his head hanging limp, his wrists bound behind him to a post. Blood trickled from a swollen wound above his right ear where his hair was shaved flat to his skull in the half moon shape. Nemattanew sat beside him in a similar position, more alert, his eyes filled with fury as they approached.

"Oh, God, Winn!" she cried.

28

Her voice sounded like the melody of warm summer sunshine as she turned backwards on her horse to laugh at him. He loved to see her smile, and when she issued her teasing challenge to race, he gladly followed. She slapped her horse on the rump and took off, and he dug his heels in to urge his horse into pursuit. A splatter of wet sand kicked up around them, splattering the bellies of their mounts, but still she laughed, calling to him to follow. Her long scarlet locks streamed wild behind her, and he could hardly wait to catch her so he could hold her in his arms.

"Winn!" she called out.

He let her win the race, as he would give anything to see her smile, and slowed his mount as she stopped the race. Her pony swung around in a tight circle, and suddenly her eyes widened and her heart-shaped face crumpled, as if a shadow of fear had swallowed her.

"What is it, ntehem?" he called.

"Winn!" she screamed.

He had tracked Nemattenew down hours before and followed him to a farm outside of town. The warrior was alone, and Winn was uncertain why he had circled back from town and then visited the farm. As Winn watched, Nemattanew arrived and argued with the English, and against his better judgment, Winn rode in to help him. Winn grimaced, knowing now the decision was a poor one, but at the time, needed to know what was going on if he had any hope of finding Maggie.

The settlers claimed Jack of a Feather killed the Elder Morgan, and they wanted to bring the Indian to James City to face the magistrate. Winn stepped in to defend the accused, but when Winn tried to intercede, the servants immediately assumed the worst.

Things escalated very quickly after that. The servants turned on them and held them at gunpoint, and the last thing Winn could recall was waking up bound to the post. He could only surmise that Nemattanew wanted to return to the farm to explain the white man's disappearance, probably in order to keep relations calm with the English as all Powhatan were under order to do. Opechancanough had been planning his coordinated attack on the whites for several years, and success hinged on the ability of the Powhatans to gain the trust of the whites. The Weroance would not be pleased to hear Nemattanew had slaughtered an Englishman for no good reason. Every local tribe under Powhatan rule knew of the plan, and each tribe had a part in maintaining good relations with the whites.

Nemattanew, however, was a loose cannon. The brave had a deep hate for the whites that often led him to rash acts, and the unfortunate Elder Morgan had been too trusting of the tricky Jack-of-a-Feather. Winn knew Nemattanew was losing favor with his uncle for his rash behavior, and his only regret was that it had come too late to prevent all the chaos involving Maggie. Given the choice, Winn would gladly end Nemattanew's life, as he was sure Nemattanew would happily do the same for him.

He woke to hands shaking his shoulders and several angry voices, but even before he opened his eyes he knew one voice belonged to Maggie. His transition back to consciousness returned in a rush, and suddenly the only thing he could think of was getting Maggie as far away from Nemattanew as possible. He tried to rise but the man pushed him back down with firm pressure on his shoulders. Benjamin. Winn shrugged off his hands and staggered to his feet as the stars clouding his vision began to fade, his hands still bound behind his back.

"What is the meaning of this?" Benjamin yelled, directing his anger at the other Englishman. Winn's right eye was swollen from the blow of a rifle butt, but he could still see Maggie as she pushed around Benjamin and pressed a cool cloth to his temple. He closed his eyes briefly to her touch, hoping the others did not notice how she wrapped her hands around his arm and pressed dangerously close to him. Winn saw a glimmer of wetness in her jade eyes and gently leaned into her to help steady her shaking.

"Thank you," he said softly to comfort her. He kept his voice low as the Englishmen argued, more worried about getting Maggie to safety than what they might do to him.

"Winn, what happened here?" Benjamin asked, reaching out to pull Maggie away.

"Untie me," Winn answered. His hands clenched into fists when he saw how Benjamin glanced at Thomas, then paused. *Was Benjamin going to forsake him and leave him bound like a dog?*

Maggie moved forward, but Benjamin snatched her hand and pushed her behind him as if Winn was a danger to her. Winn would have laughed at the irony if he were not in such a precarious position. Thomas Martin had his rifle cocked at his waist, waiting with his little pebble eyes for any move Winn might make.

"Thomas, take Maggie back to the house."

"No!" she shouted. Maggie shook off the hand that reached for her and tried to avoid Thomas, but Winn could only watch as the older man dragged her toward the house. He heard her utter a slew of oaths at Thomas as she went, and he closed his eyes against her words and prayed she would be safe until he could get to her.

"Winn…please. Tell me what you have done," Benjamin asked. He put his rifle down to lean against the wall, and he unsheathed the knife at his waist. Benjamin sliced through the bonds with one quick jab then stepped back a few paces. Winn flexed his hands as his wrists were released, then swiftly reached for his knife and spear that had been taken from him and lay at Benjamin's feet. He tucked the knife in his corded belt and sheathed the spear in the carrying harness on his back, lowering his tight jaw as he gave his answer through gritted teeth.

"Think what you will, friend. I killed no Englishman … today."

He would give no further answer to the accusations his friend posed. Fighting back his anger at Benjamin, at the English, at his uncle – in one swoop it all became clear, as if he had been living in a shadow of denial before this day.

He deserves to be a suspect, because he was guilty. No matter how much he felt friendship for Benjamin, despite the trust between them, Winn had deceived him all along with full intent to lead an attack upon the English. He had grown up believing that following the orders of his Weroance somehow made it honorable, but now, as he stared into the blue eyes of his oldest friend, he could not deny that he and the rest of the Powhatan would soon take everything from the Englishman.

Winn avoided his stare and bent to cut Nemattanew loose. He would have liked to leave him there to face the English justice but knew he could not.

"We go," he said, directing the order to Nemattanew, who Winn feared would want to retaliate. It would only bring down the rage of Opechancanough on them all if he allowed that to happen. For once, Nemattanew offered no protest. Winn took it as a sign that he knew he was beaten for now.

"I can't let you do that, Winn. Winn!" Benjamin yelled.

"Shoot me if you must, brother," Winn replied. He stepped out of the barn and scanned the courtyard for Maggie. "Where is the woman?"

"She is safe. You must tell me—"

Winn ignored his plea and stalked off toward the house. He would not make the mistake of leaving her again. Nemattanew mounted up, watching him. She stood grappling with the two servant boys, looking the victor of the group in her fury, her thick fiery hair streaming out behind her and her eyes alight with heathen rage.

"Unhand my wife," he said simply. He reached for the spear slung over his back, and both boys immediately retreated. He left the weapon sheathed and held out his hand to Maggie. Her chest heaved from her struggle, and he could hardly wait to feel her in his arms again.

"Knihelel!" Nemattanew screamed, swinging his horse wildly in circles as he cried out, lifting his fist back toward the Englishmen and screaming his promise to end them all.

Winn turned to the warrior, but before he could issue a command, Nemattanew was thrown back off his horse. The echo of the rifle came afterward, and in the melee that followed, Thomas Martin shot off another round.

"No!" Maggie screamed.

He felt the shot before he heard it, the sound trailing behind through the space of the open meadow. He hit the ground, the warm sticky sensation of his own blood running over his chest, the wound pulsing even as he tried to stop it with his hand. He sat up but fell back down, his left arm burning as if shards of glass filled the bone. He let it take him for only a moment, knowing he could not give in before he made her safe.

"Stay down! Do not move!" Benjamin ordered from somewhere above him. The voice trailed off in an echo, the sound of his heartbeat thudding louder through his ears as he winced up at the blinding sunlight. He wondered if perhaps time travel felt the same, and if Maggie had suffered when she came through to him. He would ask her that later, when they lay by his fire beneath warm furs, when he held her and whispered a song to lure her into sleep.

"Is he dead?" another voice asked.

"No…but the wound is bad," Benjamin answered.

Winn felt his chest squeezed as Benjamin placed pressure to the wound. His eyes slid open into slits to look at his friend.

"Keep her safe, Benjamin," he said, his voice strained from forming the words.

"Maggie – you mean Maggie?" Benjamin replied hoarsely. Winn grimaced when Benjamin pushed down harder on the wound, and he felt the warmth of his own blood as it ebbed down his ribs. He could smell its coppery scent and knew that too much of it had left his veins.

"She is…my wife. Let no man harm her…brother."

Winn closed his eyes.

"Catch me if you can, warrior!" she laughe•.

So she woul• make a game of it, an• he woul• chase her. Her long auburn hair streame• behin• her as she ran laughing •own the beach, the wet san• sticking to her skin. Her footsteps marke• her trail like brea•crumbs across the san•, an• he followe• it.

Should it take forever, he would find her again.

29

Maggie screamed as Nemattanew flew off the horse and Winn swung back around to face them, and before she could stop him, Thomas fired off a round and Winn fell to the ground.

"No!" she screamed, throwing herself at the rifle Thomas held. She fought Benjamin when he pulled her off Thomas, kicking and biting anything she could make contact with. Her teeth sank into Benjamin's arm and he shook her off, finally subduing her in a bear hug to avoid her sharp fingernails as she clawed him.

"Let me go!"

"Boys! Take her inside – and for God's sake don't let her out of your sight!" he ordered the servants who stood by. She relaxed and let them think she was willing, and then darted easily out of their grasp to follow Benjamin as he ran toward Winn. Benjamin kneeled down next to Winn, who lay fallen on the dirt.

"Enough!" Thomas shouted. He grabbed her by the back of her dress, and with one thick fist, he struck her across the face. The blow was a powerful one, sending her to the ground.

* * *

Maggie winced as Aunt Alice dabbed at her split lower lip with a bit of clean wool. They both jumped when Thomas entered the bedroom and slammed the door behind him.

"Leave us, good wife," he said, his graveled voice steady. She could see the menace in his beady black eyes no matter how calmly he spoke, and she knew he had nothing but harsh intention behind his mask. Alice immediately obeyed, reaching out to touch his arm before she left, but drawing back at the last moment and grasping for the door handle instead. She avoided eye contact with Maggie as she skittered away.

When the door clicked softly into its latch, Thomas took a step toward the bed where she sat. Her first instinct was to move away, but she was already sitting back upright to the plaster wall and had no space left to go.

"Ye will tell me now why ye helped those savages, girl. It will not save ye from what is to come, but God shows mercy on those who speak truth," he snarled. She curled her knees to her chest and her heart began to pound against her ribs when she saw him slide the heavy leather belt from his breeches, the brass buckle catching the light from the single lamp in the room and casting a glare as he swung it in front of him.

"Don't you dare come near me with that!" she whispered.

He breached the space and grabbed her by the hair, but then was distracted for a moment by her braid. He pulled her off the bed by using her hair like a lever, shaking her hard while his face contorted into a bright red mask.

"Ye like the savages? Should I have left ye there with them? My own niece, loyal to the savages?" he shouted. She lurched away but he was faster, his hold on her hair bringing a rush of tears to her eyes as he pulled her across the floor. Her fingernails tore and split on the plank flooring when he dragged her back, falling on her with not the belt, but his fists. He was careful in his punishment, aiming his blows to her chest and belly, anywhere her garments would cover, and finally when she lay on her side gasping for air with her arms curled around her belly, he reached for the belt.

"You'd choose them over yer own kind? It that what ye've done? Which one was it? Was it that bloody Winn, that blue-eyed devil?" he roared, striking her with the belt across her back. She clutched her side and tried to crawl away, but he was relentless in his rage. She felt a blow to her hip from the tip of his boot which sent her sprawling, and when he came back for another blow, she scrambled around and used the strength she had left to spit a mixture of blood and saliva in his face.

"He's a better man than you'll ever be!" she hissed.

"Well," he said slowly, ceasing his pursuit to gasp a few quick breaths. "He is a dead man, is what he truly is." He reached into the pocket of his brown breeches, and Maggie felt the blood and fight drain from her as she saw the object hanging from his hand. Two black feathers hung from a rawhide cord, and between them, she could see a Bloodstone set in copper.

"Yer lover is dead. I will have no harlot in my house, so if no man will contract ye, ye are going back to England." He threw the pendant at her feet. "Clean up yourself, and clean up this mess."

He wiped the back of one hand across his face and stomped out, slamming the door behind him. She sat on the floor, her chest heaving with effort of each painful breath, and although she felt the sticky wetness of blood trickle down from her mouth, she did not move.

The Bloodstone lay only a foot away, the smooth dark orb staring back at her. A crimson vein ran through its center, like a lone ray of brilliant light slicing it in half.

No. Not Winn. It coul• not be true. She knew with all the fiber of her being that he would never part with it. Not if there was breath left in his body.

But when she finally reached for the stone and felt the weight of it in her hand, coldness crept through her limbs as she brought it to rest against her heart. Her split lower lip began to tremble and a rush of tears rounded her swollen eyelids, the wetness streaking her cheeks and coursing down onto her hands.

30

Aunt Alice allowed Maggie no time for grief. In a future life that felt long lost, Marcus had shared equally the loss of Maggie's grandfather, and through the patience and comfort of the giant man she drew reassurance from the bond they shared. Although the sorrow had been harsh, the passing was natural and necessary, a final blow to seal the fate of a man who lived a good life and loved well. Winn's death held no such illusion for her. She found no meaning in his loss, and among the numbness and sheer ache that littered her bones she only could see despair, licking at the wounds created by a mallet that took slow joy in crushing her soul piece by piece. She could neither run from the pain nor stop it, nor would she, if able, because at night when she curled up in her narrow bed and cried she clung to the grief, as it was all she had left of him.

Alice, however, hovered more than usual, and though she did not ever say Winn's name, Maggie could see the sympathy in her grey eyes as the woman helped her into her dress. Alice altered a new garment by loosening a seam on the side of the bodice, and Maggie was grateful for the kindness, which made it easier for her to take a deep breath. Maggie realized by her actions that Thomas had likely beaten his wife in the past, and the woman simply knew the means to help hide the after effects.

Maggie had not left the room in two days, not from petulance but more from sheer pain, unable to make her battered body do more than use the privy pot to void or vomit. It was Alice who finally took charge, bursting into the room as if it were any other day and throwing open the shutters to the lone window. She would take no argument, Maggie was getting dressed, and that was all there was to it.

While Alice rifled through her trunk looking for a more presentable apron, Maggie felt another surge of bile rise in her throat as she sat on the edge of the bed. She reached the pot just in time, and Alice made a clucking sound as she helped hold back her red hair. Thicker and shinier since she had arrived, it was quite a bit longer, too, so she was glad for the assistance. She smiled ruefully at Alice.

"Sorry," she murmured. Alice shrugged and took the pot in both hands to dispose of the contents.

"You need to eat, child. Nothing to fret upon." Alice opened the door with a swing of her ample hip and glanced back at Maggie. "Leave that one apron out, 'tis threadbare. We will cut it for rags—for when ye have need."

Maggie nodded in acknowledgment, but when the door closed behind Alice another sickly feeling assuaged her, and this time it was not only her stomach. Rags? Well, women were still women, no matter what time one lived in. She picked up the worn out apron and stared at it for a moment, counting backward in her head.

No. It coul• not be.

"No!" she moaned, pressing the apron to her lips.

She counted again, and suddenly she felt like the passenger on a freight train when her heart began to hammer away behind her bruised ribs. Her hand slipped down over her belly, swollen she assumed from the more palatable food in town, then up to her sore and heavy breasts, which she had blindly ignored. She realized that she had not bled in six weeks, and promptly vomited into the apron.

"Oh, dear! Again? Come to the parlor and we will feed you, dear! I will clean this mess. You cannot go on without food!" Alice sighed over the additional disorder when she entered the room.

"And Margaret, Young Benjamin is here. He worries terribly for ye and asks to see ye," Alice commented as she buttoned up the back of

Maggie's dress. Maggie winced when Alice pulled the apron and knotted it at her waist.

"I don't think so," she replied.

Alice took her hand firm in her grasp. "Yes, dear, ye are leaving this room, and a fine young man waits for ye. He told Thomas of his intention to court ye, take yer comfort in that. Here," she said, taking a white linen kerchief from her apron pocket. Alice wiped it gently across Maggie's eyes and mouth and then paused for a moment with her palm on her cheek. She offered Maggie a cup of water, which helped wash the sour taste away. "He is a good man, child. He is quite different from...yer uncle."

Maggie lowered her eyes. It was probably the most the woman could ever admit to what a beast her own husband was, and Maggie appreciated the sentiment. She wondered how many times Alice had suffered the same under his twisted form of personal justice. She also wondered if the life in her belly had survived his onslaught.

Alice unlatched the bedroom door, and as Maggie peeked out from behind her, she saw Benjamin jump to his feet, his wide-brimmed hat clenched in one fist and his shoulders sprinkled with fresh snow. His high cheekbones were flushed with cherry red dimples as his eyes met hers across the room.

Maggie was relieved to see Thomas was not present, so she felt somewhat safer as she let Alice lead her into the parlor.

"Miss Martin," Benjamin said with a curt nod of his head. His eyes remained fixed on Maggie as he spoke, pained and searching, and she dropped her gaze to break the contact. She did not wish to hurt him, but she could hardly find strength enough not to run screaming from the house, let alone continue to pretend to be a compliant Englishwoman. With her head still spinning with the news of her discovery, she tried to cling to some vestige of sanity, but knowing Winn would never come rescue her from the façade left little motivation for her to continue the ploy.

"Good morning, Young Benjamin," Alice replied. "Margaret is feeling much better today. Will ye please sit with her while I fetch more kindling?"

"Of course." He dipped his head to Alice as she passed, leaving them alone in the parlor, the crack and spit of the fire the only sound between them.

"Are ye well, Maggie? Ye look quite pale."

She wanted to tell him he would look just the same, having been beaten within an inch of his life, but she bit back the retort for lack of caring or strength to argue. She shrugged.

"I'm fine. You can go away now."

She stood up and turned her back to him, her eyes focused instead on the fire. Anything was better than looking into his tragic face, full of guilt, longing, and other unmentionables.

"I'm sorry for what happened. He was my friend as well as yours. I can see it pains ye, and I wish I could—"

"You could what, Benjamin? Bring him back? Give my child a father? Get out," she whispered, the anguish spilling forth like the swell of a hurricane. "Get out. Just get out!"

She shrieked and slapped him in a reflexive response when he put his hands on her, a swell of rank fear bursting forth with memories of what Thomas has done to her. Benjamin did not block her blows, merely stood there, his hands on her shoulders as she sobbed, until finally he closed his arms around her. She hated every ounce of his touch, every gentle pat, every calming word he spoke, and finally when she lost will to continue she simply cried against his shoulder, clutching his hated chest with her fist.

"Ye carry his child?" he asked quietly. She did not raise her head, but nodded.

"Yes."

His arms tightened around her and she grimaced against the pain.

"Then grieve for him tonight," he murmured. "And tomorrow I will see ye to church."

He placed a gentle kiss on her brow, placed his hat on his head, and left.

31

Maggie walked dutifully beside Benjamin, wishing she could pull her hand away from where he had it tucked firmly in his elbow. As the stale days passed and left her aching with loneliness, she found it best to make plans on her own and decided it was time to speak with the Pale Witch. No one could help her but Finola.

She knew the time of the massacre was approaching, but her memories of history were fuzzy at best. Yes, she knew it happened in early spring, but she could not recall the exact date. For that matter, the English kept dates differently than she was accustomed to in the future so she was not quite sure how the numbers would correlate anyway. The only truth she knew for certain was if she wanted to avoid the upcoming massacre, she needed to get out of Martin's Hundred as soon as she possibly could.

Benjamin continued to press his attentions, but she was relieved he seemed somewhat shy and reserved in his courting and remained patient to gain her favor. She felt sorry for deceiving him, letting him believe she was a happy recipient of his affection, but she had no other option save telling him the truth.

Well Benjamin, soon the Indians are going to kill pretty much everyone in Martin's Hundred. How do I know that? Oh, I'm from the future. From 2012. Care for some tea with your dinner?

She was sure that conversation would not go over well.

They took a different path to town than she was accustomed, and as they passed down a lane through a narrow stretch of dense woods she wondered if he chose the seclusion on purpose. His intentions became clear when he stopped walking and took her hand more intimately in his own.

"Benjamin, we should hurry on," she began, stunned when he raised her hand to his lips and gently kissed her knuckles.

"I beg yer leave, Maggie, but I must speak to ye."

He caught her by the fingertips and held them tight so she could not flee.

"I do not wish to cause ye distress," he began. "But I fear we must act quickly," he pleaded. She shook her head, afraid of his meaning, uncertain how to placate him and extricate herself from the awkward mess.

"I don't know what you mean–"

"I ask ye to marry me. Please be my wife," he said softly. She stepped back.

"Benjamin–"

"If we do not marry soon, people will soon notice yer condition, and there will be talk."

She shook her head and turned her eyes downward, unable to meet his soft searching gaze.

"I cannot marry you, Benjamin," she murmured.

"Maggie," he sighed. "Yer uncle will disown ye, and possibly send ye back to England. I can do nothing to change that…unless ye marry me now."

"Why? Why would you ask this, when you know I carry his child?" she asked, feeling the sting of tears in her eyes as she lost patience with him.

"It matters not to me," he said softly. Shocked by his admission, and not expecting such a declaration from a man of his time, she let him hold her closer and raised her swollen eyes to his.

"Why would I hold ye at fault for such a thing? Ye were lost and injured, ye are lucky to live. It is not your doing what happened," he replied, his eyes damping with sadness. "Ye came here under contract on yer uncle's bidding. And whatever happened between ye and

Winn...he was my friend, even so. At least I can offer ye protection now."

Taken aback by his sincerity and struck by the adamant undercurrent in his words, she leveled her response with the kindest tone she could muster.

"I don't know what to say."

"He asked it of me, before he died. He asked me to protect ye. It is the last thing I can do for him...to see ye cared for."

She bit her lower lip. *No. Winn would not have asked this of her...would he?* Winn, her warrior, the man who had killed a brave for placing an ownership mark on her head? Would Winn truly have wanted this? She did not believe he would send her willingly to another man, unless...unless he knew he could no longer be there to protect her from what was to come.

"What did he say to you?" she whispered. She stepped away from him, but he did not let her leave him entirely. His eyes dipped down and he clutched her hands harder.

"With his last words, he spoke of ye. He knew the shot was fatal...he asked me to keep ye safe."

She bowed her head into her hands and her body began to shake. Memory of his promises stung her as the tears flowed.

Now you will feel no rain, for I will shelter you.

Was this his way of keeping his promise, even in death?

"All right," she whispered, the words like ice upon her tongue. He ran one hand through his unruly hair and his cheeks burned with a hint of crimson at her declaration. He raised the hand he held to his lips and kissed it gently.

"Yes, then. Good, it is settled. Come now, Miss Finola awaits us."

* * *

Finola did not take the news well. She had closed her shop to visitors, yet when Maggie and Benjamin arrived that morning, she allowed them entrance. She stepped back from the door and waved them inside, clutching a wool cloak around her as the snow whipped in behind them. She looked older than when Maggie had last visited, her face drawn, her skin an unhealthy pallor. The older woman sat down on a stool next to the fire and placed her hands close to the flames, rubbing her palms to warm them. Maggie recalled her own desire to let the flames consume her and her heart ached fresh at the thought of their shared loss.

Benjamin took her cloak from her shoulders and Maggie sank down on her knees in front of Finola. Their hands met and entwined together, and they both kept their gaze on the snapping flames of the fire. Maggie could cry no tears for Winn with Benjamin at her side, but the older woman seemed to know her heart and she patted her hand in a soothing manner.

"He was the best of them, you know. The Paspahegh, that is," Finola said quietly. She kept her eyes on the fire as she spoke, and Maggie felt each of her words like a dagger scraping slowly across her skin.

"He was," Maggie answered, the words hollow on her dry lips.

"Will Thomas Martin be punished for his crime?"

Finola turned then to look at Benjamin, and he paled considerably.

"You know there was no crime, Miss," he said, his voice breaking with the last bit of words. He shoved his hat back over his unruly curls.

"Yes, I know. No crime but the murder of my grandson."

"Take care for your words, lest someone else hear them. I will see to my business and return for ye soon, Maggie. Miss Finola." He nodded to them both in a stilted manner and quickly made his exit.

Maggie felt a surge of relief when Benjamin left the cabin, leaving her and Finola to speak openly. Finola must have sensed her urgency, because after Benjamin left she quickly closed the door and latched it securely.

"Come," she said simply, and waved her toward a separate room in the back.

Maggie followed her into the second half of the house, a common sitting room with her sleeping space in one corner. The older woman reached under her stuffed straw mattress, and after fiddling through the linens for a few moments, she withdrew a bundle wrapped in silk.

"What do you have there, Finola?" Maggie asked.

"Sit down, dear," she ordered as she unwrapped the bundle. When it was unbound, Maggie did as she was directed and sat down on a chair, nearly missing the seat but finding it with two outstretched hands.

From Finola's thin white fingers hung a pendant on a thick gold chain, the center of the setting a fat, shining, Bloodstone.

"Before ye ask, child, this is my Bloodstone. I cannot give it to ye, it does not work that way. I have the same mark as ye," she explained, holding out her palm for inspection. It was true. They shared the same brand.

"But how does it work? Why am I here?" she asked, her questions running together in an incoherent jumble of nonsense. "Tell me!"

"Aye, of course, I will tell ye! I do not know where yer stone is hidden. My grandson kept his secrets well," she said softly. Maggie felt a surge of despair at the revelation, but she knew the outcome had bound her to the time more powerfully than any shackle could. "The raw stone needs your blood to work the magic, and once you use it, it bonds to the bearer. My mother taught me how to use it long ago."

"Oh," Maggie said. "Blood...I cut my hand before I picked it up."

Finola nodded. "So it knows you now, and you cannot walk again without it."

"There has to be another way – have you tried to use another stone?" Maggie asked.

"There are other ways, with other magic, but the ways to wield that power are long lost to us. But child, if I had your stone here to give ye now, would ye truly want to use it? I think your heart lies here, and this is the time ye now call home," she said. "The babe in your belly belongs to this time, does it not?"

"But," she began, but then her lips fell silent. She wrapped her arms around her body, trying to wash away the doubt the woman brought forth. *Would she leave, if she could? Could she walk away from this time?* She shook her head. The thought of leaving Winn's memory in the past hurt more than the notion of what she left in the future, the door to the fable of her old life clicking shut with a gentle tap. By staying in the past, would her son know his father? Or would they both be better off in the time she was born to?

"Nay, no need to answer me, dear. It is as it should be," she sighed.

"What do you mean?"

"Well, the Bloodstones are curious things. They have been used by my people for generations, and have been known as potent talismans. Only the most powerful Blooded Ones can truly harness their magic, and once a raw stone is used, the Bloodstone marks its bearer, ye see," she said.

"Wait, wait a second! Blooded Ones? What does that mean?" Maggie interrupted.

"It is what my kind are called. Blooded Ones, those who can use powerful magic. Here in James City, they would call us witches," she answered.

"So the Weroance was right. You are a witch."

Finola shrugged.

"Opechancanough is an old fool, he knows nothing."

"What lies between you? He told me he spared my life, as he once spared yours," Maggie said. "What was he talking about?"

"A tale best left buried, is all. It is true, he let me leave. He fears too much what he canna understand. Enough of him," she muttered, shaking her head. "He is too stubborn to see the truth."

Maggie swallowed despite the dryness in her throat. "Were you born here, in James City?"

"Och, no! My Bloodstone sent me here many years ago, with my son, Dagr. It is a long story for another time, but it is how we arrived. My mother was a powerful Blooded One of the Five Families, and she passed her gift to me," she said softly, her eyes staring off, seeming lost in her memory for a moment. Her clear blue eyes glistened, but she shook her head a bit and continued. "It seems you have some powerful blood in yer veins, child. Who are your kin? I suspect I must know them."

"No, I don't come from—from anyone special. I don't even know my parents, my grandfather raised me after my mother abandoned me. I never had anyone else."

"Ah," she murmured. "Well, I imagine your blood came from one of the Five families, somewhere in your line. 'Tis good to know we live on and endure in the future. But now ye know where ye belong—you belong here. I saw it in a dream, Winkeohkwet with his Red Woman."

"Did you see his death, as well?" she asked, her voiced edged in more bitterness than she intended.

"No," she answered. "I did not."

* * *

Maggie let out her breath in a long sigh before she entered the parlor. Benjamin was waiting to announce their plans, eager to tell her guardians they would marry in the morning.

Benjamin stepped toward her with his gloved hand outstretched, and Maggie walked toward him, although she was unable to curb a low cry when he squeezed her bruised upper arm in his excitement. His brows darted downward, tiny creases spreading out from each corner of his troubled blue eyes at the sound of her pained noise.

"Sweetheart, what troubles you?" he asked softly. She winced when his hands closed around her shoulders, and when he pulled her into his arms and his embrace tightened around her ribs she let out a moan.

"What is it?"

"It's nothing," she lied. She shook her head, more to herself than to him, not wishing to admit aloud what Thomas had done to her.

He frowned as he looked down on her and reached a purposeful hand to her collar, which he gently pushed aside. She made no effort to stop him, letting him see the lacework of blue and purple bruises that marked her skin. He tilted her chin with shaking fingers, his lips mashed in a single thin line as he drew away. When he spoke, his voice cracked through his gritted teeth.

"I will be right back. Keep ye here until I return."

Maggie watched him swing abruptly around, his cloak whirling in a halo around him as he shoved his hat on his mass of thick black hair and left the house. Alice was nearly knocked over by his exit, and Maggie was surprised to note Benjamin failed to acknowledge Alice as he left.

Alice swatted fresh snow off her bonnet and dropped a bundle of kindling next to the fire.

"Did you chase him away, niece?" she asked.

"No. I did nothing," Maggie answered with a shrug. She had no idea what was going on in Benjamin's head. She reached back and loosened the apron at her waist, and then settled down on her knees by the fire. The flames licked her skin, casting a spreading warmth over her face as she leaned close. If she stuck her hand in, would she burn? Or would she wake up from the nightmare she was in and find her husband waiting to welcome both her – and the babe?

A baby. The last thread pulled from an unraveling yarn, a splinter from the heartwood of a forest, a pledge of his love left nestled within her. Her hand slipped down over her belly and rested there. Her condition was not yet evident, but soon, it would be.

"Well, he looks to be in a rare temper," the older woman sniped.

It was not long before the door slammed open again and Benjamin returned. This time he failed to remove his hat, and he stalked purposefully across the room to the fire where she sat. He held out one gloved hand to her.

"The minister is waiting for us now, my dear. There is no need to wait any longer."

Alice gasped. "Now, you say?"

"Yes."

Maggie looked at his outstretched hand, his long fingers covered by the fine black calfskin glove. She turned her gaze to the fire. She wondered if she could just continue to stare at the flames and forever remain there, eventually melting into its core to disappear into nothingness.

Another figure filled the doorway, his wind chapped cheeks stunted and beady eyes narrowed, and when Maggie realized it was Thomas, she quickly placed her hand into the palm Benjamin held out to her. *Stay with a violent ●evil, or take what Benjamin offere●.*

She had no choice.

* * *

She clutched her cloak around her shoulders as Benjamin hurried her toward the church, barely able to keep up with his rapid pace without jogging alongside him. His stride was long and propelled by his quiet anger, his displayed emotion clear yet much different than she was accustomed.

The church loomed up ahead, the lights blazing like a beacon to guide them. The faster Benjamin walked, the more she slowed, and finally she grabbed his arm with both hands and urged him to a halt.

"Benjamin. Stop, please, stop!" she insisted. He swung around to her, his cloak whirling, snow quickly covering the brim of his hat and the tops of his broad shoulders. His cheeks were reddened, from the cold or the anger she knew not, and his soft eyes looked pleading as he gazed down at her.

"Sweetheart, we can talk inside, after our vows," he promised. She shook her head, panicking at the realization of what she was about to do. *She woul● tell him she coul● not we● him, that her heart belonge● to her husban● even if she coul● not join him yet in the afterlife.*

"No." She raised her chin and looked him in the eye. "I cannot do this."

His brows creased and his mouth fell open with a sigh before he spoke. He still held her hand, but more tightly now, as if he could mask the sting of her words from it.

"Maggie, I –"

"I cannot," she said softly. She had no idea where she would go in the dead of winter without his protection, but she knew it would not be back to that lying, abusive, bastard Thomas. Perhaps Finola would take her in.

She was stunned when his cold hands slipped around her face and his breath warmed her skin. His eyes were tinged red about the edges as he looked at her, searching for something she knew she could never give him.

"Maggie, I love ye. I have loved ye since the first moment I saw thee in Finola's store, yer hair in braids, a pale beauty among all the rest." He bowed his head away from her gaze for a moment. "I wish I was the first man ye lay eyes on in this fearful new world. But I take thee whole, as ye are, with all that has happened. Without all those of things, I would not have thee," he said softly. He kissed her then, his lips cold at first but heated with their connection, then moistened by her salty tears. "Ye did not deserve what Thomas did to ye. I promise you, I am not that kind of man. I would never lay hands to my wife in such a way. Let me protect you, and in time—in time ye will grow accustomed to me."

She swallowed hard at the memory of the beating. Her eyes searched his, and she could see the earnest plea reflected in his gaze. What choice did she have?

"But the baby –"

"Hush. I take thee before God as my wife, and the child will be ours, just as the children that will come of our union. Now, take my hand," he said. "The minister is waiting for us."

* * *

Maggie sat with her hands folded on the edge of the bed. She was no idiot, and she was fairly certain her new husband would expect to share her bed on their wedding night. Men of the time were predictable in their ways, and when it came to both sex and religion they gave no leeway for compromise. Her bruises were tender but healing, and she knew prolonging the matter would only cause more strife. She reminded herself of the reasons, but in the end, the thought of sharing his bed felt akin to a stake through her spine.

Benjamin was a man of his time. Although he seemed more reasonable than the others and had already pledged he would not be the sort of husband to lay hands on her, she did not expect him to forgo his rights as her spouse.

When she murmured goodnight and left a chaste kiss on his cheek, he stepped into the room with her and closed the door. He reached to snuff the single candle in the room, then peeled off his calfskin gloves. Always dressed as the proper gentleman, he had several layers of clothes to shed before he took her hand again in the dim light. He turned her slowly back to him, the longing evident in his gaze and building rapidly as he placed his hands on her shift. His fingers shook as he untied the laces, plucking the delicate rounds free one by one. In her flat bare feet her head only came to his collarbone, and she closed her eyes when he bent down to kiss her, his hands sliding around her waist.

"Will ye have me, dearest?" he asked.

She nodded. Later, the silence seemed much easier to live through than listening to the ghost of her past. The demons, however, had other ideas, and when he lay sleeping peacefully beside her with his long arm thrown over her belly, she stared up at the ceiling and silently cried in acknowledgement of the devils.

32

Maggie wiped her hands on her apron as she watched the wagon approach the farm. It was not long before she spotted the two passengers, Charles Potts and Jonathon Pace, and decided she should join Benjamin in the barn before they arrived.

Benjamin lived on a small croft on the outskirts of Martin's Hundred called Wolstenholme Towne. It lacked the protection of the stockade walls, but it had a separate enclosure of shoulder-high log barriers that appeared to provide adequate security against wildlife and other dangers. Maggie knew Benjamin was quite friendly with the natives and considered them little threat. Yet she knew better than he as to the danger that would come, and she was torn with the urge to alert him to the potential disaster. Of course, she could only offer her womanly advice, for as much as that was worth in the despicable century, and bat her eyelids when he laughed off her ideas. Why on earth should she help any of them, anyway? They deserved to be run off after what the English were bound by history to do to the Natives, but the resolution seemed less clear when the victims in question were living, breathing, human beings who gave her food and shelter. They had no idea what the Indians would do to them in a few short weeks and Maggie could not fathom what her role should be in the tragedy.

Benjamin stood by the barn, shirtless and sweating and not the least bit unattractive when a wide smiled creased his face at her approach. She grabbed her skirts up above her ankles and made way toward him with his midday meal in a basket. Although married only a few weeks, they settled into a comfortable routine that she could tolerate without resistance. As long as she cooked for him and allowed him to share her bed, he was pleasant to live with, quite the contrast to what her life would have been like had she remained in the Martin household.

"Well, it is mighty fine to see yer pretty face, sweetheart," he said. He let the axe handle rest against a stump and met her halfway, wiping the sweat from his brow with the back of his forearm and grinning at her as if he had committed a heathen crime.

"Thank you, Benjamin," she replied. She glanced anxiously around him, peering over his shoulder toward the barn, hoping to get a glimpse of the new foal. She missed Blaze terribly, and longed to regain some normalcy in her very un-normal life. Spending some time with a new foal would prove quite the distraction.

"They're in the barn," he explained. He reached out as if to take her arm but pulled back, apparently unwilling to mar her new dress with his grime. She was happy for the distraction and brushed past him into the barn. She found the mother eating peacefully with the foal curled in the straw at her feet, and sat down beside them in the large loose box.

She filly nickered when she scratched her chin, and Benjamin joined her in a smile at the new life before them. He leaned over the wall of the box, watching her as she petted the foal and cooed to the mare.

"Pretty girl," he commented, a teasing twinkle in his blue eyes. Maggie ducked her head and shrugged.

"She's a nice filly, for sure," she agreed, deflecting the comment because she knew full well it was not directed at the horse. Charles Potts finally made it to the doorway, his chest heaving with effort when he entered the barn. He leaned on the doorjamb, spit out a chuck of dark tobacco, and glared at the two of them.

"Ye hardly look ready to go into town, Dixon!" he complained.

"Doona worry, Charles," Benjamin offered. "I will not take long to be ready." Charles scowled, but apparently thought better of complaining further.

"Well, then make haste, and we will go."

Her hand paused in mid scratch against the filly's ear, and Maggie held her breath in as the men spoke, wishing she could curl up into herself and disappear. If there was one thing she hated most about the century, it was being disregarded as if her presence held no meaning. She was bone tired of being told what to do every second of the day, shushed when she dared object, and generally talked down to as if she was worth little more than a sack of oats. If not for the baby she would have taken her chances in the wilderness long before, preferring the risk rather than remain stuck in such a life.

Benjamin shifted nervously as he folded his arms over his bared chest, then ran one hand through his unruly ebony hair. Maggie pretended not to pay attention, but she noticed the way he cocked his head and studied her as he spoke to Charles.

"Well, yes, of course. Would ye like to go into town with us, my dear?"

"Business has no place fer women," Charles said gruffly, his plump cheeks flushed like ripe red berries against his grey pallor. Benjamin made a low chortling sound in his throat and waved the man off.

"Then ye know not my wife, Charles. She is quite clever." Benjamin spoke slowly, his voice without waver as he stared the other man down.

"So then bring her, if ye must. There is some new ale up at the Ordinary, we mean to try it. I fear that may not please the lady, but –"

"Ah, no worry. Go water your horses, we will be along soon."

Maggie ducked her head and closed her eyes briefly, feeling her fingernails cut crescents into the skin of her palms as she clenched her fists. She could smell his scent – sweet fresh alfalfa mixed with afternoon sweat, stronger when he slipped a hand under her elbow and pulled her gently to her feet.

"I hope this arrangement pleases you," he offered. She had no idea how to answer him, or what to say to pacify him, not knowing if he spoke of the impending visit to town or of the state of their hasty marriage.

Benjamin was a confusing matter entirely. She had learned much about him in the few weeks of their marriage, and his honorable and gentle nature continued to surprise her. From what she recalled of her history lessons, life was lonely for English settlers, and with a man to woman ratio of nearly six to one, marriage was a luxury few could afford. She wondered how he had been one of the men fortunate enough to have such money to spend on a wife.

"I have no say in how things are done," she finally answered after a long silence. She pulled at the edge of her bodice and made a chore of righting it over her skirts, then bent to brush imaginary straw off her boots.

"Maggie."

She knelt down and began to re-tie her bootlaces. Not yet dissuaded, he knelt beside her and reached out, taking her hands away from the task and holding them between his larger ones. He wore gloves as he often did during the day, but his hands were still warm through the soft leather.

"We have not had much time to know each other, but many marriages start with less than what we have had." He placed his thumb under her jaw and she moved to turn away, but he tucked her chin between his fingers and met her resistance. "I am not such an awful scag, am I?"

A corner of her lip turned up, his earnest appraisal of the situation and his resultant uncertainty in his own appeal causing her to smile against her better judgment. A flush streaked his neck and he grinned, looking down and then up at her and then back to the ground again like a shy adolescent. She took his proffered hand and stood up beside him, watching curiously, as he ran a hand through his thick black hair. Standing there with the setting sun streaming across his back from the open barn door, his broad shoulders filled out a pleasing countenance and unexpectedly she ached with a pang of homesickness. Perhaps it was his kind disposition, or his gentle manner, or maybe the way his hulking form filled out the doorway, but suddenly it all reminded her of Marcus and a farm of her own that was probably falling apart without her.

"No, you're nothing of the sort," she replied.

"No? Well, then, I suppose that is a good start."

She saw his bright eyes soften as he laughed, but then his laugh slowed as he watched her chuckle. Her throat caught and she swallowed back another laugh, seeing the budding desire in his gaze and trying to think of a way to put him off. When he kissed her she did not object. His attentions were careful, controlled, treading carefully as he asked for more.

"I've held ye at night in the darkness," he said softly, "and I've felt yer body beside mine. I wonder, is it different then, when I can see ye like this in the light?"

She swallowed hard when his fingers drifted down her body. His hand brushed over the side of her neck, his thumb caressing her gently. As his lips traced a path down her throat his hand settled lower at the base of her spine. He pulled her close, seemingly eager to answer his own questions.

No, she thought. *Not here, not like this.* She could abide his attention in their bed when darkness settled and the candles were snuffed. Then she could imagine he was another, and somehow, it eased her despair. In the muted daylight of the barn, however, there was no protection from the truth. She froze at his touch and put her palm flat against his chest.

"Please, not here," she whispered.

He looked up and his hands stilled. She closed her eyes in relief when he pulled away.

"Oh, Maggie," he said, caressing her cheek. He gently kissed her lips without pressing for more. "I'm so sorry. I – I should not have – I'm sorry. Here, let me help ye."

He brushed the straw from her hair and straightened her dress, then squeezed her hand.

Feeling more than a bit deceitful, she looked toward the house and held a hand to her ear.

"Do you hear that? I think it's Charles calling, we'd better go inside," she insisted. She grabbed his hand and pulled him toward the house, her chest heaving as she tried to slow her breathing. Although he protested, he followed anyway, and for that, Maggie was quite grateful.

* * *

Maggie tapped the granite mortar against the side of the pestle, the dried herb remnants falling into a fine dust in the cup. Finola glanced over her shoulder as she often did while they worked, nodded approvingly, and then moved back to her place cataloging the various jars along the wall shelves.

She spent as much time as allowed with Finola, and although Benjamin did not entirely approve of her working with the healer, he did not move to stop their visits, so it was all Maggie could do to get there fast enough each day after church.

Maggie rose from her stool and went searching for the loose goldenseal she had brought, and realizing she left it in her gathering basket, she went into the back room to find it. She heard the door open as she rummaged through the basket, knowing it was most likely Benjamin come to fetch her as usual. When she still had not located the wayward bunch of plants, she let out a frustrated sigh and kicked the wall with her boot toe.

"Ah, Maggie, there ye are!"

She glanced up at Benjamin and forced a smile to her lips.

"I think it might be sprained," she lied, rubbing the joint with a grimace.

"Ye surely invite accidents, if I may beg yer pardon for saying so," he smiled. He offered her his arm, and she took it, letting him lead her out into the great room where Finola still hummed away as she worked on her inventory. The older woman appeared engrossed in her task, but she raised an eyebrow at Maggie when Benjamin bent to examine her ankle.

"It does not appear too damaged. Can ye walk on it, or shall I carry ye home?"

Maggie choked on her reply when Finola rolled her eyes skyward.

"No—no! I'm fine, Benjamin, I can walk just fine," she muttered.

Benjamin placed her hand firmly in his elbow and nodded to Finola on the way out with a smile. Maggie's teeth clanked together in the back of her mouth and she cleared her throat to muffle a groan.

It was not that he was unkind, or even that he was not pleasant to be around. In fact, as much as she would admit to herself, he was good company, and he certainly was a handsome young man. There were several women still unattached who had arrived on the same ship Maggie supposedly sailed on, maidens and young widows alike, and Maggie noticed the stares Benjamin garnered anytime he happened into town. He commanded a presence, from his broad shoulders and thick strapping arms to his twinkling blue eyes and boyish grin. Still showing remnants of an unsure youth in his chiseled face, but with the swagger of growing self-assurance, he would be irresistible to any lucky young woman. Had they met in another lifetime, Maggie had no doubt he would have turned her head, but fate being what it was, there was nothing of her heart left for anyone but her child. What was worse, even the thought of softening towards Benjamin felt like a betrayal of what she once shared with Winn.

Benjamin took care in leading her back to the Towne square, where the wives served a hearty mid-day meal to the men. She did not want to join them, but being they were in town for the day they could not refuse the offer Alice made.

She stumbled and Benjamin caught her, a grin on his lips at her scowl. She resisted the urge to simply lift her skirts above her heels instead of kicking through the heavy skirt, but she tried not to embarrass Benjamin in front of the other townsfolk.

A group of braves was tying their horses outside the Ordinary and she spotted Chetan among them, flanked by Makedewa. She had no objection to seeing Chetan and would like to ask how his son fared, but knowing she would see Makedewa as well put a damper on things. She had not seen either of them since the night Nemattanew abducted her, the memories of that time in the village beginning to feel like the whispers of a dream she meant to return to.

"Oh, so good to see ye back! We are nearly ready to eat, find ye a seat," she ordered, shooing them toward the long wooden table in the courtyard. Feeling a distinct rumble of acquiescence from her belly, Maggie was happy to comply and took a seat beside Benjamin on a bench. Aunt Alice joined them at the far end of the table and led them in a short rendition of grace before they all dived in.

"Would you rather rest, my dear? I will take ye in the house if you need so," Benjamin offered, passing her a basket of soft fresh corn bread. She took a helping and passed it to her left as she shook her head at Benjamin.

"I'm fine, thank you," she said. The last place she wanted to rest was anywhere near Thomas, and in fact, sitting at the same table sharing a meal with him as he glared at her with his beady black eyes was more than enough torture for one day.

"Thank ye, Miss," a voice murmured. She tried not to twist around in her seat, but instead settled for shooting Jonathon Pace a look from the corner of one squinted eye.

"You're welcome," she said, as demurely as possible under the circumstances. The man gave her the creeps, and she had nothing nice to say to him. She scooted over a few inches closer to Benjamin.

"Jonathon!" Benjamin bellowed, thrusting his arm across her face to clasp warmly with Jonathon. She leaned back away from the two men, her eyebrows raised, and shoved a piece of corn bread in her mouth. She reached over them to grab her mug of cider and hastily downed it, looking longingly across the table at Benjamin's tall cup of ale.

"Ah, uhm, I will pour ye some ale, dearest, but go easy," Benjamin said, grinning as he removed his own mug from her hands and filled her cider cup with a splash of ale. She looked down at it and hastily handed it back to him. As much as she would like to, she knew it was bad for the baby no matter what century she was in.

"So Opechancanough passed through Jamestown? Must be a special occasion for him to travel so far from his home," Benjamin commented. Maggie felt her cider and bread coming back up at the name of the

Weroance. Jonathon nodded, taking a bite of bread as he reached for a platter of fish passed his way.

He offered it politely to Maggie but she waved it off, content with her ration of boiled ham and pickled beets. Along with the fresh bread, the meal would be quite filling, and she knew with more mouths to feed it would be best to pass the meats to the men.

"Yes, he stayed only one day, but he was quite cordial to the new Governor," Jonathon agreed.

"Was there trouble?"

Maggie swallowed back an over large amount of cider and felt a distinct warmth run from her throat to toes. She hoped she could keep her stomach in check, afraid she would lose her composure in front of all the men. As bad as that would be, it would still be a welcome respite to hearing the two men squawk like a pair of roosters over a pebble of feed at their feet.

"Nay. He brought plenty of warriors with him, no one would dare speak against him. The savage surely is a smart fellow," Jonathon answered. "But those ones, the ones at the Ordinary now, they were with him."

Maggie realized he meant Chetan and Makedewa, and her interest was suddenly held. Did they plan to attack soon? She slipped a hand defensively down over her belly. Benjamin noticed the gesture and patted her knee under the table.

"Yes, he is a smart one," Benjamin agreed. "Perhaps I should speak with the natives about it. Would ye excuse me for a short time, dear? I will return soon."

She nodded wordlessly. She was surprised he would go talk with the brothers, considering the role he played in Winn's death. She was doubly shocked to see the braves in town so soon after the disaster, but sure as well it was part of their plan to extinguish the English. A flutter in her belly spoke volumes as she watched Benjamin walk toward the Indians, who were preparing to mount their ponies. Would her son ever know his people, or would they be his enemies, as most of the English looked upon them?

Relieved to see Benjamin clasp arms with both men, she tried not to appear too interested, but she abruptly realized it was all in her hands. Chetan and Makedewa were kin to her child, and she would be damned if she would be the one to break that bond. Perhaps Makedewa would not care to see her, but she was sure Chetan would, and she knew he would pass a message to Teyas who she missed terribly.

She dropped her mug to the table and went to meet them, ignoring the squawk Aunt Alice uttered and the furious glare Thomas sent her way. She cared no more what either of them thought, and she would not be kept silent any longer.

She silently practiced the Paspahegh words she knew in greeting, and finally decided that a simple *How are you* would do just fine.

"Kulamalsi hach?" she said as she approached. She noticed Benjamin appeared distressed, and for that she was sorry, but she hoped he would understand why she needed to speak to the brothers.

"Fire Heart," Chetan greeted her, bending his head toward her in respect. Makedewa grunted and crossed his arms, but it was an acknowledgement and for that she was grateful. She wondered briefly why Chetan used the name Winn had often called her, the sound of the English version quite different than she was accustomed, but still the words stung her.

"Maggie, I was about to return to ye, there was no need for ye to fetch me," Benjamin laughed, placing his hand on the small of her back. She noticed his voice tremor and ignored it, too eager to speak to the warriors, but he took her hand firmly and turned her back the way they came.

"But Benjamin, I only want to talk to them."

"Good day, brothers," Benjamin said curtly, forcibly guiding her away. She shook her head and shoved him, unable to tolerate his behavior when she only wanted to say a few words to them. Was this how it would be, whenever she wished to see them?

"No! I need to talk to them!"

"We wish happiness for you in your new marriage, Red Woman."

Maggie balked at the sound of Makedewa's cold voice. She turned back and saw Chetan glare at him and make a low barking sound as she had often heard an irritated warrior make, but Makedewa had her attention now and a sneering grin stretched across his face.

"And we will have a feast in honor of your child. May the Great Creator bless you and your husband."

"What?" she whispered as the ground seemed to drop beneath her feet. *Has Benjamin told them?* She struggled to remain unmoved at the hate in his voice and the menace written on his face. He clearly despised her, more than he ever had, and by his words she suspected he thought Benjamin was the father of her babe.

What did it matter? Winn was gone. She could never go back to the Paspahegh village. Her child would never know a father other than Benjamin.

"Let us go," Benjamin insisted. This time she let him lead her.

* * *

Benjamin seemed distracted the rest of the afternoon. The conversations between them were a mere barrage of polite responses, and when it was time to retire she was happy to put the day behind them. If he were sore at her for speaking to the warriors, she would gladly leave him to his sulking. She readied herself for bed and sank down into the deep feather mattress, her mind just as weary of the day as her tired body.

Maggie placed her hand on her taut rounded belly. Just a bulge, easily hidden under her skirts, but soon it would be more apparent and she dreaded anyone else knowing her condition.

Benjamin cracked the door and entered the room. He stared wordlessly at her now, and she could see his round blue eyes stained bloodshot, his shirt unbuttoned and skewed about his neck. He watched her as he undressed, shedding his waistcoat and shirt and stepping out of his tall boots.

"Benjamin, I am sorry if my speaking to the braves upset you," she began, but he cut her off by raising one hand and a firm shake of his head.

"No, wife. I am not upset with ye."

She inhaled as he approached the bed, working the clasp of his buckle to shed his breeches. A wisp of strong brandy, and the telltale remnants of sweet pipe smoke clung to his clothes, and she realized he must have taken his enjoyment before he came to bed. His hair was wild, frazzled in a mop that looked as if he had been running his fingers over his scalp, in his eyes a strange hollow look that reflected some sadness yet undisclosed. Perhaps he would only talk and fall asleep, as he usually did when he drank.

He slid under the quilts and pulled her gently to him, and she let out the breath of air she had been holding.

"Ye are my wife, by the King's law," he said softly, his breath hot against her neck. "My wife."

She made no answer, frozen into helplessness as she lay in his arms. He seemed to need no response, as soon his breath grew shallow and the gentle snores of his inebriated sleep filled the room, and she was content to see his attentions distracted for the evening.

33

Snow was still falling when Winn awoke. Although he could see the dark clouds overhead through the smoke hole from remnants of the last storm, he was warmed from the layers of furs that covered him. The fever had passed days ago, but his muscles still ached as if they had no strength and it was the most he could do to roll onto his side. He could only roll onto the right, lest he risk tearing open the healing wound to his left chest.

Chulensak Asuwak and Teyas tended him faithfully, taking turns cleaning the bullet wound, but despite their attentive efforts it festered anyway. When the fever took him they moved him to the sweat lodge for five days expecting either his death or recovery, he was not sure which. Whatever the intent had been at the time, he was grateful they cared enough to nurse him, since he would need to recover every ounce of his strength before he went to find his wife.

Winn expected the villagers to denounce him when he announced his bond to Maggie, but he was stunned to see that he retained their loyalty. He would never have asked it of them, knowing he risked his own life by defying Opechancanough, and he did not expect any other to stand by his side in defense of a Time Walker. Yet their love humbled him, and he gladly accepted it.

"Brother," Chetan spoke as he entered the yehakin.

Winn opened his eyes and watched the warrior kneel beside him. His eyes were downcast, and by the lines creasing his face Winn could see he was troubled. Makedewa entered a moment later, yet he hung back, his arms crossed over his chest.

"Did you get word to her? Is she well? What say you?" he demanded, his hoarse voice rising as he surveyed his brothers. Winn had only been awake less than a day since the fever broke, but his first thought had been to retrieve Maggie. He knew she watched him fall from the rifle shot, and he feared she would think the worst when he did not return for her. Somehow he staggered out of the furs and made it to the door, but his brothers stopped him and insisted they would carry a message to her.

Now as he looked at the expressions of the two anxious men, he feared to hear their tale.

"She is well, brother. Benjamin Dixon tends to her," Chetan said carefully. Winn noticed that Chetan glanced at Makedewa, who appeared ready to boil over as he waited to speak. Winn nodded with relief to Chetan and looked to his second brother.

"What, Makedewa? Does Chetan not speak truth?"

"He speaks true, brother. Yet he does not tell all. The Red Woman married Benjamin Dixon. She breeds his babe even now."

Winn felt the grip of icy fingers around his neck as his blood rushed cold.

"You must be mistaken," he growled.

"No, it is true. Benjamin told us both by his own tongue. I wanted to kill him and bring her back to you, but Chetan refused me. Give me your word, and I will go back to finish it," Makedewa ground out.

Winn struggled to sit up and was glad the braves did not move to help him. He felt his wound tear, only a minimal disruption, but the healing flesh parted and a fresh gush of blood began to spread over the dressing on his chest.

"No. I do not believe it." Winn grimaced and tried to stand, but at this both warriors moved forward to stop him.

"It is truth. I am sorry. I ask Makedewa to wait to hear your word before we act. We will bring her to you if you wish. You know she is in danger if she stays with the English," Chetan said.

Winn swallowed hard. Benjamin? The man he called brother left him for dead slung over the back of his horse, and then stole his woman? And what of Maggie – his wife, his heart? She would marry another, as if Winn had never existed? He remembered the words she once spoke during an argument.

Whore. A ba♦ woman, she had said, as if the words were most distasteful. *A woman who sleeps with any man.*

No. He would not believe that of her. He would believe the vows they spoke. He could believe nothing else, or risk slipping back down deep into that dank place the fever took him to, that soulless void bereft of light.

"Leave me, brothers," he said. "I will think on these things."

34

She tucked her hands beneath her thighs as she sat on the plank bench next to a young blond-haired girl. The girl did not talk much but Maggie did not mind, content to watch the others dance from her perch away from the festivity.

Benjamin stood across the barn with a handful of similarly dressed men, drinking from a pewter mug that he refilled at least twice from a cask at his feet. She hoped he would drink enough to ensure a quick slumber when they arrived home. He caught her eye and smiled, raising his mug up to her in salute through the crowd of dancers. She tilted her chin up to show him her acknowledgement, and he turned his attention back to the men.

A brisk fiddle beat filled the barn. It was a temporary meeting place in Wolstenholme town, sitting next to the community storehouse, serving the various needs of the citizens until more suitable accommodations were built. Although they went to church twice a day, the English spent an equal amount of time on their entertainment, finding some reason or another to drink and play music nearly every night.

"Would ye care to dance, Miss Dixon?"

She looked up at the grainy voice. Charles Potts stood beside her, hand outstretched in a most polite fashion. His stick-straight hair stood out like thorns beyond his brown woolen hat, his pox-marked face shaved clean for the evening, yet he still held an air of arrogance and she did not want to spend any time in his presence.

She shook her head demurely.

"I'm sorry, I fear I am taken a bit ill. I think I'll take some air."

"Are ye sure? Should I escort ye, miss?"

"Ah, no. Thank you," she said firmly, putting a distinct end to the near uncomfortable discussion. He gave her a quick half-bow as she stood up. She left him standing there and made her way out of the barn.

Once outside, she leaned back on the plank wall and pulled her bodice away from her breast. It was damn hot in the place, with all the warm dancing bodies and half-soused men stumbling around. She fanned her neck and chest with her hand. *There, that felt better.*

The wail of the fiddle could still be heard, the stomps of the dancers thudding off the wall she leaned against. She closed her eyes and let her head fall back, her breath misting as it left her lungs in a sigh.

She thought she heard a rustle of leaves coming from the tree line, distinct from the pounding of dancing feet, yet still the fiddles wailed and she supposed it was only her imagination.

"Ye shouldna be out here by yer lonesome, Miss."

Charles Potts stood in front of her, an arm's length away, her cloak folded over his elbow. She scowled and snatched it from him, but he held onto it and used it as an excuse to move close to her. She shrunk back into the solid wall to keep a proper space between them, suspicious of the gleam in his muddy brown eyes. Her stomach curled when he spit out a chunk of wet tobacco at her feet.

"I'm fine, thank you. I'll be going to find my husband now," she said dismissively, trying to brush past him. His hand shot out to block her exit, braced against the barn at the height of her shoulders. She did not turn to look at him, gritting her jaw as she tried to keep her voice low. If there was one thing she knew for sure about the English, it was their distaste for public embarrassment, and if she caused a scene, she knew she would be considered the one at fault, not the teetering Master Potts.

"Are ye out here meeting someone? Maybe yer savage lover?" he sneered.

"You're a disgusting sod. Let me pass!" she hissed. She shrugged off the hand he placed on her shoulder. "And keep your hands to yourself, you bloody bastard!"

The insult struck a nerve, and before she could get away he shoved her against the wall. His faced came close to hers in all its rancid glory, his breath like curdled milk tainted with ale. Her head snapped back painfully when he clamped a hand over her mouth.

"You best keep that trap shut, if ye know what's good fer ye! Yer the blasted harlot who shacked up with the savages, are ye not?"

She cursed him, her words muffled under his hand. Suddenly he let go, looking her up and down from breast to toes, nodding to himself.

"Off with ye, now. I wouldna touch the leavings of an Indian, in any case," he muttered.

She darted away, her cloak clutched in her hands. It was not the first time a man had made inappropriate advances, and she was certain it would not be the last. The colony was sorely lacking in women, and when the men drank too much they could be quite obnoxious. *Just like men of any other time*, she thought angrily.

When she reached the inside of the barn without further pursuit, she stood there for a moment, scanning the crowd. Her heart hammered like a jackrabbit through her chest as she searched for Benjamin, who she finally spotted in a crowd of men. He saw her and grinned, and raised one finger with his brows raised at her. She nodded and took her former seat watching the dancers.

The frantic squeal of the fiddle rose above the laughter, a rhythmic illusion of happiness in the air. She felt the wetness on her cheek, streaking down as she closed her eyes, wishing the numbness to take her far away.

Looking around at English, skirts rustling and cloaks flinging in dance, she let out a sob and found camaraderie in the tears. Is this how her life would be, and endless cycle of aimless dance, pleasing her husband, pleasing the townsfolk, yet helpless to fill the empty pit where her heart once resided?

Now you will never be lonely, for we will be together.

His voice smothered the noise of the celebration. She could hear it as if he were next to her, holding her hand, brushing his lips across her cheek, the sweet simple touch of the man she missed so much.

But Winn, I am lonely.

She felt a wave of nausea, that gentle reminder of the life growing inside her. She placed her hand over her belly.

She would carry on, because she must. She would endure a life in his time without him, because she must. She would protect their son with the last bit of her breath, if it was needed of her.

And she would love Winn until the day she died.

* * *

The next night Maggie watched as Finola tended the last customer of the day. She was not often present when the healer closed down her wares for the evening, and frankly was puzzled Benjamin left her at the shop for such a lengthy visit. Whatever motive was behind his reasoning, she was grateful for it, happy to relax with Finola. The only comfort she felt of late was spent in the presence of the healer, the only person who knew all her secrets and accepted her as such.

"Some tea, child?" Finola asked. Maggie nodded and rose to help her with the heavy copper kettle.

"Here, let me."

"Nay! Sit yerself, dear, I can manage." The older woman tossed her long blond braid back over her shoulder, her brows raised as she surveyed Maggie. "Has the sickness passed yet? I fear ye eat not enough to feed the babe."

"I'm eating more now, it will be enough," Maggie assured her.

"Ye thinks the wean a boy or girl? I canna see myself what it is."

Maggie smiled as Finola shook her head. The witch had been trying to see the sex of the babe for the last few weeks, eager to give an identity to the child. The English rarely asked for her predictions, so she was out of practice, and with a much more personal stake in the knowledge of Maggie's pregnancy the woman tried every method she knew of to decipher what it would be.

"If only we had an ultrasound, there would be no question," Maggie laughed.

"What do ye speak of? Tell me of this magic!"

"Ah, it's no magic. Just a ... a machine that makes a picture of the baby, inside the womb. It uses sound waves to make the image." Maggie did the best she could explaining the marvelous use of the medical device. Finola was a most avid listener, devouring every tidbit Maggie explained of the life she left behind. In their frequent talks, Maggie had already described television and cameras, so the description of ultrasound was not too far of a leap to comprehend.

"'Tis most useful then, this yulta-sound?"

"Yes," Maggie sighed, knowing she would have no such comforts of the well-being of her babe during the pregnancy. Although she had no bleeding or other indication of problems, she still worried damage was done by the beating she endured. "I would give just about anything to have an ultrasound right now."

Maggie felt Finola pat her hand, then the woman turned quickly back to the boiling kettle.

"Perhaps we should send ye back. Back to ye own time."

Maggie froze. Surely, she had not heard the woman correctly. There was no way to return, Maggie had accepted that fact.

"There is no way to return, is there, Finola?" Maggie asked, her hoarse voice rising shrill the more she spoke. "Please tell me!"

"Aye, I know no way, without yer own Bloodstone," the woman admitted, shaking her head with her eyes fastened on the mug of tea she poured. "But I will go to the Paspahegh village, and try to find it for ye, if that's what you need to be happy, child. It pains me to see you so sad."

Maggie felt the wetness on her cheeks, unaware she was crying.

"You would do that for me?"

"Oh, I would," the woman murmured, taking her into her arms. Maggie squeezed her tight, never in her life knowing what the embrace of a mother's love felt like, yet knowing her friendship with Finola echoed the spirit of it. "Of course I would. My visions told me ye belonged here, but perhaps things have been changed with all that has happened. If sending ye back to yer time would make it all easier to bear, then yes, I would."

"I don't know what I want," Maggie sniffed, feeling the comfort of Finola gently patting her back. "I don't know where I belong. Here, or in the future, I would still miss him. Can the Bloodstone take this pain away, can it make me forget? Or can it take me back..." she stood upright away from Finola, tremors overtaking her body as the ideas leapt into her mind. "Can I go back to stop it? Can I stop what happened that day, to save Winn?" She grabbed Finola's hands, barely able to contain the rush of hope. They sat down together on a wooden bench.

"No, child. It does not work in such a way. You canna live a time more than once. And if ye do not know the runes to direct ye, ye should have a bit of yer place on ye when you go, so the Bloodstone knows where to send ye. It's a tricky thing, ye see."

"Runes? A bit of your place?"

"The mark of a rune will send ye to a place, but if ye have no rune, it can work if ye have a piece of the time yer meant for. Something tied to that place. Anything will do. A button, a brooch, any small tidbit of the time ye mean to travel to. 'Tis no guarantee, but it helps to point the way."

Maggie reached into the folds of her apron and pulled out the raven. The pitted stone was heavy in her hand, but the tiny likeness felt solid. She held it out to Finola.

"Something like this? I brought it with me from my time. How could it matter, it's just a toy."

Finola reached slowly for the charm. The woman raised it up with both hands in front of her face, her blue eyes widening as she studied it. She looked at Maggie, then back to the stone raven, her mouth falling open.

"Where did ye get this?" Finola finally asked.

"I've had it since I was a child. It was a gift." She smiled a bit at the memory of when Marcus gave her the raven. "I was told the raven would chase away my bad dreams, that no one could hurt me as long as the raven watched over me. I've kept it ever since. It traveled through time with me, it's the only thing I have left from the place I come from."

"What is your family name?" Finola demanded, her eyes widening as she abruptly straightened her back.

"McMillian," Maggie replied softly. "My grandfather's name was Malcolm McMillian."

Finola opened her mouth to speak but footsteps interrupted them. They both looked up at the creak of floorboards. Benjamin stood in the doorway. His face was etched in a stony mask, his skin pale beneath his crumpled brows. Behind him was Charles Potts. Maggie stood reflexively and patted down her apron, shielding her eyes as creeping fingers of panic gripped her. *How much of their conversation had the men heard?*

"Good day, Miss Finola," Benjamin said. He nodded curtly to Finola, and took Maggie's hand firmly in his. She did not resist the pressure of his touch, even though his fingers tightened so much she feared he would bruise her.

Maggie met Finola's eyes. They shared one panicked glance before Benjamin pulled her into the street.

* * *

Maggie watched at the window for Benjamin's return. He did not speak to her on the ride home, his gloved hands fisted over the reins, and she was reluctant to spark a conversation. It was clear he overheard some of the exchange, yet Maggie could not tell how much information he gleaned from his eavesdropping.

"Get ye in the house and wait for my return. Stay inside," was all he uttered. He took a fresh horse from the barn and rode off back toward town, and it was the last Maggie had seen of him since he brought her home from her visit with Finola.

A wide bright moon lit the darkness as night wore on. After she had changed into a simple white shift and let her hair down for bed, she finally heard the pounding of hooves against earth and knew he had returned.

"Benjamin! I was worried!" she said as he crossed the room. The door slammed shut behind him with a thud and she felt the tremor of the floorboards beneath her bare feet with the force of it. He shed his cloak and hat, tossing them carelessly into a heap near the fire.

She took a deep breath to steady herself. Turning to the hearth, she reached for a bowl to ladle him a bit of stew, but stopped at the sound of his low, cold voice.

"I want truth between us, my wife," he said evenly, advancing toward her one slow pace at a time. She equaled it by stepping backward, keeping the distance as best she could. She had never seen him so affected, not certain what emotion lay beneath his features as the veins on his neck bulged and sweat glistened on the chest exposed by his half-opened shirt.

"I don't know what you mean," she replied. He reeked of spirits, but his eyes were still sharp as he latched his steady gaze on her. She had never feared Benjamin, yet the manner in which he stalked her made her heart start to thud against her bodice. They had an arrangement; he would not come to her bed without invitation, and with the stench he carried in from the tavern she was certain that time would not be tonight.

Her hand bumped the latch to the bedroom, and she sprung it, trying to slam the door shut before he could reach it. She was certain he would be more reasonable in the morning after he slept off the liquor.

She made a grave error in thinking the door would deter him, and she shrieked when he shouldered the door before she could latch it, and he stalked toward her quickly now as if the door had been no barrier at all.

"Where do ye come from?" he shouted. "Who are yer people?" He grabbed her arms then, and it crossed her mind that she was frightfully tired of men grabbing her like a sack of potatoes. She tried to shake him off, but he was strong, after all, and clearly not ready to budge.

"Stop it!" she cried. He shook her hard.

"Did Winn know? Tell me!" She flinched at mention of his name, and he read the look on her face with ease.

"Stop it, Benjamin, stop it!" she yelled, finally wrenching away from him.

"Ye are my wife, before God we were married. Have ye no love for me at all? Have ye no care to tell me? Ye lay with Winn, tell him your secrets, yet I get not even a sliver of such truth from ye!"

"Benjamin, please—"

"Did ye go to him willingly, or did he kidnap ye?"

"Stop it," she moaned.

"Tell me, wife!"

"Benjamin—"

"No more lies!" he roared.

She bit down hard on her bottom lip to quell her sobs. *What did it matter now?* Let him shout, let him prove he was her husband, let him sate his jealousy, and in the morning he would beg forgiveness and life would go on.

"Why was he worthy of yer secrets, yet I am not?" he demanded.

His shaking hands latched onto her upper arms, and she closed her eyes in anticipation against what was to come. His breath came fast on her skin, hot along her cheek as he took her face into his hands. The less she responded, the harder he held her, until his fingers dug into her tender skin and he drew away with a low uttered swear.

"I saw ye that night, when ye visited with him. I followed him into the woods. I watched him dishonor ye." His throat constricted as he swallowed. "I thought of nothing but saving thee after that," he said quietly.

"I didn't need to be saved," she whispered, tears bursting forth on her pale cheeks.

His lips twisted. "Even now, you love him, don't you? You stand here as my wife, and still, you love him."

She did not reply, but she knew he could read the truth on her face just as surely as she felt it in her heart. He dropped his hands away from her and stepped back.

"I thought I was the better man, but I am not," he said softly. "Charles told the magistrate what we heard. I could not stop him. He's accused ye of witchcraft. They want to hang thee, ye know."

"And you? Do you think I'm a witch?" she asked, her chin tilting up a notch with her words.

"Yes, my wife," he murmured. "I think…I think ye are."

He closed the door behind him when he left, and the latch clicked to lock. She sat down on the bed in the room to wait.

* * *

They came for her at dawn.

She imagined a more orderly abduction, sure the English would treat a woman prisoner in a better fashion than Nemattanew had treated her, yet she was chagrined to discover just how brutal the cultivated whites could be. Bound fist and ankle, her mouth gagged with a dirty bit of rag, she succumbed to the arrest without a fight.

Benjamin watched from a few paces away. By his side stood Charles Potts, his hand resting on Benjamin's shoulder in an apparent show of sympathy.

Someone was laughing, a frivolous, shrieking howl that nearly curled her toes inside her leather boots. It was not until they hurled her up into the wagon that she realized the laughter came from her own lips, only slightly muffled for their efforts to quiet her.

"This is ridiculous!" she screamed, the words emitted as a slur amidst her howling. Jonathon Pace bent over to tie her hands to the bench, and when he came in range, she butted her head against his with a crack. He uttered a rather feminine scream and fell back holding his nose, and then Charles leapt into the wagon.

"She hit me! The witch broke me nose!"

Charles glanced at the bleeding man, and then to Maggie. She shrugged her shoulders and rolled her eyes, and shouted a few foul responses into the rag before Charles lifted his revolver over her head.

"I'll clout ye, witch. No more trouble, ye hear?" he snapped.

Bound beyond any hope of moving, her hands tied to the bench at her side, what other option did she have? She nodded in agreement and slid back as far as she could away from them.

"It's a half-day ride to James City, best ye spend it praying fer yer black soul," Charles added. He gave his companion a kerchief from his pocket, and they all settled back for the ride.

35

Thump. Thump. Maggie grimaced at the infernal banging noise, her eyes still sealed shut from sleep.

Thump.

Damnit, there it was again. The back of her head began to ache, the steady pain washing through her skull in a rhythmic throb. She cracked her swollen eyelids and saw her hands sitting in her lap, bound by a coarse length of rope twisted into a double knot. The wagon lurched, and her head snapped back.

Thump.

The noise was her own head banging against the wooden wagon brace.

She adjusted her hips and squirmed back up against the pole, moving as little as possible when she spotted the three men resting across from her. Jonathon Pace and Charles Potts, still there. *Great, the English have sent her to death accompanied by two village idiots.* Not that it mattered anymore how her life ended, but she did take slight offense at the fact that her security team was chosen from among the incompetent.

Benjamin was the third man. While the two half-wits slumped dozing along with the rocking of the wagon, Benjamin sat across from her, his long legs sprawled so that his heels touched her toes, his arms crossed over his chest. He was staring straight at her.

Maggie bent her legs and pushed hard with her feet to shove away from him, which was not much considering that her ankles were still bound. He slowly uncrossed his arms and sat up, leaning forward toward her, and she flattened herself against the wagon brace to get away from him. His lips twisted at her evasion, but he continued to breach the space between them, placing two fingers to his mouth in a gesture to silence her. She had no reason to trust him, yet she remained quiet. He eyed the other two men, and once satisfied they slept, he swiftly moved across the wagon to take the bench beside her. His lips bent to her ear, but he did not touch her.

"Answer me this, Maggie," he whispered. "Do you love Winn still?"

Her eyes felt too swollen to shed more tears, and thankfully, they were, because the sound of his name sliced through her heart like a blade and it was all she could do not to scream herself senseless. Did Benjamin wish to torture her, as if her mind were not already filled with visions of Winn as she rode to her death? How surely she had misjudged him, thinking Benjamin had a kind heart beating inside his chest.

"I have never stopped," she said softly in reply. There was no more reason for lies between them. She expected the confirmation to wound him further, and wondered if he would be happy to see her hang. Perhaps she deserved his anger for his damaged pride, but she never imagined him such a callous beast.

Benjamin closed his eyes for a moment and then nodded, as if agreeing to his own internal dialogue. When he opened them, he took her bound hands to his lips and kissed them softly.

"Then go. Go to him."

She panicked. *What was he talking about?* She had no time to consider his request. He leaned over and cut the rope that bound her ankles. Before he could free her wrists, Jonathon Pace stood up, and when he saw what Benjamin meant to do he reached for his pistol. Benjamin was faster, and took only a moment to wrestle the gun away and then shoot him point blank in the chest with his own pistol. His blue eyes were cool but steady when Charles jumped to his feet, saw his dead friend, and threw himself at Benjamin as the wagon came skidding to a stop.

"You killed him! You'll hang for this, Dixon!" Charles shouted, his eyes darting from his dead friend to the eerily calm Benjamin.

Maggie heard horses screaming and the wagon lurched when the second shot went off, but she kept hanging onto the bench with her fingertips as the wagon tipped dangerously sideways.

With the second man wounded but still struggling, Benjamin glanced back at her.

"Benjamin!"

"Get out! Go, now!" he shouted. "So help me, Maggie, get out of this wagon! I won't see you hang! Go!"

He pointed his hand, urging her to make escape, but when he turned his palm Maggie caught her breath, her feet frozen in place. It was not often that Benjamin went without gloves, and suddenly she understood why. Singed into his bare hand, pale and aged, was a carved entwined scar.

A knot that looked exactly like her own.

The mark of a Time Walker.

"Benjamin?" she whispered. Their eyes met one last time.

"Go!" he roared, then launched himself at Charles.

She braced against the beam and looked out the back, stumbling as the wagon shifted and falling to her knees. The wagon finally slid to a stop and she took the moment to jump out, landing on her hands and knees in the frigid creek bed. She scrambled to gather her sodden dress in her bound hands and crawled forward, making it up on one leg before she tripped on the heavy fabric and fell face first again.

The sound of screams and gunfire suddenly broke from the front wagon in the caravan, the cries of both horses and men shattering the air. She spit up creek water and tried to push herself back onto her knees, knowing she only had moments before they chased her. Bracing herself on her palms, she wrenched her skirt up to her thighs and rose up on bruised knees when she heard the splashing of footsteps through the water beside her.

She slowly looked up. Two chiseled legs attached to beaded moccasin boots stood before her, water dripping off the gleaming brown skin. A familiar face glared down at her, streaked with red war paint and his chest splattered with blood. Her heart sank as Makedewa bent down with one hand and swiftly jerked her to her feet, knife in his other hand.

She knew her pleas would mean nothing to him, and she would not give him the joy of seeing her beg before he gutted her. She closed her eyes and waited for the blow. Puzzled when it did not arrive, she cracked one eye open to peer at him, and watched as he slid the blade between her wrists and cut her bonds free.

"You are much trouble, Red Woman," he growled. "Come!"

He pulled her through the shallow creek, away from the melee. She looked back at the caravan and shuddered, seeing dozens of Indians in battle with the English. One of the horses was down, struggling to rise, but caught in the stays of the wagon and unable to stand. Braves on their war ponies crashed through the water, their shrieks overtaking the cries of the English. She wondered where Benjamin was, and grabbed Makedewa's arm.

"We have to help Benjamin! He killed two men to help me escape—we can't leave him to die!"

"No! We leave now!" he shouted. She balked and twisted away when he tried to stop her, his hands like steel around her waist as he refused to let her go back.

The bellow of war cries pierced the air and the hooves of running horses sent water splashing in all directions. More warriors approached, a sorrel pony leading them, the gleaming warrior astride its back afire with rage and headed straight for them.

The warrior's chest and face was smeared with red war paint, his head flanked by a crescent of black tipped eagle feathers. His face contorted when he screamed their fierce cry, water spraying around him as he galloped down the creek bed toward them. As Makedewa's hands tightened on her waist she realized he meant to pass her off to the rider and she tried to twist away from him.

Makedewa gripped her forearms with a grunt as the rider thundered toward them, and in the moment before he thrust her upward into the warrior's outstretched arm she wondered if she imagined the flash of bright blue eyes beneath the paint.

The horse scrambled up the riverbank until it was on solid ground, and she grasped its mane to keep from falling off. Half perched, sliding against his chest, he yanked her closer as another rider approached. She recognized Chetan as the second rider in all his war glory, all trace of his gentle nature shadowed by his finery. He nodded at them.

"Go. Take her. We will finish this." Chetan issued the order to her captor and immediately spun his pony around to rejoin the fight. *Had even Chetan abandoned her, and agreed to obey Opechancanough by seeing her dead?*

She had no power to speak, afraid to utter a single syllable or to even look at the warrior behind her. The horse carried them up through a hill pass, then burrowed down deep through a valley where they put space between them and the English. They came upon a familiar formation splitting the mountains, where a waterfall graced a narrow ledge. The horse navigated the path with a steady pace, and Maggie gasped as they passed through the waterfall.

She sat soaked and shaking, but the warrior gave nothing away, and they made tracks out the back of the waterfall through a crevice which led to a sloped grassy alcove.

They had been there together once before. Unchanged since that day, yet still different than when she would live there, the site of her future home awaited them. She remembered him dancing away from the brown bear, saving her life. He took her heart into his keeping that day, and she realized with a pang of despair it was no longer hers to control.

The mouth of a cave was partially concealed in the jagged rock crevice. The rider sat back and the horse came obediently to a stop.

She thought she had no tears left, but when the warrior dipped his head to her shoulder and his arms tightened around her waist, tears came. His voice, strained and low, echoed against her ear.

"Go inside, *Tentay teh.* A fire burns. I will return soon."

PART FOUR

36

Maggie waited for Winn to return as the hours stretched on. She could not control the shaking that wracked her body, and if it stemmed from the cold or the knowledge that Winn lived, she did not know. The long muslin dress was soaked through, the fabric wrapped around her legs and the weight of the layers still pulling her down. She needed to get warm. Standing above the fire, she tried to unfasten the front of her shift, but her fingers were numb and slipped off the tiny buttons. Her teeth chattered and snapped together as the shaking overcame her again, and this time it brought her to her knees.

Winn entered the cave entrance as she gave up on her bindings and pulled a fur up around her shoulders. His blue eyes locked with hers and he slowly approached, his gaze never wavering even as the fur slid from her shoulders in a heap around her hips. The traveling sack fell out of his hand and he dropped to his knees beside her.

"You're here. You're really here," she whispered.

It was all a lie. Winn was warm and breathing and very much alive in front of her. She needed to tell him everything, tell him about the child, and tell him how much she loved him. She needed to touch him, to feel his skin, to know he was truly there. It was the only way she could be certain he was not one of her desperate dreams.

"You're freezing," he said softly.

Her eyes glazed over and Winn was a blur as he bent to help her. He kneeled beside her, and she felt the fabric of her shift give way. He tore off some of the buttons in his haste to rid her of the wet garment, and continued to shed sopping wet fabric from her body until only her thin damp shift remained. She felt him gather her against his warm skin, sharing his heat. He wrapped a dry fur around them both and sat down next to the fire, rubbing her arms to return blood to her frigid limbs.

Maggie reached for him, but his hand circled her wrist and stopped her attempt. He brought her palm upward and gently pressed it to his lips, closing his eyes.

"Oh, Winn," she whispered. He grasped her face in both hands, his eyes searing through to her soul. She moved closer in his arms, and a strangled groan escaped him when she laid a hand over the ragged healing scar on his bare chest. *It was the wound he suffered on the day she believed he had died.*

He abruptly pulled back, holding her at the length of his arms as if she burned. Confused, she bit back her unease. *Why was he pushing her away?*

"I have a gift for you," he said, his voice low. He pulled the fallen fur up over her shoulders, his motions mechanical. A measure of fear replaced her confusion, washing through her blood and leaving a sickly bile sensation in her belly, and when he held the gift out to her, she stifled her cry.

He held the Bloodstone. Although it was wrapped in copper and attached to a long rawhide lanyard, she knew it was the same stone that had brought her to his time. When she did not move to take it, he placed it in her hands and stood up, his face a vacant mask that betrayed no hint of the man she loved.

"You will use the Bloodstone to return…to return to your time," he said. "We will leave when night falls. I will see you safely home."

"No, Winn, I won't go."

"You will. There is nothing for you here."

She blinked back tears. Anger began to replace her despair, rising rapidly to snatch what control she had left. She could not believe he was casting her away, as if he felt nothing for her. Her pride refused to accept his answer, and with shaking fists clenched to her sides she glared back at his stoic face. She grasped the fur to her shoulders and stood to follow him.

"There is nothing here for me, Winn? Then why did you save me from the English?"

"I would not see them hang you. And it pleased me to take you from your English husband." His dismissal stung, but still inflamed her.

"So you *do* care," she accused, reaching for him. He grabbed her by both shoulders, the fur sinking to the ground in a heap. His eyes bored through her and his fingers dug painfully into her skin.

"Do I care you chose the Englishman? I did at one time, but no more. You went to his bed. I would not lie between your legs now where he left his seed."

She slapped him. He turned his cheek but remained otherwise still, although his grip on her arm tightened. Stunned at his lack of emotion, she moved to strike him again, but this time he grabbed her wrist and twisted it, then dropped it as if it burned him.

He turned and left her alone, stalking away out of the cave.

Stunned, she could find no words. She stared at the Bloodstone. It was her Bloodstone, the one she arrived with, the one he hid from her all along. She turned it over in her hand, felt the warmth that spread up her arm. Yes, Winn had kept the stone from her. But would a man who worked so hard to keep her trapped in his time suddenly have a change of heart? For weeks now she had thought him dead. Had he stopped loving her in that time as well? How could he abandon her when she needed him the most? He owed her an explanation. *Yes, he had suffered—but she had suffered, too.*

Maggie clutched the fur around her shoulders and followed him. The bottoms of her feet felt numb as she stumbled along the rocky path. She approached, determined to make him listen, her frustration and pain spilling forth when she grabbed his arm.

"You are a stubborn fool, Winkeohkwet. When did you turn into such a – such a half man?" she demanded. "I thought you were brave

– you said you would always come for me! Yet you *left* me there. Was that a lie, Winn? A lie from a sorry excuse for a man?"

His hands bunched into fists and he stepped back from her, his eyes flashing like black jade. She could see every muscle of his chest tense, the sinews in his thick arms straining as he listened to her taunts.

"I took care of myself when I thought you were dead," she continued. "I did what I had to do to survive. And I'm still standing." Her voice cracked with the last, and she was not sure if he would even respond by the way he looked at her. *Was that passion in his eyes, or hate?*

She glared at him, her breath coming in short gasps, and was caught completely off guard when he grabbed her. Squirming in his arms, she scowled at him, causing him to grasp her face with one hand and hold her with the other. His breath left a brand on her skin, sending ripples of electricity down her spine.

"Why do you taunt me, Maggie? Do you think I can forget? That it does not *burn* me, the thought of you with him?"

"Then release me, if you hate me so much!" she cried.

His eyes were glazed over as if he could see through her, and she could feel the torture of longing running through her starving blood. She did not recognize the man behind the embers of his eyes, his soul consumed by the raging fire, his fingers searing into her skin like burning coals. His thumb brushed over her lower lip.

"Did you tell him you loved him with these lips?"

Maggie's eyes widened when she realized what he meant. *Winn thought she wanteı Benjamin. He believeı she loveı Benjamin.*

She had to tell him the truth, make him understand it was never about love. She could not let him believe such a lie.

"Halloo! Winkeohkwet!"

The familiar call of his brother echoed in the tense air. Time screeched to a stop. Winn held her tightly, his hard gaze imprisoning her in place. The rush of water from the falls sounded so loud, nearly as loud as Winn's stilted breathing, filling the air between them. He let her go and she slowly stepped back away from him. His eyes, once crazed with anger, now echoed with regret.

She struggled to control her shaking. He shouted a greeting in reply to his brothers and stood for a moment with his back to her, his shoulders betraying emotion left unspoken as they heaved and lowered. He finally turned to her, his fists clenched at his sides and his voice cold.

"Go back to the cave. Wait there until I return."

It was far from her nature to give in when he gave such commands, but she knew she had no choice but to obey.

Winn could pretend she was nothing to him and claim he no longer loved her, but she knew him better than that. She doused her despair with the surge of anger rising in her blood, and lifted her chin as she straightened her back. She stalked away to the cave where the fire still burned, her auburn hair whipping in her wake.

Winn did not follow her. She dressed in what was left of her torn garments and watched silently as they prepared to leave.

37

Winn sat ready on his horse. His mount stomped impatiently beneath his body, as if sensing what his master would do. One of the other men gave word to depart, but Winn knew he could not yet go. Chetan gave him a hard look, shaking his head with a sigh when Winn raised his hand to stop them. His glare was full of knowing, as if his brother could read the thoughts that haunted him. The other men did not appear surprised to see Winn dismount and stalk back toward the cave. Someone chuckled, obviously amused at the warrior. Their grumbles meant nothing to him, as they were nothing to him.

He had no plan and knew nothing of what he would do when he saw her. He simmered with rage at her, yet the anger he carried in check was more for himself.

Ntehem, his heart, his love.

How could he still want her? He should not, but he did.

To have her back in his arms after all this time, to touch her soft skin, was torture. He was a liar, and a bad one at that, for he was certain she could see straight through to his soul. It wounded him to know she loved the Englishman and to know she carried the man's child. That was the crux of it, he knew—if she truly still loved him, he would take her no matter who sired the child in her womb. Yet he could not keep her when she loved another.

It was an unbearable truth, one that could not be denied. There was nothing in the world that could make her abandon her stubborn nature, of that, Winn was certain. She had not denied his words when he spoke of her English husband, in fact, it only seemed to inflame her, and Winn vividly recalled the way she once insisted she could not lay with a man she did not love.

It •i• not matter any longer. He woul• not keep a woman who love• another. The bitterness was too strong, and he knew if she stayed, he would become a man he did not wish to be and that he would do things to her that he would regret. Yes, he loved her, but he would let her go. The last gift he could give her was the safety of her own time in the future. Suddenly the only thing he knew was that he needed to make her understand.

Words failed him as he approached her. He meant to tell her he loved her and that no matter what, he always would. There were sweet words he knew would soothe her fire so she could listen, but none of the words emerged. He wanted her safe, but he wanted to ravage her. He wanted to leave her, but the thought of life without her shattered his heart. None of it made sense, the conflict driving his blood frantic through his veins, pounding in his chest.

Her half-dried hair fell in amber ringlets around her shoulders. When he entered the cave she glared at him in challenge, and he was lost. In seconds he crossed the space and was on her, eliciting a startled cry before he crushed his mouth to hers.

She pushed at his chest as if to stop him, but it was too late. He lifted her by the waist and parted her thighs with his knee as he pressed her harder against the stone wall, oblivious or uncaring of her protest he did not know. The feel of her in his arms, her skin sliding against his, sent his senses to that place between darkness and light where he could hold her forever and never account for his sins. There he could possess her soul, hold it captive, pretend she felt love for no other, let her soothe the aching emptiness she left in the hollow of his chest.

"I will have you!" he whispered in a guttural groan as he lifted her hips and plunged. He lost his breath as her slippery tightness surrounded him, and she drove her teeth to his shoulder as she cried out.

A primal moan escaped him and he succumbed to the need, gripping her hips in his hands again as he started to move. He could not bear the sweetness of her embrace, the way her mouth parted slightly open, her soft white throat thrown back so he could see her pulse throbbing at her jaw. He could need no other, love no other, and for each day he lived without her, he would picture her like that, in the final moment he gave her glorious release.

He clutched her so tightly he could feel her heart pounding against his chest, until he broke the embrace and lowered his forehead against her shoulder. She looked up when he raised his head, meeting his gaze with the beginning of a shy smile.

Her smile tore a hole through his heart.

She looked radiant. *Happy. Like a woman in love.*

But he knew better, and he hated himself for needing more from her, for needing her whole heart instead of fragments of what they once shared. *Perhaps she ha♦ stare♦ at her English husban♦ the same way.*

"Did he ever take you like that, Fire Heart?" he asked, the words seeming to come from some foreign place he no longer recognized. He knew he was a swine. Her rosy cheeks suddenly lost color and tears rimmed her eyes at his words. He deflected her blow but held her wrist tight.

"Winn..." she whispered. Winn stepped back and let his breechcloth fall, his throat tight and dry with the cruelty of his own words. She slid slightly downward on the wall as if her legs lacked strength.

He ha♦ to put ♦istance between them before his shattere♦ pri♦e begge♦ her to love him once more, an♦ he resorte♦ to taking what scraps she might bestow upon him.

"Stay here. When I return, I will show you how to use the stone and you will go home. You will be safe in your future time. There is nothing left for you here."

He turned and left.

It was finishe♦. He would send her back with the Bloodstone to the life she missed, the only gift he could give her, sending her away with the broken remnants of his blackened heart in her keeping.

* * *

It had only taken minutes for Winn to rejoin the others, but he could see from their stares they wondered what had happened. He ignored Chetan's questioning glance as he stalked to his mount and threw himself astride.

They searched the site of the ambush, but the English were long gone. One wagon remained, the horse lathered and heaving as it lay in the creek with the cold water rushing over its broken leg. Makedewa put an arrow through its skull to give it peace, and the animal ceased its struggle.

"Two whites were left. I saw them ride back to Wolstenholme Towne. They had Benjamin Dixon bound and took him as well," Makedewa said, swinging his bow over his back. "I followed them for some time. They say they will see him hang."

"Let him hang," Winn muttered, turning his shoulder to his brother. Their plan was to find The Pale Witch and bring her to safety before the attack on the whites was put in motion, and he would not be swayed. He knew his actions only drove the wedge deeper between him and his uncle, but Winn would not allow Maggie or his grandmother to die in the Great Assault. *She was no longer his wife, but he woul♦ not let her be harme♦.*

Maggie was safe. Soon Finola would be as well. If the Creator meant for him to kill more Englishmen, then he would gladly do it. Perhaps the blood would silence the shouts in his head, quell the anger he felt. It might ease the burden of knowing he had lost everything.

He walked off a few paces and pulled his breechcloth aside to relieve himself before they mounted the horses again. *Damn Benjamin, let him hang for what he ha♦ ♦one,* Winn thought bitterly as the stream came forth onto the soil. What kind of man could let his wife hang? As much as Maggie had ever enraged him, and no matter what had been left unsaid between them, he would still die himself before he watched her swing from a noose. It hardened his heart to know a man he once called brother held so little care for the woman he took such trouble to steal away from him. If Winn and his brothers had arrived moments later, they would have missed the Englishmen taking Maggie away in the wagon. *She woul◆ be ◆ea◆, because of Benjamin.*

The stream ended, and Winn replaced his breechcloth, dropping it back in place and then tightening the cord at his waist. An image of Maggie entered his vision, when he helped her shed her wet dress and she kneeled beside him in her damp cotton shift. By the Creator, he would remember her that way for all of his days, the curve of her sweet rounded belly beneath his hand, her eyes alight as if she still belonged to him. He shook off the memory before the urge to turn his horse around took over.

"What is it, brother?"

Winn did not turn to Makedewa, struggling to keep his voice even.

"Tell me again what you know. How far gone is Maggie with the child?"

"I know not. Benjamin Dixon said she breeds, but not how long."

Bile burned his throat as he realized the truth. Her protests, her anger when he taunted her about Benjamin. Her swollen belly, her heavy breasts. He had seen many women with child, and suddenly it hit him that Maggie was not newly pregnant, she looked a few months gone. In his jealous rage, he failed to realize the truth. *She was carrying his chil◆, an◆ he ha◆ ravishe◆ her like a rutting stag against a stone wall.* That is what she had tried to tell him, and he was too foolish and jaded in his jealousy to listen to the truth. He thought he would vomit. He was a fool.

"Dixon is mine to kill when we arrive." Winn walked away from him, but Makedewa followed at his flank, his face wide in astonishment.

"What mean you? I thought –"

"That one...he deserves death for his deceit." He let his words fall off, unwilling to meet his brother's eye at his rash change in plan. "You say they took Benjamin back to town?"

"Yes, he was bound and gagged. I think they beat him as well, his face looked like deer meat," Makedewa grinned, but then became thoughtful. "You know, brother, she will hate you if you kill the father of her child."

"The child she carries is my blood."

Winn scowled and Makedewa raised an eyebrow but refrained from asking any more questions.

38

Maggie left her horse ground tied in the woods, and made the rest of the way on foot. She was close enough to town, and although she knew a way to steal inside near Finola's cabin, she thought the horse was better off hidden in the brush. She knew if she was spotted there would be no way out this time. Although she tried to hide her flaming hair by dividing it into two thick braids, she would not go unnoticed by any stretch of imagination.

Winn was going to kill her if he discovered she left the cave. Well, she'd be back before he returned, and then they would pick up where they left off.

The fact that Winn was alive still stung her, and his hateful parting words left her reeling. She did not know which emotion was stronger, the frustration and rage she wished to return to him, or the desperate heartache that threatened to break her down. *How could he be so cruel?* He had no idea what she had been through. She had done what she had to do to ensure the safety of their child, yet he behaved as if she had some choice in the matter. She had no choice in being kidnapped, nor in anything else that happened – yet she was still standing, and she would still try to make Winn understand.

Yet there was one thing she must do before that happened. She heard the men talking about Benjamin. Despite what he had done in his jealous rage, he had chosen to save her in the end. After trying to reason with Winn, Maggie could certainly understand how betrayal and the pain of a broken heart could make a person do things in anger. She did not love him, but she could not leave Benjamin to die.

She came up behind Finola's cabin and peeked around a corner toward the church, knowing most of the activity took place down that end of town and people tended to gather nearby. The sun had barely risen for the day so she did not expect much activity, and she was lucky to find no prying eyes as she darted through the front door of the cabin. She slammed it closed behind her and immediately checked the lone window. Satisfied no one approached, she turned to Finola.

"Maggie?" the older woman cried, swiftly crossing the room and throwing her arms around her. Maggie clutched her in return as they cried, while Finola patted her face and kissed her cheeks in joy.

"How did ye escape them? Was it Benjamin? He promised me he would free ye! Why did you come back, girl, ye must go! Ye cannot stay here!"

"Finola, he saved me. He killed two men to set me free. We have to help him."

"Ye make no sense! Ye must leave this place! Go to Chetan, he may know where Winn hid your Bloodstone, and 'tis the only way for ye to return to your time. Please, Maggie," Finola pleaded, grasping her hands tightly in her own. "Winn would have wanted you safe. You cannot stay here; even I am no longer safe. I will move on, but you must try to return. It is the only way."

Maggie felt her throat tense. She gripped Finola's hands tighter so she could find the right words.

"Winn is not dead, Finola. He lives still." Her explanation came forth in a rush, jumbled and scattered, but the truth none the same. Finola froze at her tale, nary taking a breath, until tears began to stream down her beautiful weathered face.

"My grandson lives," Finola whispered. Maggie held her again as they both cried.

"Yes. I'll take you to him. But we need to help Benjamin right now. He—he's a Time Walker, like me," Maggie said. "We'll help Benjamin, and then join the others. Winn left me in a cave, I'm sure I can find the way back to it."

Maggie shrugged off the lingering anger she held for Winn, still overcome by relief that he was alive. Yes, Winn would be furious she left the cave, but she would be damned if she let the brooding warrior make demands after he let her believe he was dead for so long. She could stomp off in a temper just as well as he could, and if he was hell bent on pushing her away, then she would make him pay for it.

Finola considered her words for a tenuous moment, then patted her hand.

"I will bring Benjamin his Bloodstone. It is the only way to free him now."

Maggie's yes met hers.

"You knew he was a Blooded One?" she asked.

Finola nodded.

* * *

Maggie sat down hard on a bench as Finola recounted her tale. Finola was there the day Benjamin was found by the English, a skinny, mute, starving boy dressed in strange blue trousers and half mad with hunger. Adopted by Agatha Dixon, Finola helped nurse the ten-year old back to health, and he eventually found his tongue.

She kept the secrets he shared with her about the strange place he came from, a place where children drove things called bicycles and adults put their offspring in daycare all week. He spoke of a father he rarely saw, but cried when he could no longer remember his face. She kept his darkest secret safely in her cabin, swathed in silk and tucked underneath her mattress. She had found the loose stone in his pocket, a near black Bloodstone creased with a single vein of crimson, and she wrapped it in copper and hung it from a rawhide cord in anticipation of the day he might wear it around his neck.

"Benjamin was a Blooded One," she whispered, already knowing the answer. "A Time Walker. He was marked like me." She saw the brand that seared him when he set her free in the wagon, the mark that mirrored the one on her own hand. She held her scarred palm out to Finola, who nodded sadly.

"I know not from what time he comes."

"We need to get it to him. He can go back to his own time and be safe again."

The woman frowned as she considered it. "It seems that Blooded Ones in the future have lost the knowledge of the power that runs in their veins. Even if it is safe in that time, it is too dangerous, child. What if the English see you?"

"We have to try. I can't just let him die. He saved my life, even if he took his sweet time about it. If we can send him back, we have to risk it."

"Well," Finola said, looking her up and down with a frown. "Ye best change into something suitable, and take ye my cloak. Get ye dressed, and hurry about it."

Maggie nodded, wordless. Finola placed a cap over her bright own blond locks and put a cape over her shoulders, and Maggie changed quickly into one of her dresses. She tucked her hair under a white bonnet and donned a hooded cloak, which shielded her face when she kept it lowered.

She hoped they would never suspect she might return to town. Hell, she knew it was not one of her best schemes, but she found her actions fueled by pure adrenaline after the events of the day.

Finola's dress was quite serviceable yet much less appropriate for scrambling through the underbrush. It would have to do. Dressed like an Englishwoman, Maggie hoped she would blend in without much notice as they walked through town to the church.

"Let's go, before I change my mind," Finola murmured, and Maggie complied. They left the store, arm in arm, walking briskly down the street toward the church where they held Benjamin.

Maggie peered out from under her hood at the lone man guarding the church and let out a sigh. She had never seen the man before, so hopefully he would not recognize her. Even with such luck, she clung to Finola's arm and let the healer do the talking.

"I would see Benjamin Dixon to pray with him and offer him a meal. Ye would not deny the man such comfort in his last hours?"

"Nay, Miss. But be quick about it. The Gov'ner will have my neck if ye dally. What do ye have for him?"

"Ah, a bit of bread and some cheese. Would you like a taste? 'Tis plenty enough here," Finola said. The man grunted an acknowledgement and thrust his hand into the basket Finola carried, producing a thick slice of warm bread which he proceeded to stuff into his mouth. Maggie let out a sigh of relief, wondering how long the poor bloke would be passed out once the poppy extract hit him.

"Thank ye, sir. We shall not be long."

They entered the church and closed the heavy door behind them. Maggie flung the hood off her head when she saw it was empty save for Benjamin, tied neatly to a pew.

They ran down the aisle to him, with Finola fumbling for the Bloodstone as she dropped down beside him.

"Benjamin!" she hissed. "Wake up!"

When he did not stir, Maggie shook his shoulders as hard as she could, unwilling to slap him when his face was so bruised and beaten. The wood pew shuddered beneath them when he jerked upright with a groan.

"Maggie? What?" he said, seeming confused at first. He glanced around with his demeanor changed, and he glared at her as if she were the devil.

"Why are ye here?" he demanded. "Have ye not a lick of sense in yer brain? Did I set ye free for naught?"

"Benjamin –" she said, trying to get his attention.

"And you, Finola! Of all of them, ye would help her? Ah, get ye gone, the both of ye! Let me die without the lot of ye wailing about it."

"Oh, for Pete's sake, Benjamin! Shut up for one minute!" she snapped, thrusting the Bloodstone into his hand. "You can go home now, and leave this all behind. I won't let you die for this, you idiot!"

He jumped back away from the Bloodstone as if burned, his skin draining to a sickly grey pallor.

"Get that away from me!"

"Take it, you stubborn ox!"

"Nay, I will take none of ye cursed magic!"

"You'd rather die here, at the end of a rope?" Maggie asked.

"Do ye seek to punish me for my sins, witch? Yes, I knew Winn lived. Yes, I told his brothers ye carried my child, and now I will hang for what I've done. Let me hang in peace, and take that cursed stone away!"

"You—*what?*" she screamed. "You *bastard!* You knew all along? You let me think he was dead! How could you?"

Maggie leapt at him then, screeching out her anger at his deceit. He gave no resistance, letting her strike him even as welts formed across his face from her blows. Finola pulled her off him as best she could.

"Enough, child, enough!" Finola cried.

"How could you do it? You knew the whole time? You let me mourn him. Did you plan this—this whole thing?" Maggie whispered, overcome with disbelief of how he had let her suffer. She knew he heard it, she could see by the way his shoulders slumped in defeat. Eyes rimmed red, he looked up at her as she strained against Finola with intent to attack him again.

"I sent him back to the village on his horse, he was near death. I was sure he died," he admitted. "He asked me to take care of you. I thought he was gone."

"But you knew he survived. It was that day in town, when you spoke to Makedewa and Chetan, wasn't it?" she said softly, knowing what his answer would be before he nodded.

"Yes. They told me he was gravely wounded, but that he lived," he said. "I knew you would want to go to him. I thought I could keep you – I thought you might love me too, someday, when your memory of him faded. By then, you were my wife...and I did not want to lose you."

Maggie felt her knees give way and she sank down beside him on the bench.

"You did a good job hiding your scar all this time," she whispered. Would it have mattered if she knew he was a Time Walker? She did not know, but she felt like there was much more to his story than either Finola or Benjamin had revealed.

"She told me to keep it secret, as if my life depended on it," he looked at Finola. "It was easy enough to hide."

Maggie nodded. She knew how one might hide a small scar on the palm. After all, it was a chore she had grown quite adept at as well.

Finola reached into her pocket as Benjamin shrunk away from them. He could hardly move due to the binding, but he made quite an effort, so much that Maggie thought he would cut off circulation to his wrists.

If only it were his blasted lying neck, they would be through with him. Perhaps she should let him hang after all.

"Here. You will need this to return to your time," Finola said, holding the object out to him.

Maggie felt the breath leave her body as she looked at the object in Finola's hand. Sitting there, pitted and scarred, just about the size of her palm, was a stone eagle.

The mate of her raven. She had last seen it in the hand of her childhood playmate, what seemed a hundred years ago.

Marcus's son.

She was frozen in place, watching as if she had left her body, staring at the scene in front of her yet not truly living it.

Finola took a small blade from her pocket, and Benjamin held out his hand. He nodded, resigned, tears streaming down his face.

"Tell me, Finola, that I shall not go to hell by using this magic," he begged. His outstretched hand wavered until she took it into her own. Finola cut the rope from his bound wrists.

"Nay, dearest. Ye will only go back where ye belong."

With a flick of her wrist, the Pale Witch sliced his hand and placed the Bloodstone in his palm. As she closed his fingers over the stone, Maggie took the raven from her pocket.

"Oh, Benjamin. I didn't know," she whispered.

He kneeled down on the ground, the pulse throbbing in his temple as he gripped the stone, his tortured gaze boring into Maggie as if there might be some semblance of care left between them. His eyes widened with recognition when he saw the raven, and then they watched him flicker like a ghost until he was no more.

"Tell your father I love him." she said softly.

* * *

Finola patted her shoulder.

Finola ladled stew for them both into glass bowls and set them on the table. Maggie stared at it, unmoving, unwilling to acknowledge the events of the day. The healer ate in silence, casting Maggie an occasional raised eyebrow, but otherwise leaving her to her own thoughts.

They both looked up when the door opened.

"Ah, I beg yer pardon, but the store is not open today," Finola twittered as an unfamiliar brave entered the parlor. He made no sign of hearing her. The scalplock hair made Maggie nervous. She wondered what tribe he hailed from, and why he chose Finola's store when it was in Paspahegh territory.

"Perhaps ye did not hear me, sir," Finola said. The braves studied the axe hanging above the mantle. Her heart leapt into her throat when he pulled it down from its hooks.

"That is not for sale, sir!" Finola cried.

Maggie grabbed Finola's hand, and swung up the brace holding the door. Too late by far, she retreated slowly backward as another unfamiliar brave entered the house. He held a knife in one hand, and wore an empty stare as he approached, his skin smeared with not war paint, but blood. He did not look dressed for attack but his demeanor clearly spoke otherwise, and Maggie swallowed down a hard lump in her throat as he spoke to the first man. She pushed Finola back. She knew exactly what was happening. It was why Winn left her in the cave, and why he left with his brothers.

It was the day she dreaded would come.

She knew few details, the occurrence only one tiny speck amongst the inkblot of history she learned as a child, but of what she could recall, it began in an innocent manner.

In the Indian Massacre of 1622, even women and children were slaughtered. The Indians came unarmed into the homes of the English, and under guise of selling provisions, used whatever tools lay about to kill them. At Martin's Hundred, more than half were killed, and only two houses and the church left standing.

"Leave us be," Maggie demanded, her voice much braver than she felt. She gasped when Finola tried to strike the man with her knife and was cruelly knocked to the floor.

"No!" Maggie tried to get to Finola, but the first man grabbed her by the throat and shoved her back against the hearth. She clawed at his wrist as her airway was squeezed, wheezing a single breath when he took her braid in his fist and pulled her head back. He thrust his face close to hers, and she winced at his rancid breath, rapidly losing consciousness for the lack of air. The next moments were a blur. She heard the door crash open and a clamor of men shouting in Paspahegh, but she felt very little as her body slumped to the floor by the hearth.

Two firm hands pulled her to a sitting position, and she began to choke at the influx of air that suddenly rushed into her lungs. Tears flooded her vision and she reached out in a panic to ward off the one who held her, slapping and scratching like a cat. She felt her nails connect with flesh and heard a low uttered curse, but instead of the blow she expected, she was crushed against a wide warm chest.

"Maggie, shhh, stop fighting me," Winn demanded. She shuddered as she gasped for air, clutching his shoulders at first but then pushing him away.

"You!" she shouted. "Have you come to finish me off?"

His jaw hardened and his blue eyes bore down on her.

"No, *Keptchat*! I kill my kind to save your blasted white skin!" he snarled, glancing toward the two dead warriors on the floor. Chetan stood behind him, and Makedewa had Finola cradled in his arms. "Why do you not listen? I told you to stay at the cave!"

"I had to help Benjamin!"

"Benjamin? You help him, a man that sends you to hang? You would be dead right now if we did not come for Finola! Dead, woman! *Damn you!*" he roared.

Maggie struck out at him and he lunged forward on his knees, shoving her back against the mantle. He took the fallen axe at his side and pounded it into the wall where it split the wood with a sickly cracking sound beside her head. She did not flinch, glowering back at him in defiance, wordless in her fury as her chest heaved and her heart thundered.

"He's a Blooded One, like me! He came from my time!" she shouted. She could see the pulse in his neck throbbing as he grabbed both her shoulders, his fingers digging into her skin.

"So you risk your life – and the life of my son – for him?"

Chetan grabbed her forearm and hauled her to her feet, his other hand firm against Winn's chest to hold him off when Winn stood up and reached for her.

"This fight will wait," he said. "I will take her with me. We must go." Chetan glared at Winn in challenge, and Winn punched his brother's fist away.

"No. She rides with me," he growled, snatching her hand away from Chetan. Maggie scowled, but did not argue. Chetan was right, they needed to leave.

* * *

Winn held her wrist in an unbreakable grip as he pulled her through the streets of Wolstenholme Towne. She followed mutely behind as their small group navigated the clay packed path, Chetan leading the way. Shorter than the other men, with sharp eyes and a distinct sense of direction, Chetan ushered them quietly along.

The silence in the air was unexpected as they tried to steal out of town unnoticed. Maggie looked at Winn's chest, splattered with fresh blood, and wondered if he had taken part in the planned massacre before he found them. The blood did not belong to him and she could see his body remained undamaged, yet she could not fathom if that was a comforting fact or not.

As they rounded the corner of a house, a woman's scream pierced the air followed by a sickening thump. Heavy footsteps thudded over plank flooring, tap, tap, tapping as they approached. Maggie stood paralyzed as the front door flew open and Master John Boise came running out, stumbling down the stairs, his eyes wild with fear. He saw her there with Winn and his face crumpled.

"Oh, Miss! Run! Run, get ye gone!" he cried. He reached out for her hand, but before he could grab her, he fell face down to the ground with a distinct uttered sigh, a bloody axe impaled along his spine.

A warrior left the house closest to them. The unfamiliar brave approached them, his stride long and even, a tall, muscular fellow with bulging biceps and a single feather tucked in his hair, yet he stood otherwise undecorated. Maggie remembered that it was part of their plan, to arrive as any other day, and take the settlers by surprise.

She looked up at Winn, decorated more extravagantly with his war paint and feathers, looking every bit the mythical warrior, as did Chetan. She had no time to wonder why when he suddenly snatched her roughly around the neck with one arm and placed a knife to her throat. He barked something at his brothers, and she watched helplessly as they spoke.

The warrior asked Winn a question, and Winn made an equally brisk response.

"I take this one. Find your own!" Winn growled. Maggie twisted against his steel embrace, elbowing him sharply in the ribs. She felt him flinch, but he made no sound, only squeezing her tighter as she struggled.

Heavy soot filled the air carried by the afternoon breeze, clogging her throat and causing her eyes to water, even more so than Winn's grip around her neck. Houses erupted in flames around them, the roof of the house behind them devoured by fire in mere seconds.

"Help me! Help! Help!" another voice cried. Although Winn still held her, they all turned to stare at the young girl who ran screaming from the burning house behind them. A mountain of blond curls streamed after her as she flew past them, her rosy red cheeks stained with blood and tears as she cried. She stumbled and fell, leapt to her feet, and continued running out into the meadow beyond the open palisade gates.

The stranger took off after her.

"Winn, please, don't let him hurt her!" Maggie pleaded. His grip around her throat lessened and finally he dropped his hand as they watched the man pursue the young girl.

"Makedewa!" Winn shouted.

At the sight of the girl, Makedewa dropped Finola none to gently onto the ground, and took off in pursuit. He sprinted after the man who followed her, reaching him quickly. He launched himself at the man and brought him to the ground. Although more wiry than brawn, Makedewa was built like a wrestler with long lean muscles and surprising strength. By the time they reached him, the larger warrior was dead, his throat cut from ear to ear.

The blond-haired girl began to scream as Makedewa stood over her, her hysterical cries merely adding to the sudden onset of wailing from the town. She sat on her backside, her eyes frantic, her mouth agape.

"Yours?" Winn asked, eyeing his brother. Makedewa crouched next to the screaming girl. He put out one hand to touch her and she slapped him away, screaming louder as if it would have more impact with more volume, kicking her tiny feet about the sand as her cheeks flushed raw. She could not be more than fourteen or fifteen, and she was scared senseless by the looks of her.

Maggie noticed the look between the men. Winn arched one brow, and Makedewa nodded back so slightly she would have missed it had she not been looking.

She turned back toward the town as the men decided what to do with the girl.

Near the palisade gates, a young man laid, his neck in an unnatural angle. An ear of corn was shoved down his throat, the yellow silken end waving in the breeze, but his cause of death was more likely the garden hoe impaled in his chest. A boy lay beside him, a child of no more than five, his head cocked at an unnatural angle beneath his starched white collar.

A woman ran screaming down the middle of the street, quickly fallen by the blow of a well-aimed sickle. A warrior walked up behind her, snatched the sickle from the woman's fallen body, and took a path into the next house.

"Come, we must go!" Winn said. Chetan gave a shrill whistle, and their ponies came forth from the wood line. Chetan mounted up with Finola, who looked to be waking up, and Makedewa tried to get the girl to her feet.

This time she bit him when he reached for her, and Maggie held her breath. Makedewa was no softhearted brave. Although she had never seen the younger brother with a woman, she suspected he would not handle her assault well.

"Let me," Maggie said, leaving Winn's side. She kneeled down beside the girl. Although the blond-haired hellion did not fight her, she looked like a fuse about to ignite. She sat there shaking with her curls sticking out around her face, sprawled on the ground with her apron around her knees and a look of sheer terror etched on her face.

"What's your name?" she said softly. The girl stared blankly back at Maggie, then looked at Makedewa and Winn, then returned to Maggie.

"Rebecca," the girl said very softly, so low that Maggie knew the others had not heard it. Maggie reached slowly and took her shaking hand. Filthy with blood and dirt, Maggie patted it, hoping to gain her trust so they could all live to see another day.

Fires roared behind them, the flames jumping from house to rooftop, swallowing anything in its path. The blacksmith shop ignited with a bang, the explosion sending them all to their knees with hands over their heads.

"Rebecca," Maggie said, pulling the girl to her feet. "Ride with us if you want to live. No one will hurt you."

"They killed my parents, and my baby brother," she whispered.

"It was not these men. Trust me. They mean you no harm. You'll ride with Makedewa, I promise we'll be safe."

She tilted her head to Makedewa, who stood watching the exchange with Winn a few paces away. Winn swung up on his pony and held out a hand for her, and she used his foot as an anchor to swing up behind her husband.

Makedewa held out his hand to Rebecca, and this time, after one quick look back at the burning town, she took it without biting or slapping him. The girl settled behind the warrior and they prodded their horses into a gallop.

The stank odor of burning flesh clung to them as they raced away from the scene, the cries of the dying following them for miles, even as they passed long out of range.

It would take more than distance to forget such a day, if ever they could. Maggie glanced back over her shoulder at the blazing town and shuddered. She clenched her arms tighter on Winn's waist and hugged him.

* * *

The horse stopped from nearly a full gallop by burying his haunches in the dirt, his response immediate to Winn's command. The warrior pulled Maggie into his arms and jumped clear of the beast in one motion, his stride purposeful yet laced with anger as he stalked to the cave. She knew better than to argue. Her skin tingled under his touch when he finally placed his hands on her face, cupping her jaw and clenching her hair with such desperation that she could feel the anguish and fear coarse through him. His skin was stained with the scent of smoke and when he kissed her she tasted the whisky he shared with the settlers before the slaughter. *Had he obeyed his uncle? Had he participated in the massacre?*

His blue eyes clouded as he pulled back, searching her own desperate gaze for a moment. Short, tender kisses followed along her cheeks, her neck, and back to her forehead, where he rested his head against hers. She could not bear to move, her shaking contained by the way he clutched her to his bared chest slick with sweat and blood. Neither one of them dared a word. Their silent truce remained intact when he released her, a fragile stalemate created between them.

Maggie let out a whispered objection as he broke the embrace, but obeyed when he pushed her down to the furs at their feet. She let him cover her with dry furs, sitting cross-legged next to the fire he started. She worried he would never speak or that he would leave, and she felt panicked until he sat down behind her on the furs. Her eyes closed as his arms surrounded her, drawing her back to nest in his lap. She writhed around in his lap to face him when his lips caressed her ear and he chuckled, but she did not miss the edge of sadness in the gesture.

"My stubborn little Fire Heart," he said, his lips still buried in her hair. "Why didn't you tell me the truth?" he asked.

Her words caught in her throat as she returned his stare. Sad, sincere, his eyes were like windows through the warrior, a glimpse of the tormented soul within. She hated to know she caused him such grief, and although there were many more players in this tragedy to cast blame on, the knowledge was of little comfort.

"I was angry at you for being so cold to me," she whispered. "You let me think you were dead."

"I sent my brothers to Benjamin with word that I lived, but it was too late. You married him," he said quietly.

"I saw Thomas Martin shoot you. He said you were dead, he brought your Bloodstone to me as proof." She touched his face with her fingertips. "Then I found out I was carrying our child. I – I didn't know what to do."

She shook her head when he tried to interrupt. "I tried to stop Thomas from firing his rifle that day, and he...he did not take it well." She swallowed to steady her voice, omitting how Thomas had beaten her severely. "I had to get away from him – he was going to send me to England. Benjamin said he would help me. He said he promised you he would protect me. I thought – I thought you would want me to survive. That you would want our child to be safe," she paused. "I thought you were dead. If you were alive, why didn't you come for me? How could you leave me there? How could you let me *mourn* you?"

His shoulders dropped and his face creased as if the breath had been stolen from his chest, his arms tightening around her when he pressed his lips into her damp hair. He closed his eyes as he inhaled and kissed her ear very softly, then released his sigh in a low rush.

"Makedewa. He told me you carried a child and that you were happy with your husband. I would not steal you away from your happiness...even if it was not with me."

"But—" she reeled, confused. "Oh...I see. You thought...you thought Benjamin was the father. You thought I *wanted* to be there?"

He did not answer, and his silence infuriated her.

"So why not just leave me to hang then, if that's what you thought?"

"You took my pride when you married him, but still I loved you. I would not let you hang."

"But you would send me back to my own time, then? With no explanation?"

He pressed his lips against her cheek and she felt his arms tense. "You once said you would give anything to return to your time. I had your Bloodstone. It was all I could give you. It was my only way to protect you."

Maggie closed her eyes. *So much has happened.*

"Oh, Winn," she whispered. "When they told me you were dead, nothing mattered to me anymore. I never loved him, Winn, it was never like that. I wanted to die with you, and damn you, I tried! But then there was the baby...and a reason to keep breathing, at least for one more day."

She felt his wordless nod against her hair and his chest expanded as he let out a deep sigh.

"I know something of this pain." His gentle hands closed tighter, and he clutched her back against his chest, his words forced out through a half-choke, half-groan. "I wanted to explain, to tell you so many things.

Then I saw you standing there, a fire goddess, like you would strike me down before you let me touch you, I – I lost my head."

She reached out to touch his face, but he caught her hand and pressed it to his chest against his heart, where she could feel the tortured thud as it beat against her palm.

"I was a fool. Yes, I stayed away, but I knew your ghost would never leave me. I knew I would see your face in my dreams, for all my days. I am so sorry, *ntehem.*"

Maggie found no words to answer, wanting to comfort him as much as she wished to bury her face in his bared chest and weep. She closed her palms on each side of his face, touching her mouth gently to his. His fingers traced a line down both of her arms, a shudder running through her at the touch of his skin against her own. His mouth opened as he groaned and pulled her so close her legs parted and fell to straddle his hips. She sat above him, holding his head as his mouth dipped to her aching breasts, arching up to meet his kiss. He fumbled with the strings of her dress and she pushed his hands away to untie it herself, loving the way his eyes widened and he sighed as she lifted the shift over her shoulders. Her skin felt laced with fire as he grabbed her face and ravaged her lips again, a shudder running through her at the touch of his skin against her own.

"Don't stop, my heart," she whispered. It was all he needed. One arm slid around her waist, the other guided her hip, and she clutched his head to her breast as he moved. Slow, steady, a tantalizing rhythm that rapidly began to build like a wave, he showed her how to move to catch the crest, melding her buttock with his strong hand as he controlled the pace. She lost herself in the startling blue depths of his eyes, the anguish in her chest ebbing away with each touch of his hand, each needful thrust, each measure of his desire tearing down the barrier around her soul.

"*Nouwmais,*" he said softly.

"I love you, too," she whispered back.

"I could not stop, you know," he said quietly some time later, after their breathing began to slow and they lay with limbs entwined, threaded through furs and soft flesh. "When you married him, I still could not stop wanting you. Even though I knew you were lost to me. These eyes haunt my dreams," he whispered. Her eyes closed as he pressed his soft lips against each lid, and then grazed across her lips. "I betray all that I am, all that I know. I walk alone now, *ntehem*, I cannot return to live among my people. Still none of it matters. I lay here with you, and tell you I would do it again, every day of my life."

His hand closed around her face and he gazed down intently at her, his fingers firm but gentle, his face creased and his brows pinned over his slanted blazing eyes.

"Did you come to me with this power, from your future time? Why do I think nothing of betraying my people, if only to be here, with you, like this?"

"I have no power," she said softly. She briefly recalled his uncle, the legendary leader who also believed her to be a witch, but the memory passed back into the recess of her mind where it belonged. He shook his head and placed his hand on her belly, using one calloused finger to trace a line from navel to her throat, then up under her chin, where it stopped at her swollen lips.

"No, *ntehem*, no power," he whispered. "Only my lifeblood, a prisoner here," he smiled, then placed his palm against the gentle swell of her belly. "I am your prisoner, *Tentay teh*. Do with me what you will."

* * *

Maggie heard horses approach, the sounds of hooves scrambling up the mountainside unmistakable. She joined Winn outside to greet the riders, surprised to see it was Makedewa holding Rebecca in his arms. The girl slumped over, clearly unconscious after her harrowing ordeal.

"Chetan returned to the village?" Winn asked.

"Yes, he took the Pale Witch to mother, she will tend her. I brought this one here. I thought – I thought seeing more of our kind might frighten her now. Will you let Maggie see to her?" Makedewa answered.

She stepped up beside Winn.

"Of course I will. Bring her inside," she replied.

Makedewa cradled the girl easily against his chest and brought her into the cave, where he set her down on the furs next to the fire. Winn said something in Paspahegh which elicited only a grunt from Makedewa, and the two men quickly left.

She stared after them for a moment. She imagined they expected her to know what to do. After all, wasn't caring for the sick a woman's duty? Looking down at the exhausted girl before her, all she could think to do was tend to any wounds and clean her up the best she could manage with limited supplies. It would go a long way towards her tired muscles and weary mind.

She untied the girl's blood sodden apron and placed it in a pile, adding her scuffed leather boots and brown wool stockings as well. The girl did not stir. Maggie lifted her skirt to untie her starched petticoat, still not accustomed to English fashion, but thinking she could wrestle it off without waking the girl. She found the stays and pulled them loose, and then pulled the petticoat gently off.

She inhaled a quick breath and held it when she pulled the garment away. The lining was smeared with blood. As the breeze hit her skin, the girl opened her eyes and began to thrash, kicking and hissing like a cat held under a waterspout. Maggie did the best she could to deflect her blows, unwilling to hurt her further. Finally she wrapped her arms around her in a bear hug as Marcus had so often done to her when she had flown into a temper, rocking her and murmuring soothing words as she patted her back.

The girl howled against her chest, her pale little hand clenched under her chin as she sobbed.

Makedewa and Winn came to the cave opening at the screams. She held up a hand over the girl's trembling back in a gesture to stop them, and they remained a few paces away.

"Oh, sweetheart, it's okay now," she soothed her.

"I could not stop him," she cried softly into Maggie's breast. Maggie held her as tight as the girl could tolerate, rocking back and forth together, mimicking the easy sway of a babe inside a cradle.

"It's not your fault," Maggie whispered.

"I wish he killed me. Why didn't he just kill me?" she sobbed.

Maggie continued to rock her.

"I don't know," she whispered, at loss to give her any semblance of comfort.

* * *

Despite the closeness Maggie and Winn shared on returning to the cave, when dawn arrived and they went about the business of making camp, Maggie felt the slow strangle of distance growing between them. Makedewa and Chetan joined them after procuring more supplies and she was pleased to hear they would join them soon in their exile. Winn would never admit it, but she knew how much he missed his family and she was glad they would all settle together in one place to ride out the coming winter.

Maggie wondered how Rebecca would adapt. The girl followed Maggie everywhere and took a liking to Teyas, so it was a welcome relief that Teyas decided to join them. The girl was only fifteen, as Maggie suspected, and she looked at the men with tribulation most days but she was smart enough to understand they meant her no harm. They never spoke of returning her to the English, and Maggie had a feeling the girl would not go even if it were offered. Rebecca held a deep shame for what had happened to her.

"It's better off my Ma and Pa lie dead. Better dead then to know the truth," Rebecca said.

The cave served as their home and as a central gathering place, the large enclosed space adopting the usage the community long house would traditionally take in their new settlement. The men built two *yehakins* in a semi-circle outside the cave, and also a smaller house to keep their gathered food and supplies. Teyas and Ahi Kekeleksu joined them as well, and their private sanctuary suddenly was a bustling mini village. Maggie welcomed the companionship but at the same time she longed for privacy with her husband, who seemed to be slipping further away.

It was nothing she could point to that changed things. The first night the others arrived, he held her tenderly in his arms when they slept, yet he made no move to press his attention and she soon fell asleep in his embrace. However, when the next night followed the same routine, Maggie knew something was amiss, and on waking alone in the furs once again she decided to confront him.

Makedewa and Chetan worked on completing the supply house. Makedewa grunted in greeting as Chetan secured a flat bark shingle to the roof and tapped it into place with the blunt end of his iron axe, a gift he had gleaned from the English when they were all still on better terms.

"Have you seen Winn?" she asked.

"He checks the snares by the cliff. Take care if you follow him," Makedewa answered, disapproval evident in his tone.

"Thank you, I will," she smiled. She left them to their work. Stopping by the cave to grab her heavy wool cloak, she also tossed some crusty bread and some cheese into a small satchel before she set off up to the cliff in search of her husband. Although she knew the trail well, it still might take a bit of time to find him and she did not want to be trapped without any recourse if her stomach acted up. Most of her nausea had diminished in the weeks they spent in the mountain valley, but there were still waves of dizziness that seemed to get better with a bit of food in her belly.

She found him on the ridge by the cliff, standing at the edge. His ears were sharp and she was surprised he did not hear her advance as he looked out over the valley, his empty gaze searching over the tumble of green that graced the land as far as the eye could wander. His chin dipped down and he cocked his head to the side when he finally noticed her, but he did not turn to greet her.

Maggie slipped her arms around his waist and pressed a kiss to his bared shoulder. He was dressed simply in a breechcloth and leather leggings, his brown skin shimmering with a layer of fresh sweat dampening his skin. He placed one hand over hers and held her tightly as he continued to watch the valley.

"I miss you, husband," she said softly. She felt his ribs move as he let out a sigh.

"I do not go away for long."

"I'm not talking about just this morning. I miss *my husband*." She let her hand slip down over his breechcloth and smiled when his body responded to her touch.

He made a low growling sound and swung her around into his arms, and she sighed with pleasure as his lips came down upon hers. Needful and wanting, his mouth made promises, but she was left confused when he pulled back.

"You should go back to the cave. I will return soon," he said. One of his hands caressed the small of her back as he held her, and she felt the fingers of his other hand twisting in her hair. He kissed the top of her head as he often did and made to part, but she circled her arms around his waist and would not yield.

"Please tell me what troubles you," she asked. She wished it was only the uncertainty of the coming winter, or worry over storing enough food before the first snow, but when his almond shaped blue eyes fell dark and he gazed down at her in despair, she feared perhaps it was something she did not want to know after all.

"I...I will not worry you over my thoughts, *ntehem*," he said softly.

"But I would hear them anyway. What keeps you from my bed, warrior? Am I too round now for you to love?" she tried to joke, infusing a bit of humor. The corner of his mouth turned up and he did smile, but it did not reach his eyes and it was rapidly replaced with a frown.

"Of course not. I know my babe grows inside you." He broke away at the confession, and turned back to the cliff.

Maggie winced at his words and made no move to follow him. So that ghost was rearing its memory, shades of the time they spent apart, and she had no idea how to battle such things. They had not spoken of that time since they were reunited, and although she knew someday it would need to be said, she feared it was still too fresh of a wound to risk bending it.

"Do you doubt this child is yours?" she asked, the words so hoarse as to be nearly silent as uttered from her lips. His shoulders flinched and sagged, but he did not move otherwise.

"I know the babe is my blood."

"Then what are you getting at, Winn?" she whispered. She felt the sting of tears and thrust the despair away, instead embracing the rising tide of anger as a means to clear the path. He was stubborn, she would give him that, but she was even more so to a greater fault, and she would not let his accusations go unanswered.

She put her hand on his arm but he shrugged it off, turning on her. His eyes flared like beacons in a storm, his cheeks flushed, his fisted hands at his sides. The veins in his neck and arms stood out in rails along his skin.

"Tell me why you went to him. Tell me why you wed him," he said quietly. She swallowed hard before she could summon the strength to answer.

"I was afraid. I was alone and afraid. Is that what you want to hear?" she said. "I didn't know what to do. You were gone, and I didn't know what to do."

"Did you love him?" he asked. His lips thinned with the force of holding back, and his hands reached for her once but pulled away. He thrust his hands up and squeezed his head, then ran his fingers through his thick hair. "I fear to ask it, but not knowing haunts me."

"Winn –"

"I know you shared his bed. I must know – did you share his heart as well? I will hear it from you."

"Then hear this, husband," she said. "I have loved no other but you. Every moment we were apart, it was always you. Even when I thought you were dead, it was still you."

He stepped back, putting space between them, and when she reached for him he gently pushed her hands away.

She dropped her hand and turned to go when a sob reached her throat, biting down hard on her lip to stifle it as she made for the trail. Through blurred eyes she took the path back down to the cave, but instead of returning to the others, she followed the tree line to the crevice where the spring sat beneath the falls.

She wanted to be angry with him, but she could not. *Would she be any better, had he been with another woman?* She cringed at the thought of her warrior in the arms of another, and with the intensity of disgust that surfaced within her she could hardly hold him accountable for the anger he now felt.

Shedding her dress, she stepped into the shallow pool and sank down onto the flat ledge, closing her eyes to the warmth and wishing it was his arms that surrounded her instead. Was it a matter of forgiveness between them now, some demon they needed to extinguish, or was this the slow tearing of the bonds that held their lifeblood together? Should she feel shame for doing what she thought was best when she believed Winn dead, or should she hold it up and demand it be forgotten, never to be spoke of again? She had no answer for mending the tear between them.

She felt the water ripple and saw the flash of his bared skin when he dipped beneath the water. His clothes lay in a pile next to hers, and two dead rabbits tied together lay staring with blank eyes at the mouth of the crevice. She closed her eyes when she felt his hands circle her waist and he surfaced in front of her. Like a glorious heathen God, he shook the water from his hair and droplets ran down his rippled chest, dipping into the scarred crease below his left shoulder. She wanted to brush it away, but she was afraid to touch him, fearful to breathe or make a sound lest he go back the way he came.

"Winn, I'm so sorry," she whispered, pulling back slightly from his kiss. He cupped her face with two wide hands and gently kissed the tear than ran down her cheek.

"As am I, *ntehem*."

"But can you ever forgive me?" she whispered.

"Maggie," he said softly. "You once asked me if I would not do the same, if I was trapped, like you, far away from my home. Yes, I had anger at you! By the Gods, Maggie, I wanted to hurt you for marrying him!" He trembled as he spoke, his eyes skewed into shallow slits and his face contorted in a grimace, as if he pained with each syllable. "But I know why you did it, and when my head cleared, I could not keep anger at you," he murmured.

"Oh, Winn," she breathed. "I love you. It's always been you."

He pressed his lips to her hair and drew her close.

His hand slid up her back, and she could feel the sensation of something rough yet yielding against her skin. He took her hand in his and placed the object in her outstretched palm. Filled with water and scented with sweet oil, a fat sea sponge sat in her hand. She looked up at him, uncertain of his intention, and was pleased to see the beginning of a smile on his lips.

"Among my people, a story is told of the First Husband," he said softly. He brought her hand to his chest, where he guided her to make circles across his skin with the sponge. "The man loved a beautiful maiden, and this maiden was as dear to him as the sun is to the moon. He married her, and they lived as one. So blinded by his love for the maiden, he could think of nothing else but her. One day he was called away to hunt, and he left the maiden alone."

Maggie remained silent, but she followed his lead, and she continued to sponge him gently as he told the story. The sounds of the water lapping against their skin echoed in the cavern, as loud as his shallow breaths upon her skin. His hands settled on her waist and he pulled her closer as she gently scrubbed his shoulders and arms.

"The man never returned to the village and the maiden knew some evil had taken him from her, since she knew he would never leave her. Soon her family found her another husband, and she married again." At this his voice dipped lower, and he took the sponge from her to gently caress along her skin. He dabbed her face and neck, and traced tiny circles over her ribs. "Many moons later the First Husband returned, as he was not dead at all, but only lost in the woods. He challenged the new husband for his wife, and when he won she was returned to him."

His hand dropped lower to her belly where he resumed the gentle rhythm, cleansing the spot where their child grew deep inside her.

"The man took his wife to the river, and there he bathed her. He scrubbed her skin with the bark from a Cyprus tree, scrubbed until her skin lay pink. Then she did the same to him, and they lay together again as man and wife, the sadness of their time apart forgotten."

She felt a tear escape down her cheek, and smiled as he brushed it away with the sponge.

"I am clean now," he said softly. His bright eyes softened of their frantic luster, a calmness washing over him as he gazed down at her.

"As am I, my husband," she whispered.

39

"It is finished. The Council speaks, they say they give us blessing."

Maggie and Teyas both looked up as Winn entered the cave and made his declaration, the joy in his words streaming from his grinning lips. She jumped to her feet and threw herself into his waiting arms.

"Oh, Winn, that is wonderful!" she cried. She had worried for days what it would mean to him by returning to the village to speak with the Council, but with his safe return she had hope that someday they may rejoin the Paspahegh. Although they would remain in their secluded valley until the child was born, the support of the Council meant the Paspahegh would not hunt them. The threat from Opechancanough remained, but it was the best they could hope for at this point.

He kissed her soundly, kicking out at Teyas with his toe when she giggled.

"They say Opechancanough sent you to the English, so he must not need your blood. They welcome you return to the village. It is the best we could hope for."

"Well, I can't fault their reasoning, but I wish it had nothing to do with your uncle," Maggie grumbled. He squeezed her and groaned.

"Ah, woman! You know it has much to do with my uncle."

"What about Finola?" she asked. Opechancanough had banished Finola as well, but as she had no husband to speak for her, Winn served as emissary to the Council. Maggie held her breath while waiting for his response.

"If she wishes, she may remain there with the Paspahegh. But the Council fear her, and I worry she may want to return to the English."

"No! Why would she want that?" she asked, drawing back from his embrace to look up at his face.

Teyas interrupted. "She said she fears she will miss it when it happens if she is not with the English."

"Miss what?"

"The return of Pale Feather."

Winn stiffened at her words and his hands fell away from Maggie. Teyas shrugged her shoulders and went back to her work, weaving strips of cured deer hide together for a sleeping mat.

"What did the Witch say of my father?" Winn demanded, his words spoken careful but with clear authority. Teyas sighed.

"Finola sees a night when stars fall from the sky. She sees the English send men to look for the stars, and that is the night Pale Feather will return. She says she must stay with the English for it to pass."

Maggie felt a stirring in her belly and slid her hand down over the swelling. Surely, it was too soon to feel movement, but she smiled anyway and waited breathlessly to see if it would come again. Winn noticed her shift and eyed her expectantly.

"It's nothing," she smiled. He grinned and nodded, looking a bit like a wounded puppy, but kissed her cheek quickly and shook his head.

"So another vision then. She can go to the English if that is her wish, I will not keep her from them," Winn said. "But you, little one, I will keep you here in front of my two eyes, so I may never lose you again." He squeezed her and lifted her off her feet, and a squeal escaped her lips as they laughed. Teyas rolled her eyes skyward, but she also smiled.

It was a blissful peace for the moment, and Maggie was happy to bask in the glorious contentment as long as it would have them.

* * *

Maggie walked back from the waterfall, a basket of damp clothes balanced on her hip. Her belly had grown somewhat large as the birth approached, as pregnant bellies often do, and she found it harder each day to make the trek down the steep path. She managed well with the constant exercise, pleasantly surprised to see how her body responded to the activity during her pregnancy. Yet the fatigue now made even the smallest chore seem much more complicated. At times she felt afraid of the upcoming birth, but Teyas and Chulensak Asuwak were like hovering hens and they kept her too occupied to dwell on her fears too often. She was glad Winn's family had joined them at the waterfall and she hoped they would stay instead of returning to the village.

She smiled at the thought of their faces when she explained how babies were born in her time. A hospital room, male doctors, and spinal anesthesia made quite the impact on them, but once they heard all about it they assured her their ways were much better. Birthing a baby was a sacred event, and the women would take care of her as they cared for each other. Maggie was glad for their kinship, and thankful for their love.

As the cave came in sight, she looked up ahead and spotted Ahi Kekeleksu leading Blaze into the new corral. He smiled and waved, shooting his hand up so fast that the chestnut colt spooked and reared, but the spry boy dodged the animal and managed to get it through the gate.

Maggie was panting when she finally reached him, and she bent over a bit with her hands on her knees to catch her breath before she chastised him. The child knelt before her and peered up into her eyes. Rebecca came running to help him.

"*Tentay teh?* Is it your time?" he asked. His large brown eyes were round with excitement.

She could not recover her breath, and then a wave of pressure surged through her back down to her pelvis. She placed her hand on his shoulder, but he was not strong enough to hold her upright when her knees buckled, so he helped lower her to the ground.

"I need Winn," she managed to groan as another contraction coursed through her. The pains were nearly on top of each other, with no relief in between. Was it normal for labor to start in such a way?

In the movies they did things like count minutes between contractions, she thought with a grimace as another wave took her breath away.

"The warriors are hunting – I will get Teyas!" the boy shouted, taking off in a bare footed run up to the cave. She tried to get up, but the next contraction was too strong, and she uttered a scream as she sank down to her knees.

"Oh, Maggie!" Rebecca groaned, patting her back. Maggie glanced sideways at her. The girl looked terrified, and she could hardly blame her. She was close to panicked herself.

She gritted her teeth against the pressure and let out a long groan. She would get her ass up, her child would not be born in the dirt outside the cave! Thrusting both hands against her knees, she pushed up again to stand and felt a warm gush of fluid leave her body.

Relief washed over her when she felt two pairs of hands take her under each elbow and assist her to stand. Teyas grinned, and Chulensak Asuwak shook her head with a knowing chuckle.

They led her into the cave, Ahi Kekeleksu and Rebecca trailing behind them.

40

Winn noticed the yard was empty when he approached their camp, which he thought was strange since Ahi Kekeleksu despised being cooped up inside on such a warm day. Winn usually left one of his brothers with the women while he hunted, but with the birth approaching he felt more need to hunt quickly and return so he had taken both brothers with him. They returned with two fair sized deer and a half dozen rabbits, a good amount of game for one day. Hunting was more plentiful near the camp, as the English had not invaded the sanctuary yet.

The boy streaked out of the cave as they approached, his eyes wild and his face flushed with excitement. Winn knew something had happened, and he felt his stomach curl down deep into a knot. He jumped off his horse and ran for the cave.

"The baby, the baby is here!" the boy shouted.

"Maggie? Is she well?" he asked as he passed the boy. The boy grinned.

"Oh yes! She sleeps now!"

Winn let out the air from his lungs and relaxed his tight gripped fists. Ahi Kekeleksu spoke true. He sank down beside his sleeping wife as she lay on the pallet, the relief running through him as he looked at her. She was propped up with several pillows, the odd fluffy things she insisted on making before the birth, and he could see why she had wanted the things now. Her crown was streaked with damp sweat that moistened her auburn hair into tiny curls around her face, and he could taste the salt of her work as he kissed her forehead.

The child lay snug in her arms. Eyes closed in sleep amongst a round chubby face with a swatch of dark hair, he marveled at the lightly bronzed skin and tiny rounded nose. When Maggie gently touched his face, he clasped her hand and pressed it hard to his lips, so that he could have another moment to look at the child and find the right words to show his wife his joy.

"She's beautiful, isn't she?" Maggie whispered. His eyes shifted to hers.

"She?"

"Yes...your daughter," she smiled.

"Oh," he breathed. *"Kwetii."* The baby opened her eyes, blinking deep blue orbs several times until finally she stared up at him. Her bow-shaped mouth parted as he gazed at her, and then her face puckered into a hearty cry. *His ⁊aughter. She was beautiful.*

Maggie raised her eyebrows and he whispered, "It means Little One. I call her Little One," he explained.

"Shh, shhh, here," Maggie cooed, placing the infant to her breast. Winn slid beside her on the furs and wrapped his arms around them both as the baby fed.

"I am sorry I was not here," he said softly. She turned and kissed him as the baby continued to peacefully nurse.

"You're here now. Thanks for bringing more food, I think I'm hungry now," she smiled. He groaned and clutched her against his chest.

"Thank you for...for her. For you. God, I love you, woman! And yes, I will feed you...but wait. I would watch you both for a bit longer."

Maggie nodded. Winn settled back, his head resting on her shoulder as they watched their daughter.

41

Maggie heard the riders at the same time as Winn, as they made no effort to conceal their approach. She had been nursing Kwetii while sitting on the grass watching the others, but at the sight of the three men jumping off their horses she let her deerskin mantle drop lightly over the head of the child. She had grown accustomed to nursing the babe in front of her family, but her modesty was too ingrained to do so in front of strangers.

Winn greeted the riders, and by his friendly demeanor, she could see the warriors were no threat to them. They had lived peacefully on the mountain for more than six months, and although they often discussed where they would settle more permanently, Maggie secretly hoped they could stay where they were forever. Winn, however, reminded her it was too close to the English for him to feel secure, and Opechancanough would always pose a threat to them. Although his uncle had not chosen to prevent Winn from leaving the tribe, Winn did not trust the man not to retaliate at some point, and he felt very strongly they should soon move south out of his reach.

Now as the familiar warriors spoke with her husband, she wondered what news they carried from the tribe. They were clearly Powhatan, wearing the distinct scalp lock hair. A fully shaved head except for one central piece that trailed in a long braid down their back, the most honored warriors favored it. By the way Winn spoke to them, she thought he must know them, and as she approached with the babe, he offered no warning so she felt more secure.

She felt their gaze as she stood next to Winn, the surprise evident in their eyes as she stood beside her husband. Winn spoke rapidly in Paspahegh to them, nodded toward her, and then did something that startled her. He unsheathed his knife and with one quick flick, he sliced a line across the skin of his forearm. When it surged with blood, he dipped his finger into it, and then ran it across the baby's brow.

"Tell Opechancanough I will not give him my blood. I cannot help him," Winn said.

One of the warriors shook his head, his eyes widening at the words Winn spoke, and he issued a frantic response Maggie could not decipher.

"What does your uncle want?" Maggie interrupted.

Winn answered the warrior, and turned to Maggie.

"He asks too much," he said. "He wants me to join him at a feast with the English. The whites tire of the fighting, and they offer a peace treaty if Opechancanough will come eat with them."

"But does this mean your uncle forgives you for leaving?" she asked, hoping it would be a way for Winn to return to his people. Winn shook his head.

"I know not except that if I deny him, he will consider it a great insult. He asks me to sit by his side at this meal."

The thought of insulting the Weroance left a sour taste in her throat, especially considering the last encounter she had with the man. She did not fully trust the Weroance, but she could not let Winn pass over the chance to mend the strain between him and his uncle. They not only had themselves to think about, but their family as well.

"But if you insult him, he may come for us," she said softly.

"I would go, but he asks for more than I can give. He wants the Red Woman there as well. I will not take you, and I cannot leave you here unprotected. There is no other choice."

"I will go with you."

Maggie said the words and knew he would refuse, but she had to convince him it was the only way. If there was a chance to make peace with the Weroance, they would all sleep better for it, and perhaps they would not have to live always waiting for an enemy to strike.

"Please, Winn. If it will calm your uncle's hatred, I will go with you. It will make life much safer for us all," she pleaded. She tried to keep calm as he looked hard at her, and then the child. He glanced back at the cave, where Ahi Kekeleksu stood watching with Teyas. Finally, he issued a quick response to the visitors, and although they nodded in respect as they left, she could see their faces streaked with anger.

She followed Winn back to the cave, wondering what the refusal would cost them.

42

Kwetii squealed as Maggie placed her on the soft swaddling blanket, tiny feet kicking at the empty air as her round red faced puckered to make her happy noise. Maggie reached down to the child and tickled her tummy as she patted her dry. She was eager to dress her before she sat up in the dirt, which was her most favorite thing to do. Winn thought her strange for covering the child, but Maggie held fast to her ingrained notions of propriety and insisted on dressing the child instead of allowing her to roll around naked.

"Ah, more silly clothes my daughter will ruin?"

Maggie rolled her eyes at Winn as he approached. They watched Kwetii scramble onto her belly and sit up on the blanket. Her round blue eyes searched for something to hold her attention, looking up at the ancient willow tree that shaded their serene resting place. She spotted Winn standing behind Maggie and let out a screech with her two chubby arms upraised toward her father. When he scooped her up, Maggie noticed the rifle slung over his shoulder.

"Hunting?" she asked.

He nodded. "Yes, we will return before dark. How goes the packing?"

"Most of it is ready. We can leave on your word," she replied, scrunching her shoulder to her ear as he kissed her neck. His touch sent shivers down her back but she smiled. He held Kwetii at his hip with one arm and wrapped his other around her waist, lifting her up and spinning them both around as they screeched with laughter.

"Stop, stop, enough!" she laughed. Kwetii emitted a brisk hiccup through her wide toothless grin. The child clutched one long piece of hair in her hand, but Winn did not seem to mind.

Her chest heaved with the effort of catching her breath and trying not to laugh, and as she looked down at his chest where her hand rested, she could see Winn was breathing heavy as well. Warmed from the mid-day sun, his skin felt hot beneath her fingers, and she could feel the stagger of his heart beat under his breast.

"You have to leave?" she asked breathlessly.

He shifted very slightly, but enough for her to feel he could be convinced to stay if she gave him a good reason. She lifted her chin and placed a fleeting kiss on his neck, beneath his chin where she knew he was sensitive, and she smiled when he groaned and his fingers tightened on her waist. With all the preparations of leaving, they had whittled the *yehakins* down and all slept now in the cave, and under the watchful eye of five other people and one cranky baby, they had done little more than sleep at night.

"*Ntehem*," he said, his forehead pressed to hers. "I have to leave now, but I will seek your company later."

The baby let out a wail, piercing the peaceful glow between them, and they reluctantly separated. Winn placed the wailing child into her arms and Maggie did her best to soothe her, letting out a sigh when the baby sought to nurse.

Winn picked up the rifle and slung it over his shoulder by the carrying strap, then kissed her flushed cheek. His mouth twisted up into a grin, his blue eyes squinted half-closed as he looked down on the nursing babe.

"If only I could spend my day like that," he murmured.

"Like a baby?" she asked. He nodded.

"Safe in your arms? Yes, that would be a good life," he grinned.

Maggie rolled her eyes and pursed her lips together, but was unable to stifle a laugh when he enclosed them both in a fierce hug. His lips sent a shiver through her when he kissed her ear and whispered sweet Paspahegh endearments, his breath thick and warm on her neck.

"Hurry back," she said.

"You will see me at nightfall. Be good, *ntehem.*"

She watched him walk to the path at the edge of the woods, and when she could no longer see the outline of his bronzed shoulders, she took the baby back to the cave.

* * *

She rolled the letter tight and bound it with a thin piece of rawhide. Winn's pewter flask, a gift from Benjamin, sat waiting to receive the missive. It would have to do. She could think of no other way to let Marcus know she lived. Although she would be long dead before such word reached him, he would know she lived a happy life in the past.

On the outside of the rolled parchment, written with a dove quill dipped in some ink Chetan brought back from town, she left directions. It was to be given to Marcus Neilson on Saturday, October sixth, two thousand twelve, the day after the Bloodstone took her. She knew it was possible the letter would never reach him, but she had to try. It was the only way she could put the ghosts of her future to rest.

May 1623

Dear Marcus,

I can only pray that this letter somehow reaches you, an● that you can for-give me for not returning home. Believe me, I trie● to return, many times, but the longer I staye●, the more I came to see my life was meant to be live● in the past.

I'm not crazy. I ●o not write this un●er ●uress. Nothing ba● happene● to me when I ●isappeare●. I think I hear● you calling me as I left that ●ay in the barn, so you probably saw me ●isappear. Please know there was nothing you coul● have ●one to prevent it. Some things are just meant to be, an● I truly be-lieve my leaving was one of them.

It was a strange black stone that ●i● it, a shiny warm stone with a streak of re● running through the center like a bloo●y vein. It is calle● a Bloo●stone, an● it is very powerful. My husban● burie● them many years ago, a small pile of them insi●e an ol● trunk, right where our barn was built. They must have been dug up and just thrown into the foundation when they built the place. If you find any more of them in the barn, please bury them deep in the earth so no one can ever find them. Although the Bloodstone brought me here, I cannot say for sure how the magic works, so I view them with more fear than curiosity.

Please know I am safe and happy here with my husband, Winkeohkwet. We have a beautiful daughter, and I am sure the future will be filled with happiness.

I must tell you something, and though I hesitate to cause you grief, I know you would want to hear it. Your son, Benjamin, was here in the past. My friend Finola tells me he traveled here as a young boy, and then lived among the English settlers at Martin's Hundred, outside of Jamestown. We helped him use the Bloodstone to return to your time. I hope that Benjamin reached you and that he is safe. It would comfort me to know you will see him again, that your son is returned to you. He will have much to tell you about this time, but I will leave that to him, as it is his story to tell.

May your future be happy. I love you very much, and think of you often. Please take care, and rest easy, knowing I am happy as well.

Love always,

Maggie-mae

The Bloodstones sat piled inside the Viking chest, a square metal lined thing that Winn buried them in. Someday, somehow, those stones ended up in the foundation of her barn, so Maggie hoped that by leaving the flask with the stones, the letter might find its way to Marcus.

She placed the flask inside and closed the trunk. Kwetii let out a squeal from where she lay on her belly watching as Maggie shoved dirt back over the chest.

"It's all right, sweetheart," she cooed. "Everything is okay now."

* * *

Kwetii was crying, her sobs echoing against the walls of the cavern.

Maggie reaches out to the babe, but found an empty space beside her where the babe should be.

The cries became weaker, and Maggie screamed for Winn.

"Winn?" she whispered, sitting up groggily on her pallet, the furs tumbling down in a pile around her. The events of the nightmare came back in one disjointed flash, and she reached for her daughter amidst her panic. "Oh, sweetheart!" she sighed. She brushed back a tear from her eye and placed the sleeping baby against her chest.

She looked up at the sky as she left the cave. It was just past dusk, the sky slathered with streaks of purple and orange as the sun dipped low over the horizon. She must have dozed off after feeding the baby, as they often did, which was good since that meant Winn would be back soon. Maggie did not like to be alone at the settlement, but with the others tied up with preparing to leave, she found herself there with just the baby for company quite often.

Maggie placed the baby on the ground, still swaddled in a soft doe-skin blanket, and walked a few paces away into the underbrush to relieve her bladder. She hastily patted dry and rose to her feet.

They did not make a sound. Suddenly, standing over Kwetii were two familiar warriors. Maggie recognized the scalplock hair immediately, and as bile rose up from the pit of her stomach, she knew they were the men sent by Opechancanough.

"*Kwishali!*" she said forcefully, tilting her head up to address them in the few words of their language she knew. She hoped if she told them they frightened her, they would back away from the baby, but her hopes dimmed when she saw they did not budge. Their faces displayed nothing, two granite slabs staring at her and the baby as if they had stumbled onto something that perplexed them. One man glanced at the other and muttered a string of curt words she did not understand, and the other nodded and made a quick retort. When one man bent to pick up the child, she darted toward him and grabbed for her daughter.

"No! Leave her!" she screamed, punching wildly at the warrior who caught her by the upper arm. Her heart plummeted when the other man held her daughter out, as if she were a hot potato, blistering his hands.

"Here. Take the child!" the man said in stilted English.

"My husband is not here!" she said. Kwetii began to cry softly, and Maggie raised her to her shoulder, trying to comfort her while she figured out what the warriors wanted.

The first man scowled. He pointed to Maggie, then to the woods. She clutched the baby and shook her head, her eyes darting past the men to see if anyone else had returned to the cave. It was achingly quiet, leaving her to deal with the unwelcomed visitors herself.

"You go!" the native ordered again, pointing more forcefully this time toward the woods.

"No! I'm not going anywhere!" she hissed.

At her vocal protest, the men looked briefly at each other, and then the second man unsheathed the knife at his side. Kwetii squealed as Maggie stepped backward and stumbled, caught by the warrior at her side. She had no idea what intent they held toward her, and with the horror of realization rising she knew she could not fight with them without causing harm to her daughter.

She passed one more fleeting glance toward the cave in hopes anyone had returned, and then mutely went along with the two Powhatan warriors.

43

Winn dropped the small deer carcass near the fire and looked around the yard. He heard voices down by the waterfall, and recognized the gleeful laugh of Ahi Kekeleksu, probably getting one last bath from Teyas before they set out on their journey to find a new home. He wondered if Maggie and the babe were down there as well, and he smiled when he thought of sneaking up on them as a surprise.

He slid the rifle off his shoulder and meant to put it inside the cave, but when he walked toward the crevice, his gait slowed. Standing upright, stiff in the ground, was the spear of a warrior, a red tipped feather attached to it blowing gently with the breeze.

"Maggie," he called, to no response. "*Tentay Teh!*" His skin felt cold and he felt a pressure around his chest, squeezing slowly until he shouted again. "Maggie!"

Teyas and Ahi Kekeleksu came running at his frantic call, but neither Maggie nor the babe were with them. He pulled the spear from the ground and swore, swinging around to challenge the empty woods for want of any other to vent his rage on, his arms spread apart like an eagle ready to take flight.

"I will come for them!" he screamed.

44

Maggie sat stiffly beside the other women on the furs that flanked the Weroance. Opechancanough perched on the highest dais, surrounded on each side by two of his wives. One was his favorite wife, and the other his newest, youngest wife. Both were quite beautiful, decked out in all the finery they possessed, their skin stained with bright red ochre and decorated with layers of copper and silver bangles. The Weroance was most impressive of all, showing off his riches by wearing every piece of jewelry he could manage to fit onto his sinewy weathered body.

He was a tall man, and when seated his new wife was barely taller than the top of his head as she stood beside him. Maggie only noticed when the woman approached him to sit down, because women did not presume to speak or stand in the presence of the Weroance without invitation. Opechancanough ruled without resistance, and although Maggie thought of him as a vindictive, bitter warrior, his people clearly showed intense love for him by the way they worshipped his very presence.

Maggie rocked Kwetii, who thankfully slept peacefully through the pounding of drums and joyous cries throughout the long house. She dared another glance at the Weroance, who silently watched the celebration and occasionally nodded his approval. She noticed his eyelids drooped a bit, as if sleepy, and that he seemed more fatigued as the night wore on. She had no idea what they were celebrating, her understanding of the Powhatan language not much more than conversational. It was certainly not sufficient enough to risk an attempt at speaking with her captives.

She watched the proceedings from her spot of semi-importance among the Weroance's less favorite wives, and considered herself lucky for the moment that they had treated her quite well. As the night wore on, she wondered what the Weroance planned for her, and when she saw Winn enter the long house she realized the purpose of her presence.

She was bait.

He displaced the light around him when he passed through the doorway, his wide shoulders braced, his arms tensed tight to the ends of his clenched fingers. His chest marked with black paint, his face streaked and shadowed so that his teeth appeared to glow with malevolence, he carried a long decorated spear as he approached the high dais. His bright blue eyes gleamed as he stared down the Weroance, and Maggie felt her composure slip away when she realized he was going to confront his uncle.

The drumbeats stopped and the Long House fell silent. Winn raised the spear over his head with both hands and then thrust it down into the ground, where it stood shuddering before the Weroance. Maggie dared not let out a breath as she watched her husband slowly kneel down before his uncle.

Winn pounded one fisted hand to his chest and looked up at Opechancanough. He kept his breathing shallow, barely expanding his chest, and she could see his fingers clench and unclench as he waited to be acknowledged by his uncle.

"I see you, nephew, and I will hear you now," the Weroance called out. Whispers commenced throughout the crowd, and from the faces of the people around her Maggie could not tell if they were voices of admiration or disgust.

Winn remained on bent knee, but stared defiantly at the Weroance, one hand braced on the impaled spear and his knuckles standing out pale against the dark wood.

"I come for my wife," he said, slow but loud, as if he desired everyone in the Long House to hear it. Maggie was sure they all did, as the eyes of every native were fixed on the impetuous warrior as he spoke.

Opechancanough narrowed his brows, and his eyes focused on Winn.

"What will you give me for her?" he asked. "She is quite valuable to me."

Winn must have anticipated the answer, since he shot his response back in quick succession.

"I will stand by your side against the English during this treaty."

The Weroance pursed his lips, and then his creased face broke into a wide smile. Maggie wondered how he managed to eat with nary a tooth in his blasted stubborn head.

"Then join me here, nephew, and I will give you the Red Woman," Opechancanough pronounced, spreading his arms wide in a show of pleasure at the deal. The long house erupted into a chasm of relieved cries, and the rhythmic thud of the drums started anew. Winn rose up off his knee, his hand still gripping the spear.

"I have one more request."

Maggie felt the blood leave her cheeks, and the drums stopped again. Opechancanough rose from his sitting position and approached Winn. Maggie swallowed hard at the sight of the ceremonial mallet he held in his hand, knowing how easily the bastard could flip the switch of his temper and turn into an irrational sod.

"Tell me your request."

Winn glanced beyond his uncle to where the warriors stood flanking the Weroance.

"I ask for the right to challenge the warrior who stole my woman. I will take his life, and then I will stand at your side for this English treaty."

"No!" Maggie moaned, pressing her daughter to her face, the doeskin blanket muffling both her cries and that of the startled baby. Why did he have to make a challenge? Couldn't he see that both Maggie and Kwetii were perfectly fine, that the entire thing had just been to extract his compliance? Even Maggie knew if Opechancanough wanted her dead, she would have been exterminated long before now. It was clear the entire kidnapping served only as a means to bring Winn back in line.

"You may have your challenge." The Weroance flicked his hand at his wives, and they obediently rose to follow him. "We will gather by the Great Fire, and see your fight."

A long line of warriors followed behind the wives, and then the less favored wives began to file out, one of them holding onto her arm to keep her inside the pack as they walked past Winn. The remainder of the Indians in the Long House filed out in an unruly crowd, shouts and taunts bouncing through them. Some glared at Winn and some turned their backs, but most smiled and acknowledged him with a respectful nod. Maggie looked helplessly at him and longed to go to him, though she knew she could not.

His eyes met hers as she passed. She saw a flicker in his gaze, and no other sign of acknowledgement, but she was certain he saw in her heart what words she could not let loose.

The entire village gathered at the Great Fire, even the children. Faces turned toward the warriors in the circle, eyes alight with anticipation. Hands drew Maggie back inside the crowd, the wives embracing her within their ranks to watch the spectacle.

"What will they do?" Maggie asked.

"Quiet!" came a hiss from the woman beside her.

Kwetii dozed at her shoulder, the baby thankfully exhausted from the excitement, snoring while making tiny mewling sounds against her. Maggie rocked her and patted her bottom, more to give herself a task than to comfort the child. The babe slept soundly when she needed to, no matter what was going on around her, safe in her arms and oblivious to the risk her father was about to embark on.

Murmurs from the crowd abruptly stopped.

Winn pushed through a barrage of hands, reaching the clearing in the middle of the circular throng of people. He had no weapon save his capable hands, which turned white across the knuckles as he clenched them at his sides. Stripped of his clothes, he stood waiting for his opponent, wearing only a simple undecorated breechcloth. His wide chest was streaked with black paint, three lines slashed on each side of his chest, like wings stretching out from his ribs. The bottom of his face was covered with paint from ears through his jaw, the black mask heightening the whiteness in his teeth when he flashed a snarl at his opponent.

Kwetii squirmed with a sleepy squeal. Maggie looked down at her own clenched arms and immediately lightened her grasp, patting the baby to apologize. She had not realized she was gripping her harder until the baby stirred.

The village priest entered the clearing. Clad in ceremonial garb, a white fur cloak across his hunched shoulders, the man stood between the two warriors. A horned helmet enclosed his head, giving him enough height to near that of Winn, yet the diminutive man still looked fragile to her rather than fierce. He raised a feather-decorated spear above his head as if in salute, and all fell silent once again.

"Kweshkwesh and Winkeohkwet!" he screamed. "Finish this!"

Crouched low, hands outstretched, Kweshkwesh darted at Winn's knees the moment the priest left the circle. The crowd erupted into bellows and howls, and multiple drums thudded in unison around the men. Louder, stronger, the drums set the rhythm, swallowing the cries and screams, dulling the sounds until all she could hear was a distant echo as she watched her husband fight.

Arms locked on each other, the men were head to shoulder, their feet scraping the ground to find purchase as each struggled to get the upper hand. Kweshkwesh lunged with his knife, slicing across Winn's chest, and Maggie cried out at the surge of blood on his skin.

"No!" she shouted, her plea muted into nothingness among the voices of the villagers. She saw Opechancanough with his arms crossed over his chest, watching the fight as he stood next to the priest. How could he stand there and watch his own nephew fight to the death? What a bastard he was!

Winn paid no mind to the wound as he showed his own knife, slashing at Kweshkwesh in retaliation. He made contact and lunged forward, knocking Kweshkwesh to the ground, his chest heaving and dripping blood as he straddled the warrior. Winn held the knife to his throat, and as he paused in finishing the act, suddenly the noise among the people diminished and heads turned to Opechancanough.

Winn looked toward the Weroance, and then down at the man he held against the ground.

"I will not kill this man!" Winn shouted. "This man only followed orders, and I will not take his life for it."

There was a sharp intake of gasps among the crowd, but Opechancanough did not waver.

Winn stood up, his knife still clutched in his fist, his blue eyes fastened on the Weroance. Kweshkwesh slowly rose from the ground, his head hanging and his face shielded, and as two women came forward to help him, he shrugged off their hands and stalked away from the circle.

"Let it be known to all. No man will take what is mine!" he bellowed.

Winn impaled his knife in the dirt at the feet of Opechancanough and stared at the man, their gazes locked for what seemed like hours, as the villagers waited for the outcome. The Weroance betrayed no surprise at the challenge, instead merely meeting Winn's defiant stare with a pensive one of his own.

Kwetii whimpered beneath her swaddling blanket.

The Weroance straightened his back and stepped one pace toward Winn.

"We hear you, warrior!" he shouted. Before he could finish the words, shouts and whoops filled the air, and the drum began to beat out a frantic celebratory rhythm. Men and women broke off from the circle and began to dance, and the children scattered like rabbits through the mesh of people.

As villagers vanished in all directions, Maggie pushed through the crowd to get to Winn. He turned, and she could see his eyes scan the crowd for her, finally meeting her own as relief flooded his face. Damn their tribal rules, she was going to her husband and no one would stop her this time. She threw herself into his arms.

"Winn!"

"*Ntehem*," he said. He held her tight, his breath warm upon her hair.

"You could have been killed!"

"You think so little of my skill, woman?"

"You didn't have to fight him!"

"Yes," he said firmly. "I did."

She bent her head to his chest, the babe sheltered between them, and his arms tightened around them.

"The English come here tomorrow to make peace. I will stand with my uncle, and then we will leave."

"Your brothers?"

"They wait for us to return."

They passed over the celebration and instead retired to a nearby yehakin, escorted by several of the less favored wives and left with a multitude of supplies. Furs heaped on a sleeping mat, and a basket lined with down for the baby, they had all the comforts they needed for what Maggie hoped would be a very short stay. The women accompanied them as they readied the yehakin, bringing them bowls of food and stone jugs of drink, which they placed near the fire. One took the baby from Maggie and placed her in the makeshift cradle.

Maggie did not understand their words, which seemed different from the Paspahegh she was accustomed to, yet Winn had no such impediment and spoke softly to the women. One older woman in particular talked to him at length, and from the intimacy of their exchange Maggie was sure the woman was known to him. She was comely, with one long braid down her back, her oval face creased with tiny lines at the edges of her round brown eyes but betraying no other sign of her age. She placed a hand on Winn's shoulder and Maggie watched it linger before she gave him a half-bow and summoned the other women.

As she left, she gave Maggie a shy smile, and then one more nod to Winn before she was gone.

"What was that about?"

"What?"

"That woman! Who is she?"

Maggie had never seen her husband blush and she was not reassured by the sight. His neck flushed, the color creeping up his jaw and cheeks, until he met her gaze with a hooded stare.

"Sesapatae, wife to my uncle. I lived with her family when I stayed here."

"Oh. It just seemed like you – like she was someone special."

"She was the first woman I shared furs with."

Maggie sat down hard on the fur pallet.

"Oh. Oh, okay," she said. She had no idea what the proper response to such a revelation should be, so she clamped her mouth shut and pulled a fur over her shoulders. Winn said nothing as he sank into the furs beside her, nor as he wrapped his arms around her and pressed his naked skin to hers.

She should not be surprised to hear his explanation, since she was well aware she was not the first woman he laid hands on, but she was perplexed that the woman was his uncle's wife. She thought she would drop the subject, as Winn clearly had once he crawled beneath the furs, but when he still said nothing her curiosity won out.

"So how on earth did that happen?" she asked.

He moved above onto one elbow and squinted down at her.

"Like this," he murmured. He untied the laces on the front of her dress, and his other hand slid down over her thigh. His mouth dipped down onto her neck, sending shivers over her skin as he nuzzled her playfully.

"But –"

"No more talk," he whispered as he continued the path down her body. When he paused to give attention to her full breasts, she moaned at the contact, the pleasure of his touch mingled with the soreness from nursing, excruciating yet blissful pain that scattered the questions she meant to ask.

"Stop that and answer me!"

He shook his head and parted her thighs with his knee, continuing his gentle ministrations as he gave worship to her body. Slick with sweat under the heavy furs, their skin slipped against each other, his touch rising in urgency until he finally slid inside her, effectively silencing her remaining protests as he rocked her back against the furs.

"My wife and child were stolen from me today. I fought the man who stole her, and I threatened my Weroance in front of the entire village," he said, his mouth pressed against her ear. "And I am tired of talking!"

He rose up above her, his thrust boring her down, their limbs entwined. She lost herself to the need in his touch, for it was anger and despair that drove him, the sweet culmination sealing the oath of possession between their bodies as they moved as one.

Later, when he lay with his head nestled against her shoulder, she felt the breath leave him and his tense muscles finally softened. He played with a lock of her hair, absently twisting it into a ringlet, his palm resting on her breast.

"It is the way of our people," he said quietly. "I lived here when I became a man. It is custom for the uncle's wife to lead the nephew into manhood. There is no more to it than that."

"All right then," she replied, ready to dismiss the topic until another thought took root. "But you wouldn't expect me – I mean, what about Ahi Kekeleksu?" she stammered.

"It will be the wife to the mother's brother. Not you."

"Oh." She had more questions, but held her tongue.

She heard him laugh, and she reached out to smack his chest in response. He caught her hand and pressed it to his chest.

"You are too busy teaching me, *ntehem*. I will not share you with any other."

The conversation was finished, and she was glad for it.

45

Maggie watched the Englishman give his theatrical speech as she sat next to Winn.

Captain Tucker was an enigmatic speaker, his thick baritone sharp and clear as he bellowed out his pledge to the Powhatans. Maggie expected a more imposing figure that would correlate more with the tales told of the man, but instead of an invincible solider, she only saw an average height man wearing a partial suit of overly decorated armor. His girth had long outgrown the outfit, and when he stood up straight to address the crowd, a crack of his belly showed beneath the armor. Maggie smirked each time he raised his arm.

"Will this take very long, you think?" she asked Winn. He sat cross-legged next to Opechancanough, but he had been silent through most of the demonstration other than to nod in agreement with the Weroance.

"I know not," he replied.

The two opposing sides met on the banks of the Potomac, a neutral place where each felt on equal footing. Although he seemed like a psychotic beast at times, Maggie had to admit that Opechancanough was a skilled tactical leader. He had taken years planning the 1622 massacre, cultivating trust with the English so that his warriors could enter their homes without suspicion, until he took his vengeance out on them in one fatal day. Every Powhatan man, woman, and child had known the plan for years, yet he managed to keep their blind loyalty long enough to carry through with the attack.

Now the Great Weroance sat beside her husband, dressed in his finest attire, watching the Englishman pledge a truce to the Powhatan people. She could feel the tension roll off them in waves, from the sly glances they shared and the grunts of disproval from the Weroance as the Englishman spoke.

Maggie looked over Winn's shoulder to where Kwetii lay in the arms of a Powhatan woman. It made her nervous to see her daughter out of her immediate reach, but Opechancanough had insisted one of his wives hold the child. She suspected it was just another ploy to keep both her and Winn in line throughout the ceremony, and a successful one at that.

"We share this meal as we meet as friends. All who take of this food today make this promise!" Opechancanough called out, raising his hands in the air. The Powhatans hooted and hollered, and the sounds of joyful noise filled the air. The Englishmen, few as they were, and none that she recognized, joined in by clapping and nodding in agreement. She fleetingly wondered why no English women were present, but then she recalled the subservient role they played in Jamestown society and realized they would not be included in such activities.

"Business has no place fer women," Charles said. Benjamin waved the man off.

"Then you know not my wife, Charles. She is quite clever." Benjamin replied.

Maggie shuddered at the unwelcome memory. Its shadow persisted, however, nipping at her ankles like hungry fleas wanting her blood, begging for acknowledgement. Was Benjamin safely returned to his own time? She knew she might never know the answer, and it was best left in the past. She glanced sideways at Winn.

He watched the English as he ate, taking the offered bowl of food from the Taster. Winn only gave her bits from his bowl, and stopped her hand when she reached for his untouched mug of rum.

"Wait."

He handed the mug to the thin man seated behind them, who took a gulp. Winn watched the Taster for a few moments, shrugged, and then handed it to Maggie. She noticed the Weroance did the same.

Doctor Potts began passing around jugs of ale, which the Indians gladly filled their mugs with. He was another little man, yet dressed in the fine clothes of an aristocrat with a starched stand up collar and shiny new shoes with his brown hair tied neatly with a blue ribbon at his nape. His eyes followed the jugs as he watched the Indians pour out their share.

"'Tis the best we have, for our loyal friends!" Potts shouted, his arm outstretched, pointing to the clay jugs.

The Taster was given an overflowing mug, which he topped off with a gulp before handing it to the Weroance. Opechancanough grinned and raised it in salute.

Maggie looked around the gathering at the Indians seated in a circle, her mug sitting still full in front of her. Men, women, and children were present, nearly three hundred total, a token of trust to show the English they were sincere in desire for a treaty. A young brave teetered across the fire, and the women around him snickered and laughed.

Then another young brave fell to his knees.

Maggie turned to Winn, who had also seen the men fall, and then she saw Opechancanough lifting his mug to his lips. She lurched over Winn and knocked the mug from the hand of the Weroance in one quick motion, falling into Winn's arms as a flurry of activity erupted around them.

"Red Woman!" the Weroance shouted. Maggie felt hands trying to pry her from Winn, but her husband held fast and shielded her from her would-be captors.

"I – I think it's poisoned!" she told Winn. Both Winn and Opechancanough stared at her and then turned their attention to the Taster, who hiccupped and promptly fell to the ground in a heap of twitching limbs. Thick foaming bubbles of saliva began to drain from his opened mouth into the dirt.

"Liars! We will kill you all for this!" Opechancanough shouted.

Bedlam exploded around them. Warriors pulled the Weroance to his feet and shuttled him to the dugout boats waiting at the river. He barked out commands and the Indians began to mill toward the canoes, some stumbling and falling into the mud amidst screaming and crying. Maggie frantically searched for Kwetii and nearly keeled over with relief when Winn handed her the babe.

Shots rang out, and Maggie saw the Weroance stumble before he was pulled into a canoe. As the crowd surged toward the shoreline, many men fell, never to rise, all foaming at the mouth as the Taster had done. Women screamed and cried as they ran, dragging children behind them.

The English fired into the crowd, taking down more than the poison could finish off, pecking off the Indians blow by blow. She let Winn push her into a canoe, then reached up for his hand to guide him in, panicked when he kissed her roughly then thrust her away. As the bellow of gunfire roared around them, he pushed the canoe into the current instead of getting in.

"No! Winn! No, no!" she screamed.

"Go! Be safe with my daughter!" he shouted.

She clutched the side of the canoe, tears clouding her vision. He stood still for what seemed like ages, his tall warrior's body primed to fight, his chest rising only slightly with each breath, looking like some ancient pagan devil as he watched them leave. Smoke from the fires rose behind him, the flames cracking and hissing to smother the screams. He glanced up at the sky, and then she lost sight of him as he turned back to the chaos to join the other warriors.

* * *

As she took a deep breath to steady herself, the thick smoke stung her throat and her lungs rejected the influx, leading to a spasm of coughing that served to agitate Kwetii more. The babe lay nestled against her breast inside a soft doeskin sling, but even the infant knew how precarious their lives were at that moment and she voiced her dismay loudly. Sitting wedged next to two sobbing women in the canoe,

Maggie stared at the riverbank, hoping for something, anything to indicate the men would return.

Her arms ached as she paddled, the muscles in her shoulders screaming in protest at the unaccustomed labor. She closed her eyes to the pain and continued to push the oar through the murky water, grimacing when it caught on a bushel of Tuckahoe roots and she had to yank it free. Kwetii continued to wail.

"Here, I will row," the woman beside her said. "Feed the babe." Crusted with mud down her back, her one arm bloodied but intact, the woman took the paddle from Maggie and resumed the chore. Maggie glanced down at her daughter, somewhat stunned at her own inability to recognize the child's cry for milk. Her body, however, was much more attuned, and she felt a rush of milk let down as the babe latched onto her swollen nipple.

"The men will follow us. Your warrior will return."

Maggie looked up at the soft spoken voice. It was Sesapatae, and it was she who had taken the paddle from her hands. Maggie could only nod in return, not trusting her voice for fear of wavering. If she spoke her fears aloud, would it make her unworthy? Should she hold her own hopelessness inside the empty chamber where her beating heart should rest? She felt beaten and bruised, unable to raise the spirit within to battle the hopelessness, the sight of Winn walking back toward the battle etched into her mind. She could not strike it away, neither by closing her eyes nor by screaming, the hated image burning bright and clenching off all glimmers of hope.

She felt unworthy of his love, unworthy of his trust, when it would take but a gentle push to send her over the edge of madness. She could easily run screaming from the destruction, and if not for the tugging of the tiny babe at her breast, she would have done so.

The dugout canoe bumped bottom and slid onto loose sand, and they all helped pull it up onto the bank. There were three other canoes with the occupants doing the same, their backs illuminated in the moonlight as they worked wordlessly across the shimmering sand. Up ahead, she saw four men carry Opechancanough from the lead canoe and take him immediately to the Long House.

She felt a thin hand slip around her own. Sesapatae led her away from the riverbank.

"Come with me, Red Woman."

Maggie looked back toward the river. The water was calm, lapping the beach with a gentle slapping sound as it gleamed in the light of the full moon. They had left to meet the English with more than two dozen canoes. Only four returned.

She let Sesapatae guide her up the riverbank to the village. Only a few remained behind, and those who were able rushed down to help the wounded and sick. A woman walking ahead, supported by two other women, vomited up a blood-tinged froth. Several children, crying but otherwise unharmed, ran ahead, luckily among those too young to share the gift of the English rum. They were fortunate, because it seemed those smaller and weaker fell first, like the young braves who first teetered and collapsed, and the wiry young Taster. The Taster who had saved her life, and the lives of all those she loved.

She did not know she cried until the hot tears stung her splintered lip. She reached up and brushed them away with her filthy fingers, ashamed of her weakness in the face of so much stoicism among the women. With the pain of the truth hammering into her, she suddenly realized that the life she had led in the future was truly meaningless. In her own time she had been independent and resourceful, never doubting she could take care of herself. Nothing in the future could have ever prepared her for a life in the past.

Before they reached the Long House, a warrior came striding toward them, his face etched with despair. Her stomach flipped over as she realized he was coming straight for her, and she grasped her daughter convulsively to her chest to protect her from what was to come.

"Come with me. My Weroance will speak to you," he said. Sesapatae held out her arms for the baby, but Maggie shook her head. She knew the offer was sincere and that she could trust the woman, but she also knew she could not be parted from her child. If there was nothing within her power to do, she at least was sure she could protect her flesh and blood.

She followed the warrior into the Long House. There were no women sitting regally at his side this time, no warrior standing ready to pounce. He lay alone on his raised dais, his only comfort his oldest wife who tended his wound. Opechancanough bled from a wound to his stomach, and although it appeared to be more lateral to his flank, it could very well be fatal. When he turned his head and opened his round brown eyes, she could see he was well aware of that fact.

"Leave us," he commanded. His voice held a tremor, yet even in his weakness, he would not be opposed. The wife finished bandaging the wound and quickly obeyed. The Long House emptied on his command. Maggie recalled the last time she had been alone with Winn's uncle. It was a different Long House and a different village, yet the legendary man lying wounded in front of her was one and the same.

"Come closer, Red Woman. Let me see the child."

She did as he asked, although her hands trembled as she pulled back the sling and released her sleeping daughter. The child often slept like the dead when her belly was milk full, and she hoped the babe remained quiet throughout their exchange.

"I will hold her," he said gruffly. Maggie was shocked when he pulled himself into a sitting position, so much so that she rushed forward to help him when he let out a moan and clutched his side. He grunted and shrugged off her ministrations, instead holding his arms out for Kwetii.

"Not too tight," she whispered. Seeing her lifeblood held in his arms weakened her, and the only motion left in her power was to sit down next to the Weroance on his dais. He raised an eyebrow at her and chuckled, but quickly returned his gaze to Kwetii, appearing enamored with her.

"You think I do not know how? I am a Great Warrior, as well as your husband is," he said. "This life means much to me."

He ran one crooked finger along her cheek, and she opened her blue eyes to stare at him. Usually the child made her presence known by screaming upon waking, but laying there in the arms of the elder Weroance she merely studied his weathered face. Maggie let out a sigh.

"Why did you save me?" he asked, keeping his gaze steady on the babe. Maggie swallowed hard and cleared her throat before she spoke.

"I don't know," she said softly. She had no urge to lie to him, only the desire to serve him the truth as she knew it, as scattered as it was from her slivered memory of childhood history lessons. "I didn't think of it as saving you. I just realized too late that it was all poisoned. I didn't want to see anyone die."

He nodded, more to himself than to her, and patted the babe as he rocked her.

"Was this my time, Red Woman? Did you chase death from me today?"

"No," she replied hoarsely. "You won't die just yet. I know you live to be a very old man."

He smiled.

"I have ordered the death of all the Blooded Ones, and all my warriors obey my command. Yet my own nephew, my favorite, son of my sister, he defies me … for you. For one red-haired Blooded One, he defied me. And now here in my arms, is this blood of my blood, this blood of a Time Walker." He bent down and pressed his lips gently to Kwetii's forehead, and the babe continued to stare peacefully at the warrior. "I see you there, you know. You are the one who will send me to death. You are the Blooded One who will bring death to me."

Maggie put a hand on his arm. Her touch was light, yet she needed to connect to him, to show him somehow that she was no enemy.

"It will not be by my hand, and it will not be today. I can promise you that."

He winced once more, seeming in pain, and gently turned to place the babe back in her arms. She helped him lay back down, yet as he stretched back onto the furs he reached up with one hand to cup her cheek.

"Keep safe my blood, Red Woman."

She nodded. The old warrior closed his eyes, and she tucked a fur around him, placing Kwetii next to him as they both gave in to slumber. She would sit with him until his wife returned.

A shadow crossed the doorway. It was Winn, and Maggie threw herself into his waiting arms. Bruised and bleeding with the scent of smoke searing his skin but blessedly intact, he held her tight as his body shuddered.

"Don't ever leave me again!" she cried, not caring that she was smeared with blood and sweat, nor that he shook his head furiously and clutched her harder.

"Shh, *ntehem*," he whispered.

* * *

Only a few warriors returned from the peace treaty dinner. Winn was back, and he was safe. It was all she could ask for.

They spoke each night in quiet whispers as they embraced beneath the furs, seeking answers to the question of where to take their small family. Although Chulensak Asuwak decided to return to the remains of the Paspahegh village, Teyas insisted on staying with their band of misfits. Ahi Kekeleksu refused to leave, and although Maggie thought it merely an excuse for Chetan to stay, she was surprised Makedewa opted to join them as well.

Rebecca, however, was another matter entirely. She grew stronger while she lived amongst them, eventually coming to the point where she could tolerate interaction with the men without flying into a panic. Luckily her mind was sharp and she found comfort in the daily labors of living with them, and she knew the people who saved her from the Massacre meant her no harm.

For all his faults, Makedewa was still a brooding male, yet they all noticed the change in him since that fateful day. Formerly rash and loud, he became more thoughtful in his actions and made effort to speak in a neutral manner instead of round-the-clock angry. Clearly, he held more interest in Rebecca then just friendship, and Maggie found it amusing to watch him around the girl. She would have never expected him to fall for an Englishwoman, but as she watched him follow the girl around the camp like a lovesick puppy, she knew he was smitten. He knew how she had been damaged, and for all the desire in his eyes, there also burned a temperate patience he never showed before. Maggie was sure he would never do anything to harm her.

The decision on where to live, however, fell only on Winn, and for that matter, Winn demanded answers of Maggie that she could not give him. It frustrated her that she had not been a better student of history, but hindsight was a luxury she no longer dwelled on. He wanted to go south to live among the Nansemonds, where he knew they would be welcomed, but Maggie had doubts living among any Indian tribe would be safe for very long. She was fearful of relying on what she knew of history, yet Winn banked their lives on the few facts she was certain of. It was an impasse, for sure, but one that had to be rapidly resolved. Winter would overcome them soon, and to be settled well before the first frost would see much to ensure their survival.

The decision was made, however, and they believed it to be the right one. Maggie could offer no guarantee, and Winn had only his knowledge to guide them. Their destiny lay ahead, a future in the past. South, it would be.

They left on one of those lingering days of summer where the sun still scorched their skin as they worked, but the night brought enough chill to chase them beneath layers of furs. The horses stood waiting, Blaze tied to Maggie's fat older mare, the yearling nipping at her flanks and causing her to squeal and stomp.

"Ready, Maggie?" Teyas called. Maggie finished tightening the rawhide strap that held her traveling sacks around the barrel of her pony, and Teyas peered over her shoulder.

"If Winn is ready, I'm good."

"Find him, then, sister, I think he lingers too long at the waterfall."

"All right. You go on, we'll catch up. I think Kwetii will sleep some more," Maggie replied. Teyas shrugged and mounted up, Kwetii carried in front of her in a makeshift pouch. Maggie crafted it after the babe outgrew the swaddling board, and Teyas liked to use it when they rode.

The child was nearing too big to use the contraption any longer, but it would serve well for the ride, at least when she slept.

He was not difficult to find. Winn stood looking out over the waterfall when she approached, his countenance sculpted in thought, his warrior's body softened in a forgiving stance as he gazed at the crashing water. When she moved to his side and slipped her arm through his, she was surprised to see her bloodstone suspended from a rawhide cord, hanging from his hand.

"You still have that," she said softly.

"It belongs to you," he replied. He placed it in her hand, closing his fist over it for a moment before he let go.

"I belong to you."

"And I am yours, *ntehem*," he whispered. "But I wonder if it is wrong of me to keep you here. I wonder if it is wrong of me to love you so much, to want you…to make you stay in this time."

"You're a fool, warrior," she said softly. She placed her hand on his cheek and kissed him. "You can't make me do anything! Haven't you learned that yet?"

She turned abruptly. She would end his troubles, strike the worry from his heart, and tear the seeds of doubt away with one quick launch. Pulling her arm back, she prepared to throw the Bloodstone into the waterfall, but he stopped her with a firm hand around her wrist.

"No, little Fire Heart," he murmured. He placed the lanyard around her neck, then pressed his hand over the stone against her heart. "It is part of you now. Keep it with you, as I will keep you, and let the right or wrong of it be damned."

Maggie brushed her fingers over his.

"All right, then."

They could see the others downstream from their spot on the waterfall, traveling in a line beside the river. Chetan let out a holler and Winn returned it in kind. She took her husband's hand, and they left to join their family.

PREVIEW: Return of the Pale Feather

Time Walkers: Book 2

CHAPTER 1

Maggie reined her mount in closer to Winn's war pony, taking comfort in the touch of her husband's knee against hers as their horses brushed together. She reached for him, her fingers sliding against the slick skin of his golden-brown thigh. It had been a long ride on a humid summer day without rest, a sacrifice made to speed their journey home, and she was glad it would soon come to an end.

"Do you need rest?" Winn asked, placing his hand over hers. She shook her head.

"No. I just want to get back. The sooner the better."

He tipped his head toward her, a slight movement, yet she felt the sudden tension of his leg muscle under her hand as his blue eyes met hers. She wanted to ask what was wrong, but if she knew nothing of his warrior ways by now, she knew enough when to keep silent. Her own body stiffened, her response attuned to his. He slowed his pony and hers followed suit.

"I think you are right. We will stop to rest," he said, his voice louder than necessary. She felt the pressure of his fingers as he gave her hand a gentle squeeze, then slid down off his mount. Unease crept in as he lifted his arms to her waist to help her down.

He never helped her dismount, there was no need. She was perfectly capable, and he was no gentleman.

"I suppose I could use a drink," she whispered.

His eyes held hers as she slid off the horse. He kept her close, her body sliding down tight against his bare chest, and if she had not been so scared she would have been lost in the delicious sensation as he kept her shielded between him and the horse. She welcomed his touch, even knowing it was a ploy. His lips traced a path over her sun-scorched cheek to her ear where his words fell whispered in her hair as if only sweet endearments.

"We are being tracked. I think there are two men. One is behind us now. The other circles us."

She bit down over her lower lip as he pressed a kiss to that soft sensitive place near her collarbone.

"How long have you known?" she asked. His arm slipped down around her waist and he pulled her closer.

"Since we left the river."

"That was miles ago! You should have told me!" she hissed.

"There was no need for you to know!" he snapped back.

She ran her hands through his thick black hair, in part to continue the rouse, yet also to convey her frustration. He uttered a low growl in warning before he shoved her away. Stumbling backward a few paces before she regained her footing, she watched as Winn crouched into a defensive stance to face the two men who approached them.

The men were not strangers.

One stepped forward, knife raised.

~end preview~

ABOUT THE AUTHOR

E.B. Brown enjoys researching history and genealogy and uses her findings to cultivate new ideas for her writing. She grew up in Gibbstown, New Jersey, and is a proud graduate of Paulsboro High School and Drexel University. Her debut novel, *The Legend of the Bloodstone (Time Walkers #1)*, was a Quarter-finalist in the 2013 Amazon Breakthrough Novel Award contest. An excerpt from another Time Walkers novel, *A Tale of Oak and Mistletoe (Time Walkers #4)*, was a finalist in the 2013 RWA/NYC We Need a Hero Contest.

E.B. loves mudding in her Jeep Wrangler and likes to cause all kinds of havoc the rest of the time. She resides in New Jersey.

CONNECT WITH ME ONLINE:

FACEBOOK www.facebook.com/ebbrownauthor

OFFICIAL WEBSITE: www.ebbrown.net

Made in the USA
Columbia, SC
21 July 2021

42167548R00191